Playing the Bosses

AN EROTIC DRAMEDY

PLAYING THE BOSSES
BOOK ONE

JANERA MOON

SLEEPYHOUSE PUBLISHING

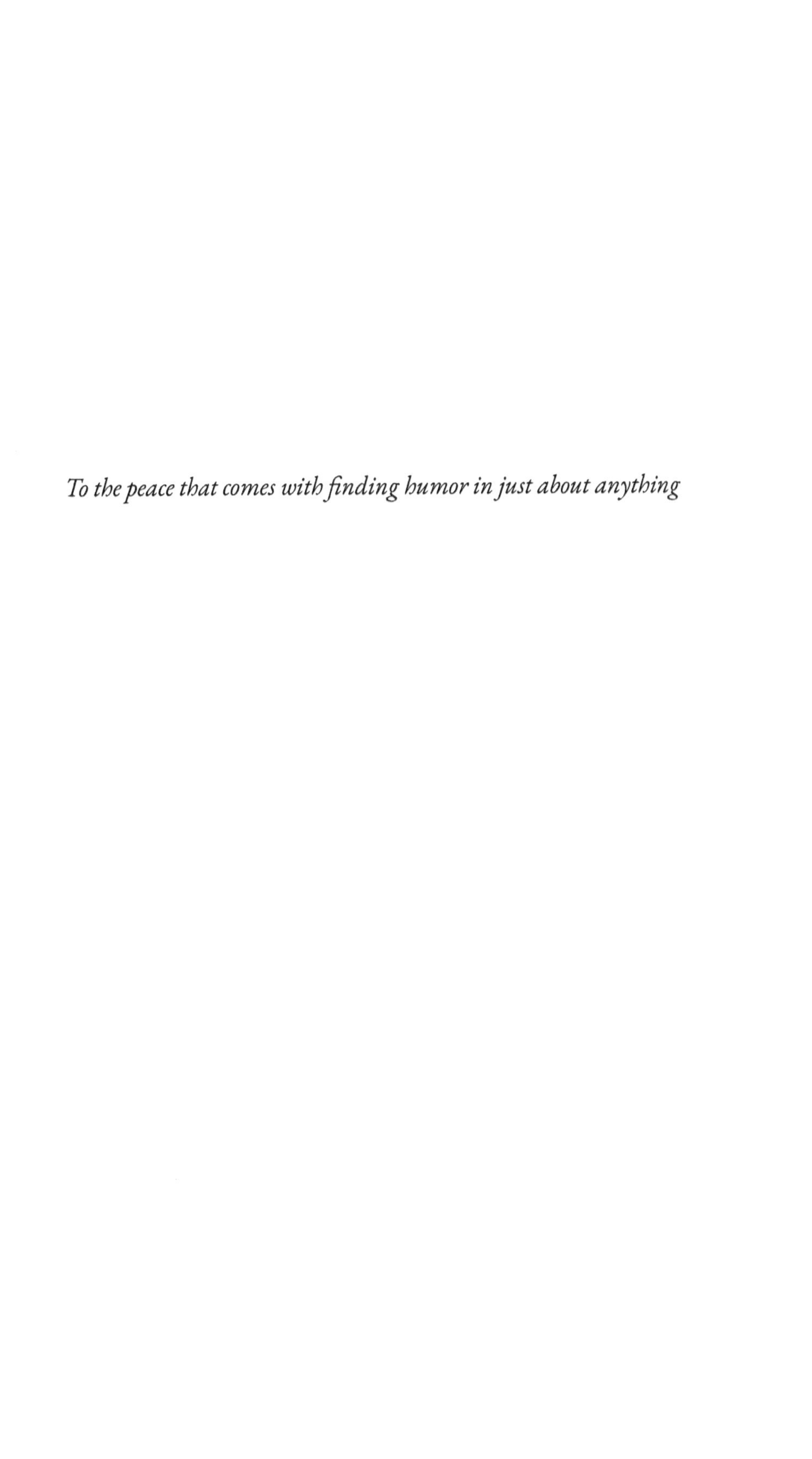

To the peace that comes with finding humor in just about anything

Contents

Warnings

This book contains some content and subject matters that may be triggering for readers, including:

- Fatphobia
- Dubious consent: While Mila otherwise behaves as herself, the men are not aware of her true identity; the disguise is solely to infiltrate their company. On the other side, there is also a power imbalance considering the men are all technically her bosses.
- Stalker ex-boyfriend

Further, this book contains light kink elements as part of some power exchanges, including:

- Degradation and humiliation
- Light breath play
- Edging
- Orgasm control

While there are some depictions of negotiation, check-ins during scenes, and aftercare, this is a work of FICTION, characters are NOT engaging in kink responsibly. By no means should this book be used as reference for real-life play.

This book also contains descriptions of sex and should only be read by people age 18 and up.

If you read this book and believe any additional triggers are not addressed here, please contact me through my website: www.janer amoon.com.

An Opening Word from the Author

Hello! Thank you so much for your openness to reading this book. As you get started, you'll notice that the chapters are referred to as episodes throughout the book—that is intentional. This story, as it is written, is meant to be consumed as if watching from the outside. Also, to make this experience interactive, there is a Playing the Bosses bingo card on my website. Take a look and join in on the fun! I hope you enjoy this book as much as I enjoyed writing it!

The Man-Eater

Mila Thompson relaxed in a large chair toward the back of the VIP airport lounge as she awaited her flight back to Lenrod City from Atlanta. In a comfortable fit for travel, she wore a scoop-neck black shirt that she tucked into a loose pair of distressed mom jeans, and she had on fresh black Chucks. Her acrylic nails were still painted beige from her friend Naomi's wedding and her dark brown hair was secured in a tight bun. With a mostly bare face, she wore a natural color lipgloss.

Even with the relaxed appearance of her outfit and lack of makeup, Mila still looked anything but plain. On the small table next to her sat a gin martini that she had been slowly nursing for the past half hour. A subtle smile on her face, she swiped through pictures of herself with her friends from Atlanta as she reminisced on the past week with them.

Mila's fond memories were interrupted by a phone call from her sister Alexis.

"What's up, sis?" she answered.

"Hey, how are you? How was your trip?"

"It was great! I'm so happy for Naomi! I mean, marriage isn't my groove, but I still love going to weddings and seeing my friends celebrated as they deserve."

"Oh, I know marriage isn't your 'groove'," Alexis replied, a hint of disapproval in her tone. "Eric still asks about you."

Mila took a deep sigh. "I can't believe you still have him as your financial advisor…"

"And I can't believe you rejected his proposal…"

"We were only dating for a year!" Mila whispered sharply. It had been months since she rejected her now ex-boyfriend Eric's marriage proposal, but her family still brought it up with her. "I tried with Eric, I really did. But I couldn't imagine spending the rest of my life with just him. I'm not built for that. Plus, we hadn't even spent that much time together while we were dating. I was always in and out of Lenrod and he was working long hours."

"Distance shouldn't be an excuse. People do it all the time. Text messages and video calls exist. Your friend Naomi did it. And weren't she and Sebastien Laurent long-distance for most of their relationship?"

"They were together for over a year. And yes, that's great for her and all those other people that 'make it work'. But, I can't do that. Anyway, what's up? I know you want something."

"Damn," Alexis groaned. "I can't just check on my little sister?"

There was a long pause without Mila replying until she heard Alexis huff on the other side of the phone.

"Okay, I do need something," Alexis confessed. "But I can't talk about it over the phone. Can you please come over when you're back?"

"I knew it." Mila scoffed. "Fine… I'll stop by tonight."

"Please be here by eight! Thank you!" Alexis chimed before hanging up.

Mila shook her head and let out a deep sigh after getting off the phone with her sister. While they did have a positive relationship, since Alexis took over the family business—Thompson Luxe Group, a luxury goods holding company—most of their interactions had turned business-related with Mila providing counsel.

Ever since she was young, Mila was a natural with the family business, but when the time came for her parents to retire, she refused to co-lead with Alexis. Growing up, Mila witnessed the type of stress her parents went through running Thompson Luxe and although she was happy to offer her input and guidance when she could, Mila didn't like the idea of spending a good portion of her life under significant stress. She also knew that she didn't have to since Alexis always dreamed of becoming CEO and had big ideas of her own for Thompson Luxe.

Just as Mila finished the final sip of her martini, another was placed on the table and she looked up at the server with a raised brow.

"From the gentleman over there," he said, gesturing toward a man sitting at the bar of the lounge. He appeared to be in his mid- to late-thirties and looked over at Mila with a slight glimmer in his eyes.

She took the martini and held it up at him as if giving a toast while mouthing "thank you" before taking a sip of the drink. The stranger took her acceptance as an invitation and soon joined Mila at the chair next to hers.

"So, gin martini? That's really your drink of choice?" he questioned skeptically as he settled in his seat.

"Thanks for ordering me this *free* drink, mister...?"

"Richards," he replied. "Logan Richards. And no need to call me 'mister'."

"Well, Logan... Why do you sound surprised that I like gin martinis?"

Logan was smiling while he unabashedly scanned over Mila as she got out her question and didn't meet her eyes again until he was ready to answer.

"I'm not surprised, just intrigued." He rested his elbows on his knees as he leaned in toward her.

Mila turned and looked at him with her chin on her knuckles and her eyes sharpened. She had a talent for reading people and as she measured him up, she took notice of his Brioni suit, freshly-cleaned Rolex, Salvatore Ferragamo oxfords, and Hermès tie. If she had to estimate the cost of everything he was wearing, she was sure it'd be north of $20,000. Analyzing his face, it was full of confidence. It was clear in his dark brown eyes that he was well aware that Mila was measuring him up.

"So, what's your read, beautiful?"

Mila let out an amused huff. "Let's see... Businessman, probably in Atlanta for meetings and my guess is that you work in banking... investment banking to be exact. You can afford these *very* expensive brands that you're wearing, but considering the mix, there's no way you work in fashion or media. I also don't take you as an athlete. And nothing about your demeanor says tech guy."

"I'm impressed," he said with a nod and pursed lips. "Also, a tad bit offended, but mostly impressed... So, what's your name? And where are you off to?"

"It's Mila," she responded casually, relaxing back in her seat and stirring her martini. "I'm off to Lenrod City."

"Mila..." He said it like he was measuring her name on his lips. "I like that name. So, are you traveling for business or pleasure?"

"You say that like the two must be mutually exclusive."

He lifted his head as if he were beginning to nod. "Ah, so Ms. Mila likes to mix her business with pleasure?"

"The two can go hand-in-hand if you're creative enough—"

Mila was cut off by an announcement that sounded through the lounge. *"Flight AA617 is now boarding... Flight AA617 is now boarding."*

"Well, I guess that's me- *oops.*" Mila's unlocked phone fell as she stood from her seat and when she pretended to reach for it, Logan already picked it up for her.

"Unlocked, too? It's probably fate..." he said as he typed his number into her phone. "Well, Ms. Mila... I tend to travel a lot, so I don't see why we can't cross paths again," he added with a wink as he handed her phone to her.

She returned his gesture before she rolled her eyes and turned to walk away. "Someone's eager..."

"Hey Ms. Mila," Logan called before she was out of earshot. "You're not the only one who can read people... take a look at my contact."

Mila heard him, but kept walking anyway. It wasn't until she knew he couldn't see her anymore that she pulled up his contact details to delete his number. She paused when something in the notes caught her eye.

Queening?

After seeing that one word, Mila hesitated and took a few seconds to weigh her options before ultimately deleting Logan's number.

EPISODE 2

The Playmaker

Caleb Peterson was with his closest friends and business partners—Justin Matsuda and Adrian Collins—sitting on each side of him in their private section at Club Ace. Finally able to relax after intense negotiations, his tie was loosened and his suit jacket was gone. His bright blue eyes were lit with excitement as he shot to his feet and punched the air triumphantly.

"Another deal for the books!" he beamed before falling back into his seat and pulling the woman standing in front of him into his lap, who in turn squealed her surprise with a wide smile on her face. Caleb signaled the bottle girl near their section and ordered the most expensive champagne they had to offer at the club. "This has got to be my favorite venue where we've made a deal so far."

"You never seem to fail," Justin replied. "A true play-maker if I do say so myself."

"I thought you were nuts when you suggested closing out a deal at a nightclub, but it looks like I was wrong." Adrian shrugged. "Who knew that almost a year of back-and-forth on negotiations just needed a fun night to seal the deal."

"The owner of that fashion line said he wanted the brand to center partying, but the holding company we *were* competing with was trying too hard to make the shit fancy. So, I showed him we're absolutely willing to have a more fun brand under our belt, and he was hooked the second I suggested we meet here."

The woman on Caleb's lap ran her fingers through his undercut, dirty blond hair and used her other hand to admire his perfectly-chiseled jawline. "You're such a genius, Daddy," she chimed.

"Of-fucking-course, I am!" He pulled her to the center of his lap and opened his legs slightly wider. "Now, give Daddy a dance to celebrate."

Adrian huffed and rolled his eyes at the way Caleb immediately started with his shenanigans. Meanwhile, Justin looked down at his phone.

"Why don't you guys get some bitches so we can have some fun tonight?" Caleb asked his friends as the woman in his lap sensually ground against him. "Shit, I might even be down for an orgy now that we've scored this deal."

"Shut up," Adrian said sharply. "And I'm not going to stay here long, I have somewhere else to be…"

"Dude, did you forget I'm in a relationship now?" Justin chided. "Ashley should be here soon. She's just getting back in from Jersey."

"Yeah, yeah," Caleb waved his hand dismissively as he kept his eyes on the woman in his lap grinding on him. He used his other hand to rub her ass before smacking it. "You guys aren't fun anymore."

"Or we have different ideas of fun these days," Adrian countered.

"I find that hard to believe," Caleb snorted. "I know for a *fact* that we have similar interests."

"Or perhaps 'had'," Adrian corrected.

"Whatever. And Justin…" Caleb turned his attention to his other friend. "When are you going to drop Ashley? Yeah, she's hot, but look at the three of us! We're hot, rich corporate executives… We're literally every bitch's fantasy and can have whoever we want. You're really gonna settle for one?"

"What did I tell you about making comments on my relationship?" Justin warned. "We can't just fuck around forever, we need to build legacies like our parents did."

"Justin, Justin, Justin…" Caleb tilted his head left to right each time he said it. "Always wanting to please mommy and daddy. You're a man. If you want a 'legacy', you wait until you're like fifty years old and knock up a bunch of chicks."

"They want grandkids soon, especially now that PMC Group his doing well."

Caleb simply shook his head and continued enjoying his dance. As the woman ground harder against him, Caleb's erection grew under her and he reached around her waist to pull her back and whisper in her ear. "You better be ready to take my cock all night."

Adrian looked at his watch yet again before getting up to say good-bye. "I'll see you guys in the office this week." He shook both of his friends' hands before leaving the club.

Justin's phone vibrated and he pulled it from his pocket. "Finally," he sighed. "Ashley is here. I'll go get her."

"Yeah yeah," Caleb grumbled as his hands wandered the woman he was with. "Boring asses."

The Pleasure-Seeker

Adrian Collins was more relaxed by the time he arrived at The Scarlet Lounge, out of his suit and in a chic button-up with his sleeves rolled far enough to expose his tattoo-covered forearms. He made a direct path to the bar where he ordered a whiskey. Other than a glass of champagne, he didn't drink much at Club Ace with Caleb and Justin. As excited as we was about them closing yet another deal, Adrian couldn't seem to feel the same enthusiasm or zest he did when they first launched PMC Group and were making back-to-back wins.

Adrian knew he wasn't depressed so much as he simply wanted more excitement in a life that had turned repetitive in many ways.

"Any scenes planned tonight, AC?" the server asked. Adrian only went by his initials when he was there, even though there was no need to. The Scarlet Lounge was one of his favorite spots. He appreciated the discretion and the clientele were similar in many ways to him—business-people looking to unwind or be themselves freely without judgement or risk of exposure. Interestingly, he'd even ended up making some reliable business contacts to add to his network from the club.

Adrian gestured at his drink. "I think I'll just watch tonight," he replied before leaving the bar to step into the other part of the club.

Large couches were scattered throughout with doors leading down various hallways for private rooms. There were people playing publicly —both out in the open and in rooms that had large windows for viewing.

Adrian's soft brown eyes scanned the scenes as he passed by them until he finally landed on one that caught his attention.

A man was laying on a table on his back, his wrists and ankles bound to it; a woman in a latex set with matching platform heels circled him. His chest heaved with his heavy breathing as her fingernails lightly brushed against his body while she walked around him. While he was laying on his back, his dick was blushed with the intensity of his erection, as if he'd been going through extensive teasing.

The woman stopped when she got between his legs and ran her hands up his thighs and back down before using a single finger to rub the most sensitive part of his tip, causing his dick to jump.

"Someone is sensitive," she teased, her low voice coming out as a purr. "How long has it been since you came, bitch?"

"Seventeen days and eight hours, Mistress," he replied, urgency clear in his tone.

"Seventeen days, eight hours, and *what*?"

There was a brief pause this time before he answered her as his gaze went up to the clock that sat high up on the wall inside the room with them. "Seventeen days, eight hours, and thirty-seven minutes..."

The woman looked at the clock before turning her attention back down to the man on the table.

"Of course the only thing a slut like you is good for is counting the fucking minutes since the last time you came... But you *did* get it right, which means a reward," she sighed. "So, let's see..."

"Isn't it amazing the way control manifests itself during play?" a woman asked, catching Adrian by surprise. When he slightly jumped, a small smile came to her face.

"She made him take note of the last time he came since he did it without permission and then prohibited him from coming again until she said he could," the stranger explained as she turned her eyes to the scene that Adrian was watching. "In the meantime, she required that he count every minute. I've seen her do this with a few of her subs and I'm always impressed."

"Hm..." Adrian hummed thoughtfully with a nod.

"You're a pleasure-seeker, aren't you?"

Adrian finally tore his eyes away from the scene to look the woman in her hazel eyes. "What do you mean by that?"

"I can tell from the way you carry yourself. You're in search of different ways to achieve new heights of pleasure... And I bet you're open to just about *anything* that might take you there."

Adrian huffed. "Pretty generic line... That could apply to anyone here."

"You've got a little attitude," the woman replied plainly. "Let me know when you're ready for me to help you fix it," she added before turning to walk away.

Adrian scoffed and shook his head before his attention returned to the scene he had been watching and his eyes immediately grew wide when he noticed what the submissive's 'reward' was. His wrists were unbound and the Domme was perched on his face while he had his arms wrapped around her large thighs as he devoured her. With the way his mouth moved diligently and pre-cum leaked from his dick, it was clear that the sub was very much into it.

And so was Adrian.

He felt himself harden at the sight as he licked his lips and gulped his desire. The only thing that broke him from his trance was his need to experience something like it himself. Adrian turned away to look around the room before he finally saw the woman who propositioned him earlier and made his way toward her.

The People Pleaser

Justin Matsuda walked into his apartment with his girlfriend Ashley, kicked off his shoes, and fell into his couch. After taking off her heels and jacket, Ashley went into the kitchen to get cups of water for them both and joined Justin.

"Why didn't you tell me ahead of time you'd be wanting me to meet you at Club Ace?" Ashley complained. "I would've at least planned my outfit better or something."

Justin's almond brown eyes that sat above his high cheekbones analyzed Ashley, reading the disappointment on her face. "You looked fine as always," he replied flatly before running his fingers through his hair and averting his gaze. "I don't know why you're making a deal out of it."

"Because, Justin, I like to be presentable and dress appropriate for occasions. If you know that about me, why can't you be more considerate of it?"

"Okay, okay... Fine," he surrendered before taking a sip of his water and turning on the TV. "I'll be more considerate of it."

Ashley had mentioned it to him several times before and it was as if her communication would go in one ear and out the other. It was like anything she did or said wasn't much of a priority for him and when she spoke, Justin seemed to only listen to reply, but not to understand.

Justin didn't speak on it further as he browsed the options supplied by the various streaming apps on his TV looking for something to put on that could distract them.

"Caleb is so vulgar all the time," Ashley commented, breaking the awkward silence that ensued between them. "And that girl he was with... I felt so bad for her. He was practically having sex with her in the club between the intense making out and heavy groping."

"She's into it." Justin shrugged. "Caleb said she's an exhibitionist and they've had sex in some wild places."

"That's weird. I understand having kinks or whatever, but that stuff should be kept between the two people who are having sex."

"You say that like you don't like it rough."

"Yeah, but rough sex is like mainstream these days, honey. Choking and spanking are pretty much vanilla."

"Only when it's done to women," Justin mumbled under his breath.

"What was that?"

"Nothing. Could we talk about something other than Caleb's sex life?"

"Oh, yeah..." Ashley tapped her finger to her chin. "We're going to see your parents in D.C. next weekend, right?"

Justin dragged a hand down the side of his face. "I forgot about that! We'll have to deal with them asking all the same fucking questions they ask every time as if the answer is going to change."

"You mean like when we'll get married?"

Justin's head jerked back at Ashley's question. "What?"

"Every time we see your parents, they ask about when we're getting married. We've been dating for a year-and-a-half now, Justin, and it seems like they're making it a more urgent issue..." Ashley took a deep breath. "Are we getting married? Like, ever?"

"Ashley." Justin sighed. "I love you, it's just that I want to focus on work for a couple of more years before you and I... get married."

Ashley crossed her arms and sunk down into the chair. "Did you notice that when you say that you love me or we're going to get married, it doesn't even sound like *you* believe those things?"

"Oh god, here we go…" Justin groaned.

"I'm just saying that if you don't mean it, why do you say it?"

"I *do* mean it. Why are you always doubting how I feel about you?"

"It's just that… Sometimes it feels like you're only with me because your parents want you to be with someone and I know how much of a people pleaser you are."

Justin rubbed his forehead and muttered something under his breath before taking Ashley's hand. He wasn't in the mood to talk to her and he knew there was one thing he could do to stop any further conversation.

"Babe, I love you. I'm just not ready for marriage right now…" He pulled her in to kiss her lips and then her jaw and then her neck, making his way down her body until he was nestled between her legs with her dress hiked up. "Let me show you just how much," he whispered before his face was buried between her thighs.

EPISODE 5

A Family Favor

Mila arrived at her sister's high-rise apartment building in Uptown Lenrod right on time for them to meet. The large penthouse had three bedrooms and two baths, a kitchen equipped with a full bar, living room and a terrace with a large pool. Mila had a similar setup at her place in Downtown Lenrod, but with two bedrooms.

"Finally, you're here!" Alexis beamed when she opened the door before she wrapped her sister into a tight hug. "Thank you so much for coming! So, here's what I need you to do—"

"Damn," Mila interrupted. "Can I at least get something to drink first?"

"Oh right, of course! What do you want? I have water, soda, juice..." Alexis drifted off as she watched Mila make a path straight to the bar.

"Let me guess, a Cuba Libre for you?" Mila asked as she went through the cabinets.

"You know me well."

"More like you *always* get the same drink. There are other options, you know?" Mila pulled out rum, coke, lime, gin, vermouth, and an orange before she started making their drinks.

"And look, you're making yourself a gin martini, as always." Alexis didn't bother to hide the judgement with a hint of playfulness in her tone. "You can stop pretending to like those just to seem interesting, you know? You're an heiress and a traveler. You have plenty going for you."

"Shut up and leave my drinking preferences alone." Mila finished making Alexis' drink and handed it to her. "Anyway, what did you want to talk about?"

"Right! So, I need your help with something for the company…"

"Okay…" Mila shook her martini and poured it in the glass before going around the bar to sit with her sister. "What is it?"

"Have you heard of PMC Group?"

Mila nodded. "Yeah, aren't they our competition? And they've been moving up pretty fast, haven't they?"

"Yes!" Alexis confirmed. "They've been acquiring brand after brand —many of which were vehemently against selling before."

"Okay, that's odd, but not unheard of…" While she'd been listening enough to her sister, Mila didn't seem too focused on the conversation, instead savoring the taste of her martini or periodically checking her phone.

"Correct, but if you're already against selling, why sell to a firm as new as PMC Group rather than a more established, reputable luxury holding company like ours?"

"I don't know. Probably some shady shit going on, but why do you care?"

"Because, we expect them to target companies that we own next."

"So don't sell," Mila said flatly. "Easy enough."

"Not that easy. We're a publicly-traded company now. We have a board and if PMC offers a sizable enough amount for one of our companies, it'll be much harder to say no."

"If they offer a sizable amount, wouldn't that benefit us?"

"Not if they chip away at us like they did with GHC Group." Alexis took a big gulp of her drink. "They started off by overpaying for GHC's smaller companies here and there and with the offers they were making, it's not like the shareholders or the board were going to let them say no. In the end, PMC absorbed GHC and while GHC's shareholders and execs got out pretty fucking rich, PMC had one less competitor."

Mila played with the slice of orange peel in her drink. "Damn, but how are they finding money to do all this buying?"

"Good question! Which is where you come in. I need you to spy on them."

That got Mila's full attention. Her head jerked back and she looked up, wide-eyed at Alexis. "What? How the hell would I do that?

Alexis gave Mila a genuine smile with her head tilted to the side as she explained, "So, I have this friend named Jen, right? And she runs a temp agency. Turns out that Caleb Peterson, Justin Matsuda, and Adrian Collins—the men who run PMC Group—need a new executive assistant and they prefer to share one. Jen is looking for someone to place in that role."

Mila's nostrils flared as she exhaled. She knew exactly where their conversation was going, but she hoped it would be a rare occasion where she was wrong. "Okay, and?"

"*And* it would be the perfect opportunity to find out exactly what the fuck they are doing to scoop up smaller companies that don't want to sell, and how they're finding the money to overpay for brands owned by other holding companies. I was thinking you could take the job as their executive assistant and find out everything we need to know!"

"No," Mila responded curtly.

"Please, Mila?" Alexis put her hands together in a begging motion. "You're the only one I trust to do this and my face is known. I have no chances of going undercover. Even if I did, the board would have a fit."

Mila took a sip from her martini. "You've got me fucked up if you think I'm about to play assistant to three rich boys."

"Mila," Alexis groaned. "You say that like you're not a rich girl."

"You know what the fuck I meant," Mila said sharply. "People are disrespectful as fuck to assistants and I'm really not about to let that shit slide so I can spy on the competition. Not to mention the legal risks."

"Mila, please..." Alexis pleaded. "If they do to our company what they're doing to others, we may cease to exist just so our shareholders can get a big payout."

"I told dad he shouldn't have taken Thompson Luxe public," Mila griped. "Yeah, it brings in more money, but you also lose control of your own fucking company and now we—actual Thompsons—are beholden to some shareholders just because they have deep pockets and inflated senses of self-importance."

"Well, you were nine years old at the time, so don't blame him for not taking your sound business advice," Alexis replied sarcastically. "But please, please, *please*, can you help, Mila? You'd only have to suffer through it temporarily."

"No! I could go to jail for like corporate espionage or some shit!"

"You won't go to jail," Alexis assured. "I've got us covered."

"How?"

"Alright, so have you heard of the Davidson family?"

Mila pondered for several moments trying to figure out the familiar name before it finally clicked. "Oh! You mean the family with all those so-called 'business ventures' when it's likely just cover for some criminal shit?"

"Damn, you figured that out?"

"Yeah." Mila shrugged. "Who has *that many* ventures unless you're doing something illegal? Anyway, why do you mention them?"

"They own people pretty high up in the government, it's why they can get away with anything. One of the heads of the family—Sean Davidson—he owes me a favor!"

"Favor for what?"

"He launched a fashion line a few years back, but he was running it with dirty money to keep it afloat. As a favor to him, I had Thompson Luxe acquire it so now it's legit."

"Why would he care about it being legit when, like you said, his family can do whatever with impunity?"

"He has a daughter," Alexis explained. "You know how people get when they have kids. He wants her to be able to chose between following in his footsteps with their 'family business' when she gets older or separating herself, and the fashion line would be a legit business for her to make clean money."

"That's sweet of him. I didn't know crime families were so... considerate." Mila's dry tone when she said it was borderline mocking. "So, if some shit goes down, the Davidsons would get us out of it?"

"Yup! So, can you please do it? I know it's a big commitment, but as soon as you can gather information on how PMC is pulling off these deals as well as getting as much dirt as possible on them, you can just quit! Hell, you can ghost them for all I care. And we'll have regular check-ins on your progress."

Mila took a deep sigh and downed the rest of her Martini. She thought about her family's business. While Alexis was doing great job in her role as CEO, Mila hoped that one day, either Alexis or herself would find a way to take the company private again so that they didn't have to answer to shareholders. The fact that her family—a Black family from Lenrod City, North Carolina—owned a luxury goods holding company in an industry where most companies were hundreds of years old and based out of Europe was an unprecedented accomplishment and a testament to her grandparents'—who founded the company—hard work.

"Fine..." Mila agreed.

A wide, toothy smile immediately grew on Alexis' face. She clasped her hands together, making the sound of a single clap. "Great! So, I've already told Jen that you'd take the position and you don't have to worry about an interview or anything, though I imagine the three of them will want to talk to you on your first day or something."

"You already volunteered me? How did you know if I'd even say yes?"

"Oh, I had a whole list of contingencies until you said yes."

Mila scoffed. "Of course you did... When do I start?"

"Tomorrow!"

"*Tomorrow*? The fuck you mean I start tomorrow?"

"Sorry!" Alexis raised her hands defensively. "I know it's short notice, but that was the only way Jen could make it work!"

"Jesus Christ," Mila muttered. "You're buying me a new car— no! You're buying me a fucking condo in this fancy ass building or some shit."

"Deal!" Alexis chimed and wrapped her sister into a hug. "You'll be great, I know it! Oh! And one last thing... Your name will be Mila *Nelson*."

Twenty-Third Floor

Mila spent almost all night doing research on PMC Group. Although she was reluctant about taking the assistant job to spy, when she did do something, she wanted to be great at it. So, Mila learned all she could about Caleb Peterson, Justin Matsuda, and Adrian Collins as well as the culture of the their company.

Caleb Peterson was the Chief Executive Officer of PMC Group. At 32, he was one of the youngest CEOs in their industry other than Mila's sister Alexis. He came from a wealthy family in Pennsylvania and earned a degree in business administration from UPenn.

Justin Matsuda, 34, served as Chief Operations Officer and like Caleb, he came from a rather affluent family as well that owned a chain of high-end hotels throughout the world. He got his degree in management from UPenn.

Adrian Collins, who was the Chief Financial Officer, was 33 years old and held a degree in accounting from UPenn. Unlike Justin or Caleb, Adrian came from a more modest upbringing—his family didn't seem to own anything and it appeared he was a first generation graduate.

It was obvious that the men met at university and began their various business ventures from there. Even with families as wealthy as Caleb's and Justin's, Mila questioned how they were able to afford their failed ventures in food, hospitality, and tech before finding success in opening a holding company for luxury brands. None of it made sense.

She also took a look at their social media to get a sense of their personalities. Caleb's photos were abundant—he regularly posted pictures of himself working out, relaxing on the beach, or in swanky restaurants or hotels. Justin's posts were much rarer than Caleb's and mostly included photos of him with his girlfriend or with family. Adrian's social media was more active than Justin's but less than Caleb and he'd mostly post images of furniture he built as a hobby.

Following additional research on PMC Group, Mila was sure to dress accordingly for her first day—the photos and employee reviews of the company indicated it was an uptight environment. As such, Mila decided on a chic all black suit with a skirt modest enough to fall below her knees, back seam tights, and black pumps.

When she arrived at the high-rise office building, she was directed to the twenty-third floor where she'd meet with an administrative assistant who would direct her to her desk and train Mila during her first week there.

"Hi!" a perky blonde beamed when Mila reached the PMC Group offices that took up the entire floor.

"Hi," Mila replied. "Are you—"

"Shannon!" she chimed. "Yes! And I'm assuming you are Mila Nelson? I am going to train you this week. Welcome to PMC Group! Let me show you to your desk first so you can set your bag down and then I'll give you a tour of the office!"

"Oh, okay... thanks." Mila was thrown off at Shannon's enthusiasm because the rest of the office seemed rather dry and based on her research, the work environment sounded toxic.

With her cheerful demeanor, Shannon seemed to be talking a mile a minute as she continued to greet Mila. "I'm so glad that you're joining our firm. Jennifer said great things about your work ethic and I know you'll do an awesome job. I've been handling misters Peterson, Matsuda, and Collins' schedules since their previous assistant quit. But doing it on top of my existing work has been tough, honestly. Trust me when I say that you'll be plenty busy!"

"Great! I'm looking forward to it." Mila feigned her excitement.

"So, what's it like working for them? I know you mentioned it's tough, but anything else?"

"It's been good. I mean, they're pretty young executives in their early thirties leading a rapidly growing luxury goods holding company, so as I'm sure you can imagine, there are excessive amounts of press engagements on top of meetings and travel that you'll need to handle for them and all three of them have their own quirks and can be a bit particular about different things."

"I see..."

"Don't worry," Shannon assured. "I've already made an onboarding binder for you with notes on each of them that should help you quickly acclimate to their preferences. I'll also give you the rundown at lunch today. Normally, I don't leave, but the big three—that's what we call them since saying all their names can be a mouthful—will be at a conference until about three o'clock and my actual boss, the Chief Marketing Officer, is on vacation this week. It all works out so I can focus on training you until she returns next week."

"Awesome, thanks."

As they toured the office and Shannon introduced Mila to more of their colleagues, Mila noticed that other than Shannon, no one was particularly talkative. However, they seemed friendly enough when doing introductions and offered to answer any questions as Mila transitioned into her role.

"Here's the copy room where you'll probably spend a lot of time," Shannon explained. "The big three like physical briefing binders for big meetings and conferences. And for certain documents, there's a printing and disposal protocol. And then next to here is one of three break rooms in the office and this one is typically used by the other receptionists and entry-level staff."

"So the break rooms are based on your level at the firm?" Mila asked.

"Kind of? All the executives have rest areas in their own offices equipped with couches and a coffee table. They sometimes take naps there or hold more casual meetings without using the common areas. As for everyone below them, we tend to gravitate to people with similar job titles and levels. It just makes it less awkward than being on break with your boss, if you're even allowed to take one."

"Got it." Mila nodded. "That makes sense."

"Right, so let's get started on some of your training and then we'll go to lunch before the big three come back."

MILA STRAIGHTENED up in her seat when she saw Caleb, Justin, and Adrian enter the floor. The first thing she noticed was the way they held themselves with absolute confidence—not surprising given that they owned the company.

"We fucking killed that!" Caleb exclaimed triumphantly as soon as they walked in before lowering his voice and explaining something to Justin and Adrian while the three of them made a path toward their offices.

The way it was set up, Mila's desk as their assistant sat front and center of the big three's offices. Adrian's office was diagonally back and to her right, Justin's was on the left, and Caleb's was at the center. Anyone entering their offices would have to pass Mila first.

Mila hated faking smiles, but she reluctantly pushed a cheerful one to her face to greet them once they neared her desk. She wasn't looking forward to meeting the men or working for them, but Mila reminded herself that she was there for her family, so she'd fake whatever jovial demeanor she needed to accomplish her mission as quickly and effectively as possible.

"Hello, Mr. Peterson! I am—"

"You're our new assistant?" Caleb Peterson cut her off to ask. He had a slight look of disgust on his face as he scanned over Mila.

She nodded, maintaining her fake cheerfulness. "Yes! It's nice—"

"Large coffee, black, Colombian origin," he said curtly and continued into his office.

"Same for me, but with two sugars," Justin Matsuda added, following Caleb's lead, but not even bothering to look at Mila.

Mila furrowed her brows at the two men as they walked away. Immediately agitated with their shortness in speaking to her, Mila had the urge to march into the office and tell off Caleb and Justin. While she didn't consider herself to have much of a temper, she wasn't the type to tolerate disrespect. Mila took a mental note that she'd have to teach her new 'bosses' all about that, while keeping herself from getting fired.

"Sorry," Adrian Collins said once the other two men went into Caleb's office. "They're a bit busy and can sometimes forget their manners. Do you remember their orders? If not, I can write them down for you. It's always the same thing."

Mila shook her head. "It's fine, I remember. Did you want anything, Mr. Collins?"

"Oh, um... Yes, coffee for me as well, but with two creamers and one sugar."

"Okay, I'll get right on that."

"What is your name?" Adrian asked.

"It's Mila. Mila Nelson."

"A pleasure to meet you, Mila Nelson, and thank you in advance for dealing with our three crazy schedules and demands," he replied with a warm smile.

"Adrian!" Caleb called from his office. "Bring your ass here! And tell the assistant to hurry up with the coffees!"

By the time Adrian turned to Mila to apologize for his friend again and say goodbye, she had already gotten up from her desk and was making her way to get the coffees. He swallowed as he watched the way her wide hips swayed while she walked away with almost a strut and his eyes drifted further down, taking notice of the lined seam of the tights she was wearing—a style for which he had a preference—and her high heels that she almost seemed to float in.

"Adrian!" Caleb called again and broke him out of his trance.

"Geez, I'm coming," Adrian grumbled before going to join the men in the office. When he got inside and sat with Justin and Caleb in the lounge area of the office, he said, "You couldn't have been nicer to our new assistant?"

"Why would that be necessary?" Justin questioned.

Caleb snorted. "You act like she'll still be here next week. I bet she thinks it's an easy job and she can just sit her fat ass at that desk and eat all day. When she's too busy for lunch a few days in a row, I'm sure she'll quit."

"Whatever," Adrian huffed. He was used to Caleb making obnoxious comments and learned it usually wasn't worth challenging him on.

"Anyway, on to business..." Caleb leaned back in his seat and propped his feet up on the coffee table. "We have less than one year to set ourselves up nice and pretty before we go for our next target: Thompson Luxe Group."

BBE

It had been a long, uneventful first week for Mila at PMC Group and she was happy to make it to her first Friday. Looking at her clock, it was seven minutes past three o'clock and she felt like the afternoon had been dragging on. Despite it being her first week, Mila was kept busy. She wasn't only responsible for Caleb, Justin, and Adrian's schedules and taking their phone calls, Mila also had to help with personal tasks like arranging gifts to be sent, handling expense reports, organizing travel, and ordering food.

While Mila scrolled aimlessly on her phone awaiting the time to pass, Shannon approached her desk with a wide smile. "So, how has your first week been?"

"It's been great!" Mila replied, hoping she didn't sound too fake with the way her voice went up a few octaves. "I really appreciate you training me all week, it's been super helpful and thanks to that, I'm quickly getting the hang of things."

"You're welcome, I'm glad I could help. My executive will be back next week, so I'll be tending to her specifically again, but if you ever have any questions about dealing with the big three, I'm just a phone call, email, IM, or walk across the office away."

"Thank you, Shannon. So, do you have any fun plans for the weekend?"

Shannon smiled and bit her lip. "Well... I'm actually going to the beach with my boyfr- I mean... with someone special. He has a house out there."

"That sounds lovely."

"What about you? Anything exciting for the weekend?"

Mila sighed with a shrug. "Not much. It's looking like a chill weekend for me. I'm getting drinks with some friends tonight and then tomorrow, I'm going to my favorite spa."

"Shannon," Caleb called impatiently from the doorway of his office. "You're five minutes late. Is it because you were running your mouth with the assistant?"

Mila rolled her eyes. Caleb refused to call her by her name all week and talked about her like she wasn't sitting right there and could hear him. Her brows then tensed when she realized he didn't have anything about meeting Shannon on his schedule.

"Wait," Mila tilted her head at Shannon. "Did I miss something about you being on the schedule?"

"Oh no, that's not on you. Mr. Peterson and I are having a quick, informal meeting about my performance overall working with him, Mr. Matsuda, and Mr. Collins before my boss gets back."

"Oh." Mila nodded. "I see..."

"Shannon," Caleb repeated, still with clear agitation in his voice. "Let's go, I've got other shit to do and you're holding me up."

Shannon smiled at Mila and quickly walked over to Caleb's office. Before he closed the door behind them, Caleb turned his attention to Mila.

"Hey, assistant... Instead of gossiping or whatever it is you were doing, why don't you do your job and check your email? I have a stack of documents you need to print out and organize for me. And they need to be done before you leave today, got it?"

"On it," Mila replied through clenched teeth. Out of the three men she was working for, Caleb was the one who annoyed her most and she'd already come close to losing her job at PMC Group on several occasions that week due to encounters with his attitude. She often had a mind to tell him off or would think about the different ways in which she could embarrass him in front of the office.

However, it gave her some comfort knowing that once her mission was accomplished and PMC Group was taken down, it would be the sweetest revenge.

Mila looked at her computer to see three emails from Caleb with around fifty pages worth of materials that needed to be printed and ordered. She noticed that they used *a lot* of paper at PMC Group and were very selective on what they'd keep digital copies of. In fact, there was a policy among senior staff that required them to delete much of their materials after printing it out, with only handful being permissible to keep digitally. As for the printed materials containing whatever confidential information they had, employees would have to put them through the cross shredder.

When Mila heard of the policy, she thought that it could mean there was some incendiary information in the documents she printed out, but all the information seemed innocuous so far.

Mila's phone chimed and she looked down to see a text from her friend Jade.

JADE

Hey girl! Are you still good to have drinks tonight with me and Greg?

MILA

Yeah, and I'm gonna need like 30 after the week I just had.

JADE

That bad?

MILA

Mostly annoying and stressful.

JADE

Well hopefully we can drink that all away lol!
We'll see you in a few hours, girl.

MILA

Yeah, see you.

Mila sent the documents Caleb shared with her to the printer so she could put them together for him.

While she waited for the prints, Mila went to the break room to refill her water bottle where she came across two other assistants she'd often see together. Both of them looked over her when she walked in and Mila couldn't quite decipher their expressions, but she also didn't care for what they may have been thinking.

After greeting her, they both returned to their conversation in a hushed tone. Mila couldn't make much of what they were saying, but she did hear Caleb's name, a gasp, and the word 'when.'

Mila assumed at least one of them had slept with Caleb, if not both. She regularly saw him flirting with women in the office, especially the assistants. In fact, Mila was one of the few women who Caleb didn't flirt with and whenever he did look at her, it often seemed to be an expression of subtle disgust. She figured he was the type of man who didn't like women he found unattractive—that he was the type of man who thought women were only on this planet to be appealing to him and took offense to anyone who didn't fit his mold of attractiveness.

After filling up her water bottle, Mila picked up the finished stack of papers and returned to her desk to put them in order.

MILA SAT at a table toward the edge of the bar with her friends Jade and Greg and she had just taken her fifth shot with the two of them. While Mila enjoyed a good party, she wasn't usually the type to drink so much.

"Damn," Jade said. "You must've had a *really* rough week..."

"Did you not believe me?" Mila questioned.

"I mean, it's not like you work a job or anything, so what do you have to be stressed about?"

"Being a bad bitch *is* a job," Mila replied, flipping her hair in an exaggerated motion.

Greg chuckled as he shook his head. "It's been a while since you came out with us. Your ass has been *traveling* traveling."

"I have, but now I'm ready to stay in one place for a bit. Maybe if I sit still, I'll figure out what I want to do with my life."

"What do you mean?" Jade asked.

"I don't know, all my friends have dreams and goals and shit. You're going to law school and Greg is out here recording music. Meanwhile, all I'm doing is fucking and traveling."

"Bitch!" Jade exclaimed. "Fucking and traveling sounds like a damn good life."

"I mean, yeah, but I just feel like I should be doing more."

"Don't put too much pressure on yourself," Greg assured. "What's for you is for you."

"He's right." Jade nodded. "And it sounds like you're too much into your head. You have the luxury of enjoying a soft life, so take it all in."

"Yeah, you're right..." Mila agreed with them so they could move on from the subject—she regretted bringing it up in the first place. She never felt inadequate, but she had moments where she worried about not doing enough in her life.

Unlike the people she surrounded herself with, Mila never had big dreams. She didn't want to take over the family business, she didn't want to get married, and she didn't want to have kids. The closest Mila ever got to a 'dream' was traveling the world, and now that she'd done that, she had no idea what 'next steps' would be for her. She'd been growing bored with her life after finishing her travels, and even when she did switch things up with new partners or by visiting friends in other parts of the country, Mila found her life starting to feel redundant, and she didn't like it.

"Anyway," Mila sighed before she cut her eyes in the direction they'd been going most of the night. "What do y'all want to drink? Next round is on me... Kinda."

"What do you mean 'kinda'?"

"You'll see..." Mila straightened up in her seat and turned her lips into a small, flirty smile just when the man she'd been exchanging glances with since they first arrived at the bar came up to them. He appeared to be older than Mila, about early- to mid-forties with a solid build and standing at close to six feet.

"Hey," he said to Mila. "I'm Julian. What's your name?"

"It's Mila," she replied, batting her eyelashes before gesturing to her friends. "And this is Jade and this is Greg."

Julian smiled and nodded. "A pleasure to meet you all. So, may I buy you a drink?"

Mila lightly touched his arm and tilted her head to the side. "That's so sweet of you. I'll have a gin martini. Jade, Greg? What do you two want?" Mila figured Julian was only referring to her when he asked about buying a drink, but she wanted to see what would happen when she put him on the spot—whether he'd attempt to correct her and risk embarrassing himself, or if he would just go with it.

She was impressed when he did the latter and listened to Jade and Greg's orders before heading to the bar to order them drinks.

Jade's mouth was agape as she watched him walk away. "How the hell do you always do that?"

"When you got it, you got it." Mila shrugged nonchalantly. "I don't know... Ask Greg, he dates women. Maybe he can give some insights."

Jade turned to Greg, clasped her hands together, and leaned in, inviting him to answer the question.

"I mean..." he started. "Mila is just one of those people who has natural sex appeal. I've said this before, but if we weren't such close friends since childhood and almost felt like siblings, I'd probably hit on her too. She gives off big dick energy, but like... as a person without a dick."

"He means bad bitch energy," Mila added with a wink. "And I wear a dick sometimes."

Jade bursted out laughing. "Mila! This is not the time for any pegging stories. Speaking of which, is whatever his name was gonna get any tonight?"

Mila pursed her lips and looked around as if she were weighing the options. "Not tonight. I'll give him some good conversation and see where it could go from there. Best case scenario, he might get some another day if I'm feeling it. Plus, Mother Nature is pissed at me again for not getting pregnant this month and this bitch is choosing violence."

Greg shook his head amused. "You are a whole mess."

"Isn't she?" Jade agreed.

Mila mockingly flashed a toothy smile. "And y'all love me, anyway."

Oh, For Real?

Mila was laying on her couch on a video call with her friend Naomi Laurent. They'd been growing closer over the past year or so and had reached the point of speaking on the phone at least weekly.

"I'm surprised you're calling me from your honeymoon, Naomi," Mila teased. "Sebastien gave your kitty a break?"

"More like I gave him a break," Naomi replied. She turned the camera to Sebastien who was laying asleep on the bed.

"Ohhhh! Get it, Mrs. Laurent! Not you put his ass to sleep."

Naomi giggled and shook her head. "I wore one of the sets you put in that 'fun bag' you gave us for the wedding and he got a bit carried away."

Mila sat up with her excitement. "Wait. Which one? Was it the red piece?"

Naomi nodded. "It was."

"Shit! I'd get carried away too! That was my favorite set I put in there. I was about to buy one for myself."

"You should!" Naomi agreed. "Anyway, how have you been since you got back to Lenrod City? Thanks again for coming out to the wedding and for all your help, girl. I really appreciate it."

"No need to to thank me. That's what friends do. And it's been... interesting. I've been helping Alexis out with some business stuff and just took on a big project. She's actually stopping by soon so we can talk about it."

"Oh nice! What are you doing for it?"

"It's a mix of administrative stuff and uh... research. A bit of competitive analysis. It's daunting right now, to be honest, but I have some ideas for ways to spice it up and have fun."

"Really? What did you have in mind?"

Just as Mila was about to answer Naomi's question, she was cut off by loud knocking at her door.

"I know that SWAT team ass knock anywhere," Mila groaned. "That's Alexis. She's early... I'm sorry, Naomi."

"It's okay!" Naomi assured. "I'm about to take a nap myself anyway. I'll talk to you later. Love you."

"Love you too," Mila replied before hanging up and going to open the door.

Alexis, Mila's ever serious older sister, stood in the hall with her arms crossed and tapping her foot impatiently. "Hey Alexis, you're early."

"Mila, you know how I am. Am I not always early?"

"You're right," Mila surrendered and turned to lead Alexis inside.

As she followed Mila into her apartment, Alexis' eyes went wide when she saw bouquets of roses on every surface. "Damn, Mila. I know you have your fair share of suitors, but did all the men send the same flowers?"

"No." Mila bit out. "These are from Eric. I told his ass to leave me the hell alone, but as he did when we were dating, he ignored my requests. He's hell-bent on getting back together."

"Wow. And don't you hate roses?"

"Yes! I told him that several times while we were dating. He never paid attention to shit I had to say."

"You'd think he would do better if he wanted you back so badly."

"That's what I've been saying!" Mila exclaimed. "Did you at least tell him to stop asking about me?"

"Why would I do that? I only see him once every couple of months. It's not like he's keeping tabs on your day-to-day."

"Fair enough. It's weird to me that we ended things a while ago and he's still sending me flowers and cards and shit at least once a month."

"That *is* creepy," Alexis agreed as she relaxed on Mila's couch. "Just keep ignoring him and then maybe he'll finally move on when he realizes that you're not going back to him."

"Yeah, I hope so... Wine?" Mila offered.

"Do you have any sweet whites?"

"Of course I do. I keep a bottle chilled just for you."

"Oh, you're such a great little sister," Alexis said sarcastically.

Mila hummed her agreement and poured her sister a glass before joining her on the couch.

"So, how did your first week at PMC go?"

"That whole office is a mess! I swear the only reason they haven't been sued or exposed to the media is because of those ironclad fucking NDAs. And messiest of them all are the execs. Do you know how much tea the other assistants have already given me? Nearly all of the married execs are cheating on their spouses! Hell, some of the men even have whole ass families that their wives know nothing about."

"Yikes!" Alexis cringed. "Do you think what you've seen already is enough to take them down?"

Mila shook her head. "Unfortunately, no... Hostile work environments are so common. They'd probably just bury it under other stories. And the personal life shit is juicy, but not really enough to take them down. We need to uncover something that'll piss off investors."

"Yeah, you're right. What other updates do you have? What are the three you work for like?"

"First off, Caleb is an asshole," Mila explained. "You can tell he's a spoiled rich boy who always got what he wanted. Plus, not only is he filthy fucking rich, he's also hot—which I hate to admit, but it's objectively true. I can almost promise that he has never experienced a consequence ever in his life, nor has he ever been denied what he wanted. But no one in the office cares because he is the playmaker and makes the company good money."

"Damn, he sounds like he was born to be a douche."

"Yup. And I'm stuck having to behave like a 'good assistant,'" Mila said mockingly. "What's fucked up is that by my third day, he was already throwing me curveballs and shit like he wanted me to fuck up. Like, he'd ask for his usual coffee, but when I return with it, he'd say he asked for something different and I know damn well that he didn't. He keeps playing these obnoxious games, but I got something for his ass in due time."

"You're probably right. And the other two?"

"Justin is very focused, it seems—business always comes first and after that comes his parents, and then his girlfriend. She's beautiful and a sweetheart, but something feels off about them. I can't really place my finger on it, though. It's probably rooted in him being a people pleaser, which I've read right off the bat because he is constantly on edge about getting shit right and satisfying *all* PMC Group stakeholders as if that's realistic."

Alexis nodded attentively.

"As for Adrian," Mila continued. "He's the coolest of the three and super courteous. He's like the polar opposite of Caleb. He greets me when he comes in and always has a warm smile on his face. He also calls me 'Ms. Mila' and I'm not gonna lie, that shit kinda turns me on. There's also something about him that gives pleasure-seeker vibes, I bet he's a freak on the low. I'm surprised that I've never run into him at any dungeons or sex clubs in the city. Then again, with traveling and all, I haven't been much into the scene."

"You gathered all of that in just a week?" Alexis gawked. "You've always been damn good at reading people to the point that it's scary... And I'm going to forget about that last part of what you just said."

"It's one of my many talents. But yeah, you're gonna owe me a lot of shit after I finish this mission you have me on, especially considering that I have to deal with Caleb's rude ass."

"I thought you said you had something planned for him 'in due time'?" Alexis asked, raising a challenging brow.

Mila waved her off. "Yeah, yeah... But I still have to keep it tame, don't I? Like being on my best behavior or something?"

"You told me it seems like an anything goes culture." Alexis shrugged. "So if that's the case, then do you. I just need for you not to lose your job or get caught. And I trust you enough to know that you won't, especially since Thompson Luxe Group could possibly be on the line."

"Oh for real?" Mila leaned in toward Alexis with an amused grin. "Then let the games begin."

Still Here

Adrian entered PMC Group's offices with two coffees. It was the second week with Mila as his new assistant and he had already grown fond of her. Just from her first week, he noticed how quickly she adapted to the new environment and she seemed to be doing well with handling the often unreasonable demands of attending to him, Caleb, and Justin.

"I bought you coffee," Adrian chimed as he approached Mila's desk. "You like iced lattes, right?"

Adrian was often the first of the three men to arrive and he preferred to start his day with Mila in his office going over his schedule with him. Meanwhile, Justin would have Mila print out his schedule and tape it to his desk before start of day and Caleb requested she send an email at the beginning and middle of the day providing updates.

"Thanks, Mr. Collins." Mila accepted the coffee and followed Adrian into his office.

She sat across from him with a tablet in her hands while he unpacked his laptop and connected it to an extra monitor.

"So Ms. Mila," he said to her with a smile. "What's on the calendar for today?"

"Right, your first meeting is with David Greyson II of Greyson-James law firm..."

As Mila went on, Adrian was barely paying attention to her words as he admired the woman herself. From the moment he first saw her, there was something about Mila that drew him in. She was a beautiful woman, no doubt. Her full lips were often decorated with gloss or lipstick—a bold red being his favorite shade. She had a small, barely noticeable diamond stud that pierced her cute broad nose. And her brown skin had a deep golden undertone to it that gave it a natural glow.

Mila's heavenly curves embodied Adrian's view of femininity itself and since they first met, he'd often have to fight back thoughts of showing her just how much he appreciated every inch of her form.

She also leaked pure sex appeal with her underlying confidence that slightly intimidated Adrian—only making him more attracted to her.

There was a pause in her listing off his meetings and Adrian broke himself out of his trance to scan Mila's face. "Is something wrong?"

"No. This name just looked familiar and I can't remember why. Logan Richards?"

"Ah, Logan! You've probably heard me mention him or have seen his name on old copies of my schedule. He's a friend of mine and we have lunch at least once a month when he's not traveling. He recently returned from a trip to Atlanta and then he was playing catchup at work last week and now we're finally getting around to seeing each other today."

Logan was one of the business associates that Adrian had first met at The Scarlet Lounge and they immediately clicked. It was useful that Logan was an investment banker as PMC Group could always use funding opportunities and the company's final goal after demolishing competition was to launch their IPO.

Mila nodded. "I see... Well, let's get through the rest of these. You have a long day ahead."

AFTER MEETING with Adrian and putting Justin's schedule on his desk, Mila returned to her desk to email Caleb his list of meetings. As soon as she logged into her computer, Caleb entered the floor and Mila was immediately annoyed by his presence. The week prior, she'd experienced nothing but attitude from him when he wasn't straight up ignoring her.

Mila wanted to put him in his place several times—predicting she could probably break him in a week or two if she wanted—but she ultimately decided on a longer-term strategy... A quick one wasn't good enough for her and he made the perfect target for mind games.

Caleb normally ignored Mila, passing her desk to enter his office when he arrived in the mornings, but this time, he acknowledged her.

"Oh, you're still here?" he questioned sarcastically. "Damn, now I owe Justin a hundred bucks. I thought sure you'd be gone by now, especially after having to work through lunch every day the second half of last week."

Secure in her plans for him, Mila looked up from her desk to make eye contact with Caleb.

"Mr. Jeffries will be here shortly, Mr. Peterson," she replied cheerfully. "The rest of your schedule for the day is in your inbox and I'll be sure to follow up with more updates mid-day, as per usual."

"Whatever." Caleb scoffed without saying anything else and went on to his office. He was used to receiving more of a response from people, whether it be positive because of his money or looks, or negative —which was very rare—because of his attitude. However, Mila treated him as if he was ordinary, and Caleb didn't like that at all.

A snide look came to Mila's face, satisfied that she was already getting under his skin. Just as she suspected, he'd likely be the easiest to crack. Showing a narcissist like Caleb indifference was the best way to bring him right where she needed.

Soon after Caleb went into his office, Justin entered the floor. Typically, when he arrived he would at least have the decency to give Mila a curt greeting using her name. However, he approached her this morning.

"Good morning, Mr. Matsuda," Mila greeted. "How was your weekend?"

Ignoring her greeting, Justin went straight into his request. "Mila, I need you to get things prepared for visitors I have coming here for meetings a month from now. I'm going to email you the contact information for their assistants so you can coordinate with them. They're coming in from Japan for a business summit and they're carving out time to meet with me."

"Yes, of course."

"And this needs to go perfectly, Mila," Justin said sternly. "There can be no hiccups in any of the logistics. Their time is limited and I really need to make this connection with them. Do you understand?"

Mila was irked at the patronizing tone, but maintained her attentive demeanor.

"I understand, Mr. Matsuda."

"Okay, like I said, I'll send you the contact information for their assistants. You're also going to need to do some research to make sure that you know proper Japanese etiquette for greeting them when they come to meet with me. I won't have time to hand-hold you through it all and you need to take care not to offend our guests."

If this uptight asshole does not get the fuck out my face in ten seconds... Mila thought.

"I'll check in regularly to make sure you're on this," Justin finished before going to his office.

"This job can't be over soon enough," Mila muttered to herself.

MILA WAS SITTING at her desk eating a yogurt when Logan arrived on the floor to meet with Adrian for their lunch. As he got closer, Logan recognized her from the airport.

"Well, we meet again, Ms. Mila," he greeted with a knowing smile. "Funny seeing you here."

Mila met his smile with her own and reached for the phone on her desk to call Adrian.

"I'll let Mr. Collins know that you're here."

She was only on her second week at PMC Group, but Mila was ready to start playing games, especially after realizing that the company had an 'anything goes' culture, ironclad NDAs, and a non-existent HR department. The coincidence that Adrian just so happened to be friends with the stranger who asked Mila about queening not long ago was the perfect opportunity to begin.

"Yes, Mila," Adrian answered when she called.

"Mr. Richards is here for your lunch."

"Excellent, could you let him know I'll be out in five minutes? I'm just finishing up an email."

"Of course," Mila replied before removing the phone from her ear and placing it on the desk. She allowed the sound of the impact to make it seem like she hung up, but the call was still connected.

"So, you remembered me?" Mila asked, directing her question at Logan.

"Men don't often forget meeting a woman such as yourself."

Adrian was just about to hang up the call when he heard them and his curiosity was sparked as to how Logan may have known Mila.

"Of course you don't. Anyway, Mr. Collins will be out in five."

"You never did call me. Was my read wrong?"

Mila then leaned forward with her elbow on her desk, rested her chin on her knuckles, and looked up at Logan. "You mean about the queening?"

On the other side of the call that was still connected, Adrian's eyes went wide when he heard Mila. He was very much familiar with the term and knew it was something that Logan was into. His mind began to wander, curious if Logan actually prepositioned Mila, whether she understood the request, and if it was something she might be into. And if she was, Adrian wondered if she'd done it often, what her thighs might feel like on each side of his head, if she was more the dominant type or...

His thoughts were interrupted when Logan responded to Mila's question.

"Yes, about the queening," he said.

"Hmmm," Mila was obviously feigning ignorance as she tapped her finger to her chin. "Could you explain to me what that is, exactly?"

Logan leaned against the reception desk and closer to Mila, licking his lips. From her demeanor, he knew that Mila knew what queening was. She was clearly challenging him to say it out loud. And he had no shame in doing so.

With a confident sneer, he narrowed his eyes at her. "Queening: As in I want you to sit on my fa—"

"Hey!"

Logan was cut off when Adrian walked out of his office and approached.

"Sorry I kept you waiting, Logan. I just needed to get an email out."

Logan's face fell and his shoulders slacked. Turning to his friend with a fake smile, Logan greeted Adrian.

"Damn, man... That five minutes was rough," he quipped. "Poor Ms. Mila here was trying to keep me entertained so I wouldn't bore myself to death."

"Whatever," Adrian scoffed before his eyes connected with Mila's. "Thank you for keeping this one entertained, Ms. Mila. I'll make sure you won't have to suffer through that again."

Mila giggled and shook her head. "It's all good, Mr. Collins. Mr. Richards was just about to give me a valuable vocabulary lesson. We'll have to pick up from there next time."

"And that, we very much will," Logan replied with a wink.

The men made their way to the elevator and when it closed with just the two of them in it, Adrian turned to Logan.

"Do you know my new assistant?"

"I'm working on it," Logan said. "Ironically, I ran into her at the airport when I was in Atlanta. I chatted her up a bit, but I assumed she was traveling to Lenrod City for fun or something. I didn't consider that she might live here."

Adrian nodded. "What did you talk to her about?"

"And why do you need to know that?"

"Hey, she's our new assistant and I'm trying to figure her out."

"Well, you've been around her. You're not getting the same read I got from her, Adrian? C'mon, man... Don't forget where you and I met in the first place."

"What do you mean?" Adrian tried his best to maintain his bluff. "What read?"

"Oh please... The woman gives off a *certain energy*, if you know what I mean," Logan commented suggestively. "If I was an asshole of a friend and cool with making shit awkward for you and her, I'd invite her to The Scarlet Lounge for some play... Her presence alone is strong enough to practically put me on my knees."

"That's because you're easy," Adrian replied, shaking his head.

"You only say that because she works for you. If you ran into her in a different setting, like at The Scarlet Lounge, what do you think the dynamic would be?"

"I'm not going to answer that."

"Yeah." Logan snorted. "I thought so."

EPISODE 10

Not Worth Fitting Into

"Only on week two and I'm working late? What the fuck?" Mila grumbled to herself as she printed out copies of briefing papers for her three 'bosses'. "I can't wait to finish this so I can just go on with my life. I need to speed this shit up."

Mila finished printing the papers and went back to her desk with three binders to put them in order before heading to each of the men's offices to deliver them.

Starting with Adrian, his door was already open, so Mila knocked on the frame and he looked up at her with his characteristically warm smile. She approached his desk to hand him the binder and it was never lost on Mila the way his eyes would often linger on her form and it emboldened her to sway her hips just slightly more than usual.

Once she reached his desk and sat down the binder, Adrian's eyes finally met hers. "Thank you," he said softly. His lips parted like he was about to say something, but he closed them again and Mila turned around to go to her next stop.

"Wait," Adrian called.

Mila turned around and tilted her head. "How may I help you, Mr. Collins?"

"You can call me Adrian."

"Okay, how may I help you, Adrian?"

"Oh, I just wanted to apologize for having you work late already. For what it's worth, it *is* a sign that you're doing so well at your job that we're trusting you with more responsibilities just on week two."

"Awesome," Mila chimed. "My goal is for you three to trust me completely, so it looks like I'm making decent progress," she added with a wink before turning and walking away. She didn't need to see it to know that Adrian's eyes were glued to her.

Approaching Justin's office, Mila knocked on his closed door. "Come in," he answered. When Mila opened it, he signaled to her that he was on a call and she held up the binder to show him why she was there. He nodded and pointed her to the coffee table across the room in the small seating area before returning to his call.

Mila took her time walking over to the table so she could hear as much of Justin's conversation as possible. He was speaking Japanese and little did he know, Mila was fluent in it. From what she heard of the conversation, Justin was touching base with one of the representatives from the small luxury fashion line in Tokyo that would be visiting in a month. Unsurprising to Mila, it turned out that they would indeed be discussing the prospect of joining PMC Group at their meeting.

After leaving Justin's office, Mila took a deep breath as she approached Caleb's door. He grew more obnoxious with each day. He was rude and disrespectful, but that's not what got to her. What bothered Mila was that even though she was working on it, she wasn't in a position to put him in his place just yet. She already had specific plans in mind for him, but in order break him down in the way that she wanted, Mila knew that it required time and patience.

She knocked on Caleb's door a few times, but he never answered.

Assuming he'd gone home for the night and she missed him while she was in Adrian or Justin's offices, Mila opened the door and as soon as she did, she knew exactly why Caleb wasn't answering.

Muffled moans filled the room and a woman was bent over Caleb's desk while he took her from behind. Unfazed by the scene, Mila walked further into the office and when Caleb noticed her, his eyes went wide, but he didn't stop what he was doing. She held up the binder and he flicked his wrist, gesturing toward the opposite side of the room for her to put it there.

Caleb wrapped the woman's long blonde hair around his hand, yanked her head back, and smacked her ass. "Close your eyes, slut," he commanded, though they were already squeeze shut.

When Mila saw the woman's face, she realized it was Shannon and the reason her noises were so muffled was because it appeared her own underwear were stuffed in her mouth.

Mila removed her heels at the door so that she could walk across the room without making a sound. She figured Shannon would be mortified to see that Mila walked in on them and wanted to spare her the embarrassment.

While Caleb continued to fuck Shannon, his eyes narrowed at Mila —something about how unbothered she was at the fact he was mostly naked and in the middle of sex, offended Caleb. She always seemed to be indifferent to him and it pissed him off. He slammed his hand on Shannon's ass loud enough for it to echo through the office and started pounding her harder. "Take my cock you fucking whore," he told her and Shannon let out a muffled squealed when he got even rougher.

To Caleb's disappointment, Mila didn't react at all, walking back to the door and grabbing her shoes before leaving.

When she returned to her desk, Mila saw a note in Adrian's handwriting.

Be sure to charge your ride home to the company.
Thanks again! ~Adrian

Cute, she thought to herself and smiled when she looked at the note. She'd already planned to charge an Uber Black to PMC Group for keeping her in the office late, anyway.

It was the next morning and Mila had gone through her usual routine of meeting with Adrian, putting Justin's schedule on his desk, and emailing Caleb. Sitting at her desk, she started writing her to-do list for the day when Caleb walked in.

"My office, now," he instructed without stopping or looking at Mila.

She took her time gathering her tablet and getting up from her seat. Caleb was used to people jumping at his beck and call and while it was Mila's job to do so as well, considering she was his assistant, she refused to show any signs of eagerness toward him. To Mila, Caleb was just another task and it was obvious to him that she did not have any personal stake in impressing him—yet another thing about her that got under his skin.

When Mila finally walked into Caleb's office, she sat in the chair across from him at his desk while he appeared to be getting his computer set up and then going through emails. As she waited for him to say something, Mila played around on her tablet to keep herself busy. She knew her approach to Caleb was an effective one. So, rather than expending energy on asking him what he wanted, Mila was going to pass the time until he spoke.

About ten minutes went by of the office being mostly silent other than the sound of Caleb's typing and Mila's nails making contact with her tablet screen until he finally spoke.

"I bet you saw something last night that you liked," Caleb said without removing his eyes from his computer.

"Something last night...?" Mila said softly as she pondered to herself out loud. She gave it some thought as if she'd forgotten about walking in on him, and her act was so well that Caleb believed it. After her long pause, Mila said, "Oh, you and Shannon?"

"Yeah, keep that shit to yourself..." He momentarily shifted his eyes to her before his gaze returned to the screen. "And you won't need to worry about anything like that happening between you and I. When it comes to the category of assistants I'd fuck, you don't exactly *fit*."

"*Someone's* overconfident," Mila mumbled. She did so just loud enough so that he could hear it, but low enough so that it didn't sound intentional.

Caleb's eyes cut over to her again and he gave her almost a glare. "What did you say?"

"Oh nothing, Mr. Peterson," she said with a smile. "It's just that there are certain categories not worth fitting into, you know?" Mila was satisfied when she saw the surprise quickly flash across Caleb's face before it returned neutral.

"Anyway..." she sighed. "I should get going. You have a meeting in fifteen minutes and I know you like to prepare ahead of time. I've already emailed you a biography on Mr. Romano."

"Right," he affirmed before waving Mila off. "You're dismissed."

When she got up and turned away to head toward the door, Caleb watched her with his eyes narrowed. Mila pissed him off, but he couldn't bring himself to fire her as he had done to assistants in the past.

He would never admit it to himself, but the woman intrigued him. The way she carried herself as if completely unbothered by him was unusual for Caleb and he wanted to see just how long it would take until he could get under her skin. He wanted to evoke some sort of emotion—positive or negative—from her other than the aloofness she often showed him.

Once Mila returned to her desk, she noticed a missed call from reception downstairs. "Shit," she whispered to herself. She dialed the number back, hoping that whomever was waiting hadn't been waiting too long.

"This is reception," a man answered.

"Hi, this is Mila Nelson with PMC Group. You called me earlier. Is there a visitor downstairs for one of my execs?"

"Yes, her name is Ashley Kirkland and she said she is here to see Mr. Justin Matsuda. You're down as the primary contact for him."

"Right. You can send her up. Thank you."

After hanging up, Mila then called Justin's desk.

"Hello," he answered. "What is it?"

"Ashley Kirkland is here to see you, Mr. Matsuda. She'll be up shortly."

Mila heard him groan from the other side of the phone before letting out a deep sigh.

"I told her I wouldn't have time today and of course she shows up anyway," he grumbled. "I have a few more things I need to take care of before I see her. You can let her in and just keep her in the waiting area."

"Will do," Mila replied.

By the time Ashley reached the twenty-third floor, Mila was standing at the elevators to meet with her.

"Hello," Mila greeted with a smile when Ashley walked through the doors. She carried a large bag from the eatery around the corner and Mila figured Ashley was bringing Justin lunch.

Ashley returned Mila's smile with her own. "Hi, how are you? You must be Justin's new assistant."

Mila ignored the fact that Ashley seemed to forget that the two of them met briefly before during Mila's first week at PMC Group. "That's correct, I'm Mila. He's actually tying up a few things right now and will be coming to see you shortly. For the time being, you can sit out here in the waiting area by my desk."

"Thank you so much!"

After about twenty minutes went by, Mila grew concerned that Justin may have forgotten Ashley was waiting for him, so she dialed his number and the trills of the phone went on for so long, she thought sure it'd go to voicemail before he answered at the very last moment.

"Hi Mila, I know Ashley is waiting and I'll be out soon," he said curtly, hanging up before Mila could say anything.

Mila huffed after hanging up the phone. *Looks like Caleb isn't the only one who needs to learn... Another one for the long game.* She thought to herself before turning her attention to Ashley.

"Ms. Kirkland. Sorry about the wait. Mr. Matsuda said he'll be out shortly. I hope your food doesn't get too cold, but we have microwaves in the break rooms if you need them."

"No, it's fine," Ashley assured. "I made sure to get us salads, anyway. This isn't the first time something like this has happened. Justin just gets so wrapped up in his work all the time and I'm used to it."

Mila wondered why a woman like Ashley would put up with a man who seemed to have no interest in prioritizing her.

Another ten minutes went by when Justin finally came out of his office to meet with Ashley.

"Babe," he said as he approached her, a hint of agitation in his tone. "I told you I was busy and wouldn't have time for lunch today. Why'd you come?"

Ashley held up the bags carrying their salads with an apologetic smile. "I just wanted to do something special for you, honey."

"Well, we need to make it quick. I'm preparing for some upcoming meetings and it's important that I nail these."

"Right, of course! Which is why I decided to come here. I really wanted to see you..."

Justin exhaled and guilt hit him as he analyzed the sadness in Ashley's eyes. He'd been telling himself that he loved her, or at least, it would make the most sense for him to love her, especially since they'd been dating for eighteen months and both of their families seemed to approve of the other. He was also tired of his parents constantly being down his throat about getting married and Ashley was his best option at getting there as quickly as possible.

"It's fine, babe," he assured. "Thank you for thinking of me and for bringing the lunch. I'm sorry for being short with you."

"I know how stressful work can be, honey. It's okay."

Once Justin and Ashley went into his office, Mila shook her head.

"Oh, he is *definitely* going to need an attitude adjustment," she noted to herself.

Interest Piqued

Nearly a month had passed since Mila joined PMC Group and she'd gotten into a decent groove while she tried to gain enough trust from Caleb, Justin, and Adrian to learn more about *how* they'd been able to come up so quickly in their industry. Although she had access to their files and schedules, Mila could tell that she was missing a big piece of the puzzle. And whatever that piece was, it would likely be enough to effectively sabotage PMC Group.

As for her interactions with the three men, little to their knowledge, Mila was in complete control every time.

When it came to Adrian, he would tell her to call him by his first name rather than "Mr. Collins," but Mila would only do so on occasion, positioning it as more of a treat for him instead of a given.

For Caleb, Mila's plan of showing him indifference continued to be an effective one. She could tell that he was becoming increasingly frustrated with her lack of emotion toward him and knew it was only a matter of time until he'd make more obvious efforts to get her attention.

With Justin, Mila was still formulating a plan for him. Unlike Adrian or Caleb, he didn't seem to have many obvious desires outside of doing well at work and impressing his family, so Mila knew that her approach would have to differ from what she did with Adrian and Caleb.

"Hi Ms. Mila," Adrian greeted with a smile when he arrived for their usual morning meetings. Mila knew that he meant it playfully, but she still found herself slightly turned on whenever he said it.

And when he *did* call her that, he would receive his small reward.

"Good morning Adrian." Mila returned his smile with her own before getting up to follow him into the office.

As Adrian set up his desk, Mila took notice of a new tattoo on his forearm.

"Did you get a new one?" Mila asked, pointing at Adrian's arm.

"Yeah, I did." He turned out his arm so that Mila could have a better view of his new tattoo, which was a black and gray image of a moth with its wings spread and a pattern on the body that resembled a skull on the back. It was covered with a clear saniderm patch to protect it for its first few days of healing.

Mila gently cradled under Adrian's arm to hold it, being sure not to touch the tattoo itself, even though it was covered. When she made contact with his skin, he couldn't help but enjoy the feeling of her soft hands on him and the way her fingertips caressed other parts of his arms while she admired his tattoos.

"These are all really good," she commented. "Do you have a specific artist you typically go to?"

"Yeah," Adrian gulped as Mila continued to lightly run her fingers over his arm while he spoke. "There's this guy in Wryston who does all of my work."

"Well, he is very talented." When she let go of Adrian's arm, it felt too soon for him and he grew increasingly aware of just how attracted he was to her.

"What about you, Mila? Do you have any tattoos?"

"I do." She nodded. "I have a quote tattooed on my thigh."

"And what does it say?"

Mila gave Adrian a small smile while she had a slight glimmer in her eyes. For a split second, he interpreted the nature of her gaze as flirtation until she let out a small giggle and shook her head.

"I got it when I was like sixteen," she started. "It says: 'If you obey all the rules, you'll miss all the fun'."

"Why do you act like it's something you're embarrassed about?"

"I'm not *embarrassed*. I just think if I'd gotten it a few years later, maybe I would've made the words more complex or something. But, the sentiment is still there. It's definitely my life motto."

"So you're a rule-breaker?" Adrian questioned with a raised brow.

"I can be." Mila shrugged. "Many of life's greatest pleasures are guarded by society's most arbitrary rules. Shame is often associated with the things in life that we find most pleasurable. For example..." She touched Adrian's arm very lightly and traced over another tattoo. "Your tattoos are something enjoy, right? But an arbitrary societal rule says they're unprofessional and that they should be hidden."

When she again pulled away, a sharp breath crossed Adrian's nose before he pursed his lips and nodded. "You make a good point..." He thought about his tattoos as well as other things he knew gave him pleasure and the shame with which they were often associated.

"I try," she chimed with a wink. "Oh! Speaking of rules... Would you mind if I took my full lunch break today? Away from my desk?"

"Of course! I'm actually sorry that you're stuck taking most of your lunches at your desk because we have you so busy. In fact, why don't you take an hour for your lunch break today?"

"Thank you, Adrian."

"So, does this mean you have special plans, or something?"

"I have a date," Mila responded .

Adrian's first reaction was a tensed jaw before he eased up and reminded himself that Mila was an employee. *She is your secretary, Adrian,* he thought to himself. *It doesn't matter if you're attracted to her. You shouldn't feel anything about her going on a date.*

"That sounds lovely," he responded through a fake smile. "So, you're meeting with your boyfriend for lunch?"

"Nah, I'm single. It's just some guy I met at a bar."

"Oh, I see..." Adrian held himself back from prying further. "I hope you enjoy it. Now, let's have a look at my schedule for today."

~

MILA WAS COUNTING down the minutes until her lunch break. She had a decent enough conversation with Julian after he'd bought her, Greg, and Jade drinks at the bar and they agreed to make plans to meet up sometime.

Mila very much enjoyed dating. She liked reading people—it was something she was good at and it would often keep her entertained as she'd make her initial assumptions and assess which ones were correct upon getting to know the person.

Her eyes went up when she saw from her peripherals someone approaching her desk and Mila didn't bother to smile at the the man who came up to her. It was Ben Davies, a mid-level associate at the company who she noticed spent more time kissing up to the big three than doing his job.

She read him as a social climber when they met her first week. He was often short or impolite with assistants unless he was trying to set up a meeting with one the executives through them.

Ben's obvious shallowness reminded Mila of Caleb, but his arrogance was still nowhere near the disdainful CEO she was working under. Also, as much as Mila disliked Caleb, she could admit that the quality of his work was immaculate, while what she'd seen of Ben's was subpar and it was clear he'd gotten by in life with a mix of his privilege and superior schmoozing skills.

"Hi Mila," he greeted when he reached her desk.

"Hello Benjamin," she replied dryly. "Can I help you with something?"

"Yes, you can. Mr. Matsuda put out a request for anyone at mid-level who speaks Japanese to join him at his meeting with those executives from that Tokyo-based fashion line in a couple weeks."

"Yes, he did send that email."

"Right, well I'm the only one who happens to speak Japanese. I studied for my first two years of college and passed all my classes with flying colors."

"Interesting..." Mila knew where the conversation was going, but had no intention of showing Ben any sense of urgency.

"Do I need to spell it out for you?" he said sharply with a change in his tone.

"Have you spoken to Mr. Matsuda about joining his meeting?" replied an unbothered Mila. "He's keen on it going perfectly."

"Yes, I am well-aware of Mr. Matsuda's high standards and I am more than capable of meeting them. He and I have already chatted briefly about this and he's invited me to the meetings."

Mila sighed. "Let me just confirm with him..." She picked up her phone to dial Justin who quickly answered.

"What is it, Mila? I don't see anything on my calendar until around two o'clock. Did something come up?"

"No, I just need your confirmation on something, Mr. Matsuda. Ben Davies is in front of me and said that you'll be allowing him into your meetings with the execs from Japan. Is that true? And if so, would you like me to schedule some time for the two of you to prepare together? I know you've expressed numerous times that you want this go perfectly and—"

"Ben is an excellent worker who is on the fast-track at this company," Justin interrupted. "I trust his testament of his skills and I'm sure he'll be well-prepared for the meeting without me needing to hand-hold him. Thank you, Mila."

After Justin hung up, Mila had to catch herself before rolling her eyes and instead met Ben's gaze. "Mr. Matsuda confirmed, so I'll be sure to add you to the meeting. Please make sure that you are at least fifteen minutes early."

"Of course," Ben huffed before turning and walking away.

Mila shook her head and added Ben to the meeting. While she waited for twelve forty-five to come, Mila scrolled through Caleb, Justin, and Adrian's meetings, taking note of with whom they were speaking. She took note of any connections to the brands her family owned. She knew that this undertaking wouldn't be quick or easy, but she hoped to at least find some hints to start putting together theories on what shady tactics PMC Group was using to acquire so many companies.

"I thought you had a lunch date?" Adrian asked, coming out of his office and approaching Mila's desk on his way to lunch.

"I do. It's not until one o'clock, so I won't leave here until twelve forty-five."

"I see, so it's not too far from here?"

"Nope, we're meeting halfway at some 'American fine dining' spot just a few blocks over."

"Oh! I knew exactly which spot you're talking about. Smith's Restaurant, right? I can recommend some menu options."

"Let's go, Adrian. I'm fucking starving," Caleb groaned as he exited his office. "This intermittent fasting gets me ravenous as soon as the hour hits when I can eat."

Adrian cut his eyes at Caleb, annoyed that he interrupted him and didn't bother acknowledging that Mila was sitting right there while they were obviously having conversation.

"Did you really need to cut me off like mid-sentence?"

"What are you talking about? Oh..." Caleb turned and saw Mila sitting at her desk. "Can't you just send whatever you need from her in an email?"

"It wasn't about business. I was just about to give Mila some lunch recommendations."

An amused grin pulled at Caleb's lips and he looked down at Mila. "I have a recommendation and it's right downstairs. You can go to Saladworks and get the spring mix with a light vinaigrette."

An unfazed Mila replied, "I much prefer topping my salad with avocado and a bit of lime juice."

It was clear to her why Caleb was suggesting a salad, but she responded as if he was making a genuine recommendation to her, taking away the power he thought he'd have with the snide remark.

"Whatever," Caleb mumbled before walking away, leaving Adrian behind.

"Enjoy your lunch, Adrian," Mila said loud enough for Caleb to hear and he was immediately agitated at her use of Adrian's first name. He thought that it was normal for Mila to treat all of three of the men like a chore as she did with Caleb, but it turned out that was not the case. In fact, Caleb was the one of the three who seemed to receive the least response from Mila and he wondered why the others warranted more attention from her than he did.

Caleb turned to Adrian as soon as the elevator doors closed. "So, you're on a first name basis with the assistant?"

"Yes, she's been working for us for almost a month now and there's no need to go overboard with formalities."

"Don't let her get too comfortable or she'll take advantage of you and try to get special treatment or some shit."

Adrian huffed. "Funny coming from the guy who's fucking half the assistants in the office."

"Hey, they come to me," Caleb reasoned. "I just accept what is offered."

"Bullshit. Anyway, what's your problem with Mila? She's good at her job and very friendly."

"Friendly?" Caleb challenged with tense brows. "She seems unengaged more than half the time. Maybe she has a crush on you or some shit. I bet if you buy her a burger or a milkshake, she'll suck your cock."

"Or maybe she's only unengaged when it comes to *you*," Adrian countered. "Mila is relatively social with many other people in the office. It could be that you just don't pique her interest."

Caleb scoffed. "Oh, please... I'm a young and hot billionaire. I pique everyone's interest."

"Evidently not Mila's," Adrian taunted.

"We'll see about that."

Join Us

The day had finally arrived for Justin's meeting with the executives from the Tokyo-based fashion line. Mila came into the office two hours early to ensure the conference room was properly set up, reserve one of the elevators for the day, and confirm that lunch was set to be delivered on time.

Justin also arrived early, but still about an hour after Mila and he was pleased to see that everything already appeared to be in order. With pursed lips and a slow nod of approval, he scanned over the conference room that was perfectly set up for the meeting. He'd been impressed with Mila's work throughout the time she'd been at PMC Group and she was the longest he'd gone without having any complaints about an assistant.

"This looks good, Mila," he commented. "I'm going to do some last minute prep up until it's time for our meeting. Ben should be getting here not long before our guests arrive, so you just have to greet them and hand them over to him."

"Easy enough," Mila replied calmly before heading back to her desk. Given that she was so early for work and had essentially finished her morning tasks other than meeting with Adrian who hadn't arrived yet, she scrolled through her missed texts from the night before.

ALEXIS

Hey sis, how's that thing I asked you to work
on going?

Mila rolled her eyes at the vagueness of her sister's message. Alexis would often speak in code in any written correspondence about Mila working at PMC Group to avoid creating any proof of what they were doing.

910-555-0923

Did you get the roses I sent? Can we please
talk sometime soon? I really want to
reconnect.

Again, Mila rolled her eyes. From the unsaved number and the content of the message, she knew it was Eric. After she rejected Eric's proposal, the two of them broke up and that was it for her. She didn't know what else there was to discuss. They simply were not a good match and Eric seemed oblivious to that. In fact, Mila had been planning to dump him right around the time that he proposed and in the back of her mind, she wondered if it was some strong-arm attempt to save their failing relationship.

LOGAN

I'm back in town next week. What do you
think?

Mila released an entertained huff and shook her head. Logan was a bold man who'd made it *very* clear to Mila that he wanted to please her, but he was too easy. She enjoyed a bit of a game beforehand, but she still kept in contact with him in case she was in the mood some day.

JADE

Hey girl! Have you heard of this dungeon
and lifestyle club called The Scarlet Lounge?
It's the most exclusive one in the city and I
just got an invite. I know you haven't been in
the scene as much since you've been back,
but do you wanna come as my plus-one?

Mila pondered Jade's offer for a few minutes. She used to be more involved with the community, attending play parties and other events, but she'd lost interest. It was fun and she'd often encourage her other friends to get involved, which was why Jade had entered the scene, but Mila's sex drive was oddly out of wack over the past year. She still had a roster of people she'd some times hook up with, but she was able to go weeks or even months without having sex.

MILA

Hey girl! How about you go a few times with Greg or someone else and get a good read on the energy and let me know?

After finishing her text messages, Mila turned her attention back to her computer and scrolled through emails as people entered the office for work. Ben had arrived and oddly didn't meet with Justin before the representatives from the Japanese company were set to get there. Mila was surprised that a micromanager like Justin didn't want to meet with Ben every day leading up to the meeting, but she also recognized why that was probably the case.

Finally, Mila got the call that she'd been waiting for notifying her that the Japanese guests were downstairs. She sent Justin and Ben an email that she was going to retrieve them.

JUSTIN HAD BEEN PACING his office and going over his latest notes about the executives from the Japanese boutique luxury brand he'd be meeting soon. PMC Group had been aiming for more international acquisitions and this would be their opportunity to finally enter the Asian market. Justin's family name and connections helped him get in contact with the brand in the first place and he wanted to be directly responsible for what he hoped would end in PMC Group acquiring the company.

As soon as he received Mila's email, Justin made a path directly to the coat closet in his office, put on his suit jacket, and then called Ben to meet with him in PMC Group's lobby to receive their guests from Mila.

The elevator they'd rented for the day chimed and the doors opened to Mila and the three executives chatting it up—much to Justin's surprised. From what he could overhear, Mila was speaking Japanese almost without accent, and he was impressed that she did the homework of learning a few phrases of small talk in the language. He guessed that she probably watched a lot of videos to make herself sound so fluent.

After handing the guests off to Ben, Mila returned to her desk while he, Justin, and their Japanese visitors went into the conference room to start their meeting.

~

MILA EXHALED AS SOON as the door shut on the highly-anticipated meeting. And she planned to take another long exhale along with a stiff drink whenever the meeting finished and she would be completely free of the stressful task.

"Good morning, Mila," Adrian greeted with a warm smile when he came in. "How are you?"

"Good morning, Mr. Collins. I'm doing much better now that Mr. Matsuda is in his meeting with his guests from Japan."

"He's been so on edge about that for the past several weeks and he already puts too much pressure on himself as it is. Hopefully all goes well... That reminds me, we won't be able to have our morning meeting."

"Why not?"

"Justin asked me to skip it today so that you're at your desk in case they need anything. Is that alright with you?"

"I guess it makes sense." Mila sighed. "I'll type up a quick email for you with a summary of what your day should look like."

"You are perfect," Adrian complimented and Mila looked up at him with a satisfied expression.

"Thanks, Adrian. I get that a lot," she quipped.

Adrian smiled and shook his head. A few seconds of awkward silence ensued while he hovered around Mila's desk before finally asking the question that had been on his mind for weeks.

"So, how did your lunch date a couple weeks back go?"

"It was alright. At least the food was good."

"Oh, you didn't enjoy your company?"

Mila shrugged. "He referred to himself as an 'alpha male' and that was my cue to not go on another date with him."

Adrian tilted his head curiously. "Why not?"

"The whole 'alpha male' thing is a myth, first of all. And besides, I much prefer men who know how to... *behave*."

The way Mila's voice smoothed out at that last word in a manner that sounded suggestive caused Adrian to gulp as he wondered if it was on purpose.

"What do you mean by th—"

Adrian was cut off at the sound of the conference room door opening and a furious Justin scolding Ben.

"What the fuck was that? You offended our guests and embarrassed me and this company! Did you seriously lie about being fluent in Japanese just to get in on this meeting? It sounds like you did two weeks of a language app or some shit and thought it would fly."

Mila and Adrian exchanged a wide-eyed glance before their gazes returned to the scene.

"Mr. Matsuda," Ben chuckled nervously as he tried to recover. "I'm just a bit rusty is all—"

"No, that wasn't 'rusty'," Justin cut him off, still speaking sharply. "That was shit and you insulted their CEO. Get out of here... And don't expect us to let you back in."

"But sir—"

"I told you to get the fuck out!" Justin snapped.

Heeding the anger in his tone, Ben quickly scurried away and made a path straight for the elevators.

Justin muttered something under his breath as he ran his fingers through his hair. Mila audibly gasped when she noticed the disgruntled guests leaving the conference room before Justin turned back to them, bowing and apologizing profusely in Japanese.

Right when Adrian looked like he was going to jump in to help, Mila raised her hand to signal to him to stand down.

"I got it," she assured before getting up to help the guests gather their coats.

With his jaw tensed and swallowing a mix of his anger and regret, Justin watched as Mila assisted the guest. He noticed that she continued to speak with them in perfect Japanese and came to the conclusion that perhaps she *didn't* just pick up a few terms. Suddenly, his hope started to return when he noticed the CEO who had just been offended by Ben was conversing with Mila and had a big smile on his face—he even started laughing about something she'd said.

When he heard Mila ask that the executives at least stay for lunch and they agreed, Justin pulled her to the side while they again removed their coats.

"You speak Japanese?" he questioned skeptically.

"Yes, I studied Japanese for like five years and then I lived in Japan," Mila replied without thinking about it. "And it turns out that the small, rural Japanese town where the CEO is from just so happens to be where I lived for eighteen months while I rounded out my Japanese studies."

"Really? That wasn't in your resume."

"Oh, um... I didn't think it'd be that helpful for an assistant job," Mila chuckled innocently and rubbed the back of her neck. "My parents always told me that Spanish or Mandarin would've been more beneficial."

Justin twisted his lips as he mulled over what to do next. He looked between Mila and their guests before grabbing Mila's tablet off of her desk and pushing it into her hands.

"Well, it's extremely beneficial now because you may have saved us from completely fumbling this business opportunity. Please, join us for the lunch meeting you just secured and take thorough notes."

Mila nodded as she accepted her tablet.

"I owe you one, Mila," Justin added with a whisper.

Small Talk

Caleb, Justin, and Adrian sat in couches at the cigar bar they frequented. It had now been close to four months of Mila working for them and she'd already captivated each of the men in three very different ways.

Caleb's intrigue was toeing obsession. He found it frustrating that Mila seemed more interested in everyone except him and wasn't used to being treated with such indifference. He wanted to do anything he could to get *some* emotion out of her—whether that be positive or negative—just so he could say that he won, that he had some type of power over her.

After Mila saved Justin from a total loss at his meeting with the Japanese executives some months back, he was so appreciative and impressed that he started having her join all his meetings that were in Japanese. He noticed that she wasn't just good for note-taking—Mila also seemed to have keen business sense in her recaps of their discussions.

Adrian had accepted the fact that he was deeply attracted to Mila, but knew it would be wrong to pursue anything with her considering he was her boss. He'd at times have to fight back his fantasies about her, especially when he realized the way she seemed to respond when he called her *Ms.* Mila. Her conversation with Logan that he'd overheard before had Adrian wondering if she ever took up Logan's officer, but he knew he had no business asking since he wasn't supposed to hear their conversation in the first place.

"So, what do you guys think about Mila?" Justin asked Caleb and Adrian before taking another puff of his cigar.

"I'm gonna fuck her," Caleb answered bluntly.

Both Justin and Adrian immediately looked at him, their eyes wide with surprise.

Justin groaned. "I swear you're going to get us sued one day."

"What?" Caleb raised both hands defensively. "I told her I wasn't gonna fuck her, but I heard fat chicks give good head and I'm sure she'd be honored to have my cock in her mouth."

"What the fuck?" Adrian spat.

"Oh, she walked in on me and Shannon a while back." Caleb shrugged. "I told her she didn't have to worry about something like that happening between us, but now I'm curious about what a fat cunt feels like and she clearly needs to get laid. She wears heels *everyday* and the way she constantly swings those wide ass hips... Obviously she's looking to get fucked."

"You're an actual pig, you know that?" Adrian scolded.

"That's hilarious coming from you! You didn't always think of me like that..."

"Whatever."

"Anyway, I haven't decided if I should do it on the couch or floor. She'd probably break the desk. I know I'm going to have to do all the fucking work, though, because I'm sure she just lays on her back and can't do anything else."

"What does that even mean?"

"That means her fat ass won't be able to ride my cock—I mean, I doubt she has the stamina. So I'd have to fuck her on the floor or something."

"You're wrong," Adrian retorted, shaking his head.

"About what? Her riding? Are you saying you've fucked her? I wouldn't be surprised since she's in your office every morning."

"No, I'm saying you're wrong by implying that she's somehow physically incapable of doing that and you're wrong by thinking you're going to have sex with her."

"And why's that?"

"For one, there's no way she'd want to have sex with you... Out of all of us, she seems to be the most distant from you. Either way, both Justin and I have warned you about having sex with our colleagues and you're doing it so much that it's turning into a liability. And two, Mila works out almost every day."

"First of all, this is why our NDAs are so fucking strict. And second, bullshit!" Caleb exclaimed. "You expect me to believe Mila's fat ass is in a gym somewhere? Ha! I highly doubt that."

"You're just as ignorant as ever, Caleb," Adrian countered. "You can't assume someone's physical activity or health from their size alone."

"He's right," Justin noted. "She actually goes to that gym not too far from office. It's just a few blocks away and she was telling me that she recently started going in the mornings since we keep having her work late."

"What? So the assistant is complaining to you?"

"Not that, we were just chatting and it came up."

"Oh, so you have 'chats' with her too now?" questioned an annoyed Caleb as he was reminded that Mila seemed interested in everyone *but* him. "And she's all buddy-buddy with Adrian these days with their inside jokes and shit."

"We have small talk now that she's in on all my Japanese meetings," Justin explained. "We need something to fill any silence before or after. And why do you sound so hostile about it?"

"I'm not being hostile. I'm just saying you gotta be fucking kidding me if you think I'll believe that she's in the gym regularly."

"Anyway..." Justin shook his head and turned his attention from Caleb to Adrian. "What do you think of Mila?"

"She's good at her job and I think we should keep her around and *not* act like total douchebags," Adrian aimed the last part at Caleb who in turn flashed his middle finger at him. "What do you think, Justin?"

"Mila's alright, plus it's useful that she's fluent in Japanese," Justin answered flatly. "She hasn't messed up so far, but let's just keep an eye on her performance in case we need to reassess her employment."

"Fair enough." Adrian nodded. "Now, on to our next order of business. I've been looking at our numbers and I think it'll just be a few more months before we can start taking on Thompson Luxe Group."

Wide grins grew on Caleb and Justin's faces.

"Excellent..."

~

IT WAS YET another day of another week at PMC Group and Mila was just finishing up her lunch when she received a notification that it was time for her 2:00 p.m. meeting with Justin to prepare for an upcoming conference call they'd have with more Japanese executives in a few days.

Sitting in meetings with Justin became a regular routine for Mila and she started spending just as much time with him as she spent with Adrian, if not more. And with each meeting, Mila was completing two tasks in one. Her very thorough notes were impressive to Justin and she was also able to feed the information she gathered to Alexis.

"Hi Mila," Justin greeted when she entered his office. "How are you doing this morning?"

As she approached to take her seat, Justin scanned over her as he often did since spending more time with Mila. He admired her sense of style and the way she managed to dress professionally, yet still with an alluring undertone that he wasn't quite sure was due to the outfits or the woman wearing them. Also, Justin didn't understand why, but he often found his eyes drifting down Mila's legs and lingering on her heels.

"I'm great," she replied with a small smile as she sat across from him. "And you?"

"I'm fine, just hate this time difference we have with Tokyo. I'm glad they were willing to chat even though it's evening their ti—"

Justin was cut off by his phone ringing with a distinct tone that made him stiffen in his seat.

"Hey, babe," he answered. "I'm in a meeting, can we talk later?"

Mila figured it was Ashley, though she couldn't hear what she may have been saying on the other side of the phone. All she knew was that Justin looked agitated to be speaking to her.

"Okay, okay," Justin said quickly, trying to rush Ashley off the phone, but she kept going until his tone turned sharp. "I told you I was in a meeting. I'll call you back later."

A few more seconds went by, and after he finally hung up, Mila gave him a curious look.

"What?" he questioned. "Why are you looking at me like that?"

Mila had no qualms with asking such a personal question, but she knew she'd have to feign timidness in her approach. "Well, Mr. Matsuda... And I don't mean to pry or be inappropriate..."

"Go on," Justin urged.

"Ashley is your girlfriend, right? I think you told me before that you two have been together for a couple years... But it doesn't seem like you like her that much."

Justin's eyes went wide before he cleared his throat and straightened himself up. "What makes you say that?"

"Whenever I see you interact with her, you seem annoyed and you never get excited about her calling or coming into the office. You just treat it like another chore or work task for the day."

"Interesting observation," he said coldly.

"Like I said, I didn't mean to pry..."

"No, it's okay," Justin assured. "With Ashley and I, it's just that... It's that we..." He huffed to move past his hesitation. "Mila, we're speaking plainly right now, right? I mean, you asked me a question and I want to answer you thoroughly, right?"

"Oh, um... okay?"

"Ashley and I... She's a nice woman and I like her and all. We make sense as a couple, I mean, we have similarities in what we like to read and watch and we both fit in the same tax bracket and come from wealthy families. But there's just not much of a spark like there was before when we first started dating. I'm not sure if we're just used to each other now or if it's something else."

"I see..." Mila nodded thoughtfully. "You could always reignite the spark, though. Do something new, something fun... Maybe take a three-day weekend or full-on vacation and go somewhere exotic. Maybe all you need is a change of scenery."

"We've tried that..." Justin twisted his mouth while his eyes remained on Mila's. "I think it's the sex," he blurted and Mila's head jerked back. "Shit... Sorry, Mila... I'm not trying to make things weird, I've never told anyone... and it just slipped out."

Mila was partially surprised at Justin's revelation and partially annoyed that he would bring up being unsatisfied with their sex life, feeling embarrassed on Ashley's behalf.

"My advice still mostly stands," Mila said flatly. "Just change things up in the bedroom. I'm not sure what the dynamic between you two might be, but in any relationship, you should be able to be open with your partner about your sexual desires. So, if you're feeling unsatisfied, you should talk to her about it and be straightforward with her about what you're interested in trying or how you think you could improve the sex."

Justin considered Mila's words before he released a low chuckle and scratched the back of his head. "Sorry, I guess I did a bit of oversharing, but I do appreciate the advice."

"Of course," Mila replied with a smile. "Like I've told you before, I'm here to earn your trust and as your assistant, I want to make sure I'm as helpful as possible, even when it comes to things in your personal life like this."

"Thanks, Mila."

After her exchange with Justin, Mila started thinking back to her relationship with Eric and the way the two of them 'made sense' just as Justin had explained about himself and Ashley. She and Eric were both business savvy and came from affluent families. He was also nice enough and showered her with gifts, but something still didn't mesh with their relationship.

Mila couldn't bring herself to develop feelings for Eric, no matter how hard she tried, and she wondered if perhaps Justin was in the same predicament.

Keep Them On

With the new week, Caleb was ready to work his charm on Mila. He'd never been denied by a woman before and Caleb was sure that once he started flirting with Mila, she'd be on her knees in his office before the end of the week, if not that same day.

He strolled into the office with a closed-mouth smile and a twinkle in his eyes, looking at Mila.

"Good afternoon, Mila," he said when he reached her desk with a large drink in his hand. "I bought you a caramel frappuccino with whipped cream and extra caramel."

Mila hadn't looked up at him and appeared to be focused on something on her computer screen.

"Afternoon, Mr. Peterson," she greeted dryly without removing her eyes from the screen. "I've emailed you your mid-day update." That was one of Mila's standard lines for him the rare times that they would interact. It was obvious to Caleb that she didn't listen to a word he said.

Hiding his agitation, Caleb sat the drink on her desk and Mila finally looked up at him curiously.

"I bought you a drink, Mila."

She raised a confused brow because she was sure it was his first time calling her by her name since she started working there.

"A drink," he repeated. "It's a caramel frappuccino with whipped cream and extra caramel. I'm not sure what you normally get, so I had to guess."

Mila picked up the drink and looked over it with an aloof expression. "Thanks, Mr. Peterson," she said, her tone still detached.

"Call me Caleb," he said with a wink and Mila had to hold herself back from rolling her eyes.

While Mila knew he was still in earshot, she said, "I need to throw this cheap nasty shit away," before getting up from her seat with the frappuccino and searching for a trashcan away from her desk.

Caleb didn't visibly react, but something about the way she pretended to accept his offering before insulting it and throwing it away bothered him to the point that he felt it in the pit of his stomach. It was as if she was trying to spare his feelings like he was some sensitive child while underneath her fake smile, she was annoyed by him.

Mila made Caleb feel average. Even worse, she made him feel inadequate.

And he hated that.

JUSTIN BACKED Ashley into his bedroom as their mouths eagerly moved against each other and they only broke away to remove their clothes. By the time they fell over on his bed, she was in nothing but her panties and heels and he was in his boxers.

Kissing and sucking at Ashley's neck while he was on top of her, Justin pulled one of her legs up and caressed the side of her thigh.

"Justin," she breathed. "Let me take my shoes off."

"No," he rasped against her ear. "Keep them on."

Ashley found it an odd but harmless request, so she kept her heels on as he'd asked.

Justin turned them over so that she was on top. With the way his hands glided down her back and griped at her ass and her thighs in a more intense way than usual, it felt like he was grabbing for more than was there.

When Ashley sat up, still straddling him to tug at his boxers, she realized that his erection had grown faster than usual and she assumed it had something to do with his request for her to keep her heels on and the way he'd been groping her more heavily.

Once she freed his dick, Justin put his hands gently at her sides rather than holding them and taking the lead as he normally did.

"Why don't you take control tonight, babe?" He took one of her hands and guided it up his body until it was at his neck and Ashley looked down at him confused.

"You want me to choke you?"

Justin nodded. "I want to try it with *you* being more dominant."

"Oh um... Okay?" She slid her panties to the side before lowering herself on his dick and rocking her hips.

Her hand was wrapped very lightly around his neck while she rode him slowly and she could tell that he wasn't as into as he seemed when he first asked her to choke him.

"Tighter," he said and Ashley only very lightly tightened her grip around his neck.

Justin put his hands on her hips to guide Ashley's movements so that she would ride him faster, but he was still unsatisfied with the lack of control she was taking and he could feel himself softening inside of her.

Finally, he gave up on the power exchange and turned Ashley over so that he was on top and started pounding her the way she liked to be fucked with his hand around her neck and leg on his shoulder.

She bellowed his name and was obviously enjoying the experience, but Justin was mostly out of it, keeping himself just hard enough to fuck her until she hit her orgasm.

After Ashley came and Justin went soft without coming—as had been happening for the past several weeks—the two lay in bed, looking at the ceiling.

"I like it better when you're control," Ashley admitted. "I prefer when the man is dominant. And to be honest, if you want to try something new, could you at least raise it beforehand, like when we're not having sex?"

Ashley made a fair point, Justin could admit. He wasn't the spontaneous type, but his desire to be more submissive had been increasing over past several weeks and it emboldened him that night. "I'm sorry," Justin replied before closing his eyes to go to sleep.

Lunch Plans

"Very nice." Mila nodded approvingly as she and Adrian sat down in the restaurant. "It looks like you remembered when I told you about the pho spot that I love so much here in East Lenrod."

Mila had been with PMC Group for six months and it was the longest anyone had lasted as an assistant to the Big Three. To celebrate her breaking the record, Adrian decided to take Mila out for lunch at one of her favorite spots.

Hoping to make it look less like a date, he had invited Caleb and Justin, but Caleb declined, still feeling bitter that Mila wasn't receptive to any of his advances, and Justin had a scheduling conflict that prevented him from joining.

"Of course I remembered," Adrian chimed. "How could I forget considering it's one of my favorites as well?"

"You did tell me that, didn't you?" Mila replied with a smile. "Well, it looks like this celebratory lunch is off to a good start already."

It didn't take long for the pair to be served and as lunch went on, they lost track of time as their conversation flowed naturally. Also, with the change of setting, Mila and Adrian spoke even more casually than usual.

"So…" Adrian leaned in toward Mila and rested his chin on his hand. "I do have a question for you and I want you to be as honest as possible."

"Go for it," Mila said calmly before taking a sip of her tea.

"What are your goals with PMC Group? Why did you decide to work for us?"

"I've got bills," she replied, partially honest. "And PMC Group had an opening."

Adrian tilted his head. "That's it?"

When he noticed Mila cut her eyes at him with a slight glare, he tried to quickly recover. "I-I just mean… You work so hard that it doesn't seem like you see this as *just* a way to pay bills."

"What is it that you want me to say, Mr. Collins?" she questioned. "This sounds more like you're digging for something else."

After several moments of pausing while locking eyes with Mila, Adrian finally asked. "What are your dreams, Ms. Mila? I'm sure you're passionate about *something* that doesn't involve tending to our schedules."

Mila shrugged. "I don't have dreams. I simply live my life and take whatever pleasure from it that I can."

"C'mon," he urged. "There's got to be *something*."

Mila released an entertained scoff at his stubbornness and shook her head. "I guess I'd say something I'm passionate about is empowering women, specifically fat women."

Adrian's eyes went wide at Mila's casual use of the word 'fat'.

"I use 'fat' as simply a descriptor, Mr. Collins," she clarified when she saw his reaction. "As a fat woman, that's how I view and use the word, though other people prefer different terms and I don't blame them. Especially considering how the word has become synonymous with ugly in this bullshit society we live in… It's so fucking dumb."

Adrian couldn't help the small smile that came to his face. While he and Mila had spoken plenty and were very friendly with each other, it was his first time seeing her show any passion while talking about something.

"What?" she asked.

"I see that you *do* have something you're passionate about," he replied as his soft brown eyes bore into hers.

"Oh..." Mila broke eye contact when she noticed an unfamiliar feeling in her stomach. "I guess I am... I mean, it's just so ridiculous how poorly people are treated over something like that."

"I agree with you one hundred percent. It's something I've never understood either—the same way I've never understood why we tie the value of individuals to their looks. I know it's an ironic thing to say considering I'm an executive and co-founder of a firm that owns fashion companies."

"Well, it also puts you in a position to change things for the better. Why be the problem when you have the option of being a solution?"

"You make a great point," Adrian agreed. "I'll be sure to work on that."

"Don't get ahead of yourself," she teased.

"What? I've thought about it before and I already have a few ideas in mind on what we could do to support more initiatives that empower everyone to feel good about themselves and maybe undo some of the damage that the fashion industry has done."

A grin flashed across Mila's face.

"Good boy," she cooed softly without thinking about it.

Adrian's immediate reaction was a gulp and he scanned over Mila's face wondering if he heard correctly.

"W-what was that?"

Mila realized what she had done as soon as he asked, but she didn't care.

"I said, 'good boy'," she replied casually. "I just mean it's good of you to take such initiative. I hope you go through with it."

"Oh uh..." Adrian cleared his throat. "T-thanks, I gu- Er... I mean... The 'boy' part kinda threw me for a loop." He chuckled nervously.

"Oh, that?" Mila's tongue slightly peeked through her lips and retreated before she went as far as licking them. "Force of habit... Anyway, you were talking earlier about your hobby of building furniture. Tell me more about that."

"R-right... I um..." Adrian was still trying to recover from his reaction to what Mila said about the use of 'good boy' being out of habit. He wondered in which context she may have meant it.

"Go on," Mila urged.

"Y-yeah. It's just that I um... I really enjoy doing things with my hands, so building furniture is very satisfying, you know? Creating something of your own? Also, it's just a nice skill to have generally. Whenever I want a very specific piece of furniture that I may not be able to find, I can just make it on my own."

"That *is* a useful skill. Do you have pictures of anything you've built? I'd love to see it."

"I do," Adrian replied as he pulled his phone from his pocket and went to his photos. "This is my most recent piece. A couch with a bookshelf attached on the back and at the sides."

When he turned his phone to face Mila so she could look at the piece, she scanned over the image with admiration. "This is petty cool. I don't use social media like that, but I imagine this is something that'd be popular on Pinterest."

"I guess I'll take that as a compliment, Ms. Mila."

"As you should," she said with a nod.

MILA AND JUSTIN had just finished a call with a fashion executive based in California. Since her note-taking had been so well in their Japanese meetings, Justin began pulling her into other ones from time-to-time.

Although they'd usually go over their notes following a meeting, Justin had something else he wanted to discuss with Mila, though he wasn't sure if he should jump into it too quickly.

"Nice work on making it through this first six months. Have you been able to make friends in the office okay?" Justin asked, trying to open up a casual conversation.

"Yeah, everyone has been nice for the most part and I get approached a lot. I mean, I guess a big part of that is because I'm the assistant for you three and they know if they get in good with me, scheduling a time to kiss your ass might be easier."

Justin bursted out laughing at Mila's response. "Well, I'd appreciate if you keep us from too many of those. I'd much rather spend my time making deals."

"Oh, *you* don't need to worry about that. Not many people come asking for you," Mila replied frankly.

"What?" Justin questioned with a gasp.

"I just mean that everyone knows you're all about business. You're pretty curt with most of the staff if they try to speak with you on anything unrelated to business."

"Wait, do I really do that?"

"Yes, you've never noticed?"

"But you and I talk about non-business stuff, just like we're doing right now."

"Mhmm," Mila hummed. "But this is right after a meeting. Before you found out that I speak Japanese and could be helpful as you try to expand PMC Group, you were the same way with me."

"Really?"

"Mr. Matsuda, when you first gave me the assignment to prepare for the Japanese executives, you said, and I quote: 'I won't have time to hand-hold you through it all and you need to take care not to offend our guests.'" Mila mocked his tone and intonation perfectly.

"Wow," Justin gasped softly. "I didn't even realize..."

The room fell silent after that, as Mila had nothing more to say and instead read through her notes to see if she could find anything of value from the meeting to share with Alexis.

"Hey Mila," Justin said, breaking the silence. "Can I ask you for some advice?"

"Go for it."

"I noticed that you wear heels every day and I've been thinking about buying a pair for Ashley. She wears them sometimes, like for special occasions and stuff, but she always complains about them hurting. I'm hoping to find her some that she can wear for longer periods of time."

"I see..." Mila looked up with her finger to her chin as she thought about which brands had the most comfortable heels. "Oh!" she exclaimed with a snap before rapidly typing something on her tablet and going to the website.

"Take a look at this..." Mila handed the device to Justin and showed him the website. "This is one of the best brands for comfort and I buy from them often. They have a wide range of sizes and styles, and even price ranges. What style do you have in mind for Ashley? What does she like?"

"Well..." Justin rubbed the back of his neck. "I'm not totally sure. I know I want to see her in high heels and I like the platform look..."

"So, this is for you to look at? Not for Ashley?"

Justin was caught off guard by Mila's questions. "What? I mean, I was just thinking that she might li—"

He was interrupted when Caleb walked into the office and the CEO's glare was immediate when he saw Mila sitting across from Justin and leaned in toward him with tablet in her hand. The two of them appeared too friendly for Caleb's taste.

"Justin, did you forget that we have a three o'clock meeting? Isn't it the assistant's job to remind you..." Caleb caught himself before changing his tone, hoping if maybe he was nice for just a bit longer, Mila would give in to his efforts to charm her. "Er, I mean... It looks like you and Mila got a bit carried away in your conversation. It's time for our meeting."

"R-right..." Justin was clearly thrown off at the shift in Caleb's tone. "We'll chat later, Mila."

"Alright," she replied before getting up to leave the room.

Caleb unabashedly scanned over her as she walked toward the door and passed by him while scrolling through her phone. "You look nice today, Mila."

Ignoring him, Mila turned back to Justin. "I'll send you some links to my favorite stores, Mr. Matsuda."

"Thanks, Mila."

She gave him a small smile before finally leaving the room, all without acknowledging Caleb.

"You're best friends with the assistant now, too?" Caleb asked Justin as soon as Mila left. "You and Adrian are so soft."

"Oh please," Justin replied through his chuckles. "You're just mad because she's so uninterested in you, that you don't even exist to her outside of her normal work duties."

"Whatever. Let's just talk about this goddamn California meeting next month... And where the fuck is Adrian? He's always disappearing lately."

WYSOWM

Caleb was pissed that none of his advances toward Mila were well-received, and she didn't even give him the courtesy of outright rejecting him. Instead, she seemed to tolerate him, only agitating Caleb more because it felt like an extension of her continued indifference toward him.

He'd never experienced such a lack of interest from anyone before and he was growing more obsessed with the idea of somehow getting a rise out of her. All he needed was *one* time for him to be satisfied. And he had just the idea in mind.

Normally, Caleb didn't get up so early, but this morning, he woke up at 5:00 a.m. to go to the gym where Mila would be.

After learning from Justin and Adrian that Mila frequented the gym just around the corner from PMC Groups offices most mornings, he figured he would go there and watch her struggle with working out to be reminded that she wasn't as intriguing or "cool" as she seemed. He even considered embarrassing her at the gym by showing up as if he were trying out the establishment and calling her out on how poorly she was doing.

Caleb arrived around 5:20 a.m. in his own workout clothes to blend in and searched for Mila. He scanned over the floor until he saw her in the weightlifting section of the gym and his eyes narrowed as they often did when they landed on Mila.

She was doing weighted squats and to Caleb's surprise, the woman had perfect form. Her feet hips-width apart and toes pointing forward while holding the barbell across the back of her shoulders, Mila lowered herself to a sitting position and then came back up. Caleb's eyes were glued to her ass and he instinctively licked his lips.

While he watched Mila, an idea came to mind. Caleb would record a video, edit it, and share it with the office to embarrass her. He knew it was immature, but he also didn't care. It was worth it if he could get a rise out of her at least *one* time. He just wanted proof that he could have such an effect on her.

Caleb pulled out his phone and started recording and as he focused on her movements, he couldn't admit it to himself, but he felt blood rushing to his dick.

"Fuckin' weirdo," a deep voice rumbled, startling Caleb and breaking him out of his trance. "You're seriously recording girls working out, you creep?"

Caleb stuffed his phone in his pocket and met the man's glare with one of his own. "No, I'm not recording anybody and either way, what I do is none of your fucking business," he spat.

"Actually, it is considering I work here. Are you even a member? I've never seen you here. Get the fuck out!"

The man's outburst attracted the attention of some of the nearby gym-goers, though Mila was too focused on her workout to notice anything going on. Caleb locked the employee in a staring match, considering challenging him, until deciding not to make a bigger scene than he already was.

"Whatever," Caleb huffed before turning around and making his way toward the exit.

Since he was close to the office anyway, he decided to go in early and changed into his work clothes once he got there.

Caleb sat at his desk looking at the video he took of Mila and he was pissed at how much of a hold she had on him. However, he was prepared to be persistent in his efforts to get a rise out of her and he figured that video would be the final straw for her.

Analyzing the clip, Caleb couldn't keep his eyes off of Mila's form and he was particularly focused on her ass throughout. The way the fabric of her leggings would strain and her ass was more pronounced when she went down into the squat before coming back up had Caleb holding himself as he watched.

"Why the fuck does she have perfect form?" he whispered sharply. As he continued to watch the video, he found himself mesmerized by Mila's movements, almost as if he were in a trance. In a motion that felt subconscious, Caleb kept adjusting himself in his pants as he grew more strained against them.

Just when his mind was about to wander, Caleb finally stopped the video after watching it for a fourth time.

"Whatever," he grumbled to himself as he switched to his contacts and started scrolling. "It's probably because I haven't fucked anything in like a week. Let's see... Shannon? No. Casey? Possibly. Fiona? Maybe. Oh... How about Casey *and* Fiona?" Caleb nodded approvingly. "That's what it will be."

"SHIT!" Mila spouted when the stack of papers she'd just finished copying fell all over the floor. "Why can't they be environmentalists?" she muttered to herself. "All of this shit can be put on a tablet, but no, they want to kill the trees."

"For what it's worth, we do recycle."

Mila jumped when she heard Adrian's voice. She didn't realize he was in the doorway.

"Here, let me help you," he said as he approached and crouched to the floor with Mila to pick up the papers. "Sorry to have you working late again."

"It's fine, I'm used to hard work," Mila said with a smile while she internally rolled her eyes because she was *not* used to hard work. "Can you get the rest of these while I put the pages I have in order?"

"Yes, of course."

Mila walked over to the counter in the copy room and leaned forward as she started organizing the documents.

Adrian's jaw tensed as he looked at her. The woman *always* wore heels and the taller, the better for him. His eyes then drifted up to admire her sheer stockings before they met the part of her that his gaze was often glued to—her ass. She was switching between bending one knee and locking the other in a motion that he interpreted as anxious, but it kept him mesmerized with the way her hips moved and she had a slight bounce with it.

"Can I help you with something, Mr. Collins?" Her head was turned, looking down at him while she was still bent over the counter.

A subtle hint of pink came to his cheeks with his embarrassment, knowing how obvious it probably was to her that he was staring at her ass. "Sorry, I didn't mean—"

"You're welcome to keep looking, darling. I know you know how to behave. You won't touch without permission, will you?" she added with a wink.

"N-no," he choked out.

"Then why don't you continue picking up those papers?"

"R-right..." Adrian continued gathering the papers, but he was practically moving in slow motion as his eyes remained on Mila. He didn't realize when it happened, but he was suddenly in arm's reach of her and he wanted nothing more than to touch her.

"M-may I touch you?" he asked softly.

"Hm?" she hummed inquisitively. "What was that?"

"M-may I *please* touch you?"

Mila didn't respond for what felt like an eternity to Adrian, almost as if testing his self-control to see if he would touch her before she agreed.

"You may touch me, darling," she finally said and Adrian's hands were immediately against her.

On his knees behind her, he gently rubbed his finger tips up her sheer tights and back down, each time, reaching higher and higher up her skirt. When he noticed how much closer he was getting to her pussy, he felt the urge to ask, "May I touch you here, please?"

"Very well behaved," Mila purred. "You may."

Adrian's fingers brushed against her heat and when she didn't object, he placed his thumb there and applied more pressure while he rubbed her through her stockings and panties.

When he heard a sharp breath escape her, Adrian's pants grew even more strained knowing she was responding to the way he was touching her. He started placing gentle kisses against her legs and he soon realized he made a mistake.

Mila lifted her foot, placed it against his chest—her heel slightly digging into it—and pushed him back.

"And you were doing so well..." She sucked her teeth with disappointment before pulling down her skirt and standing up straight. "No more for you."

"Wait!" he pleaded. "Please, give me another cha—"

"Is something wrong, Mr. Collins?" Mila broke him out of his daydream and looked at him curiously. She was still in her position at the counter, but Adrian was not in arm's reach of her.

"Oh, um... no." He quickly gathered the papers from the floor and stood up to hand them to her. He placed one arm across his crotch in an effort to hide his erection.

Mila scanned him from his feet up until she met his eyes. "You sure nothing's wrong?" she asked with a raised brow.

"Yes, yes. I'm fine!" he replied before rushing out of the room and returning to his office.

He locked the door behind him when he entered and his daydream along with other images of Mila filled his mind. Adrian knew he had no other choice and unzipped his pants before pulling out his dick.

Before he could even begin, a knock at his door interrupted him and he heard Mila from the other side.

"Adrian," she called. "Is everything alright?"

"Y-yes!" he replied quickly as he put himself back into his pants. "I'm fine."

"I have your documents in order. Did you still want them tonight?"

"Right, I'll be right there..." Adrian readjusted himself several times as he approached the door to hide how strained he was in his pants before opening it for Mila.

"You good?" she questioned with a raised brow, analyzing his face. It was in a state she knew all too well—Adrian was holding the expression of a man who *needed* to relieve himself and she imagined that he'd do so as soon as she left his office.

Naturally, that gave her reason to linger just a bit longer.

"Yes." He gulped. "I'm fine."

Mila walked further into his office and looked around as if she hadn't been in there hundreds of times by now. "There was something I wanted to ask you, Adrian."

"Sure, go for it."

"While you, Mr. Matsuda, and Mr. Peterson are on your LA trip next month, do you mind if I take those days off? I'll keep my cell with me in case of an emergency, but I don't see a point in coming into the office when none of you are here."

"Y-yeah... That makes a lot of sense. Sure, you can take off."

"Great." Mila nodded. She sat the stack of documents on a table in Adrian's office and as she walked toward him to go to the door, her eyes unabashedly raked up and down his body and Adrian could tell that she likely noticed his erection.

The expression that flashed across Mila's face when she met his eyes again sent a shiver down Adrian's spine. He knew that expression—it reminded him of the mistress he'd been playing with a few months ago.

Mila was always alluring to him and she had natural sex appeal. There were also moments—whether it was her clear satisfaction with him calling her 'Ms. Mila' or that time she called him a 'good boy'—that made Adrian think about something Logan had said before.

"If you ran into her in a different setting, like at The Scarlet Lounge, what do you think the dynamic would be?"

At the time, Adrian refused to respond to Logan's question, although he knew the answer. Had he met Mila in such a setting, he knew he'd be interested in playing with her. Even having not met her in The Scarlet Lounge, Adrian wanted to play with Mila, but was forced to hold himself back considering he was her boss.

Mila herself knew she was attracted to Adrian and it would've been no question that had she run into him on the scene they would've likely played. She found him to be well-behaved and he had a soft, warm temperament about him. It was also clear to Mila that he was the type who liked to serve.

Before reaching the door, Mila stopped in her tracks in front of Adrian, looking up at him.

"C-can I help you with something?" he choked out.

"Oh, Adrian..." Mila tilted her head to the side with a sneer as her eyes held his. "Always the behaved one..."

"W-wh... What?"

"You heard me... *darling*."

With those words, Adrian lost his last bit of self-control and his lips were against Mila's. To his surprise, she accepted his move, but she somehow gained control, teasing him and denying his tongue each time he tried to slip it into her mouth. Suddenly, she held his face and slightly pulled away so that their lips only lightly brushed against each other.

Mila opened her eyes to see the desperation in Adrian's and a small, satisfied smile came to her face before allowing him to close the distance between them again. When she finally stopped teasing him and opened up enough for *her* tongue to enter *his* mouth, Adrian moaned against her lips as he tried to deepen the kiss.

Just when his hands drifted down her body, Mila broke away.

"Did I say you could touch me?" The coldness of her low whisper only caused Adrian to be further strained against his pants.

"N-no."

"'No', what?"

Adrian swallowed hard. "N-no... Ms. Mila."

Mila was deeply turned on and traced her thumb across his lips as ideas filled her mind of how they could be put to use, but she caught herself before she was too far gone.

"This is *very* inappropriate. Isn't it, Mr. Collins?"

"Bu-But I..." Adrian blinked several times as he returned to his senses. "Oh god!" He backed his way against the door and held his hands up. "You're right. Shit. And I'm your boss... I'm sorry, Mila. I am *really, really* sorry. This is totally inappropriate. I didn't mean to take advantage of you. That was not my intention."

Mila let out an entertained sigh and walked toward Adrian without saying anything. He was frozen in place as his eyes remained wide and intent on Mila.

When she was just as close to him as she was only moments ago,

Adrian parted his lips to speak, but Mila interrupted him before any words left.

"I'm just getting the door, Mr. Collins. If you could move..."

"Oh, um... Right! Right." Adrian stepped to the side. "I'm sorry again, Mila. Please forgive—" Adrian was unable to finish his sentence as Mila had already walked out the door without saying anything else.

He looked down at the large bulge in his pants and let out a frustrated huff.

"*Damnit!*"

Fantasies

"Fuck! I can't believe I did that," Adrian chided himself as he entered his apartment. He'd left the office immediately after kissing Mila. "I hope I didn't fuck up too bad... I mean, Mila *did* kiss me back. Hell, she was in total control when we were kissing... Then again, *I'm* the one who initiated it... But she called me 'darling' and then got all... *authoritative.*"

He ran his fingers through his hair and pulled off his shirt as he went into the bathroom and turned on the shower, figuring a cold one would be best. While he would at times fantasize about Mila, Adrian never went as far as masturbating to his fantasies, though he had come close. He was afraid that he'd throw himself into more dangerous territory and have an even harder time resisting Mila.

"Whatever, I've kissed her at this point," he said to himself before turning off the shower and deciding to relieve himself beforehand.

Adrian sat at the edge of his bed and pulled out a small bottle of lubricant from his nightstand before putting it on his hand and holding himself with it. He closed his eyes and started slowly stroking himself.

"Such a good boy," Mila cooed as she approached Adrian. *"Always so well-behaved..."* Once she was close enough, she took his chin between her fingers and lifted his head to meet her gaze.

"Why have you stopped?" she questioned when her eyes drifted down to his dick in his hand. "Keep going for me, darling."

"Yes, Ms. Mila," Adrian breathed before he returned to pumping his hand.

Mila traced her thumb across his lips, just as she had when they kissed in his office. "You know that I've already got a read on you, right darling?"

"What read, Ms. Mila?"

"You like to serve. Don't you?"

Adrian nodded and sped up the pace of his hand. "I want to serve you, Ms. Mila," he confessed.

"I know that you do," she replied softly.

His eyes finally parted from Mila's to look at what she was wearing and he groaned at the sight. She wore an all red set with a caged bra, matching panties, and platform heels.

Adrian licked his lips at the sight and he felt Mila's hand push against his chest for him to lay down. Once he was on his back, still stroking himself, Mila crawled on top of him on all fours with her face hovering just above his. He didn't realize it, but his hand slowed to almost a stop as he anticipated Mila's lips meeting his once again.

"Did I tell you to stop?"

"No, Ms. Mila."

When Adrian started stroking himself again, Mila met his lips and just as she'd done when they kissed before, the woman was in complete control. He nearly came when she wrapped her hand around his neck and he winced when she broke away.

"You always kiss me so eagerly, darling... Is it because you want to put your lips somewhere else?"

"Please, Ms. Mila..." Adrian gulped. "May I?"

With a sultry relaxation to her face, Mila crawled further up his body until her knees were on each side of his head.

"Stick your tongue out," she directed and Adrian did as he was told.

"Good boy," she purred as she started grinding against his tongue, still with her panties on. The vibrations caused by his moans against her caused Mila to release some of her own.

"You want more than this, don't you, darling?"

Adrian's response was muffled against her core and he nodded while his eyes locked with hers.

"Your desperation really turns me on..." Mila pulled her panties to the side so that Adrian's mouth could make direct contact with her lower lips.

The moment he tasted her, Adrian couldn't help but start eagerly moving his mouth on his own.

"Did I say... you could... do that?" Mila said through light moans, but Adrian was already too far gone, focusing on eating her out.

Those were the last coherent set of words he heard from her before bringing Mila to her climax, her sounds and trembling body pushing Adrian to his own.

"Fuuuckkkk," he groaned as he came all over his hand and abdomen. Once he finished, he regretted his decision to masturbate to a fantasy of Mila because now his desire for her only became more intense.

～

"So, what do you think, babe?" Justin asked Ashley when she put on the *very* tall black pumps that he bought her. He was sitting on the couch as she stood in front of him wearing the heels along with an all black leather lingerie set he also purchased for her.

"They're really cute and comfortable," she beamed. "How'd you manage to pick these out?"

"I just did some research and found a few sites that people online recommended as having comfortable shoes."

"Well, you did a great job. So..." Ashley joined Justin on the couch and straddled him. "Now that we've talked about it in more detail, I'll try this control thing."

"Oh really?" Justin questioned with a hopeful glint in his eyes, looking up at her and holding her hips.

"Yes, I'll at least try it. I've never been interested in dominating, but I figure I can give it a shot since you want it so much."

"I appreciate the effort, babe." Justin readjusted, sinking further into the seat so that his dick aligned with Ashley's core.

Ashley wrapped her hand around his neck, holding it tighter than last time and started to move her hips to grind against him while Justin caressed her thighs.

She leaned in to kiss him and Justin remained mostly still to allow her to take the lead, though she had a hard time doing so. However, in an unexpected move, she pulled his bottom lip between her teeth and Justin felt his dick twitch when she did it.

"Did you like that, honey?"

"I did," Justin whispered.

Ashley continued to grind against him as she began placing kisses on his neck. Justin's hands moved up her thighs and he started grabbing her ass aggressively as he'd been doing for the past few months. Ashley liked when Justin was more dominant, but something about the way he seemed to try groping her more heavily when they were intimate bothered her. It was as if he didn't realize he was touching *her*, like he was thinking about someone else.

Between that and not being totally comfortable with dominating, Ashley stopped him and pulled his hands off of her.

"Why do you keep doing that?" she asked, not hiding the agitation in her tone.

"What do you mean?"

"Lately, you've been grabbing at me in such a weird way, like it feels like you're handling my body as if it were larger or something. You open your hands up wider and when you grip my ass or thighs, it feels more aggressive."

"I don't understand. You like it when I'm rough with you."

"But what you're doing isn't exactly rough, it's just different and it makes me uncomfortable."

Justin let out a deep sigh. "I'm not trying to make you feel uncomfortable, babe. Sorry about that."

Ashley huffed, got off of him, and started walking toward the bedroom.

"What is it now?"

"Everything you say to me feels rehearsed, Justin. It's like you only say what you're *supposed* to say, but not what you actually *want* to say. None of it feels genuine."

"But babe..."

"But nothing," Ashley snapped. "I don't know what is going on with you, but I need a break until you figure out what the hell it is."

"Ashley, please…" He pleaded unconvincingly.

It wasn't lost on her that Justin was still in the exact same position on the couch and didn't make an effort to follow her when she left him.

"You're so full of it," she sighed. "Let's just take a week or so to think about it."

❧

CALEB WAS in the bathroom showering while Casey and Fiona—the women he'd told to come over that night—sat in his bed talking about the evening they just had.

"Is it bad that I'm shocked he made both of us come this time?" Casey asked Fiona.

"Not at all," she replied. "I'm surprised too. Usually it ends up you and I having to get each other off, but Caleb actually seemed *somewhat* interested in our pleasure this time. Who knew a jerk like that could eat pussy?"

"Right," Casey giggled. "That had to be the most surprising part. If his personality wasn't so shitty, I'd be in love. He's hot as fuck on top of all that money."

"I know, right? He could be a model himself—"

"The fuck are you two still doing here?" Caleb interrupted when he walked out of the bathroom and found Casey and Fiona still in his bed. "Both of you have been here plenty of times to know the rules."

The green-eyed blonde and freckled brunette exchanged a look before getting out of bed and quickly putting their clothes back on.

"And there it is," Fiona whispered sharply. "Asshole."

"Yeah," Caleb scoffed. "And you were just licking mine not even an hour ago while Casey had my cock in her mouth."

"Whatever," she said under her breath.

"Anyway… I already spoke to Madeline and you'll be able to model her pieces for Paris fashion week."

"Thanks," Casey replied dryly before she and Fiona finished getting dressed and walked out the door.

Caleb was still annoyed even after the women left. He realized that for the past several months, he'd been more frustrated than usual and his ongoing failure at gaining more attention from Mila only made it worse.

"Those girls don't know their fucking place," Caleb grumbled as he walked over to the kitchen to mix up a protein shake. "Speaking of people who don't know their place..."

He pulled out his phone and open the video of Mila that he took before, hoping to get ideas on ways he could edit it. However, his reaction as soon as he started the clip was the one Caleb had hoped to avoid, especially after relieving himself with Casey and Fiona.

Sitting on his large sofa with his phone in his hand, Caleb found himself readjusting again as his dick got harder.

"What is wrong with me?"

As the video repeated on its loop, Caleb completely forgot about planning his edits and went into almost a trance at the way Mila's body moved. Without even noticing, his hand was in his shorts and he was holding himself. He refused to admit it, but he was attracted to Mila— she carried herself with such an unshakeable confidence and managed to have a domineering attitude that was subtle, yet effective.

Caleb's resistance in that moment faltered as he became harder and before he knew it, lotion was on his hand and it was wrapped around his length.

"I see this is why your ass goes to the gym," Caleb jeered as Mila rode him. He was sitting on his couch while she was on his lap, facing forward and bouncing up and down his dick. "So you can ride my cock like a good slut."

"Yes," Mila moaned in response. "I want to make you feel good!"

Caleb groaned with pleasure and sped up his movements as his eyes closed and his head fell back.

"Then keep going," he growled and smacked her ass. He firmly held her hips and admired the way her ass moved each time she came down. "Be a good whore for Daddy."

Caleb began twisting his hand while stroking himself as he raced toward his release.

"Yes, Daddy!" Mila started moving faster. "Anything for you."

"Shit!" Caleb grunted as he came all over his hand.

"Shit!" he shouted after realizing what he'd just done.

~

"Good morning, Mr. Collins," Mila greeted casually when Adrian walked into the office. It was the day after he'd kissed her and Mila had no feelings about the incident while Adrian was very obviously nervous.

"M-morning, Mila," he replied without looking at her. "Could you um... C-could you maybe... Can we talk?"

"Sure thing, Mr. Collins. What did you want to talk about?"

"I me-mean in... In my office."

"Okay," Mila shrugged and got up to follow Adrian. She wasn't surprised that he continued to avoid eye contact, even after closing the door behind them and going to his desk where she sat across from him.

"So..." Adrian began. "About last night..."

He paused for a long time, fidgeting with his hands as he appeared to try to put the words together.

"I wanted to apologize to you again. It was completely out of line and as your boss, that makes it even more inappropriate."

The room returned to silence after his apology. Mila didn't have a response. She enjoyed the kiss and wouldn't exactly object to more. However, she didn't want to give Adrian the pleasure of knowing that. Plus, his obvious discomfort amused her—Mila found Adrian's times of shy awkwardness to be endearing.

Following the long pause, Mila finally said, "Is that all, Mr. Collins?"

For the first time since they kissed the night before, Adrian looked into Mila's eyes. "In addition to apologizing, I also wanted to check in with you. Are you okay?"

"I'm fine, Mr. Collins. Why wouldn't I be?"

"You can still call me Adrian... If that's okay with you. Are you sure you're fine?"

"If the underlying question here is if I'll file an HR complaint or sue you, you don't need to worry about that," Mila said flatly. "Besides, what you did is nothing compared to Mr. Peterson having sex with numerous employees in his office and somehow PMC Group has yet to be the subject of a workplace harassment or assault lawsuit."

"Oh geez," Adrian groaned. "You know about that?"

"It's not exactly a secret. Plus, I'm your secretary, it kind of comes with the territory... Anyway, did you want to go over your schedule?"

Adrian scanned Mila's face for any signs of discomfort. He'd planned to stop their one-on-one morning meetings out of fear of making her uncomfortable or losing self-control again. But now, given the fact that she seemed unbothered about the moment they shared last night, he wondered if it might be okay to continue.

However, before allowing himself to consider it further, Adrian opted to go with his original plan to cease their daily meetings.

"Actually, I think after last night, it might be better if we limit the amount of time we spend alone together. So let's just change our system to something like what you have with Justin and you can print out my schedule and put it on my desk before I come in."

"Oh, that was Justin- I mean Mr. Matsuda and I's old system. We do one-on-one meetings as well now, especially since we spend so much time together on calls and what not... Anyway, I get what you mean and it's no problem. I'll do that from now on."

Adrian knew it was wrong, but he was bothered by Mila's lack of resistance to his request and it also irked him that she seemed to be getting closer with Justin to the point that she'd called him by his first name before correcting herself. Adrian was also hurt by the way she appeared unfazed by their kiss and Adrian's decision not to have their regular one-on-one meetings that had turned into one of his favorite parts of the day.

"Right..." His jaw tensed as he clenched is teeth and tried to hide his uneasiness. "Thank you, Ms- Thank you, Mila."

"Have a nice day, Mr. Collins."

Simp

Mila was annoyed at yet another late night in the office. She never expected an assistant job to require her to work so many hours and she was especially agitated given it was Friday night. She had plans to meet with Jade at a bar and Mila was glad that she brought her outfit for the evening with her.

She had just returned to her desk after changing and was bent at her hips, lacing up her thigh-high boots when Caleb walked out of his office and immediately choked at sight of her from behind. He pulled his bottom lip between his teeth as he scanned over the rest of Mila's outfit. With the boots, she wore a short dress that hugged her curves and it was clear she wasn't wearing any panties.

After securing the last tie on her boot, Mila was still bent over to look into the mirror on her desk at eye-level as she applied a dark burgundy matte to her full lips. While admiring her reflection, she noticed Caleb behind her with almost a primal look in his eyes as he stared at her.

Without changing her position, Mila asked, "Is there something I can help you with, Mr. Peterson?"

Caleb cleared his throat when she broke him from his trance, but couldn't seem to avert his gaze. "What you're wearing is not appropriate for work…"

"Neither is fucking one—no wait—*several* of your employees in your office," she countered, still looking in the mirror as she used her finger to clean the excess lipstick from the edges of her lips. "And it's eight-thirty on a Friday night. I'm obviously not wearing this for work. You've kept me here late again and I'm going straight to the bar."

"You've got a fucking mouth on you," Caleb spat.

Mila stood straight up, smoothed out her dress, and turned to look him in the eyes. "Now *that* I do have," she sneered before making her way toward the elevator. "I've finished my work for the night. Everything is lined up for your morning departure. I've sent backup copies of your briefing binders to your emails, and the associates at the office in LA are all aware of your food and drink preferences so you'll be well taken care of."

Caleb simply glared at Mila as she walked away after listing off what was done. He didn't want to fire her because she was damn good at her job, but she also pissed him off—he hated her ongoing indifference toward him outside of her work duties. And he still hadn't forgotten the way she had the audacity to reject his advances, very much to his surprise.

Before he knew it, Caleb was following behind her and just before Mila reached the elevator door, he pulled her into one of the small meeting rooms in the office.

"Mr. Peterson, the fuck is wrong with you?" she snapped.

"*You* are what's wrong with me," he snarled as he caged her against the wall between his arms. "You piss me off and you don't know your place."

Mila's brows raised and she let out an entertained chuckle. "Don't know my place, you say? I know exactly where the fuck I belong and there isn't shit you can do about it."

"Do not *fucking* test me," Caleb asserted with a low tone as he wrapped his hand around her throat.

Mila immediately kicked him in the groin and he fell to his knees holding himself. She looked down at him and began to circle Caleb—

the only sounds in the room being his groans of pain and the the sounds of her heels hitting the floor.

"You see... *This* is where I belong." She stopped when she was in front of him again. "Above you."

Mila leaned against the wall behind her for balance and put her foot under Caleb's chin to lift his head so he could look up at her as he still held himself with his face twisted from the pain. Something about being in that position—staring up at her as she seemed to be examining him with disgust—caused blood to rush to his dick, despite the fact that he was in pain.

She put her foot back on the floor and Caleb's eyes drifted down from her face, to her form, to finally latching on to the thigh-high boots she was wearing. He jumped at the loud sound when she suddenly stomped.

"Sit up straight," she instructed and Caleb did so willingly, sitting back on his heels with his back straight as he looked up again to meet her devilish gaze.

"So," she purred. "The pet *can* listen."

He couldn't quite understand it, but something about Mila calling him 'pet' only seemed to turn him on more.

"You've been eyeing my boots since you first saw them. You like them, don't you?"

Caleb nodded as his gaze immediately returned to the black latex that wrapped around her legs. When Mila got off the wall to come closer to him and ran her fingers through his hair, Caleb released a groan of pleasure and his pants only tightened further.

"You should wear those boots everyday," he said confidently. "In fact, I'm going to make it a requirement th—"

He was cut off when Mila yanked his head back by his hair and forced him to look up at her. "I will wear what I want, when I want..." She tilted her head to the side and narrowed her eyes at him. "And, while I have you here, you will not speak unless I ask you a fucking question and you will keep your hands to your-fucking-self. Now, put them at your sides."

Although he had yet to admit it to himself, Mila had a hold over Caleb from the moment he met her. At first, he didn't understand why she was so confident at her size and after that, he'd grown increasingly obsessed with the *only* person who seemed to deny him the attention that he wanted.

Now, with her standing over him and *finally* giving him attention in a way he didn't expect to enjoy so much, Caleb was ready to relinquish complete control to Mila.

When Mila squat down to meet him at eye-level, Caleb's eyes immediately drifted to try to get a peek between her legs, but she roughly grabbed his face and brought him back to up to meet her gaze. "Eyes up *here*," she said sternly.

Her hand traveled down to his tie and she pulled his face closer to hers. When he tried to kiss her, she moved her head back, denying him what he wanted. "Do you want me to remove this, pet?"

He gulped, completely entranced by the woman before him. "Yes."

Slowly, only putting Caleb more on edge, Mila loosened his tie and brought it over his head. She admired the fabric in her hands and the design of it.

"Hermès?" she questioned, already knowing that it was, before she threw it to the side. Mila studied Caleb's face as she toyed with the first button of his shirt. "Do you want me to undo this, pet?"

"Y-yes," he let out with a shaky breath.

She repeated her question each time she reached the next button until she got to the final one and the front of his shirt was open, revealing his bare torso.

"Unimpressive," she sighed as she looked over his firm chest and abs. When she caught sight of his erection, her acrylic nail dragged its way down his torso until she met his waistband.

The anticipation was killing him, but Caleb couldn't seem to bring himself to disobey Mila's orders, so he kept his hands at his sides and did not speak unless asked a question. It felt like forever that he was waiting for Mila to part her lips and ask him the question he was already prepared to say yes to.

"Do you want me to undo this, pe—"

"Yes!" Caleb replied urgently, cutting her off.

Mila let out a deep sigh. "I didn't finish my question."

"I'm sor—"

Caleb's apology was interrupted when Mila covered his mouth. "You are *not* to speak unless I ask you a *fucking* question," she scolded. "I have something for pets like you who don't listen... In fact, it's right at my desk."

Caleb gulped and a chill went down his spine at the promise behind her words.

"Tell me, pet." She removed her hand from his mouth. "Would you like to redeem yourself?"

He nodded urgently. "Yes."

"Close your eyes and count to thirty."

Without question, Caleb closed his eyes and began counting. "One... two... three..."

Mila stood up with a satisfied smile on her face, straightened her dress, and walked out of the small meeting room to continue the path to meet with Jade at the bar, leaving Caleb there alone.

And Then?

"The fuck is this shit?" Caleb boomed as he thew the cup of coffee on the ground. "I only drink *Colombian* origin coffee!"

"I-I'm sorry, Mr. Peterson!" the startled assistant from PMC Group's Los Angeles office replied urgently. "I'll get right on that and be back with a large coffee, Colombian origin ASAP."

"You better make it faster than that! You need to be back here in two minutes with the *correct* coffee or I will make your life a living hell!"

After the young man scurried out of the conference room, both Adrian and Justin looked at Caleb with disapproving gazes.

"Caleb," Adrian groaned. "You've been even more of a jerk than usual since we got here. I thought you'd be in a better mood considering this is your favorite city and you even had the entire weekend to relax after our flight."

"I don't know what the fuck you're talking about. I'm annoyed because our assistant has a simple fucking job and she clearly can't even do that correctly. She told me she emailed the LA office with all of our preferences, but left out coffee? We should see about firing her."

"Calm down," Justin urged. "And besides, Mila *did* do her job. If you looked at the email she sent to the assistants out here—the ones that she copied us on—you would've seen that she was correct about all the preferences. It was that guy who got it wrong. And don't even think about firing her. She's good and I like her."

"What the fuck is that supposed to mean?!" Adrian said sharply, cutting his eyes at Justin.

"Whoa, whoa, whoa..." Justin raised both hands defensively. "Now you're starting to sound like Caleb. I'm saying that I like her as an assistant. She's by far the best we've had and neither of you can argue with that. If she wasn't, she wouldn't have lasted this long."

"Oh..." Adrian cleared his throat and straightened up in his seat. Ever since his and Mila's conversation about their kiss, he'd been on edge and especially weary of Justin given that she seemed to be on a first-name basis with him. "I guess that's true. She is excellent at her job. And I um... I like her too."

"That doesn't mean much coming from you," Caleb chuckled. "You like everyone. You're ridiculously soft."

"Soft? You sure about that assessment?" Adrian countered with a raised brow as he locked eyes with Caleb.

Letting out a frustrated huff with flared nostrils, Caleb swallowed hard and turned away. "Whatever..."

"I wish you two would work your shit out. And besides... Why the hell are you guys even more tense than I am?" Justin questioned. "I still can't believe Ashley put us on break. I don't get it."

"Why are you upset about it? If I were in your position, I would've spent this weekend fucking mad bitches and lined up shit for this week too," Caleb replied. " I mean, Ashley is hot and I'm sure she's a decent enough fuck, but you mean to tell me that you've been fucking a *single* pussy for like two years?"

"Not all of us are assholes with commitment issues, Caleb."

"Hey! I don't have commitment issues. I am *committed* to doing what the fuck I want in life."

Justin rolled his eyes and Adrian let out a sarcastic scoff before the room fell into complete silence.

Caleb, Justin, and Adrian originally flew to LA on Saturday morning, as they'd planned to go out that weekend and have fun in the city, but ended up spending most of their time in their hotel rooms, using "work" as an excuse, as they were all deeply upset.

All three of the men had spent their weekend frustrated, with Mila being the root cause of it all. Caleb was furious that Mila had left him in that office alone, Justin was upset about Ashley putting them on break for reasons he didn't understand, and Adrian was agitated at Mila's lack of reaction to their kiss and the fact she seemed to be warming up to Justin too well for his taste.

The door to the conference room slowly opened and the assistant walked in with shaky hands carrying Caleb's coffee. Meanwhile, Justin and Adrian were focused on their devices—Justin going through emails and Adrian debating whether or not he should try to look up Mila's page as he scrolled Instagram aimlessly.

"H-here you are, Mr. Peterson."

Caleb scanned over the assistant as he sat the coffee on the table in front of him with his jaw tensed.

"What's your name?" he asked.

"Um," the assistant gulped. "I-It's um... Joseph, sir."

"Joseph..." Caleb nodded with pursed lips. "I didn't see you last time I was here. Are you new?"

"Y-yeah. I actually moved down from San Francisco recently and started working here. I was unemployed for almost two years because of this big um... *misunderstanding*. But I finally found some luck when I applied here to PMC Gr—"

"Okay, I didn't ask for your fucking life story," Caleb interrupted. "I guess you better go looking for more of that luck because you're fired."

Joseph's eyes went wide and darted around the room with his confusion. "I-I'm sorry, sir... What was that?"

"You. Are. Fired," Caleb repeated. "You can't follow simple instructions... This coffee is wrong *again*. Plus, there's something about you I don't like."

Joseph gawked with disbelief and looked around the room at Adrian and Justin, who were too into their phones to notice what was happening.

"M-Mr. Peterson... Please," Joseph pleaded. "I didn't mean to—"

"Our meeting is about to start. You're dismissed."

Caleb shewed him away and Joseph surrendered and left the room.

~

"Alexis and Mila!" Monica Thompson beamed when her daughters entered the restaurant for their periodic brunch. "Come here! I have someone I want you to meet!"

"Oh god, this is what I get for networking," Alexis groaned when she recognized the woman sitting beside their mother. "Now mom thinks she's going to be on *Mob Wives* or some shit."

"What are you talking about?" Mila questioned.

The sisters approached and joined their mother and the mystery woman at the table. Immediately, once Mila was in her presence, she admired her. The woman was slightly older than her mother, and had an overwhelming air of confidence that radiated off of her. It was clear to Mila that she was likely the owner of a company or ruled some other large organization and based on Alexis' comment, she imagined it was criminal in nature.

"Hi, Mrs. Davidson," Alexis greeted. "My mother must have forgotten already that *I'm* the one who introduced you two..."

"Oh, that's right!" Monica chuckled, clearly tipsy from her mimosas. "It's just that Tina and I have been getting along so well, it feels like we're old friends."

"Tina Davidson..." Mila whispered to herself before it finally clicked. "Oh! Sean Davidson's mom?" she asked Alexis.

"I'm right here, child," Tina commented. "And yes, I'm Sean's mother... Simone's too."

"Sorry," Mila said with a small smile. "It's nice to meet you Mrs. Davidson."

"You can call me Ms. Tina."

"Damn, they greeted you before saying hello to their own mother," Monica griped playfully.

"Mother," Mila greeted with a dry tone.

"Hi mom," Alexis chimed.

"Hi Lexi! And Mila... I haven't seen or heard from you in weeks. You don't think you could be more attentive to your mother?"

"Sorry, mother. I don't mean to neglect you."

"Mhmmm," Monica hummed unconvinced. "One day, I won't be here anymore and you're gonna regret not spending more time with me. Anyway, how's your love life? You dating? Or are you at least going to give Eric another chance? He was such a good man. I can't believe you messed that up!"

Mila rolled her eyes at her mother before she shook her head and drank her entire mimosa.

"Honestly, mother," Mila sighed. "Finding love isn't a big priority for me right now. I am doing some dating, but mostly want to figure out what to do with my life."

"What's the point of dating if not for love?" asked a baffled Monica.

Mila took a deep breath as she poured more of the mimosa sitting at the middle of the table into her glass and drank. The reason she avoided speaking with her mother was because it seemed like the most important thing to her was for Mila to find love, which is something that always felt elusive to her.

She lost count of how many people she'd dated and despite Eric being close to perfect on paper, Mila didn't love him — she had never fallen in love with anyone and she wondered if perhaps something was wrong with her. The way her mother brought it up nonstop only made Mila feel more uneasy.

"Can't we talk about something else, mother... How's that angel investor thing going? I know Naomi will be here in a couple days and her app is giving you good enough PR so that you can dabble in ventures that might be a bit more morally questionable, yet very profitable."

Monica placed a calming hand on her chest. She was bewildered when Mila rejected Eric's marriage proposal. While she was aware that her youngest daughter was a bit of a free spirit, she never expected her to turn down a seemingly perfect man. Alexis was also single, but considering that she was running the family business, she had a better excuse as to why she didn't have enough time to date, though Monica suspected that something might be going on between Alexis and Sean Davidson.

"You didn't need to say all that," Monica grumbled. "And yes, Naomi's app is doing very well and getting us plenty of positive press.

We have a few fintech companies in the pipeline who we expect to pitch us soon that are actually focused on financial literacy and access to capital for underprivileged communities so no, nothing morally questionable."

Tina Davidson watched the exchange between Mila and Monica with a subtle smile on her face.

"You know what, Mila? You remind me of my daughter Simone."

"But at least Simone stays in contact with you and actually listens to your advice," Monica commented.

Tina shook her head. "Not always. That girl isolated herself from the family for ten years of her life."

"What do you mean ten years?" Monica gawked. "How'd she pull that off? How'd you get through that long?"

"Long story short, we were busy ourselves with business and respected her space, probably too much. But when we needed her, she came through..." Tina cut her eyes at Mila. "I'll have to introduce you two when she gets back from Italy with her husbands."

Mila leaned in toward Tina, wondering if she'd heard correctly. "*Husbands* as in plural? And is that even legal."

"Yeah, she has two husbands... And chile, do you think I care about 'legal'?" Tina finished with a raised brow.

"Two husbands sounds like a lot of work," Mila replied. "But I would love to meet her whenever she gets back."

"Great. I'll make it happen."

EPISODE 20

Please...

"Well, if it isn't my favorite couple!" Mila beamed when Naomi and Sebastien arrived at the restaurant. She got up and made a path straight to Naomi and pulled her into a tight hug.

"I've missed you so much, girl!" Naomi chimed, returning Mila's embrace.

"I can't believe I haven't seen you since the wedding! It's been what? Eight or nine months now?"

"It's been eight and a half months," Sebastien answered with a warm smile. "It's good to see you again, Mila. Naomi's been excited for this dinner since we first made plans to come here."

"Wow, time flies!" Mila shook Sebastien's hand after she finally let go of Naomi and nearly bursted out laughing when she stepped back and got a better look at what they were wearing. It appeared that the couple coordinated their outfits. Naomi wore a mustard off-the-shoulder dress that fell below her knees and Sebastien's stripped button-up shirt had lines of the same color to complement the brown and white.

"I know that face," Naomi commented when she saw Mila's expression. "This was not on purpose." She gestured at her and Sebastien's outfits. "It's just been happening a lot lately."

"Probably because *you're* the one who's been picking out my clothes whenever we go shopping, love. If you want to coordinate, just say so," Sebastien teased.

"Whatever, babe..." Naomi playfully rolled her eyes and followed Mila to the table. "I just needed to get you out of those plaid shirts."

"I thought you loved my plaid shirts?" Sebastien gasped, feigning offense.

Mila giggled and shook her head at their exchange as she took a seat at their table. "Anyway... I know that both of you enjoy Thai food and this is my favorite spot in the city."

Naomi and Sebastien joined her and she had a small smile on her face looking at them. Sitting side-by-side, they appeared to have locked hands under the table and shared a menu as they looked for what to order.

Mila remembered in college when Naomi swore off dating after assuming that she would never find love and it wasn't worth expending the energy for a lost cause. When Mila learned on a visit to Atlanta that Naomi was dating Sebastien Laurent, and upon hearing more about him and their relationship, she was ecstatic that her friend had found a good man.

"You always pick such great spots," Naomi said. "So, how have you been? I remember you telling me that you took on a big project for your family recently?"

"I've been good. And yeah, that um... Research project has been going really well, actually. Everything is lining up even better than I originally planned."

"I'm not surprised. You're one of those people who always seemed to be good at whatever you do!"

"I don't know about all that," Mila chuckled. "But I'll admit that my skills all happen to fit perfectly with this project. Anyway, enough about me, how have you two been? How's married life and building empires and all?"

"Married life has been good." Naomi moved her free hand across herself to rub Sebastien's arm. "And I don't know about empire-building. I just want the app to continue to do well and Seb's investments to keep prospering."

"I agree with Naomi," Sebastien replied. "Empires are overwhelming and stressful, so we're just enjoying our ongoing projects, as well as each other."

Mila looked between the two of them. "You are perfect for each other, I swear it... And speaking of 'enjoying each other', did you fill out that stuff I sent you?"

"For The Scarlet Lounge?" Naomi questioned with almost a whisper. "Yeah, turns out Sebastien is friends with the owner, and we'd been thinking about going on our next trip to Lenrod, so it works out well."

"Perfect! My friend Jade has been hounding me about it and this guy I actually met when I was leaving Atlanta after your wedding is a member. We were talking about meeting there tomorrow night."

"Oh?" Naomi raised a perfectly arched brow. "And what is this man's name?"

"It's nothing serious, girl... I just think I need to change things up with someone new. His name is Logan."

"YOU'VE BEEN MOPING every day since we got to LA. Go get laid or something," Caleb said to Justin. The two of them were with Adrian in his hotel room in what was meant to be a time for them to unwind after several days of meetings. However, the three men were still deeply frustrated about what'd occurred for each them before their trip.

"No. I'm still with Ashley and I'm not going to cheat on her."

Caleb scoffed. "I doubt she feels the same. It was her idea to go on a *'break'.*" He used the term mockingly. "She probably went out with her friends this weekend and already hooked up with another a guy. You should be doing the same. Go out and get some pussy."

"Shut the fuck up," Justin chided. "Why do you always have to say such rude shit all the time, man?"

"Because it's obvious that you don't like Ashley and the only reason you're so upset about this 'break' you guys are on is because you feel like it's some type of failure on your part and you'll disappoint your parents.

You need to start living for yourself and that's what I'm trying to get through your thick ass skull."

"Why the hell do people keep saying that I don't like Ashley?"

The room went quiet after Justin asked the question. Adrian stirred his glass of whiskey, avoiding eye contact, while Caleb leaned back in his seat with his hands clasped on the top of his head.

"What?" Justin gasped. "Adrian? What do you think?"

Adrian's gaze finally went from his glass, and he first exchanged a glance with Caleb before meeting Justin's eyes. His jaw tensed and he let out a long exhale through his nose.

"I mean... There's not really much chemistry between the two of you and it's been obvious for a while now, to be honest with you."

Justin took a sip of his rum and looked between Adrian and Caleb as he considered their words. He couldn't admit it out loud, but they weren't wrong. He and Ashley immediately hit it off when they first met, but as months went on, that spark gradually diminished. However, they'd been together for around two years and he wanted to make things work because Ashley had earned his parents' approval. He didn't want the time invested in their relationship to go to waste.

"See!" Caleb gestured toward Adrian. "Even Adrian agrees. And you said other people have told you the same thing? Obviously, it's true."

"Okay, so not exactly *'other people'*," Justin clarified. "More like the two of you and Mila have said it."

As soon as Mila's name came up, both Adrian and Caleb again turned tense. Adrian downed his whiskey and Caleb his vodka.

"Sounds like you and Mila are getting pretty fucking close," Adrian spat.

"Sounds like she's overstepping," Caleb commented with his eyes narrowed at Justin. "I still think we should consider firing her."

"Whoa, whoa, whoa..." Justin held both his hands up defensively. "Why are you guys getting all combative? All I said is that Mila had the same observations as you guys. She's very perceptive, you know. And why do you keep suggesting we fire her, Caleb? She's the best assistant we've ever had. Did something happen with you two?"

"No, nothing fucking happened," Caleb quickly answered. "I just think we should just try out someone else. I need better eye candy."

Adrian stood from his seat and walked over to pour himself more whiskey. "We're not firing Mila. Justin is right that she's the best assistant we've had."

"Yeah, yeah… That's because she gives you a hard-on, Adrian. You think we don't see you staring at her ass all the time? Yeah, I'll admit it's fat, but that only makes sense because so is she. And you *always* have her in your office, laughing and shit together."

Adrian had poured just enough whiskey for a shot before he downed it and gave Caleb a snide look. "Jealous, Caleb?"

In response, Caleb flashed his middle finger at Adrian.

Justin shook his head as he huffed his annoyance. "And now here you two go with your shit. You know what?" He rose to his feet and walked toward the door. "We usually have fun in LA, but this time's a fucking a bust. I'm going to bed and sleeping until our afternoon flight tomorrow. And then I'm going to directly to Ashley's place."

"Wait," Caleb called and quickly went up to Justin. He placed a comforting hand on his friend's shoulder and looked him in the eyes. "I know that I don't always word shit the best way, but all I was trying to say was that I care… And I can tell that you're never going to be happy with Ashley."

Justin placed his hand over Caleb's and gave him an affirmative nod. "I know that you care, man… I just need to get my head together. I'll see you guys tomorrow."

"See you tomorrow," Adrian said.

After Justin left, it was just Adrian and Caleb in the room. Caleb walked over and stood next to Adrian at the counter as he poured more vodka into his glass.

"Why do you keep making those snide ass comments?" Caleb questioned.

Adrian's gaze snapped over to him. "Are you serious? *You're* the one who keeps talking shit, all I'm doing is responding. What's up with you? It's like over the past year or so you've been such an asshole. I mean, you were kind of a jerk before, but it's even worse now."

"You can't really be asking me that question. Did you really forget what happened a year ago?"

"Why do you always act like you're the fucking victim here?"

"Because you never explained anything to me! It was like we were fine one day and then the next, you acted like nothing happened."

"That's because nothing happened," Adrian said softly. "Nothing needed to be explained."

Caleb put down his empty glass and walked in closer to Adrian with his arms crossed. His blue eyes bore into Adrian's brown ones. "That's really all you have to say to me?"

Adrian analyzed Caleb's face. His brows were tense and jaw clenched as his nostrils flared with the deep breaths he was taking. His Adam's apple bobbed when he swallowed, appearing as if he was trying to hold something back.

Caleb let out a huff and shook his head before turning around and walking away from Adrian. "This is such bullsh—" He was cut off when Adrian grabbed him while he was still within arm's reach and pulled him in for a deep kiss.

Holding Caleb's face as their bodies pressed against each other and mouths moved eagerly, Adrian was in complete control of the kiss. He took Caleb's bottom lip between his teeth and pulled it, earning a groan of pleasure before he made a path to Caleb's neck.

Caleb's fingertips traced along the bottom hem of Adrian's shirt before making their way under it and caressing his bare skin.

Suddenly, Adrian pushed him away and Caleb stood there in almost a daze before blinking rapidly regaining his focus. Just as he was about to go off again, Adrian stopped him.

"Take your shirt off."

"What?" Caleb gulped.

"Don't make me fucking repeat myself."

Caleb removed his shirt and Adrian his before their lips connected again, now as they walked toward the couch. The two of them fell over, into the sofa, Adrian on top and between Caleb's legs as the two of them ground against each other. Caleb's breathing was hard and ragged when Adrian finally broke away and lifted himself up to look down at Caleb.

"You're hard for me already," he said, his voice low and raspy.

Caleb reached down and cupped Adrian through his jeans. "And so are you, for me."

Adrian grabbed Caleb's wrists and pinned them above his head before going back down to kiss and suck at his neck. Caleb couldn't help the light moans that came from him as they continued to grind against each other.

"Please," Caleb breathed.

"Hm?" Adrian hummed inquisitively, knowing exactly what Caleb meant with that single word.

"Please..." Caleb pushed Adrian back and reached for his belt. "I—"

He was interrupted when his phone went off in his pocket. Not wanting the two of them to stop, he pulled it out and threw it on the floor. However, when it landed face up and Adrian saw who was calling Caleb, he came back to his senses and took a deep breath.

"You should get that," he said coldly as he stood to his feet and went toward the mini bar to retrieve his shirt.

"Hey, what the fuck?" Caleb snapped. "You started this and now you're—"

"Yeah, I'm stopping it. I'm not about to make this fucking mistake again. Just get your phone, some chick named Rachel is calling you."

"So? I don't give a fuck."

"You should, because that the only way you're getting your dick wet tonight."

"You serious right now?" Caleb stood up and walked toward the mini bar. Before he could get there, Adrian threw his shirt at him.

"Yeah, I'm serious. Now, get out. We should just keep shit between us platonic and business-focused. Besides... You and I have had too much to drink." Without another word, Adrian turned away and went into the bathroom.

Caleb contemplated following him and protesting further, but instead, he quickly put on his shirt and snatched his phone off the floor.

"This is bullshit."

Someone Else

"It's about time you got your ass out here, girl," Jade said when Mila arrived at The Scarlet Lounge with Naomi and Sebastien. Mila opted to wear something simple for the night—a black dress with cutouts just under her breasts along with a pair of red pumps that matched her nails and lipstick. Sebastien and Naomi were again inadvertently coordinated—Naomi in a dark blue dress and black heels and Sebastien in a button up of the same color with black slacks.

The club was dimly lit, but enough to see what was going on. It was a week night for open play, so the place wasn't too busy. They got there a couple hours after opening and scenes were already going on around the club.

"I promised you that I would come," Mila replied. "I'm just finally getting around to it. Besides, I knew that you'd be playing with your Dom anyway and I wanted to make sure I at least at something lined up."

"Oh?" Jade raised a brow and looked at Naomi and Sebastien. "You back on your unicorn grind these days?"

Sebastien's eyes went wide when he heard Jade and Naomi started snickering, shaking her head.

"No!" Mila exclaimed. "You know Naomi. And remember, she and Sebastien got married a while back."

"Yes, I remember! You were so excited for their wedding like it was your own. But that still doesn't answer my question. You act like you don't have sex with friends."

"Goddamn. Telling everybody my business," Mila chided playfully. "And no, I'm not playing with Naomi and Sebastien tonight. I'm meeting someone else here. What about you? You meeting with your Dom, like I said?"

Jade hummed her confirmation. "And who've you got lined up?"

"This guy named Logan who conveniently got an accurate read on me and boldly offered his face for me to sit on."

"Damn, that easy? You usually don't go for those ones, do you?"

"Nah, not normally, but some things have happened recently that've made me think I should try someone different. Anyway, hey Naomi, did you..." Mila paused when she turned around and realized Naomi and Sebastien were no longer behind her. She quickly scanned over the space before she noticed they'd already gotten to the opposite side and appeared to have been going into one of the private rooms. "Naomi's husband has a crazy sex drive for a man in his forties," she commented with almost a whisper.

"If you wanna change things up, why don't you try subbing?" Jade suggested as the two of them started walking toward one of the free couches and sat down.

"I do sub sometimes."

"You know what I mean, girl. What about subbing with a man?"

"Fuck no." Mila shook her head. "It's not something I've ever had a desire to do. I'm switchy with women, but when it comes to men, I just can't bring myself to do it."

"See, I can't do that. I *love* it when a man gets rough with me, so I'm strictly subbing."

"I don't see how those are related. Just because a partner is submissive, doesn't mean they can't get rough with you. You ever had a partner *begging* to choke you? That shit is sexy."

"Oh," Jade gasped lightly. "I didn't know that was a thing."

"Many things are things." Mila shrugged. "There's no one-size-fits all when it comes to sex and power dynamics. People always try to make some bullshit 'standards' and say if you like one thing then you won't like another… They don't get that it's a lot more complex than that."

"Hey, Ms. Mila," a deep, familiar voice sounded from behind the couch. While Mila welcomed the title, it didn't come from the person she most preferred to hear it from.

"Hello, Logan." She watched him as he rounded the couch to sit next to her. "This is my friend Jade," she gestured to her friend on her other side.

"It's nice to meet you," Logan said. He reached his arm across Mila to shake Jade's hand. "You've been here before, haven't you? I feel like I've seen you around."

"Nice to meet you too, and yeah, I've been here a few times. You must be the one who finally convinced Mila to come because I've been on her ass for weeks about trying this place out."

"Is that so?" Logan questioned. "And to think, at one point I wasn't sure if she would give me a chance. I think the fact that I'm friends with her boss probably saved—"

Mila placed her hand over Logan's mouth to stop him and Jade's brows knitted together. She'd never known of Mila working a day in her life other than helping with the Thompson Luxe Group business.

"You have a boss?" she asked Mila. "Are you helping Lexi with something?"

Mila realized that she miscalculated how this would play out. She assumed that Jade would be caught up with the guy she'd been playing with for the past few months and didn't expect Logan to bring up knowing Adrian so early in the conversation.

"I'll tell you about it later. In the mean time…" Mila gestured at a man sitting at the bar who'd been eying Jade. "Why don't you do some mingling before your Daddy arrives? I'll keep an eye on you from here to make sure he's not on some creep shit and it'll give Logan and I a chance to talk one-on-one."

Jade turned and looked at the man, gave an approving nod and got up to walk toward him. "Y'all have fun."

Mila turned back to Logan and finally removed her hand from his mouth.

"What? You don't tell your friends about work or something?"

"No. Theres no need. Anyway, let's talk about why we're here..."

ADRIAN, Caleb, and Justin arrived in Lenrod City late evening and each went their separate ways. An exhausted and agitated Adrian went straight home, a deeply frustrated Caleb did the same, and a confused Justin made his way to Ashley's apartment.

"Ashley, please..." Justin pleaded from outside of her door. "Just open the door so we can talk about this."

"I told you we need a break," she said from the opposite side.

"Please, babe... I know you were upset with me, but I honestly didn't understand why. Please, can we at least talk this out and clear things up. I feel like it's all probably a misunderstanding." Justin pressed his forehead against the door with his eyes closed as he took deep breaths.

After a long pause with not a noise from Ashley on the other side, the silence was broken at the sound of her unlocking the door. When she opened it, Justin felt guilty as soon as he saw her. She was wearing a robe and her hair was disheveled and mascara was running, her lipstick was slightly smeared and Justin assumed it was from her wiping her nose while she cried.

She stepped out of the apartment, barely able to make eye contact with him and said, "Fine. But you're not coming in and you have five minutes."

"Babe, I'm really sorry for making you feel like I don't want you to the point where you needed to take a break. That wasn't at all my intention..." Justin paused for a few moments, further analyzing her face. "I love you, Ash. And I don't... want to lose you."

Ashley let out a deep sigh after listening to his very brief speech. "I hear you, Justin, but you've been acting strange for the past few months." She hesitated for several moments before making eye contact with him for the first time since he showed up at her apartment. "Sometimes, with the way you've been touching me lately, it feels like you're thinking of someone else... *Is* there someone else?"

"What?" Justin gawked, taken aback by her question. "Of course not. I can assure you that there's no one else. I'm even willing to take a lie-detector test or you could hire a PI to follow me or something. Babe, you and I make sense and I don't want to lose that. I'd never endanger what we have by cheating on you."

Ashley studied his eyes as he spoke and lightly nodded when he finished. "Yeah... We do make sense, I guess."

"Great!" Justin exclaimed, but when he leaned toward Ashley to kiss her, she dodged him and turned her back to him and faced the door.

"We can start a clean slate... Tomorrow. How about you call me then?"

"Oh, okay..." Justin found Ashley's behavior weird, but he was too caught up in getting another chance to care of take notice of anything else going on. "I'm glad we're on the same page again. I'm pretty beat from this trip, so I'm going home."

Ashley looked over her shoulder to watch him walk toward the elevator.

"Everything is always business with him," she spat before opening her door, walking back in toward the bedroom, and removing her robe.

Adrian entered his apartment and blew out a deep breath through his mouth. He thought about his interaction with Caleb the night before, feeling guilty for stopping it in the middle while also internally chiding himself for starting it.

He knew that he could be impulsive at times, but it seemed to have become much more common since Mila started working at PMC Group. The two of them had great chemistry and while they managed to hide it from others, when it was just the two of them inside Adrian's office, the sexual tension was thick and the day Adrian decided to kiss Mila was his clearest sign that he should stop their alone time.

However, it didn't change the fact that he still very much desired those one-on-one meetings and often found himself wondering what things might be like between him and Mila if she wasn't working for him.

Adrian liked the way she seemed genuinely interested in whatever he talked about and how her thoughtful responses proved that she was actively listening to him. She asked him questions about building furniture, how he got into it, what his process was like, and if he saw it as more of an art form or trade.

He liked the way that he seemed to be the only one who could pull her out of her indifferent state and earn her excitement—it was part of the reason that he decided PMC Group would start a grant program for little-known plus-size designers to support them in growing their brands and making more size-inclusive fashion. The bright eyes and wide smile she gave him when he told her about it made it all worth it to Adrian.

The way she seemed to have such a hold on him made Adrian increasingly worried, but he still couldn't bring himself to pull away from her completely and draw a platonic line as he did with Caleb. On top of it all, he was even more conflicted because he had lingering feelings for Caleb and strong ones for Mila at the same time.

"Maybe I should take a vacation," he said to himself. "Between what happened with Mila and then with Caleb, it's obvious I need some sort of outlet... Or maybe I just need someone else to help me get over all this..." Adrian pulled out his phone and started scrolling through his contacts until landing on the name of a mistress he played with several months ago.

CALEB SAT in his couch with his computer on the coffee table in front of him and his dick in his hand. On the screen was a video showing a woman bent over in doggy style with the side of her face on the bed while a man was on top of her with his fingers tangled in her hair and the other smacking her ass while he roughly pounded into her.

Stroking himself while he watched the video, Caleb couldn't seem to really get into it. After a few more minutes passed without reaction, he reluctantly typed something else into the website's search bar.

His jaw tensed as the video got started, and wanting to get straight into it, he skipped over the skit at the beginning and went to the middle of the video. It featured one man with dark brown hair and matching eyes taking another from the back while the bottom ate out the woman who was with them. The top was rough, smacking the bottom's ass, who in turn moaned into the woman he was eating out. With the sight of the scene, Caleb's dick finally started to grow harder.

"We have such a good bitch serving us, don't we, honey?" the woman said. *"He's making such great use of himself."*

"Maybe we'll... let him... come today," the man replied through his grunts.

"Fuck," Caleb breathed as his strokes picked up pace. Several minutes passed and he hit his release much sooner than expected. The video was just what he needed after the past week he had between his interactions with Mila and Adrian.

However, and Caleb refused to admit it to himself, the woman's body wasn't quite what he was looking for and he knew that he wouldn't find the exact image that he wanted to see. While the video managed to send him over the edge, he still didn't feel anywhere near satisfied after watching it. So, he pulled out his phone and went straight to Shannon's contact details.

"Whatever, someone else obviously needs to take care of this for me and I'll be over it."

Gifts

Mila knew it would be an interesting day when she woke up to see an email she received at 4:23a.m. from Caleb asking her to see him in his office first thing in the morning.

As she usually did, Mila arrived to PMC Group about thirty minutes before her "bosses" were to come in and she prepared their schedules—placing Adrian's on his desk, printing Justin's for their morning meeting, and preparing to email Caleb.

Adrian was the first of the three men to walk into the office and a smile naturally pulled at his lips as he approached and greeted Mila. No matter how much he tried to deny it to himself, Mila was one of the brighter parts of his mornings and he missed her while he was away.

"Welcome back, Mr. Collins," Mila greeted cheerfully. "How was your trip?"

"It was wonderful and everything went smoothly," Adrian replied as he held up a tall, slim gift bag and sat it on her desk. "In fact, I even had time to get you some wine."

"Oh?" Mila questioned, locking eyes with him as she took the bag. "Based on the email I got from Mr. Peterson at four this morning, I'm sure it's going to be a long day and this wine will definitely come in handy this evening."

"Oh, geez," Adrian groaned. "What's he up to now? I'm sorry he gives you such a hard time. He can be difficult."

"I assure you, Mr. Collins, there's nothing I can't handle when it comes to Mr. Peterson. Besides, the nice part about long days is that I'll have an excuse to take a long, hot bath while I down a bottle of Napa Valley wine."

"Well, I admire your positivity, Ms. Mila."

Adrian didn't realize what he said until the title crossed his lips out of habit already. "I mean- er... I mean- Mila."

"'Ms. Mila' is fine," she teased with a wink before changing the subject. "Anyway, I've placed your schedule on your desk per our new system. Just email or call if you have any questions or need any assistance."

"R-right... Have a nice day." Adrian noticed how Mila had a way of catching him off guard with her comments that felt flirtatious before quickly, but smoothly changing the subject. It was like she knew exactly how to tease him without being so overt about it and he wondered if she'd read him as submissive.

"Enjoy your day as well, Mr. Collins."

Not long after Adrian went into his office, Justin arrived and also had a gift bag in his hand for Mila. As had become their routine in the mornings, she greeted him in Japanese and they exchanged some small talk before going into his office.

"I didn't want to forget to give you this," Justin chimed, handing the gift bag to Mila. "Just a little something I got you from California as a thank you for being such a great assistant."

"Thanks, Justin," Mila replied as she opened the bag and pulled out a personalized license plate with her name on it. Looking over the gift, it wasn't really her taste and she didn't like it, but she appreciated the thought and pulled a fake, small smile to her face and gave Justin a nod of approval before putting it back in the bag.

"Are you and Adrian trying to spoil me or something?" she questioned playfully.

"Hm? What do you mean?"

"Oh! He didn't tell you? Adrian bought me a bottle of wine from Napa Valley as a souvenir."

Justin didn't understand why, but something about hearing that Adrian also bought Mila a gift slightly bothered him, especially knowing that the wine was likely more expensive than the license plate he purchased.

"Well..." Justin cleared his throat. "That was nice of him. I didn't realize he bought you something too."

"He did. Also..." Mila leaned in toward Justin with a flirtatious glimmer in her eyes to whisper, "Don't tell Mr. Peterson this, but you and Adrian are my favorites."

Justin couldn't help the grin that pulled at his lips and he leaned in toward Mila with their faces mere inches apart. "And don't tell Adrian or Caleb this, but *you're* my favorite." As soon as he noticed a slight tense in Mila's brows, Justin realized his mistaken wording and tried to recover. "I just mean that you're my favorite colleague... You know?"

"I know what you mean," Mila assured. "Anyway, let's discuss your schedule for today..."

Mila and Justin went through his schedule relatively quickly and she left his office in time for Caleb's arrival.

Without looking at Mila, Caleb continued the path to his door and said, "I know you saw my email, so let's go."

Reluctantly, Mila followed him to his office.

Taking her seat across from Caleb while he got settled at his desk and pulled out his computer to connect it to the monitor, Mila relaxed in her chair with her legs crossed and scrolled aimlessly through her phone. She had a snide look on her face remembering what occurred Friday night.

"And what's so fucking funny?" Caleb asked sharply, breaking the silence.

Mila didn't bother looking up from her phone. "Oh nothing, Mr. Peterson. What was it you called me in here for?"

"You know exactly why the fuck I called you in here."

"No, I don't," she replied. "Could you explain?"

Caleb slammed his hand flat on his desk, breaking Mila's focus from her phone so she would finally look at him. "What type of fucking game are you playing?"

"I don't know what you're talking about, Mr. Pet—"

"Do not fucking lie to me!"

"Calm down," Mila said with a sigh. "Why so hostile?"

"Because you're playing dumb like you don't know why the fuck I called you in here! You piss me off."

Mila released an entertained huff. "You tell me that I piss you off and you act all annoyed at me, but you still have yet to fire me... Why is that?"

Caleb crossed his arms and sat up straight in his seat. "That's because you're the first assistant I've had who isn't incompetent."

"Do you know what I think, *Mr. Peterson?*" she said the name mockingly as she stood up and leaned forward against his desk toward him. "I think you won't fire me for the exact same reason you were on your knees in front of me Friday night with 'yes' and the numbers one through thirty being the only words in your vocabulary."

Caleb shot to his feet to meet Mila's eyes and they both stood there in a staring match for several moments before he was the first one to break, just as Mila expected. He grabbed her by the back of her head and smashed his lips against hers.

Mila had a moment of weakness when she felt how skillfully his tongue moved as soon as it entered her mouth and she wondered where it would feel elsewhere before finally pulling away and grabbing his face.

"I didn't say you could put your mouth on me. You haven't earned the privilege."

"Too late..." Caleb licked his lips with a snide smirk. "I've already had a taste now."

"And that is the last one you'll get," Mila replied curtly, pushing his face away and walking toward the door.

"Yeah, right..." Caleb scoffed and settled back into his seat confidently as he watched her walk away. He didn't expect to kiss Mila. In fact, he'd brought her into the office to fire her and planned to deal with any backlash from Adrian or Justin later.

However, her boldness in challenging him about Friday only seemed to turn him on and when she was standing above him again and looking down at Caleb, he had a strong desire to relinquish control to her. When he stood up to meet her gaze before, he hoped to get rid of that desire, but when he saw she was nowhere near backing down, he couldn't help himself anymore.

And now that he'd tasted her, he only wanted more.

"The fuck did I just do?"

Caught Off Guard

Mila groaned when she arrived at her apartment after a long day of work and saw yet another bouquet of roses at her door. Eric had been sending them regularly despite the fact they'd broken up for almost a year and when they were together, she'd told him multiple times that she preferred lilies.

"The hell am I gonna do with these?" she spat as she struggled to open the door. She had her purse in one hand and the wine Adrian had bought her in the other.

"I don't know, maybe decorate? Set them on a table?"

"Oh shit!" Mila gasped when she heard the familiar voice and turned around to see Eric standing behind her. A former tight-end who played on his college football team, he had a tall, muscular structure that was overbearing, even with Mila's own height. However, instead of going into professional sports, he landed on a career in finance as a wealth advisor.

"It's just me, Mila." He held up both his hands defensively and walked up to her with a toothy grin as he reached for her keys. "Here, let me help you."

Mila let out a long breath of annoyance when Eric took the keys from the side of her purse before she could smack him away. "Overstepping as usual… Do you not remember me telling you I don't like roses?"

"Is that the way you greet me and thank me for your gift?" he questioned before opening the door and letting the two of them into the apartment. He picked up the bouquet of roses and carried them to Mila's kitchen where he put them on the counter.

Eric looked around her home, admiring the expensive taste of the woman he loved. She was on the top level of an uptown apartment where she had floor-to-ceiling windows and a view of Babineaux Park, the largest in Lenrod City. With an open floor plan, the area to the far right corner was used for the living room and marked by an elegant white leather couch that sat by the windows. A TV divided it from the dining room, where an eight-person glass dining table was set up with a white china set that had rose-gold trimmings.

"Your new place is nice," Eric commented. "But, I still miss you at our apartment. It gets so lonely without you."

"I didn't have a reason to stay," Mila replied coldly as she joined Eric in the kitchen and pulled out the bottle of wine that she got from Adrian. "I'm still pissed at my mother for giving you my address without my consent."

"It's only because she loves me. Remember… Like you used to? Like maybe you still do?"

Mila took a deep sigh and pulled out her corkscrew to open the wine. "Eric… It's been almost a year. You still haven't moved on?"

"Of course I haven't moved on. Mila, you're my first and only love. Maybe my proposal wasn't the best timing, but it's hard for me to believe that you didn't love me back. I know that you still love me—"

The bottle popped when Mila pulled out the cork, interrupting him. "Eric," she said, finally meeting his eyes. "Please, I really don't want to have this conversation right now. I told you I was sorry…"

"I'm not asking to have the same conversation again, Mila. I'm here to ask you to give me another chance. To prove to you that you *do* love me. I know that you have commitment issues. Hell, I called it the day you asked about having an open relationship, but I know I'm the only one for you and you're the only one for me."

Mila poured herself a glass of wine and took three gulps, trying to calm her nerves. She was uncomfortable with the way Eric had been sending her flowers regularly and him showing up unexpected and uninvited to her apartment only made it worse.

"Eric, this is not—"

"Please, I promise I won't take long." Eric cut her off and created space between them, hoping to reduce some of Mila's uneasiness. "I'm just asking you to take one last chance with me, Mila. All I need is one more time to prove that you and I are worth it, baby…"

Mila repositioned herself so that she was she was within arm's reach of her knife block. "Eric, you need to leave. I didn't give you my address for a reason."

Eric again held up his hands defensively as he did when he first arrived outside of her apartment and backed away toward the door. "I didn't mean to scare you. I just thought that maybe us speaking in person would help, especially since you won't take any of my calls or texts or emails…"

"Because I want you move on, Eric. Find someone who can love you in the way that you want them to. You deserve someone who loves you, truly loves you."

"I deserve *you*, Mila. I love you and I *know* you love me too."

Mila took a deep breath and leaned back against the counter where the knife block sat so she could quickly grab one if needed. "Eric, I'm asking you to leave. I know you're a persistent man, but this isn't the time for it. You're in my home uninvited and you need to *go*."

"Mila, please…"

"Get out!" she snapped, pointing at the door.

"I'm going, I'm going…" Eric said urgently, grabbing the doorknob and stepping out of the apartment. "Just please… think about it. I love you, and I know you love me too."

After Eric left, Mila massaged her temples and paced her apartment before finally going to her purse to pull out her phone.

MOTHER

Hey, I told Eric to go visit you today. Give him another chance! I want a wedding and grandbabies... it doesn't necessarily have to be in that order... you're not getting any younger.

Mila threw her phone on the couch and went into the bathroom to run water into the tub.

Mila sat at her desk searching online for security systems to add to her apartment when Adrian walked up to her. As he approached, he noticed the personalized license plate with her name on it sitting on her desk and he immediately recognized it from the LA trip. Justin had been looking at them and he assumed that he was getting one as a gift for Ashley.

"Hey, Mila how are you?"

"Hi, Adrian," Mila greeted with a smile. "I'm well. Thanks again for that wine, by the way. It went perfectly with my long bath last night."

"I'm glad I could be of service..." Adrian eyed the license plate on her desk and pointed to it. "Where'd you get that?"

"Oh, this?" Mila held up the gift. "Justin got it for me while you guys were in LA. You didn't see him picking it out?"

"Oh, um... I saw him looking at the license plates to get one personalized, but I thought he was doing it for Ashley... Never mind... Speaking of Justin, is he ready for our ten-thirty meeting?"

"Yes, he is." Mila nodded. "Mr. Peterson isn't here, but I'm sure he's on his way."

"Always the late one," Adrian griped before leaning against Mila's desk and tilting his head to the side as he held her gaze. "I meant to ask, how was your vacation while we were away? I know it was only a few days, but I hope you were able to make the most of it."

Mila rested her chin in her palm while looking up at Adrian. "It was wonderful and I absolutely did make the most of it."

"Oh? So, I'm guessing you did something special?"

"I did, but it's kind of a secret," Mila teased. She bit her bottom lip and maintained eye contact with Adrian.

He caught on the challenge behind her words and before he could stop himself, he said, "I'm good at keeping secrets, Ms. Mila."

At his response, Mila eyed Adrian up and down. It was clear in her expression and the way she grazed her own thumb across her bottom lip that her thoughts were anything but innocent as she examined him.

"Well, my friend would not shut up about this, um... *very* special club," she started and Adrian listened to her attentively. "I don't need to get into the details, but it was a *great* time despite it being a weeknight, so I'm grateful for the vacation..."

"What was the club called? I'm always looking for new spots to have fun."

"I'm not sure if you've heard of it. I think it's only for a *specific* clientele..."

"Go on," Adrian urged.

"It's called..." Mila paused, feigning hesitancy with a pursing of her lips. She didn't continue until she saw Adrian's head leaned forward toward her, along with the rest of his body. "The Scarlet Lounge. Have you heard of it?"

Adrian immediately choked at Mila's answer. He felt a knot in his stomach and his heart started pounding rapidly. Even worse, he had conflicting feelings upon hearing where she went.

Part of him was thankful he wasn't there that night.

Part of him *wished* he was there that night.

Part of him was questioning if their conversation had just reached inappropriate territory.

Part of him was ecstatic to learn Mila was involved in the scene.

"You okay, Adrian?" Mila asked. "You look uneasy."

"O-oh... Sorry- I um... I've never- I don't..." Adrian was all over the place and he took note of how easily Mila managed to have such an effect on him. He often found himself tripping over his words with her. "I've never heard of it," he finally choked out.

"Okay," replied a clearly unconvinced Mila. "Anyway, your meeting with Jus- Mr. Matsuda and Mr. Peterson, remember?"

"R-right. Yes. That meeting is supposed to be happening right now.

But Caleb... Well, he's a- always late. He can just catch up, I guess." Adrian pushed himself off of Mila's desk and went toward Justin's office. "Thank you, Mila."

She hummed an affirmative. Mila had many ways of entertaining herself when it came to her three 'bosses', but the times she'd catch Adrian off guard were among her favorite moments.

Meanwhile, as Adrian walked to Justin's office, he didn't bother knocking when he entered. He walked straight to the couch on the far end of Justin's office while Justin finished a call. Adrian bounced his leg and took deep breaths, calming himself from Mila's mention of The Scarlet Lounge.

"Hey man, how's it going?" Justin asked when he went over to join Adrian at the couches.

"It's alright, just stressed as hell. I've got a lunch with Logan early next week to double check if we're in the right place financially for our next acquisition. We're looking good for it, but still..."

"You don't have to do that. You know PMC Group will *always* be good for it. Even if the funds aren't necessarily there."

"We need to be legit as much as possible," Adrian replied. "Also... This is random, but did you get Ashley anything from LA?"

Justin's eyes went wide at the question and a sharp breath crossed his nose. "You know what? I didn't even think about it. Damn! And we have a date tonight. She's taking me back, I think. Maybe I could just buy something in the city and say it came from there."

"But you bought something for Mila?"

Justin paused as his gaze darted around the office. "Yeah, but it's different. I mean... She was top of mind since she's our assistant and handled the logistics for everything."

"More top of mind than the woman you claim to love?"

"Whoa, chill out," Justin replied. "Why does it feel like you're getting hostile all of a sudden?"

"I just think it's weird that you thought of our assistant before your girlfriend..."

"I'm hearing some suggestiveness in there, so do you wanna tell me what you're getting at?"

Adrian took a deep, exacerbated breath. "You spend a lot of time with Mila in your office, you thought about her before your girlfriend when buying a gift, and you two are on a first name basis."

"Okay... Other than the girlfriend part, it's the same for you two. I still don't understand what you're implying here."

"We don't do one-on-ones anymore and it's not like I bring her into business meetings like you do."

"She's a great employee and her Japanese is perfect, so of course I'm going to have her on my calls with these Japanese companies. It's all business. Adrian, why are you so worried about that? You almost sound jealous."

Adrian quickly readjusted, leaned back in the couch, and crossed his arms and legs. "No, that's not the case at all. I'm just thinking about the company and don't want to risk some sexual harassment lawsuit or something."

"Okay, you just jumped like twenty steps. Mila is simply a great employee and that's all. Besides, you don't have that same concern with Caleb. And he's *actually* sleeping around the office."

"Well, maybe we should be concerned." Right after his response Justin's door flung open to a visibly hungover Caleb, who walked in with sunglasses and messy hair, still smelling of alcohol from the night before.

"Dude, what the fuck?" Justin questioned.

"None of your fucking business" Caleb replied sharply. "Let's just get this fucking meeting over with so I can take a nap in my office."

"Well, you're in a shittier mood than usual."

"Yeah, I wonder why..." Caleb grumbled, looking toward Adrian. "Anyway, let's just get on with these weekly updates."

He Tried

It had been a week since Caleb, Justin, and Adrian returned from California and Caleb confronted Mila about leaving him in the office alone. No matter how hard he tried, he couldn't seem to forget about that night in the office—the sound of her heels clicking, the look of disgust she had while standing over him, the way she firmly held his face when scolding him, and the darkness in her eyes when she'd falsely promised him punishment.

Caleb also couldn't stop thinking about the softness of Mila's lips after feeling them for the first time and he remembered when she faltered, even if it was only for a few moments, and returned his kiss.

However, none of that could cover up the frustration Caleb felt toward Mila. First, she refused to acknowledge his existence beyond her regular work duties and when she *did* finally acknowledge him, it was just enough to leave him wanting more. He was also well aware that she'd be steadfast in denying him.

But Caleb had a plan. He was still her boss, so she'd have to come when he called. And he intended to call her until she gave him what he wanted.

"Mila," he greeted, approaching her desk. "I hear from Justin that you're useful in meetings, so join this call I have and be sure to take thorough notes."

Without responding, Mila stood up and followed Caleb into his office. When he settled at his desk, he was thrown off when he saw that she had taken a seat on the couch in his office several feet from him.

"The hell are you sitting way over there for?"

"The couch is more comfortable than that chair and I can hear you fine from here," Mila replied without looking up from her tablet.

Caleb considered joining her on the couch, but he refused to follow her. *She needs to come to* me, he thought to himself.

"Whatever," he mumbled before dialing the number to begin the conference call.

As the meeting went on, Caleb was distracted throughout most of it as he kept looking over at Mila. She was completely focused on taking notes, her head down and typing the entire time. Unlike him, she wasn't stealing any glances and didn't appear to be resisting the urge to do so.

Who the fuck is this woman? Caleb's thoughts about Mila continued. *She had me on my knees and was undressing me and now she's back to ignoring me? And why the fuck is it bothering me so much like I don't have more than enough options?*

The call had finished and Caleb was still glaring at Mila, growing even more frustrated when she still didn't look up even after the meeting ended.

"You better have taken good notes," he said. "I won't tolerate half-assed scribbling and short-hand."

"Sure thing, Mr. Peterson," Mila replied dryly as she stood from the couch and walked toward the door. "I'll clean these up and have them to you in the next forty-five minutes."

"Make it twenty minutes. If you *really* took notes correctly, it shouldn't be hard to clean them up."

"Twenty minutes it is, then."

Just when she reached the door, Caleb called out to her again.

"Mila."

"Yes?" She turned to look at Caleb for the first time and her face was void of any emotion, only disappointing Caleb further.

He gestured to one of the seats in front of his desk. "Come here."

"No."

"What?"

"No," Mila repeated.

"I told you to come here."

"If it has nothing to do with my job, Mr. Peterson, the answer is no."

"Oh, so you're playing hard-to-get now like I haven't already had a taste of you?" Caleb challenged with a raised brow. He stood from his seat and walked over to her at the door. "Don't act like you didn't kiss me back."

"I don't 'play' hard-to-get, Mr. Peterson. If I want something, I make it happen."

"And you want me." Caleb grabbed Mila's arm, but didn't go as far as pulling her to him.

She looked down at his hand on her before she met him with a chilling glare that sent shivers down his spine.

"Get your hand off me," she said coldly and something in Caleb told him to heed the warning in her tone. "Touch me again without my consent, and you *will* regret it."

Without another word, Mila walked out of Caleb's office.

Again, he was left behind by the woman who completely baffled him.

MILA AND JUSTIN sat alone at their table in the private room of the restaurant where they had finished a dinner meeting with executives from another Japanese fashion line. Mila had become Justin's go-to for any of his Japanese-related business and she had nearly earned his full trust.

Their guests had left and the two of them were recapping the discussions with each other to make sure their mental notes were aligned and so that Mila could write things down. They'd reached a pause in their conversation as Mila typed everything on her tablet and Justin couldn't help but examine her face.

He found that his thoughts of Mila would at times consume him and he would wonder things about her that went outside of their professional relationship. There were nights and weekends when Justin would wonder what Mila might be up to with her free time and he had an urge to call and check in on her. There were times when they'd go a few weeks without having their one-on-one meetings because he'd been on travel or get too busy and he noticed that he'd miss her in those periods.

Justin knew that he liked Mila... *a lot*. She was confident, friendly, and charismatic. She also had a natural allure that Justin figured was a mix of those three things along with the way she dressed. He admired the way she regularly wore high heels and how when she walked, she seemed to almost float.

She was also one of the few people with whom he felt comfortable talking about his stress.

"What?" Mila questioned when she looked up to see Justin giving her an intense stare. "Why are you looking at me like that?"

"Oh- oh!" Justin blinked rapidly and straightened up in his seat. "Sorry, I was kind of in a daze."

"Don't worry, I'm used to having that effect," she joked and Justin chuckled at her response.

"You know... You're *really* good at this stuff, Mila," he commented.

Mila looked at him curiously and rested her chin on her knuckles. "Care to expand?"

"I just mean that you're really good at these business meetings and this work we've been doing to expand PMC Group's reach to Japan. Not only are you charismatic, but you have excellent business acumen and while I haven't put you in a situation that requires negotiating, I have no doubt that if I did, you'd do an excellent job... You're a domineering woman and I admire that a lot."

When he finished, Mila simply looked at him with a small smile on her face and he returned her look with a confused expression.

"Sorry, Mila. Was that too much? I don't want to make you uncomfortable or anything..."

"No, not at all," Mila assured. "Keep going," she gestured her hand for him to continue. "I like what I'm hearing."

With a grin on his face, Justin continued to give Mila praise. "You really are a gem, Mila Nelson. I'm glad we hired you. I know that year-long contract with the temp agency is about to expire, but what do you think of working for us permanently?"

"Hm," Mila tapped her chin thoughtfully. "I'm not sure, honestly. I'd need to think about it."

"Okay, we we have a few more months, but you've really been an asset to all of us, including Caleb even though he won't admit it, since joining this company. So, I'm sure that the guys will be in agreement about keeping you."

"Well, you can put some thought into that offer, and we'll see what happens."

"Oh, you know that I will. I don't want to risk losing you."

"Mhmm..." Mila took a sip of her wine before changing the subject. "Now that we've made it through this dinner meeting, please tell me that you're doing something *other* than working this weekend."

"I am, actually!" Justin chimed. "I'm heading up to D.C. to visit my parents."

"Oh, nice! Is Ashley coming with?"

"No. Oddly enough, *she's* the one who has to work this weekend. Funny because it's usually me, but Ashley has been so busy lately."

"I see. Is everything alright, though, work isn't stressing her out too much, is it?"

"No, I don't think so. She's in event planning and it's convention season, so I understand. At least she doesn't have to travel since she covers Lenrod-based events for her company. What about you? Any fun plans?"

"I just want to spend my weekend sleeping, though I do have a brunch with my mother on Sunday."

"You don't sound too excited about that."

Mila shook her head. "She's been having weird expectations for me lately. It's kind of personal..."

"C'mon Mila," he urged. "You and I have had some *very* personal conversations. I honestly hate that it feels one-sided with you giving me such useful advice while I have nothing to offer you. And trust me, I know what it's like dealing with parents and expectations."

Mila let out a long breath. She hadn't really had a chance to talk about how much it had been bothering her that her mother was on her back about Eric. She'd complained briefly to her sister Alexis, who didn't seem to care, and she hadn't had a chance to bring it up with her friend Naomi.

"She's been pressuring me to get married to someone I have no interest in being with," Mila admitted. "And I don't get it. I'm still young and marriage isn't something I want to even think about. It's just not something I really aspire to do."

Justin nodded as he listened to Mila. Her predicament sounded familiar considering he was facing the same pressure from his parents about Ashley.

"May I give you some unsolicited advice, Mila?"

Mila leaned in toward him with a narrowed gaze. "Go for it."

"Parents are important, but when it comes down to it, it's *your* life, not theirs. I mean, I'm sure your mom wants what's best for you and that her intentions are pure, but something like who you'll spend the rest of your life with shouldn't be up to her. And it's definitely something you shouldn't rush into because of pressure from other people."

A smile pulled at Mila's lips and she raised a brow. "You gonna follow your own advice, Justin?"

"What do you mean by that?"

"You're a people-pleaser, aren't you? At least, that's the read I've gotten from you and I'm pretty good at reading people."

"Yet another skill of the talented Mila Nelson," he replied playfully. "So... How'd you read me as a people-pleaser?"

"You work dutifully for PMC Group, but there's no passion there. You work hard and you take all the right steps, going through the motions, but there always seems to be something missing. What are you passionate about, Justin?"

The air grew heavy with Mila's question and Justin sat there analyzing her face. He didn't have a good answer for her. He knew she was perceptive, but didn't realize just how well she'd read him. Either way, Justin wasn't sure what to say. He didn't know what he was passionate about because he'd never had the opportunity to explore such things.

There was a lot Justin wanted to try, but he never did because it was considered off track for the life he *thought* he wanted to have. While he did face pressure from his parents to a certain extent, most of the pressure he faced came from himself.

Finally, Justin twisted his mouth before responding. "I don't have a good answer for you, Mila. I'll confess that I can be a bit of a people-pleaser. I mean, PMC Group's work *is* interesting to me, but I'm admittedly not really passionate about it."

"I appreciate your honesty, Justin."

"Hey, Mila... While we're being honest with each other, there's something else I've been wanting to ask you about. Is that alright?"

"Let's hear it."

Justin hesitated. Right after he made the request, he regretted it. He had gotten too caught up in the casual and open nature of their conversation and he was about to take it a step too far. Justin wanted to ask Mila for more advice about his and Ashley's sex life, but he knew it was wrong when he brought it up for the first time months ago. And he feared that asking at this time would ruin the moment they were having.

"Well?" Mila pressed, interrupting Justin's long pause.

"I um... I wanted to ask, uh... So, you're enjoying your time with PMC Group so far, right?"

Mila let out an amused huff and shook her head. "Something tells me that wasn't your original question, but I'll let it go. PMC Group has been good so far and I've gained some useful information by working here. I'm looking forward to learning a lot more as soon as possible."

"That's great to hear, Mila."

Overstepping

Mila sat at the table across from her mother Monica as the older woman went on about Mila's distancing from her. The two had met for brunch, as they did on a quarterly basis. They were waiting on Alexis, who often acted as a buffer between them, to join. It was unusual for Alexis to be late, and Mila wondered if Monica had told her older sister the wrong time on purpose.

"I can't believe you moved and you refuse to share your address with your own mother. Do you really want me out of your life that much?" Monica asked Mila.

"I don't want you out of my life, mother," Mila replied. "But considering you're the reason I have to move in the first place, it only makes sense for me to not give you my new address."

After Eric showed up at her apartment unannounced, Mila started by looking at new security systems before ultimately deciding to move altogether. Something about the energy she was sensing from Eric made her so uneasy that she was losing sleep and Mila figured it'd be best to move across town and not tell her mother her new address.

"You don't think you're overreacting? Eric popped in on you at my request. It's not like he did it randomly."

"Right, but before that, he'd been sending me roses and letters nonstop despite the fact that I was ignoring him and then he went on to show up at my apartment begging for me to go back to him. I wasn't getting a good vibe, I felt unsafe, and you put me in a really tough posi- tion... Even dangerous, I'd say."

Monica rolled her eyes in an exaggerated motion before she sighed and took a sip of her mimosa. "He's harmless, Mila. He is just a man in love who desperately wants you back."

"Mother, Eric and I will never be together again," Mila said sternly "I don't love him and I never did. I'm not sure what's been going on with you, but this obsession with marrying me off needs to stop. Can't you see that's what's been pulling you and I apart?"

"I just want you to be happy," Monica reasoned. "I want you to meet a good man to take care of you. Do you know how nice it is to have a person to go to sleep with and wake up to? And then the joy of having children! Don't you want kids?"

Mila's jaw tensed and she huffed her frustration. "I don't care about getting married and I absolutely *never* want to have kids. If I meet a man *or woman* who I want to be with for the rest of my life, great, but I refuse to give up my solitude for someone who isn't worth it."

Monica was taken aback, astonished by her daughter's words. "What do you mean you don't want kids? And you don't care to get married?"

"Exactly what I said. I don't want kids, ever. And marriage isn't a priority for me, there are so many other things in life."

Monica shook her head with disapproval. "I just don't understand."

"All due respect, mother, it's not for you to understand."

"Mila, you are impossible..."

"Could you two please not argue!" Alexis chided as she walked up to their table. "You know there was a point in our lives when you two got along, right? In fact, for most of our lives, you two were close... What happened?"

"That *is* the question..." Mila said, leaning back in her seat and looking away from her mother.

"Mila just needs to do more thinking about her future," Monica noted softly.

"Whatever."

~

It was late evening on Monday and Mila was in a horrible mood. Not only was she still agitated about her Sunday brunch with her mother and Alexis, Mila was also stressed about moving to another part of the city and the recent slowing of her progress in collecting intel on PMC Group. Despite the fact that the men were trusting her more, Mila still couldn't seem to gather anything strong enough to take them down *and* keep them from pursuing revenge against Thompson Luxe Group.

On top of it all, she was working late... again.

She let out an exacerbated sigh when her phone started ringing and she saw it was Justin. It was already a long day for her and most of the staff had gone home except for Mila, Justin, and Adrian. She still couldn't wrap her head around how often she stayed in the office late as an assistant.

"Yes, Justin?" she answered.

"May you come to my office, please?"

"Okay." As she stood up to go to his office, Mila wondered what work Justin wanted to add to her already full plate.

"Hi Mila, how's it going?" Justin asked casually when she entered his office.

"It's alright. How may I help you?"

Justin's brows tensed when he noticed the lack of energy in her tone and the difference in her demeanor compared to usual. She seemed a bit dejected—something very unusual of her.

"Are you sure you're alright?"

"Could we keep our conversation focused on work?" Mila asked. "I really can't talk about anything else today, and we're already here late. I imagine you want to get out of the office too."

"Oh um... right, of course... I actually called you in here for advice, if you don't mind."

Mila had to hold herself back from snapping. *Did he really just call me in here to ask for fucking advice? It better be business-related...*

"What... is it?" Mila struggled to get the words out in a level tone.

"Well, um... You see... I've been following your advice about communicating with Ashley, but things aren't really changing. There's still not a spark left. Do you have any other pointers on how we could reignite things? To be honest, I've been trying to get her to be more dominant." He rubbed then back of his neck. "Sorry, it's just that you're the only one I can seem to talk about this stuff with."

Mila exhaled deeply at his question, and it wasn't lost on her Justin's reiterating of his desire that Ashley be more dominant—something he'd recently complimented Mila about. And it wasn't his first time making hints that Mila's personality aligned with his interests.

Mila thought she was making progress with Justin, especially given the conversation they'd had Friday after dinner, but she couldn't believe that he *actually* had the nerve to call her into his office after hours to ask for relationship advice.

What made it worse was that Justin and Ashley had a failing relationship. It was clear to everyone that he didn't love Ashley and Mila wasn't sure if Justin even *liked* his girlfriend. Also, he'd often bring up his dissatisfaction with their relationship—whether it be directly or indirectly.

But today was not a day that Mila was capable of showing her usual patience.

"Well then dump her," she said flatly.

Justin looked at Mila in wide-eyed disbelief. "W-what?"

"Dump her, break up with her, whatever. Ashley deserves better than a significant other who's going to complain about their sex life to his secretary." The agitation was clear in Mila's voice. "Just because Ashley isn't into certain things, she shouldn't be shamed for it. If you two are sexually incompatible, then fine. Just stop trying to pretend you care about saving your relationship and end it already."

"I-it's not that easy..."

"What's so hard about it? You obviously don't want to be with her. And like I said, she deserves better."

"What do you mean I 'obviously' don't want to be with her?"

"It's clear as day. You're constantly complaining about her to me and act annoyed whenever she visits or calls... Then again, those have been less frequent recently. And haven't you told me that she's been busy with work yet somehow in a *great* mood despite the stress? Interesting..."

Justin's entire body grew tense with how cold Mila was behaving with him, he'd never experienced that from her before and he felt a tightness in his gut.

"W-what are you getting at?"

"I think you know…" Mila stood from the chair and turned to walk toward the door. "It's late and I still have like ten more things to do for you three before I can leave the office. I don't have time to listen to your problems right now." With those final words to him, Mila left his office.

When she returned to her desk, Mila audibly groaned when she saw a text message from Alexis.

ALEXIS

Hey sis… The company that shall not be named is really gaining on us and you're coming up on a year. It seems like we should've been done by now. We need to get this finished ASAP.

"Whatever," Mila muttered to herself. She stiffened in her seat when she heard Justin's door open and his footsteps approaching her.

Although she saw him standing next to her from her peripherals, Mila didn't bother looking up at him.

"Um…" Justin cleared his throat. "Mila?"

She didn't respond and instead started typing something on her computer.

"Mila," he repeated, this time with a more solid tone, but it didn't make a difference. "I just wanted to say…" Justin took a deep breath. "I'm sorry for overstepping like that. Our conversations have just been… It feels like you and I are… Ya know, like friends—" he choked on his words and felt a lump grow in his throat when Mila was still unresponsive to his apology. "I'm sorry, Mila…" He said softly and hurried out before seeing if she would respond or not.

Mila sighed and finally lifted her gaze from the computer screen to watch Justin walk away. "You need to figure yourself out, Justin," she whispered too low for him to hear.

Mila had never faced so much stress in her life. Her mother was relentlessly pressuring her to get married, Mila was reminded by Alexis' text that her plans for PMC Group were taking longer than anticipated, and Mila didn't want to admit that it had something to do with the soft spot she'd been developing for Adrian. On top of it all, she was in the process of moving because of Eric's stalker-like behavior and there was a constant underlying uneasiness that she'd been feeling since he first started sending her flowers.

Mila looked at her unfinished to-do list and let out an agitated huff. "Fuck this."

She pulled out her phone and opened her text conversation with Logan.

You free?

❦

"I hate Mondays," Adrian groaned, dragging his hands down his face. He looked at the company instant messenger to see if Justin was still in and felt even worse when he realized that it was just himself and Mila left online. Whether it was Caleb trying to make her life more difficult or simply a busy period, Mila would work late at least once a week and Adrian felt guilty for how much they would put on her.

"I'll go see if I can at least buy her dinner to make up for it," he said to himself.

Adrian walked out of his office and toward Mila's desk from behind. As he got closer, he saw that she had her messages up on her tablet along with Logan's name. He assumed the two of them had been texting a lot based on the thread on her screen and Adrian was immediately hit with jealousy.

"Hey, Mila?" he called.

"Yes?" she replied without looking up from her conversation with Logan.

"May you please come to my office?"

After a long pause, she turned to look at him, expressionless. "Sure."

Once Mila got into his office, Adrian leaned against his desk and she stood in front of him several feet away.

His brows tensed, the concern clear in his face. "Is everything okay? You've seemed kind of down all day."

"Yeah, I'm fine, just really stressed. I'm also not a fan of working late all the time." Mila shrugged. "Is that all?" She'd recently been rushing their private interactions, hoping less time with Adrian would help her get over whatever softness she felt toward him.

"No, there's something else..."

"Yes?"

Adrian's jaw tensed and his gaze was intent on Mila. "Have you been with Logan?"

"None of your business, Mr. Collins," she answered coldly.

"Adrian," he corrected. "I said you can call me Adrian... If you *have* been seeing him, that is *very* unprofessional."

"As unprofessional as when you kissed me right here in this office just a few weeks ago?"

"And I apologized for that because it *was* unprofessional. Mila, you should know better than to have sexual relations with any of our business associates."

Mila's eyes narrowed at him and she walked over to Adrian so that their faces were mere inches apart. She was just about to scold him for trying to scold *her* when she had another idea.

"Are you jealous that someone else is pleasuring me, Adrian?"

Adrian's head jerked back. "N-no," he choked out, shaking his head anxiously.

"Okay," Mila replied nonchalantly before turning to go for the door. While she was still within arm's reach, Adrian stretched out to grab her wrist.

"Wait... What if I said that I am?"

Mila turned back to him and tilted her head to the side while raising her perfectly arched brow. "What if you said you're what?"

"What if I said that I *am* jealous that someone else is giving you pleasure?"

"But you haven't." Mila snatched her hand away. "I don't do what-ifs."

Adrian knew that Mila wouldn't hang around waiting for him, so he finally blurted it out.

"I can pleasure you better than he can!" Adrian confessed.

Mila's expression mostly went unchanged from its aloof state. "Hm?"

"Let me prove it... please."

Mila crossed her arms and analyzed his face before her eyes scanned over the room and landed on the couch. She was a woman who knew what she wanted and she'd been wanting Adrian for some time. Despite deluding herself into thinking she could resist her desire for him, all it took was Adrian finally being direct about wanting her for Mila to give in.

"Couch. Shirt off. On your knees," Mila instructed and Adrian didn't need to hear any more than that as he began unbuttoning his shirt and walking over to the couch before getting on his knees. He didn't notice until he was already in place that Mila hadn't followed him. He looked over at her still standing by the desk and just when he was about to ask if she was coming, Mila put her finger to her lips to shush him.

Adrian watched her take her time walking over to the door of the office to lock it before she turned and approached the couch to sit on it in front of him. Mila held his chin and lifted his head so he could look at her.

"How would you like to pleasure me?" she questioned softly while tracing his bottom lip with her thumb.

"However you please."

Mila smiled, impressed that he was so ready, so eager for her. Between that and the mix of desire and desperation in Adrian's face as Mila held it and looked down at him, heat was rushing to her core.

"Let's start with this..." Mila's lips lightly brushed his before Adrian closed the distance. Both of them got lost in the kiss, savoring the other's lips until Mila finally parted hers and allowed their tongues to meet. Neither of them knew how much time passed, but when Mila finally pulled away, it was too soon for Adrian and he let out almost a wince.

Their eyes connected and taking in her lustful gaze, Adrian knew that he was completely at her mercy. Mila was the first to break contact, looking down at his lips and admiring their fullness. They were his favorite feature of hers after his soft brown eyes.

Adrian gulped his nerves before they could overwhelm him. "May I please eat your pussy... Ms. Mila?"

Mila enjoyed being a tease, but she allowed her curiosity to take the lead tonight and she needed something to relieve her stress, anyway. She leaned in and nibbled at his ear before whispering, "Let's see what you can do without me walking you through it... Prove you can pleasure me better than he can."

Adrian knew that meant Mila would allow him to eat her out uninterrupted and he planned to show her how badly he'd been wanting to do just that.

As eager as he was, he also wanted to take his time. Pulling off her tights first, Adrian then kissed Mila up and down the insides of her legs, savoring every bit he put his mouth on. Mila's stress gradually escaped her as Adrian's kisses went on and a sharp breath crossed her nose when she felt his hand against her pussy through her panties.

Adrian pants grew even more strained at the sensation of her becoming increasingly wet as he continued rubbing her and placing kisses along her inner thighs.

Finally, he was ready to taste what he'd been craving for so long. Adrian leaned back and pushed Mila's legs together so he could pull her panties off. The moment he parted them again and saw her pussy for the first time, he audibly groaned and spread her lips apart.

"You're so beautiful," he muttered before his tongue was moving up and down her inner lips and he eased a single finger inside of her.

As soon as Mila released a light moan, Adrian's mouth grew more eager. He added another finger and flicked his tongue against her clit. Using his free hand, he unbuttoned his pants and used his pre-cum to slowly stroke himself.

Mila tangled her fingers in his hair as he ate her out and when she pulled at it, Adrian began pumping his fingers faster. He gave her clit the attention it deserved, going between using his tongue and his lips.

"Ssshhhhit," Mila breathed, trying to keep her sounds at bay as she felt herself approaching her release.

However, the way Adrian's skillful tongue worked in sync with his fingers, Mila was forced to cover her mouth when she hit her orgasm and he moaned into her as he took every bit she had to give.

Coming down from her high, Mila looked into Adrian's eyes while he slowly moved his tongue up and down her lips before finally pulling away. She wasn't going to admit it to him, but it was already clear to Mila that Adrian could pleasure her better than Logan.

Mila swallowed and just before she was about to say something, another bold request crossed Adrian's lips.

"Please... May you sit on my face?"

Mila was surprised at his ongoing directness, but she had no objections. The two of them repositioned so that Adrian was flat on his back laying on the couch while Mila straddled his head and faced his torso.

She didn't realize it while he was eating her out before, but he'd been freed from his pants and he was stroking himself with a steady pace. His lips met her lower ones again and he lightly sucked her clit.

"Look at that," Mila started as she looked down at his curved dick in his hand. "You're this hard just from eating my pussy?"

Adrian's answer was muffled against her pussy. He refused to pull away enough to give an intelligible response.

Mila leaned forward and spit on his dick and Adrian let out a groan of pleasure at the sensation.

"Faster darling..." Mila started moving her hips in slow circles to ride his face and Adrian sped up his strokes just as he was told.

"You've been wanting this for some time, haven't you?" Mila continued. "You're moaning more than I am."

"Yesmsmila..." His response was again muffled, but Mila knew exactly what he was saying.

"Good boy... You know exactly how to address me." Mila teased him, tracing her acrylic nails along his pelvis and then lower toward his dick, but being sure to avoid touching him. "Do you want me to touch you, darling?"

"Mhmm," he hummed into her pussy.

"You'll need to earn it." Mila got up off of Adrian's face, which immediately tightened to a frustrated expression at the interruption. She turned around and straddled his face again so that she could look down into his eyes momentarily before she returned to riding his face. "Stick your tongue out."

Adrian did as he was told and Mila held his hair with a tight grip as she moved her hips back and forth, pleasuring herself with his tongue. The vibrations of his moans only pushed her closer to her release.

"So... fucking... good," she moaned. Mila noticed how Adrian's lips began to keep closing instinctively and slowed her hips. "Go ahead... Eat my pussy."

Adrian's mouth returned to working diligently at Mila's pussy. She leaned back and spit on her hand before reaching to massage his balls while he stroked himself. She had a loud outburst when Adrian started focusing on her clit and she knew she'd soon come again.

"Fuck," Mila hissed and her entire body shook at her climax. She felt something warm hitting her wrist and hand and turned to see that Adrian was coming at the same time.

She lifted herself off of him and looked down to see Adrian with an expression just as satisfied as hers.

"Thank you, Ms. Mila."

Long Time Coming

Justin found himself standing in front of Ashley's door late on a Monday night with Mila's words consuming his thoughts. He'd already called her before to tell her he was on the way and he even mustered the courage to knock when he arrived. But as he waited on her to answer, the nerves were getting to him.

He knew Mila was right. Ashley deserved better than the way Justin treated her. I didn't really like her—he'd been hanging on to their relationship because it made sense. He wasn't in love with her and despite their compatibility on paper, the reality was that they weren't compatible. Their different styles of communication and processing emotions didn't work well together.

Justin was considering turning around just when Ashley answered the door.

"What's going on?" she questioned.

On Ashley's part, she knew what was about to happen the moment she saw Justin. But, she couldn't bring herself to care much. There was a point in their relationship—in the first year when it felt like there was still some level of excitement between them—that Ashley would've dreaded this moment. But with Justin, who was normally overly formal, for once looking more raw that she had ever seen him, Ashley felt a level of comfort. So, she urged him on.

"Justin," Ashley called out to him after he took too long to answer the first time. "What's going on?"

"R-right," Justin croaked. "Well, I'm here because I really wanted to talk to you... Could we sit down?"

"Sure." Ashley shrugged and led him into the living room where they sat on the two opposite ends of the couch. "You ready to talk now?"

"Y-yeah..." Justin paused again before blowing out a quick huff and trying to hold on to the bit of courage he'd mustered earlier when he asked Ashley if he could come over. "I wanted to talk about *us*. I know we just got back together, but it feels like... Maybe it was..."

Ashley grimaced. She had hoped that he would get straight to it. She hoped that raw emotion in his face mean he was ready to be bold for once.

"Go ahead, Justin. Get it out."

"I think... Maybe getting back together was..." Justin took a deep breath before finally getting it out. "I think we should break up."

"You're the one who was at my door a few weeks ago begging for us to get back together," Ashley reminded him. Despite her words, her voice was monotoned and what she was saying felt more like a rehearsed reaction, rather than genuine.

"You're right, but now I'm not so sure..."

"Of course you're not sure. When are you ever sure about anything outside of business?"

"I'm sorry, I—"

"There's no need to pretend you're sorry. It's fine... Could you just, like... leave?"

Justin slowly rose from the chair. While he could admit to himself that at times, he missed emotional signals, it wasn't lost on him that Ashley didn't seem to have any emotion at all when reacting to him dumping her after they had *just* gotten back together.

"I really am sorry," he repeated. "Do you want to talk about it? Like, more?"

"Get out," replied an exacerbated Ashley without looking at him.

Justin quickly left her apartment and as soon as the door closed behind him, guilt began to flood in as he thought about how his parents might react. He didn't want to disappoint them, but he also knew it was wrong to continue his relationship with Ashley. Although Mila's words were harsh and stung him, everything she said to Justin about his relationship with Ashley was correct.

I am an adult, he thought to himself. *I'll tell them when I'm ready.*

A Visit

It was Friday and Adrian and Justin were sitting in Adrian's office as Caleb arrived late for their leadership meeting.

"Believe it or not, I would've been on time for once if Shannon didn't fuck up my schedule," Caleb complained as he entered Adrian's office. "When is the assistant coming back? She's been out since Monday. Did her fat ass get stuck in bed or something?"

"Don't talk about her like that!" Adrian and Justin said in unison and the two of them immediately made eye contact with each other. Adrian gave Justin a sharp glare, but didn't say anything.

"Damn, what's got the two of you so on edge? Adrian, I expect to hear that from since he's so far up Mila's ass, but this is a first for you Justin... Still in a bad mood because you broke up with Ashley? You should be proud of yourself!"

"No," Justin snapped. "I'm just tired of you disrespecting Mila. She's obviously *very* valuable to the three of us and this company considering it feels like so many things have gone to shit just with her being out for a few days. My schedule is a mess and I'm stuck doing these calls and meetings with Japanese executives alone."

Adrian remained silent, simply bouncing his knee while his eyes were still cut at Justin. He'd been on edge since Tuesday when Mila first called out sick. He'd eaten her out in his office the Monday night before that and when she didn't come to work the next day—which was very rare for her—he began to panic, wondering if it was because of him. Adrian had enough sense to text Mila and she assured him that she truly wasn't feeling well and needed to take some time off.

"I can admit that she's not a total fuck up," Caleb said. "But it's Friday and she only came into the office on Monday. Hard to believe she's been sick this whole time. She's probably lying about it and off on vacation or some shit. I've been looking at some resumes and I have some pretty good candidates to replace her. I'll send—"

"You're not getting rid of Mila," Justin interrupted, his voice cold. "If you *really* wanted her gone, you would've done it by now. Plus, I won't let you fire her. Like I said, Mila is a true asset to this company. Actually, I've been meaning to bring this up with the two of you, but we should offer her full-time work once her one-year contract is up in a couple of months."

"Well, we have time to think about that." Adrian finally spoke up. He wanted to get off the topic of Mila out of concern that Justin and Caleb would pick up on his uneasiness while they were talking about her. What he did Monday night was extremely uncharacteristic of him, but he also had no regrets. However, he now wondered what that meant for his and Mila's interactions moving forward and he'd been resisting the urge all week to show up at her apartment.

"Adrian's right," Caleb agreed. "Besides, I already told you that I have some other resumes we could look at. I don't think we should keep her as a permanent employee and I refuse to make it easy."

Justin scoffed. "I'm calling bullshit on Caleb, but like you said, Adrian, we have time to think about it. For now, let's focus on business."

"This show is fucking wild," Mila muttered to herself. She was on her couch in front of the television watching Octopus Games, and she'd been binging it all day. After a few weeks of mounting stress and the long Monday she had, Mila decided to call in sick Tuesday. It started off as simply a mental health day, but turned into mental health *days*.

Right when she was starting a new episode, Mila's phone chimed. The app for her building was notifying her that a visitor rang her apartment. Mila opened the notification and she was surprised to see Justin on the screen.

"What is it, Mr. Matsuda?"

"Hey, Mila. I just wanted to check on you... with you being sick and all." He gave an innocent smile to the camera and held up a plastic bag that appeared to have a container of soup inside.

"Okay, you can come up."

She pulled off her blanket to look down at what she was wearing, which were a pair of panties and an oversized tee-shirt.

"I guess I should be decent enough to put on some shorts..."

After doing that, she went to the door and opened it to see Justin waiting outside.

"Hey, I bought you some soup from the store..." Justin was distracted when he entered Mila's apartment and saw how nice it was. He was already surprised she was in a luxury building in a trendy neighborhood in Lenrod, but walking in and seeing that it was a large apartment that appeared to have more than one room and a decent view of the city surprised him.

"This is a really nice place, Mila." He continued to scan the apartment with its large windows that allowed natural sunlight, fully-equipped kitchen, and living room where Mila had the television mounted on the wall. "Do you have a roommate or something?"

"No," she replied curtly. She didn't want to give up her lifestyle and she figured giving a fake address would be more trouble than it was worth in case someone from PMC Group would decide to drop in unexpectedly as Justin was doing. Mila was good at making up excuses and she already had one for as to why she lived in an obviously expensive apartment despite the poor pay she received.

"But how can you um..." Justin trailed off as he seemed to struggle to find the words.

"Afford this place despite the shit pay you guys give me?" Mila finished. "I have a *very* generous older friend." The suggestiveness was clear in her voice and as she intended, Justin assumed she was hinting at having a sugar daddy, which led to more questions that he refrained from asking.

"Oh, great! That's cool... I guess?" He walked over to her kitchen and placed the plastic bag on the counter. "This is the soup they serve at that lunch spot by the office that Caleb always goes to. It's really good."

"Thanks, that was nice of you."

"How are you doing? You've been out for several days, so I wanted to check on you in person to make sure things are okay."

"I'm fine and I'll be back next week. I just needed some time to rest."

"Oh, okay. That's great to hear."

The room went silent and Mila's face grew tense as Justin lingered. Now that it was obvious she was fine, she was hoping he'd leave.

"Well, thanks again for the soup." She started walking toward the door to open it so he'd take the hint. "Have a good weekend and I'll see you—"

"I broke up with Ashley!" he blurted, cutting her off. He walked over to her living room and fell into the couch.

Mila let go of the door and went to join him. "Okay... Is that the real reason you came here? To tell me that?"

Her question seemingly caught Justin off guard. "Oh, um... I don't know. I guess I wanted to let you know that I took your advice. You were right that it was wrong of me to talk about her in that way. She deserves better than a man who's just using her to satisfy his parents."

"Cool, so you came here 'worried' about me, but of course end up talking about yourself. I read you as a people-pleaser before, but maybe you're just self-centered," Mila spat.

Justin shot to his feet. "No, I didn't mean it like that, I just..."

"You just what? Thought you'd come here and tell me you dumped your girlfriend so now I can fuck you the way that you want?" questioned an agitated Mila. "That's so shitty..." she approached Justin, who was still on his feet, to look him dead in the eyes and show him her displeasure.

"I-it's not like that..." he murmured.

"It's not? Then explain to me why you felt the need to tell me that you and your girlfriend weren't aligning sexually, hint at the idea that maybe you and I would be a good sexual match, proceed to break up with her, and then come alone to my apartment to tell me about it?"

Justin struggled to find the words for Mila. "W-well I- I mean, I didn't realize that it came off like..."

"That it came off like what?" Mila challenged, moving in closer to him. "Like you've made it *abundantly* clear that you want a rough fuck? That you want a woman who will get on top and ride you with her hand wrapped around your neck while you come undone? One who will remind you who's *really* in charge each time you even *think* about trying her? One who will take you all the way to the edge and *just* when you think you can meet your release, she'll tell you to *fucking* hold it?"

Justin gulped at her words, completely entranced by the woman in front of him. She was obviously pissed off, but the darkness in her eyes combined with her words both intimidated him and turned him on.

Suddenly, Mila pressed her hands against his torso and pushed him back on the chair. Before Justin knew it, she was straddling him and holding his face with hers dangerously close. When he tried to lean in to close the distance, wanting to feel her lips for the first time, Mila stopped him

"Is this what you wanted?" she said softly as her gaze darted between Justin's eyes and lips.

"Yes," Justin replied and Mila's lips were immediately against his.

With the way she held his face and how every movement of her mouth felt intentional, Mila was in full control of the kiss. She teased him, closing her lips each time they parted and denying his tongue. When Justin ran his hands up her thighs to hold her hips, Mila broke the kiss and his eyes fluttered open to meet her disapproving gaze.

"Put your hands at your *fucking* sides." While her voice was almost a whisper, her tone was stern and it sent chills up Justin's spine as he removed his hands from her and did as he was told.

When Mila returned to the kiss, she finally allowed their tongues to meet. As she felt Justin growing hard under her, Mila began moving her hips to grind against him and Justin let out a light groan of pleasure.

As she continued, Justin's moans became more persistent and his pants strained. He dug his fingers into the couch, doing his best to keep his hands off of her.

When Mila broke this kiss only to move down to his neck while she ground harder against him, Justin's swallowed hard, trying to keep himself in check.

Mila's hand slid from his chest down to his erection and then moved back up. "I was right... You wanted me to take control," she muttered between placing kisses and lightly sucking Justin's neck. "And you want more, don't you?"

"Yes," Justin breathed.

As her lips continued to scour Justin's neck, Mila's hands wandered his body until she reached under his shirt and her acrylic nails caressed his bare skin.

Right when Justin was about to lose control and put his hands on her again, Mila abruptly pulled herself away and stood up to look down at him expressionless.

"You can leave now," she said flatly.

"Wh-what?" Justin looked up at her in disbelief. "Bu-but I thought you were- You just- I'm um..." his eyes went down to the tent in his pants.

"Right..." Mila shrugged. "Cold showers are decent enough at taking care of that for you. Like I said, you can leave now... And don't make me repeat myself."

A flustered Justin heeded her words, grabbed his jacket, and went for the door.

"See you Monday," she cooed right before he left.

After kicking Justin out, Mila plopped back onto the couch to continue the show she'd been watching. However, by the time she finished the episode she'd started before Justin showed up, Mila was again interrupted.

"I swear if its Justin again, I'm- oh..." When she opened the app and saw on the video who was visiting her, she was surprised for the second time that evening. Pressing the intercom button, she spoke to her unexpected guest.

"I'm not home, Mr. Peterson."

Tea Time

Mila snickered, looking at Caleb on the screen with a frown on his face and his hands stuffed in his pockets. He leaned in toward the intercom and whispered sharply. "Don't lie to me. I know you're in there. Now, let me up."

"But Mr. Peterson, I can answer you from anywhere using this app. And I'm away at the moment." It was clear in her very performative tone that Mila was playing games with him.

"You expect me to believe that fake ass voice? Let me up there now."

Mila didn't respond and simply looked at him through the camera.

"Did you hear me?" Caleb said impatiently. "Let me up there."

"Even if I *were* home, Mr. Peterson, why would I let you into my apartment?"

"Because I'm your boss and I have something important to discuss with you."

"That can't be done over text or email? I prefer written correspondence if it's something work-related."

Mila could tell that he was getting increasingly frustrated as he couldn't seem to stand still while waiting at the door and she was only further entertained.

"Mila, just let me—"

"The fuck are you doing here?" a familiar voice interrupted Caleb. Mila watched through the camera as she saw Adrian approaching.

Caleb straightened up and turned to him.

"I'm here to tell the assistant that she needs to bring her ass in for work or else we're firing her."

"Why is that you *always* chose to be a douche bag?" Adrian questioned. "Nine out of ten options will be ones of decent people and you always select the path of the jerk."

Caleb didn't show it, but he was offended by Adrian's suggestion that he wasn't a decent person. "Whatever, I'm not being an asshole. The asshole move would be to fire her without notice... And besides, the fuck are *you* doing here? Is that food? Trust me, I don't think eating will do her any good."

"Shut the fuck up," Adrian snapped. "She's sick and I brought her some soup."

As the men went back and forth, Mila studied their body language. She'd only really seen the two in work interactions, but with them being in an informal setting and having a heated discussion, she noticed things she hadn't seen before. Caleb's shoulders seemed somewhat hunched, while Adrian's chest was more pronounced as if asserting himself. She saw the way Caleb for once seemed to falter in his often arrogant stance and now she was intrigued.

"Hello, Adrian," she said, interrupting their exchange. She couldn't see it through the camera, but Caleb's nostrils flared when he heard how she was immediately so friendly with Adrian.

"Hi, Mila. I'm sorry that you had to hear all this. I came to check on you. Are you home?"

"Yes, you can come up."

"What the fuck?" Caleb blurted. "You kept saying you weren't home."

Mila ignored Caleb and clicked the button to open the door downstairs. She had on an oversized shirt and athletic shorts that she'd put on when Justin came over before, but she went to her room to quickly change into shorter shorts and remove her panties. The tee-shirt she switched into was still oversized, but not long enough to cover her shorts.

This is about to be very interesting, she thought to herself.

When she heard the knock at her door, she took her time walking over and opening it. The last time she'd seen Adrian was when he'd eaten her out that Monday. She greeted him with a small smile.

Adrian swallowed when he saw Mila answer the door in her dangerously short shorts and shirt. If Caleb weren't standing behind him, he'd give Mila a very different greeting than he currently was.

"H-hi, Mila... I brought you some soup." He held up a large blue thermos and handed it too her.

Mila gawked. "Is this home-made?"

Adrian nodded happily. "It's my mom's chicken soup recipe."

"Wow, way better than the the store-bought stuff Justin dropped off earlier."

Immediately Adrian's body went stiff and he ground his teeth together. "Justin what?"

"Oh, yeah... He stopped by not too long ago and dropped off some soup."

"Why the hell did he—"

"I know for a fact that we give you shit pay, so how can you afford a place like this?" Caleb interrupted, pushing past Adrian to enter Mila's apartment. She cut her eyes as she watched him enter the space and look around with a pensive expression.

"Go back to the doorway and take your shoes off," she said calmly.

"What?"

Again, Mila maintained a calm tone. "I don't like to repeat myself, Mr. Peterson. This is my home, and *I'm* the only boss here. So, if you want to stay, go the door and take your fucking shoes off. Otherwise, get out and don't come back."

Adrian couldn't help the smile that teased at his lips at the exchange, and it grew into a full-on grin when a pouting Caleb grumbled something under his breath as he walked over to the doorway and took his shoes off. Adrian then did the same and the two of them followed Mila to the living room.

She could feel that both men were staring at her behind, and so she took her time walking them over. Caleb was having flashbacks to the video he'd recorded of her at the gym while Adrian was thinking about that Monday night.

"Are you feeling better, Mila?" Adrian asked. She sat on the couch, one cushion over from him while Caleb sat on an accent chair across from the pair.

"Yeah, I already told Justin I'd be back on Monday."

Every time Mila brought up Justin, it irked Adrian. The two of them seemed to be growing close and he was beginning to question the nature of their relationship. At first, it just seemed like the average Justin move of only getting friendly with someone who could benefit him from a business perspective. But between the way they'd laugh while speaking to each other in Japanese, the time they spent together alone, and learning that Justin also showed up to Mila's apartment to give her soup, Adrian wondered if there might be more there.

"So um... What did you do while he was here?"

"What do you mean?"

"I just mean was he here for a while. Did you guys chat? Did he catch you up on everything that happened in the office this week?"

"He wasn't here long," Mila replied plainly before changing the subject. "I meant to ask, did you want anything to drink, Adrian? I have water, tea, juice."

"You have two guests here," Caleb commented and Mila didn't react.

Adrian wasn't thirsty, but he wanted to stay at her apartment a bit longer and hoped that Caleb would soon grow frustrated enough to leave the two of them alone.

"Yeah, do you have lemon ginger tea?"

"I do, actually... And I could go for some of that too. I'll make both of us cups."

Caleb let out a long breath as he watched the way Mila continued to only acknowledge Adrian. And just as he did when he took his shoes off at the door, he again surrendered. "Could I have a cup too... please?"

Mila turned to look at him and while he hadn't earned a smile from her, her expression *did* tell him that she approved of his approach.

"Sure, I'll make you one too."

A frustrated Adrian gave Caleb a sharp glance before his gaze returned to Mila. Both men were almost in a trance as they watched her. Mila started by reaching up into the cabinet to take out three teacups and the tea itself before looking for her teapot, which sat in a lower cabinet beside her stove.

Caleb readjusted himself and Adrian nearly choked when Mila bent at her hips to reach down into the cabinet for the teapot. Based on the way her shorts hugged her and rode up, both men determined that she wasn't wearing any panties. When she stood up straight again to turn on the stovetop, Adrian finally tore his gaze away from her to look at Caleb whose eyes were still on her ass with an intense stare.

The expression on Caleb's face was one that Adrian knew well and as his eyes went lower, he saw that Caleb was holding himself over his pants. Meanwhile, Caleb didn't even notice that Adrian was looking at him as he focused on Mila. It wasn't just her appearance that had him in a trance at that moment, though, it was Mila's entire demeanor. The way she scolded him when he first entered the apartment and put him in his place; the way no matter what she wore, even now when she was in simply a tee-shirt and shorts, she always carried herself with an over-whelming confidence; and the way he could tell by her energy that she *knew* she was in control of the current situation.

Despite the memories that flowed into his mind, Adrian managed to keep himself from growing hard to the point that it was noticeable, though Caleb couldn't do the same thing.

When Caleb saw Mila walking back over to the living the room while the water heated up, he crossed his legs and rested his hands in his lap.

"The water should be hot enough soon for the tea."

"Thank you, Ms. Mi—" Adrian caught himself before it came out. "Thank you, Mila... This is a really nice a apartment you've got, and in this neighborhood, at that. How'd you come across such a great find?"

Mila shrugged. "Internet."

"But how can you afford it?" Caleb questioned. "There's no way you're living here on what we pay you."

"Oh, that?" Mila went on to give him the same response she gave to Justin. "I have a *very* generous older friend."

Adrian's brows tensed and Caleb let out an entertain huff.

"What?" He snorted. "You trying to say you have a sugar daddy? Highly doubt a man is taking care of *you* like that."

"You might be surprised to learn that some men are capable of more than simply sitting on their knees and counting to thirty."

As soon as Mila made the comment, the teapot let out a high-pitched noise to signal it was hot and she got up to finish making their tea.

Adrian looked at Mila and then back to Caleb. "What was that about?"

"I don't know." Caleb crossed his arms and glared over to her. "Just a weird ass comment from a weirdo."

Mila returned with a tray holding their teas and both Caleb and Adrian froze at what she did next.

Standing directly in front of Adrian, Mila bent forward at her hips to place the tray on the table and take the cups off it. Frustration immediately hit Adrian, knowing he couldn't do anything because Caleb was there, and Caleb narrowed his eyes from across the room at the two of them, catching on to exactly what Mila was doing.

Mila was only in that position for a second or two, but Adrian took in every bit of the moment that he could, focusing on the outline of her pussy in her shorts with the way she was bent in front of him. And as a result, the erection he'd been holding back was now visible against his dark blue slacks.

"Um, Mila..." He choked out. "W-where's your bathroom?"

She pointed over at the single hallway in the apartment. "Down the hall and to the left."

"Th-thanks..." Adrian stood, slightly hunched over, and quickly scurried to the bathroom.

Once he figured Adrian was no longer in earshot, Caleb turned is attention to Mila. "What? You trying to make me jealous or something? Don't think I didn't notice what you just did..."

Mila scooted over to the last seat in the couch so that she was closer to Caleb. She rested her chin on her knuckle as her elbow sat on the arm of the chair and gave him the snide look she always did when she teased him.

"Make you jealous of *him*... or of *me*?"

Caleb's eyes immediately went wide at Mila's comment and he started coughing when he choked on his own saliva.

There's no way she knows about me and Adrian, he thought to himself. He didn't realize it, but when he tried to regain his composure, he'd uncrossed his legs and his hands had moved out of the way to reveal his erection. When he went to cross his legs again, Mila placed her bare foot on his knee to stop him.

"It's too late, pet. No need to hide it now."

Damnit, that fucking word again... Caleb analyzed Mila's face as her eyes drifted down his body and landed on the tent in his pants.

"How long have you had this?" she questioned as her foot inched it's way up his leg. "Was it before or after you got here?"

All he could do was gulp and sit completely still, unsure what Mila was about to do, but prepared to receive whatever she was willing to give. Caleb let out a sharp breath when her foot made contact with his erection.

"You're so pathetic, you know that?" she said softly as she slowly moved her toes against him. "You come into *my* apartment and attempt to disrespect me, only for you to be sitting in front of me hard *again* for a body you pretend isn't desirable..."

"I-it's not like th—" Caleb winced with pain when Mila pressed her foot harder against him.

"Shut up," she said, her tone cold, before she started massaging again. "Any bets on what Adrian's doing in the bathroom? I'm sure we both know..." Mila then slightly increased the pressure of her foot, just enough for Caleb to grunt with pleasure. "It's probably the same thing you did when I left you the office alone that night," she continued. "Or after you left the gym the day that you were stalking me like the fucking weirdo that you are."

Caleb gasped at her last comment, but couldn't bring his body to do anything other than respond to the movements of her foot. He found himself pushing forward toward the edge of the seat to present more of himself to her.

"I bet you thought you got away with that one, didn't you?" Mila continued. "You see, Dave, the guy who caught you, and I are really, *really* good friends and he told me about some blond-haired, blue-eyed all-American looking punk bitch who was recording me on his cell phone... You've been jacking off to that video, haven't you?"

When Caleb took too long to respond, Mila's foot stopped.

"I asked you a question, pet."

"Y-yes," Caleb nodded urgently, hoping it would bring him some relief, but Mila continued to withhold it.

"Tell me."

"I'vebeenjackingofftothevideoofyouatthegym," he said breathlessly and let out a light moan when Mila started moving her foot again.

"Fucking pervert," she teased. Caleb began moving his hips, practically humping Mila's foot.

"Fuck," he breathed out and in that moment, Mila abruptly pulled her foot away. Before he could protest, she already started calling Adrian.

"Hey, Adrian!" Mila shouted toward the hallway. "Everything okay in there? You've been gone for a while."

There was a long pause before he finally replied with a shaky voice. "Y-yeah... I'm um... I'm... I'm fine. I'll be r-right out."

The sound of the sink running followed soon after.

Caleb's face was a subtle red. "Keep that shit up and—"

"You'll need to beg harder than that," Mila interrupted before scooting back over to her spot on the couch further away from him, picking up her tea, leaning back, and taking a sip.

When Adrian came out of the bathroom, the tent in his pants was gone and he looked between Mila and Caleb awkwardly. Caleb had his arms and legs crossed with a deep frown on his face, and he hadn't even touched his tea. Meanwhile, Mila had a completely different posture, appearing relaxed and content.

Now that he'd gotten himself off and it was clear that Caleb wasn't going to allow him and Mila to be alone together for the night, Adrian figured it'd be best to just leave.

"Hey, Mila... I'm going to head out. I didn't mean to take up your time by popping in on you like this, I just wanted to deliver the soup that I made."

"Well, it was very sweet of you to make that soup. I'm sure it'll be delicious."

Mila got up to lead Adrian to the door and without saying a word, Caleb stood to his feet with his hands in his pockets and followed.

Mila and Adrian exchanged their goodbyes while Caleb was awkwardly silent. After she closed the door and the two of them walked over to the elevator, Adrian let out a breath of relief and closed his eyes. Mila already made him nervous, but the way she teased him in front of Caleb, knowing they couldn't do anything about it made it worse.

When Adrian opened his eyes again he saw Caleb giving him an intense glare.

"What is it now, Caleb?" he asked, exacerbation in his tone. "You know, this visit wouldn't have been so awkward if you weren't such an asshole to Mila."

"It's what she deserves."

Adrian let out an entertained huff. "She's *really* gotten to you, hasn't she?"

"The fuck is that supposed to mean?"

"You know exactly what it means. You *hate* to see a woman at Mila's size so sure of herself, don't you? It makes you—"

"Shut up," Caleb interrupted. "Please." He sighed. "Let's just change the subject."

Adrian knew he hit a chord with Caleb and obliged.

"Sure. Do you want to go get drinks?"

The elevator chimed and Caleb turned his back to Adrian to walk out of it.

"I would like that."

Soft Gaze

"Do you always have to be such a dick to Mila?" Adrian questioned as he and Caleb sat at the bar. The two of them were a few beers into their awkward silence and Adrian was finally ready to ask questions he been wanting to pose to Caleb for some time.

"Stop treating her like she's some innocent victim," Caleb replied. "There's no way you're *that* far up her ass that you really think she's some sort of saint."

"Whatever the tension is between the two of you, you're the one who started it, Caleb. Since the first day, you were insulting her. You've always been rude to our assistants, but you're so much worse with Mila."

"Because she deserves it."

Adrian's head jerked back. "What the does that even mean?"

Since Mila started working for them, Caleb put in extra effort to make her job more difficult. Not only was he generally rude to her, he also sabotaged her work and would wait until the end of the day to unload tasks on her that would keep her in the office late. On top of it all, he often made offensive, unnecessary comments about her body, which especially got to Adrian.

"It means she fucking deserves it," Caleb said sharply before taking a swig of his beer. He continued to face forward and looked up at the TV over the bar where a basketball game was on. Meanwhile, Adrian's eyes were on Caleb, taking in his hunched over posture and the way he avoided eye contact. Whenever Mila came up as a topic of conversation, Caleb always seemed to grow defensive.

"Does it have anything to do with that bulge in your pants when we left her apartment?"

Caleb finally tore his eyes from the TV and turned to look at Adrian. He took a deep breath and his nostrils flared as he held his gaze before looking away again and sipping his beer.

"I don't know what you're talking about."

"Is that your final answer?" Adrian challenged.

"Don't fucking talk to me about a goddamn bulge in my pants like you didn't jack off in her bathroom."

Adrian's gaze cut away from Caleb and he took a deep sigh,

"Yeah," Caleb scoffed. "Did you forget that I know exactly what your face looks like after you come? All clear-eyed and shit."

"In the same way that I know what you look like when you've been denied something you want?" Adrian retorted. "So, you wanna tell me what's going on with you and Mila?"

"You first."

Again, a silence ensued between the two of them and they simply sipped their beers as they'd been doing after they first arrived at the bar. Caleb and Adrian had been friends for over a decade, having met when Adrian was a sophomore and Caleb was a freshman in college. They knew each other well and they both suspected that the other had something going on with Mila. And after learning that Justin had stopped by her apartment to drop off soup, they guessed it could be the same for him too.

"Another round," Caleb called to the bartender and he brought more beers over for the two of them.

"Did you sleep with her?" Adrian asked, finally breaking the silence between the two of them.

"No," Caleb huffed. "Pretty sure you'd know if I did... Did you?"

"No."

"The 'not yet' is silent, isn't it? I bet you two would've fucked if I wasn't there. I saw that move she pulled before you went to the bathroom... And it obviously worked."

Adrian shook his head. "No, we wouldn't have."

"Oh? So you're saying I'm wrong about you obviously wanting to fuck her?"

"The hell do you have to be so crude about it for? Whatever, we should just get off of this Mila topic... It feels like we're fighting all the time lately."

"Yeah..." Caleb replied softly.

There was another long pause between the two before Adrian spoke again.

"How are your parents? It's been so long since I've seen them."

"They're alright, I guess. Finally getting divorced," Caleb said with a shrug.

"Oh shit, why didn't you tell me anything?"

"It's not a big deal. They've hated each other since I was a kid and that shit was annoying growing up, especially with me being the only child and all. Maybe now they'll be less miserable."

Adrian's face pulled to a deep frown. "I'm sorry, man."

"Like I said, it's not a big deal," Caleb assured. "Your turn. How are your mom and sister?"

"They're doing pretty well. I was able to find my mom a nice house in a suburb around Raleigh and Jamie is doing her residency at Duke."

"That's awesome, Adrian," Caleb chimed. "I remember becoming a doctor was all Jamie would talk about, even when she was in like high school. It's great to hear that she's achieving her goals."

"Yeah, I'm glad that I'm finally in a position to be able to give them whatever they want... I never even dreamed of making it like this. Money not being an object now?" Adrian shook his head. "I remember the days my mom was barely getting us by."

"I'm sure she's proud of you. Looks like the sixth venture was the charm because PMC Group is killing it. Thanks for not giving up on me and Justin. I know you were about to."

"Of course I was!" Adrian chuckled as he was flooded with memories of the three of them starting their various business pursuits. "Here I am, some poor kid from North Carolina at UPenn on a scholarship trying to start businesses with two rich guys who *definitely* got into the school because mommy and daddy's pockets are so deep. I was afraid that I let that Ivy League mentality get to me and got in over my head."

"Shut up!" Caleb bursted out laughing as well and shook his head. "Justin and I bankrolled most of it... Or our parents did, at least. We just needed your smart ass around because you were always damn good with numbers. Your financial know-how is what really got us to where we are now."

"Oh please... I've had plenty of fuckups with those numbers. Or did you forget when we tried to open up that pizza place off campus and I was off by an entire digit in predicting profits?"

"You mean when you thought we'd make thirty-thousand a month feeding one dollar pizza slices to drunk college kids, but it turned out to be just three-thousand and not even enough to cover our overhead? Nope, I didn't forget, but you made it up with our business idea after that."

"Oh, our first dip into the world of retail when we were selling textbooks after illegally reprinting them? You're right, that one definitely wasn't *my* fuck-up..." Adrian cut his eyes over to Caleb.

"How was I supposed to know that counterfeiting books was a big enough crime to get the attention of the fucking FBI? They only cared because I'm sure some corporate asshole was crying to them about not being able to scam college kids in like three cities out of thousands of dollars... Who knew that cougar I was hooking up with was actually an undercover agent?"

"I told you I didn't trust her."

"Yeah, yeah... At least Justin's family has damn good lawyers and got us out of that mess."

"It was still your fuckup," Adrian teased. "Why'd we decide to make you CEO of PMC Group again?"

"Whatever," Caleb scoffed. "You know I was born for this position."

"Hm, I guess you *do* have what it takes to be a CEO. Let's see... You're stubborn, vulgar, reckless..."

Caleb's head jerked back with offense.

"... a total douche bag, selfish, superficial..." Adrian turned his body so that he was facing Caleb with an assuring, small smile on his face as he leaned in toward him. "... proactive, smart, charismatic... Oh, and let's not forget—confident to a fault."

Shaking his head, Caleb couldn't help the smile growing on his face as he listened to Adrian's last few words. It had been some time since the air between them felt so relaxed and to hear Adrian complimenting him put Caleb in a much better mood.

"You had me in that first half, not gonna lie," Caleb quipped and playfully pushed Adrian's shoulder.

"I mean... None of what I said was a lie." Adrian shrugged. "You've good and bad in you, Caleb. All of us do."

Caleb chuckled and shook his head before finishing his beer.

"What?" Adrian asked.

"Nothing... It's just that this is the first time in a while that it doesn't feel like you hate me. Even when we go to lunch together, it feels like you specifically focus on business the whole time, like it's a meeting."

"I don't hate you, Caleb. It's just that you've been..."

"An asshole lately. I know," Caleb finished. He let out a long sigh and turned to meet Adrian's eyes. "I really have missed these time with you, Adrian."

The men had lost count of how many pauses happened between them that night, but this was the first one that didn't feel negative. They held each other's gazes as memories they shared began to come to both of them.

Adrian gulped and he was the first to break eye contact. Raising his hand, he signaled the bartender.

"Close my tab."

Caleb tilted his head to the side curiously, analyzing Adrian who reached over and placed a hand just above his knee.

"You're not far from here, right?"

∼

As soon as they crossed the door into Caleb's apartment, Adrian pressed him against the wall. He very gently wrapped his hand around Caleb's neck and started by teasing him, only allowing their lips to meet for brief moments. The teasing continued until Caleb grew more eager, pressing his lips harder against Adrian's and trying for their tongues to meet.

Finally, Adrian's hand moved behind Caleb's head and tangled in his hair before he brought him in for a deep kiss. Immediately, their tongues started to tangle and they breathed heavily against each other. When Adrian broke their mouths apart to focus on licking and sucking Caleb's neck, Caleb ran his finger's through Adrian's wavy brown hair as he savored the moment.

Moving through Caleb's apartment as they took off each other's clothes, they were down to nothing by the time they got to his room and they fell on the bed together with Adrian on top.

Caleb moaned against his lips when he felt Adrian's hand wrapped around his dick and Caleb did the same to him. They stroked each other, moaning against one another as their tongues danced. Caleb then pushed Adrian back, who hovered over him. As Caleb looked up at him, taking in the man's soft brown eyes, the barely noticeable freckles that spread across his nose and cheeks, a warm sensation in Caleb's chest reminded him of how deeply he felt for Adrian.

"I missed you," Caleb whispered.

Adrian stared down at Caleb, the vulnerability clear in his eyes, Adrian held his face. It was times like this he was reminded of why he liked Caleb in the first place. While Caleb could be brash and offensive, he also had a softness inside of him that resonated with Adrian in the rare times he exposed it. The two of them had more in common than they cared to admit.

"I missed you too," Adrian said softly, rubbing Caleb's cheek with his thumb. He pecked his lips one last time before sitting back up. "Now, on your knees."

Caleb did as he was told and sat on the floor in front of Adrian, looking up at him expectantly as he repositioned himself on the edge of bed with legs open and feet planted on the floor on each side of Caleb.

Adrian hissed at the feeling of Caleb taking him into his mouth. He started at the tip of his dick, teasing it with his tongue and lightly sucking it before he started bobbing his head and taking Adrian deeper with each turn.

By the time Caleb started choking on his dick, Adrian's head was thrown back and his own bottom lip pulled between his teeth as he relished in the pleasure Caleb was giving him. It had been so long since the two of them were intimate, and Caleb still knew Adrian's body so well.

But Adrian wasn't the only one who remembered. Taking Caleb's hair into a tight grip, Adrian thrusted his hips up, hitting the back of Caleb's throat, making him choke on his dick.

Turned on by the way Adrian was fucking his face until saliva was dripping down his chin, Caleb started stroking his own dick.

When Adrian felt the added sensation of Caleb humming against his length, he could feel himself quickly approaching his release. Reluctant to stop in that moment, Adrian kept fucking Caleb's face until he was right on the edge of his orgasm and then stopped, pulling Caleb's head away, and looking down to meet his eyes.

The way his gaze roamed up and down Caleb's body, it was clear what was on Adrian's mind.

"I'm assuming you're not prepped..."

Caleb shook his head.

"It's fine... Get on the bed like this."

Positioning himself the way Adrian gestured, Caleb lay on his side so that he and Adrian's heads were aligned with the other's groin. At the same time, they both took each other's dicks into their mouths.

With the way Adrian's moans intensified, Caleb knew he was on the edge of his release and moved his head back and forth faster. Adrian was losing himself to the pleasure that Caleb was giving him and in a move that felt natural, he spit on his fingers and started toying with the rim of Caleb's entrance.

The vibration of Caleb's outburst on his dick sent Adrian over the edge and feeling of Adrian's finger pressed against him pushed Caleb to hit his orgasm. After taking every bit the other had to give, the two of them realigned to share a deep kiss.

"Will you spend the night?" Caleb asked softly after they pulled away.

Adrian paused for several moments with an indecipherable expression on his face. That was the first good night they'd had together in a long time and while he wasn't sure if it was the best choice to stay, he didn't want to ruin the mood.

"Sure. Let's take a shower."

What Happened

"I still can't believe that happened," Justin muttered to himself as he ran his fingers through his hair and paced his office. Monday had arrived and he hadn't spoken to Mila since he went to visit her Friday and they kissed in her apartment. Over the weekend, he typed out texts or emails to her and ended up erasing them before pressing send. His anxiety caused him to wake up unusually early and he was in the office two hours before the work day was set to start.

"How the fuck am I even going to make eye-contact with her after that?" he asked himself. "Fuck! We're going to have to talk about it..." Justin plopped into the couch, laying on his back as he rested his arm across his eyes. "And I can't stop thinking about her. It was a lot before, but it's even more intense now."

Subconsciously, his other hand drifted down to the front of his pants. Every time he closed his eyes, flashbacks from Friday would fill his mind. It wasn't just the kiss itself that consumed his thoughts. It was everything that came with it. The way Mila spoke to him with such authority before pushing him onto the couch, the way she took initiative and remained in control the entire time, and the way she knew exactly what he wanted, even if he didn't. And finally, the way her body felt when he held her for the first time—her fullness, her softness—it was like he'd been wanting that feeling all along, but didn't know until it happened.

When Mila abruptly broke away and kicked him out of her apartment, Justin was frustrated that their moment ended so quickly, but most of all, he couldn't help but desire more. And although he was left to make his way home while hiding his erection, he felt *satisfied* in an odd way, for the first time in a long time.

With the thoughts of Mila that flooded his mind while his eyes were closed, he didn't realize until he audibly groaned that he'd been rubbing himself without thinking.

Stop it, Justin! he snapped internally before standing up. He returned to pacing his office and took deep breaths to calm himself

"Am I into Mila?" he whispered before shaking his head. "No. We are going to talk this out like adults and clear the air. I'll send her an email now."

CALEB STROLLED INTO THE OFFICE, arriving much earlier than usual with a small smile on his face and a pep in his step. He was in a great mood following the weekend. However, he'd woken up earlier than usual hoping to catch Mila first thing in the morning so he could keep her in his office for the entire first half of the day taking notes for him during meetings. He'd planned to take her before Adrian or Justin could get her in for one of their meetings.

Looking at the office doors, his brows tensed. "The fuck? Are both of them already here? The office hasn't even opened yet..." His small smile grew into a noticeable one when he thought about the fact that Adrian was already there and they could have some time alone before starting the day. Adrian left Saturday morning and Caleb hadn't heard from him since then, but Caleb didn't read too much into the lack of contact.

"What's up, Adrian?" Caleb greeted walking into his office and locking the door behind him. "How was the rest of your weekend?"

"Why did you lock the door?" Adrian asked, ignoring Caleb's greeting.

"Oh, you know..." Caleb came up closer to Adrian, but when he reached out for him, Adrian stepped back. "What now?"

"I didn't want to say anything this weekend, but..." Adrian looked away and toyed with a folder on his desk. "We shouldn't have done that."

"What the fuck? You initiated it."

"And that was a mistake. I don't want to lead you on, Caleb." Adrian's tone was detached, it sounded almost as if he were conducting business.

A heaviness came over Caleb along with a tightness in his chest as his stomach seemed to feel hallow. "You can't be serious right now, Adrian. Really?"

"Yes, really. You and I... We should just stay platonic. Getting feelings involved... It wouldn't be good for business."

"You know what?" Caleb leaned over the desk so he could get in Adrian's face. "You and everyone else try to make me out to be the bad guy but *you're* the real asshole. One minute, you're making out with me and the next, you kick me out of your hotel. And then, you come to my place and we hook up just for you to tell me you don't want me two days later? The fuck is that?"

"Don't word it like that," Adrian said softly. "It's not that I don't want you, it's just that... Like I said, getting feelings involved like this could be bad for business. I mean, look at the tension it's already caused."

"No, Adrian... That's tension that *you* caused being hot and cold with me."

"Caleb..."

"No, you know what? Fuck it. You want to be platonic, then we'll be fucking platonic. I don't deserve this shit. You're the only one I've ever—" Caleb choked up and he sniffed before turning away and walking toward the door. "Whatever. Fuck it. Fine... Platonic it is."

Adrian swallowed hard as he watched Caleb walk away. He felt guilty about the mixed signals he gave him, but he was conflicted. Adrian knew that he had feelings for Mila and in the time that he'd known her, the woman completely won him over and he was enamored with her. At the same time, he and Caleb had a long history as friends that bloomed into something more at one point, but quickly fizzled out just a few months before Mila started working at PMC Group. However, the romantic feelings Adrian had developed for Caleb still lingered and he knew it was the same for him.

"I *am* the asshole," he whispered to himself.

∼

MILA LET OUT a deep sigh when she got into the elevator to go up to PMC Group's floor. She'd received a text from Adrian and emails from Justin and Caleb all asking to see her 'first thing Monday.'

All three of the men annoyed her for different reasons.

Justin came off as self-centered and she didn't like the way he came to her apartment to 'check on' her only to discuss his relationship—or lack thereof—with Ashley again. Mila knew from the way Justin would often stare at her with an intense look in his lust-glazed eyes that he was into her. And when he came to her apartment and easily succumbed to her, it gave Mila the last bit of confirmation she needed.

With Caleb, it was obvious. He was obnoxious and constantly tried to sow doubt in Mila's mind about her body, but it never worked. And it was clear that he was into her with how easily she had him on his knees. Also, his approach to pursuing her—which was forcing her into his meetings while he simply stared at her like a creep the entire time—both angered and entertained Mila. While she could admit he was an attractive man and a good kisser, she was much more interested in tormenting him than anything else.

Adrian annoyed Mila in a unique way. He was kind from the first day they met almost a year ago and she thought of him as a sweetheart. It was easy for him to make her smile and Mila found herself thinking about him a bit too much outside of work, even when she distracted herself with other men. The unfamiliar fluttering she had in her stomach when they spent time together caused Mila discomfort and she hated the way she'd developed a soft spot for him. Logically, she knew what those sensations usually meant, but she refused to put a name to them.

When Mila reached her desk, she looked at the three doors and to her surprise—especially when it came to Caleb—all three of the men were already in the office. She shook her head and sat down in her chair to log into her computer and ultimately decided not to go to any of their offices.

Am I dragging this on too long? Mila thought to herself. *Maybe it's time for me to actually focus on taking them down.*

Mila's computer chimed and it was her reminder that the men had their Monday morning meeting, which was often the longest one between them each week, and she would bring coffee for the meeting. When she heard one of their doors crack open, she got up from her desk to go to the cafe and order their drinks.

ADRIAN SIGHED when he walked out of his office just when Mila was leaving her desk. He had the urge to call her, but decided against it and continued his path to Justin's office. A week had passed since he ate her out in his office and the two still hadn't discussed what occurred.

When he saw Justin, he was reminded of what Mila told him about Justin bringing her soup. The jealousy immediately hit him.

"Hey Adrian," Justin greeted. "How was your weekend?"

"Fine," Adrian replied curtly before sitting in one of the chairs in Justin's office.

"Okay...?"

When Caleb entered the office, he was also cold with both Adrian and Justin, not bothering to say a word and simply sitting in one of the chairs in the meeting area.

"Is there a reason you guys are being so weird right now?" Justin questioned. When he saw the way Caleb and Adrian immediately looked at each other and then away, he shook his head. "Oh, I know what it is. You guys hooked up again, didn't you? You need to grow up and deal with whatever is going on between you like adults."

"Don't lecture me about shit," Adrian spat.

"I'm just saying you guys need to figure out what is *or isn't* going on between you two. And what's with the hostility toward me? I haven't done anything to you, Adrian. You're starting to act like Caleb."

"That's bullshit," Caleb interjected. "I don't snap at you like Adrian keeps doing. He pretends to be the sweet, innocent guy, but he's a total dick, too."

"Whatever." Adrian leaned back in his seat with his notebook in his lap. "Let's just get on with this meeting."

"You're right. Maybe focusing on this next big move will get us out of this... whatever it is we're in... I've taken a look at Thompson Luxe Group's companies and identified the lowest hanging fruits for us to target first. I have a meeting this week with—"

Justin was interrupted by the sound of a knock at the door and the voice that followed.

"I have your coffees," Mila called from the other side. "I'm coming in." When she opened the door, all three of the men had their eyes on her and fell into silence. The tension in the room was thick and there was a slight smugness on her face knowing she was likely the one who caused it.

"You guys are quiet," she commented as she sat their coffees in front of each of them. "Is everything alright?"

"Y-yeah," Justin answered without making eye contact. "Everything is fine. Thanks for the coffees."

"Thank you, Mila," Adrian said and gave her a warm smile.

Caleb remained quiet, simply looking at her with narrowed eyes until she left the room.

After Mila walked out, the men did not resume their conversation. Instead, they all sat there for several minutes without saying a word and only sipping on their coffees.

"That's it!" Caleb shouted after the silence went on for too long. "I'm invoking PMC's third commandment: If thou hast shit to deal with, thou will lay it out on the fucking table!"

Since the three of them first started pursuing business ventures in college, Caleb, Justin, and Adrian created a set of rules for themselves in an effort to avoid major falling outs.

"Not really sure that's the correct wording..." Justin mumbled.

"You know what the fuck I mean. Whatever is going on with us, I bet that assistant is at the root of it..." Caleb let out an annoyed sigh. "Like we set up in the rules when I got to be the first name in our acronym, I have to be first for confessions, so here it is..." He paused and looked over at Adrian before shifting his eyes away and staring out the window. "I kissed Mila."

"You kissed her?" Adrian snapped, rising to his feet. "You talk so much shit about her and you mean to say you fucking kissed her? I know Mila's too smart to fall for any of that bullshit show you put on when you were trying to sleep with her, so what the hell did you do? Did you force her?"

"No! I didn't fucking force her! She kissed me back!"

"Bull-fucking-shit! I don't believe that!"

"I kissed her too," Justin confessed, cutting between the two of them.

Adrian turned to Justin with flared nostrils. "I fucking knew you were trying to move in on her! You were treating her better than Ashley!"

"That's not true! And besides, *she* kissed *me*!"

"What the fuck? Why would Mila kiss *you*?"

"What is that supposed to mean?" questioned an offended Justin. "You think she wouldn't want me?"

"No," Adrian grunted.

Justin shot to his feet and stormed up to Adrian. "You know what—"

"Stop!" Caleb put himself between the two of them and turned to Adrian. "Clearly there's something going on between you and Mila with the way you're blowing the fuck up. You've always had a jealous streak in you. Now, what the hell happened between the two of you?"

Adrian took a deep breath and when he breathed out, it sounded almost like a low growl. He glared at both Caleb and Justin as his eyes switched between the two of them and he thought about the fact that they *both* kissed Mila.

"I... kissed her too," he said with almost a mumble.

"That's it?" Caleb questioned. "You only kissed her and you're freaking out like this?"

"Yeah."

Justin scoffed at Adrian's reply and plopped back down into his seat while Caleb turned back toward the window and crossed his arms, now with an angry glare upon learning that the other men kissed Mila as well. He waited a few more minutes until Adrian calmed down and also returned to his seat.

"So, none of us have fucked her?" Caleb asked.

"No!" Justin and Adrian said in unison.

"Good. So, how are we handling this? Fire her?"

"No!" Again, Justin and Adrian exclaimed the word simultaneously.

"You two are whipped..." Caleb swallowed his relief. He didn't want to fire Mila and was glad that neither Justin nor Adrian called his bluff. "She's not *that* great of a kisser."

"You *know* that was a lie. Also, it's not that." Justin's jaw tensed as he ground his teeth while he mulled over his next words. "It's just hard to find a good assistant, especially one who can handle all three of us at the same time... You know what I mean."

"So, what are we gonna do?" Caleb questioned.

"I think we should set out some rules to make sure none of this... *progresses*," Adrian suggested. "We're adults, we can control ourselves."

"You're right," Justin nodded. "And I think it can be a simple rule. None of us kiss Mila."

"Or fuck her," Caleb added.

"We should also limit any alone time with her."

"Fair enough. So to make it clear, no physical contact with Mila beyond a simple handshake and we all will limit our alone time with her... That means you need to cut back on having her in your meetings, Caleb."

"Same goes for you two," Caleb countered.

"Fine. I'll keep it to my Japanese meetings only. And Adrian?" Justin turned to him.

"Yeah, I'll make our one-on-one meetings shorter and less frequent."

"Well then, we're all set," Justin concluded. "Now, back to what I was saying about Thompson Luxe Group..."

Their meeting went on for another hour as they solidified their plans to overtake Thompson Luxe Group, starting from the bottom with its smallest companies and working their way up until they could target its most profitable firms. PMC Group's end goal was for

Thompson Luxe Group to first fall below them in rankings of luxury and fashion holding companies, before absorbing the conglomerate.

Once they were finished, Adrian was the first to get out of Justin's office and he made a path straight to Mila's desk. When he approached, she was sitting there, seemingly focused on her computer.

"Mila," he said, grabbing her attention. "Can we talk in my office, please?"

"Of course, Mr. Collins."

F**k the Rules

Mila and Adrian sat in his office across from each other at his desk. He looked over at her with a smile on his face and Mila couldn't help the small one that came to hers. She was trying her hardest to ignore what she felt for him, but it was growing increasingly difficult, especially after their intimate moment the week prior and his kind gesture of cooking her soup from scratch and bringing it to her apartment.

"How was the rest of your weekend, Mila? I hope you're feeling better now."

"I'm fine," Mila replied. "I just chilled, which was a nice change of pace compared to the past few weekends. What about you? Did you spend it with Mr. Peterson?"

A sharp breath crossed Adrian's nose and he cleared his throat. "W-what do you mean... Er, I mean... We got drinks after leaving your place and I talked to him about being less of a dick to you, but I otherwise also had a chill weekend."

"Interesting..." Mila muttered.

"Um, so I actually wanted to talk to you. Well, I've *been* wanting to talk to you about what happened last week... in here..."

Mila tilted her head to the side and looked at him attentively.

"Look, Mila... It's just that I- I recognize I'm your boss and this isn't *exactly* appropriate, but I don't regret what happened. I mean I- I um... I enjoyed it and I know— er I think you enjoyed it too?"

"Go ahead... Get to the point," Mila encouraged.

"Well... I just... I don't want that to be *it* between us. I don't care if it's considered 'inappropriate,' Mila. I..." Adrian took a deep breath in an attempt to steady his voice. "I like you, Mila," he confessed. "We've known each other for almost a year now and we've spent a lot of time together. Getting to know you has been so worthwhile and you're a refreshing person to be around."

Mila remained silent. Her lips fell into a neutral position as she listened to him.

"Mila, you try to play cool, but you're a kind and caring person. You're honest. You know how to handle any situation thrown at you and no matter what, you always seem in control. Not only does that take a ton of strength, but it also takes being headstrong and having trust in yourself and your ability to see things through. I am never *not* impressed by what you do."

"Not to mention..." Adrian continued. His hands were shaky and it took every bit of strength to keep his voice from doing the same. He swallowed in an effort to kept his breathing consistent. "You have a natural allure about you. You're a beautiful woman inside and out and I like you... And I think you like me too."

Mila felt her face heat up and knots tied in her stomach. The feelings that Adrian cause in her felt almost foreign.

Maintaining her façade, Mila asked, "What are you getting at, Adrian?"

Adrian felt a pain in his chest at Mila's lack of reaction to everything he'd just confessed to her, but he *knew* that she felt something for him, too.

"What I mean is that I don't want what happened last week to be a one-time thing. I also don't want it to be the *only* thing, Mila..." Adrian scanned over her face, trying to catch signs of any bit of emotion from her, but her expression was indecipherable. "I mean that I'd like to see where this goes... I-if that's okay with you. We obviously can't risk anything in the city, but, I'd like to take you on a date. A real date that isn't just us getting lunch or coffee together. I had a couple of ideas like maybe dinner on a boat or we could go up to New Y—"

"I'm going to stop you there, Mr. Collins," Mila interrupted. "I appreciate the gesture, but I'm not interested in taking it that far."

Adrian's face fell. He gulped, trying to push down the lump that immediately grew in his throat.

"I-is it because you kissed Caleb and Justin?" he asked. "Do you have feelings for them too? Or maybe you don't like me at all and this is some game you're playing."

"No. I don't have feelings for them."

"Then why'd you kiss them?" Adrian choked out.

"I am a single woman. I can kiss who I want." Mila kept her voice calm and her expression neutral. She had the urge to explain that at least she didn't purposely kiss Caleb considering he was the one who forced it on her, but she also refused to explain herself to Adrian.

Silence fell over the room and she had a hard time maintaining her demeanor when she saw Adrian's reaction and Mila never wanted to comfort someone so much. She got up and walked over to his side of the desk to stand next to him. Mila reached out and softly ran her fingers through Adrian's brown hair.

"What I mean is that I *really* enjoyed last week. And I think we're at a good pace..." Her hand went from his hair down to his chin as he looked up at her. Mila took note of the tightness of his face and she wanted to relieve that for him. She leaned forward to press her lips against his and Adrian moved his hand to the back of her head to deepen it. It was unlike the kisses they'd shared before. The exchange felt equal, as if they were both pouring something into each other. Both were unsure of how much time had passed, but as soon as Mila felt like she was about to lose herself further, she broke away and stood back up.

Looking down at him with a small smile to cover what she was really feeling, Mila used her thumb to wipe the lipstick from his mouth.

"How about we stick with what we have now, Adrian?"

Nodding, he gulped. "Right. That's fine with me."

Mila rubbed his cheek before turning away and walking out of his office without saying another word.

Once she got out, one of the last voices she wanted to hear called for her.

"Hey assistant," Caleb said from the open door of his office. "We need to talk."

Mila ignored him and went straight to the bathroom. She took a deep sigh of relief that no one was in there and she looked in the mirror, immediately annoyed at the sight before her. Her eyes had turned glossy and tears brimmed her lids. She took a deep breath through her nose and grabbed some paper towel to gently dab the almost-tears away. Mila continued with a few more minutes of breathing exercises to calm herself before looking back into the mirror at her now clear eyes.

"Get your shit together, Mila," she whispered to herself. "You can't fall for a man whose life you're going to ruin."

With that warning to herself, she relaxed her shoulders and straightened up her dress. After leaving the bathroom, she went straight to Caleb's office and stood in the doorway.

"You called, Mr. Peterson," she said dryly.

He scoffed. "Like ten minutes ago. The fuck were you doing? Getting a snack or something?"

Mila didn't react to his comment. She pushed herself off the doorframe and turned to walk back toward her desk when she was interrupted.

"I said that I need to speak with you, so get your ass over here."

Still not facing him, Mila huffed her frustration. She then pivoted to return to his office, shut the door behind her and locked it. Walking over to him, the sounds of her heels clicking reminded Caleb of that night she left him in the conference room alone.

He gave her a snide look and said, "About time you listen—"

Caleb was cut off when Mila cupped his face with her thumb and index finger digging into his cheeks. She lifted his head up so he was looking straight at her.

"Shut up," she said calmly, despite the clear disapproval on her face. Mila sat on Caleb's desk in front of him while he remained in the chair. "I was expecting you to come in today in a much better mood. Didn't I warm you and Adrian up before leaving my apartment? I thought sure you two would hook up this weekend..."

Caleb gasped and his eyes went wide. "H-how d-did you kn—"

He was again cut off by Mila, who tightened her grip on his face.

"I told you to... *Shut. Up.*" The sternness in her voice was enough for Caleb to keep his mouth closed.

How the fuck did she end up having this much of a hold on me? Caleb thought to himself. He was in a horrible mood between what happened with Adrian and the argument that the two of them and Justin had earlier about Mila. But from the moment she showed that she was annoyed with Caleb and stormed up to him, he felt a complete change in his attitude.

"Most people may not be able to see it, but I realized it this weekend. You and Adrian have a past. And something there hasn't been resolved... You were hard and needy when you left and Adrian definitely had just come, but was *still* in the mood, so what happened? Either you didn't hook up; you almost did, but something interrupted; or you *did* hook up, but had some sort of falling out soon after... Regardless of what happened, here you are, still being a douche bag."

Caleb remained silent, but allowed his face to rest in Mila's hold while, out of pure instinct, he parted his legs.

Mila sighed and placed her foot on the seat of Caleb's chair between his legs as she continued talking. "And now, you keep speaking to me like I don't have you exactly where I want you... And you know it, too. Not too long ago, you were on your knees counting to thirty wanting me to *punish* you. Three days ago, you were humping my foot, and now here you are, wanting to do it again." Her eyes drifted down to see how Caleb had already pressed himself against her foot.

She let go of his face and leaned back, still sitting on his desk and removing her foot from his seat. Reaching back out to him, Mila caressed the side of Caleb's face, her acrylic nails running down to his chin.

"You're actually somewhat tolerable when your mouth his shut, pet."

Caleb still refused to admit it to himself, but he was at Mila's mercy. He kept quiet when she told him to, even though he desperately wanted to ask her something. All he needed was permission to do so.

He scanned her from head to toe, from the dark red lipstick she wore over her plump lips, to the way her navy blue dress hugged her curves, to her perfectly manicured nails, to the ankle-strapped heels she wore. When his gaze finally came back up to her eyes, Mila could tell from Caleb's expression that he had something he wanted to say.

To his surprise, she allowed him to speak.

"What is it, pet?"

Caleb's jaw tensed and he let out a small huff. "What... do I... have to... do?"

"That's a cryptic question. Maybe I should've made you keep your mouth shut."

"I- I mean..." Caleb swallowed hard before blurting it out. "What-doIhavetodototasteyouagain?"

Mila giggled at the way he asked. She could tell that Caleb knew himself that he was slipping into his surrender and was still attempting to fight it.

"I pretty sure I told you that was the last taste you'd get," she pondered out loud as she looked up and tapped her finger to her chin.

Caleb's eyes returned to wandering Mila's form when he spoke again. "Please," he said softly.

He let out a shaky breath at the feeling of her foot against him again. Mila moved it slowly, teasing him as she spoke.

"So, pet wants to know what it'll take to taste me again, hm? Pretty presumptuous to think that's an option in the first place..."

Caleb grabbed the arms of his chair and braced himself as he moved his hips to increase the friction with Mila's foot.

"Normally, desperation turns me on, but yours is just pathetic. It's not even noon yet and here you are, humping my foot again. You're a needy one, you know that?"

Caleb grunted with pleasure when Mila increased the pressure as she felt him growing hard under her shoe. From his experiences with her, he knew that she wouldn't keep it up much longer and he was attempting to enjoy every moment while he still could.

He didn't realize it, but Caleb's mouth had opened as he let out light moans while grinding against Mila's foot and he winced when she moved it from his partial erection to under his chin to close his mouth.

Mila tilted her head to the side as she rested her foot on his chest and watched the way he stared down at her leg. Heat rushed to her core as she took in the sight. She practically owned him.

"You want a taste that bad, pet?" she questioned and Caleb nodded urgently.

A sneer grew on her face and she lifted her foot again.

"Then here you go." The heel of her stiletto was aligned with Caleb's mouth. He met the darkness in her eyes and held her gaze as he lifted his hands up to cradle her calf. Maintaining eye contact, Caleb slowly took the four-inch heel of Mila's shoe into his mouth and began moving back and forth as he sucked it.

Mila pegged Caleb as the biggest degradee of the three men and she was right. It was also one of his few redeeming qualities because Mila found herself deeply turned on as she watched him suck her heel. Her other leg moved to side so that they were open enough for Caleb to get a peek up her dress and his eyes drifted down to stare at her panties while he continued.

When Mila felt how wet she was becoming, she pulled her leg from Caleb's grasp and brought it back down to cross over her other one.

"So..." Caleb gulped. "Can I... taste you again?"

A big grin came to Mila's face and she bursted out laughing.

"You just sucked my heel!" Mila was almost hysterical. "You really think I'd want your dirty mouth on me now?" She shook her head and hopped off his desk. "Pathetic, as always."

Completely bewildered, Caleb was at a loss for words. "Bu- But..."

Mila placed a silencing finger over his lips. "Don't forget what I told you, pet. You're actually tolerable when you don't speak."

He kept quiet and Mila turned away to leave without another word. Once she was out the door, Caleb looked down at his erection and breathed his frustration.

"Damnit!"

AFTER HER INTERACTIONS with Adrian and Caleb, Mila was able to return to her work uninterrupted for the rest of the day, as Justin was in meetings that he hadn't invited her to. She was finishing up her final task when the last of the trio called out to her.

"Hey Mila," Justin called, approaching her desk. "Sorry to bother you at the end of the day, but would you mind coming to my office, please? So we can talk?"

"Sure," Mila sighed, rising from her desk and following him into his office. Rather than leading her to his desk, Justin led Mila to the couch in his office and they sat on two opposite ends of it.

"How was your weekend?" Justin asked. "Are you feeling better?"

"I'm fine."

"R-right. So, I'm sure you can guess why I brought you in here..."

"About Friday?"

"Yes, exactly! I just... I wanted to clarify that when I went to your apartment, delivering the soup and checking on you really were my only intentions. But also... I don't regret what happened."

"If those were your 'only' intentions, why did you plop yourself down on my couch to tell me you dumped Ashley?" Mila asked.

Justin's brows tensed and he leaned in toward Mila. "Because, you're the one who told me to do it. And I wanted you to know that I followed your advice. Also... I thought we were friends, Mila. I mean, we speak so casually with each other. And you're one of the only people I truly feel comfortable around other than Adrian and Caleb."

"Well, I'm your assistant, so that's part of the job."

"And kissing all three of us? Is that part of the job, too?" Justin countered.

Mila rested her arm against the back of the couch. "Are you upset?"

"Honestly..." Justin took a deep breath and scooted closer to Mila. "I am, but I know that I shouldn't be. Do you... like them?"

Mila scoffed and shook her head. "That's a loaded question and it's none of your business. *But* if it gives you any comfort, you're the only one I initiated a kiss with."

Justin's face immediately brightened before he could catch himself. Meanwhile, Mila knew exactly what she was doing with the statement. She could admit it was a character flaw of hers, but she enjoyed playing games with men. And despite the fact she was grappling with the soft spot she'd grown for Adrian, she still had every intention of entertaining herself with her three 'bosses'.

"Really?" Justin said softly. Now that he was closer to Mila while her legs were crossed, he was able to reach over and caress the outside of her calf.

She hummed her confirmation with a nod.

Again, Justin scooted closer to Mila so that her face was within reach of his. She raised a surprised brow at his boldness, but didn't move from her spot, allowing him to advance as he wanted.

"Mila," he whispered, leaning in closer to her. "May I kiss you?"

I swear half of my decisions today have been led by my fucking hormones, Mila thought to herself before closing the distance between them. Justin's breathing grew heavy as their lips moved against each other and before he knew it, they were laying in the couch and he was on top of her. He gripped one of her thighs and brought it to his side while Mila kept a hold on his face, denying his tongue each time he tried to slip it into her mouth.

Finally, Justin broke the kiss first and whispered in Mila's ear, "May I touch you?"

That was when he felt her hand press against his chest and he sat back up, hovering above her.

"Don't get ahead of yourself," Mila replied. She reached up to push her middle and ring fingers in his mouth. Justin didn't realize it was something he'd be into, but the lust in her eyes as she moved her fingers in and out of his mouth, only caused him to grow harder.

Still holding himself over her, he watched Mila as she took her fingers, now covered in his saliva out of his mouth and slid them down into her panties. She maintained eye contact with him as she began touching herself and Justin's pants turned painfully tight.

He nearly lost it when she released a light moan. Justin moved one of his hands down so he could help her and she grabbed his wrist with her free hand.

"Did I say you could touch me?" The coldness in her voice reminded him of the previous warning she'd given him in her apartment and he heeded her words. "Stay where you are," Mila instructed and Justin did as told.

With the position they were in, Justin could take in every tick of Mila's face while she pleasured herself. The scene only gave him more images for his fantasies about her, the sight of her coming undone under him.

The way Mila's face twisted in pleasure, the way her lips parted as she released the sweetest moans Justin ever heard, the way he imagined her essence mixed with *his* saliva while she played with herself... Justin was painfully hard and everything in his body was screaming for him to free his dick from his pants, pull Mila's panties to the side, and slide into her wet pussy.

"Jesus, Mila..." he muttered, trying to keep himself together. He was so entranced that it didn't register how tired his arms were getting as he tried to keep himself up. And, while the desire to touch himself was there, he didn't want to ruin the show Mila was giving him. He could tell that her hand was moving faster and that she was nearing her release with the way her neck extended as she threw her head back.

"Fuucckkkk," Mila moaned when she came.

She pulled her hand from her panties and her fingers glistened. Justin dipped his head down to take them in his mouth, but before he could, Mila pulled her hand away. He brought himself back up over her and watched as Mila sucked her own orgasm off her fingers.

She gestured him down with her finger so that he could get a small taste of her from her own mouth, and pushed him away before he could deepen the kiss.

Speechless, Justin looked on as Mila got out of the couch, pulled her skirt down, and walked out of his office without saying another word.

Avoidance

Mila was sprawled out on her couch with her phone in her hand while she was on a video call with her friend Naomi Laurent. Two weeks had passed since Adrian confessed his feelings for her and even though they kissed after, he'd been avoiding her since.

The first few days, Mila was unbothered as she continued her games with Caleb and Justin, but after a week, she found herself feeling upset that he wasn't paying her any mind beyond a passive greeting in the mornings.

The thoughts consumed her so much that she needed someone to talk to, and so she revealed as much details as she could to Naomi without telling her that she was spying on competition. Instead, Mila told her that she decided to try working a 'real job', since she never had before. Naomi didn't buy it, but assumed that Mila had a good reason for keeping part of what she was doing a secret.

"I've never experienced anything like this before, girl," Mila groaned. "He's been avoiding me for the past two weeks and the shit is actually bothering me! Me! Can you believe that I am anything but unfazed by a fucking man? A man!"

Naomi giggled and shook her head. "Mila, you did reject the man and from what you told me, he was pretty hurt. I mean, on the verge of tears at work? He obviously had very, very deep feelings for you."

"Had?" Mila sat up in the couch. "You think they're already gone? If these 'feelings' were so strong, then how would they go so quickly?"

"Mila, Mila, please... Calm down. I admittedly worded that poorly. I'm not saying that he doesn't feel anything for you now."

"There's a 'but' coming, I can feel it."

"But... He might be in the process of getting over you. I mean, they say only time can heal a broken heart, so that's probably why he's avoiding you. So he can have time to heal."

Mila audibly gasped. "You think I broke his heart?"

"Mila!" Naomi exclaimed. "Of course you broke his heart... At least, that's what it sounds like based on what you told me."

"Damnit! Why the fuck do I even care if I broke his heart? Fuck his feel- Shit! I can't even bring myself to finish that sentence! What is wrong with me? I don't get it! I've never felt this way about someone before. I couldn't even bring myself to feel this strongly for Eric, no matter how hard I tried."

"There's nothing wrong with you, Mila," Naomi assured. "You have known him for a year. Is it possible you're in lo—"

"Okay, chill out, Naomi," Mila interrupted. "We don't drop any L-words around here unless we're talking about lesbians."

"Fine, but you can't deny that you have feelings for him, too. Everything you've described to me—the butterflies, tightness in your chest, lump in your throat... It all says that you like him and your entire body is screaming it at you."

Mila was silent, stubbornly staring at Naomi through the phone with a pout on her face.

"Mila," Naomi sighed. "Why not give him a chance?"

"Because I don't understand how this shit works. I like dating and I like fucking, but I always took pride in the fact that I've never had feelings for anyone before... It made my lifestyle easier, and a lot more fun."

"But haven't you been having fun with this guy? You can like someone and still have fun with them... that's kind of the point."

"Yeah, but liking him also means that I actually care about losing him. That shit is annoying. I like dating so much because I don't catch feelings and I don't have to worry about heartache... You know what? Do you think this is some sick karma because I never developed feelings for Eric?"

"I don't think it works like that, Mila... Just give this guy a chance."

"I can't."

"I understand being scared to get hurt, Mila, I experienced the same thing with Sebastien. And I almost lost him because of it."

"It's not just that..." Mila drifted off. She couldn't tell Naomi that she was there to bring down the company and consequently ruin Adrian's life, which is what really gave her pause. The fear she felt about getting hurt wasn't strong enough to keep her from giving him a chance, but her fear of hurting him was what truly scared her.

"At the end of the day, I know you'll do what's best for you, which is what I want for you, as well."

"Thanks, Naomi."

Mila sat at her desk counting down the minutes until the end of the day. It was only two o'clock and she was bored out of her mind. Caleb was at a day-long conference in downtown, while Justin was on a work trip to Los Angeles. He'd tried to bring Mila with him, but Adrian and Caleb objected, claiming that he didn't give a strong enough reason to take her with him. Meanwhile, Adrian was around, but he was still avoiding Mila and had been calling on entry-level staff or other assistants to come to his meetings when he needed a notetaker.

She'd been scrolling aimlessly through her phone when her computer chimed with a reminder that Adrian's two-thirty meeting was coming up. She knew that it was at an office in the financial district, but to her surprise, he hadn't left yet and would be late if he didn't do so soon. She always knew him to be prompt.

"Why the fuck am I nervous about speaking to him?" she whispered to herself as her hand hovered over the phone on her desk. "This is starting to piss me off. It's my job to remind him he has a meeting... Men don't make me nervous. Why the fuck am I nervous? Fuck it."

She finally picked up the phone and dialed his extension.

"Mila?" he answered.

"Yes, Mr. Collins. Your two-thirty meeting in the financial district, remember? If you leave now, you can still make it on time."

"Y-yeah..." There was an awkward pause before Adrian could be heard taking a deep breath before he spoke again. "I'm um... I'm actually having a hard time finding someone to come with me to take notes..."

"You have an assistant right here, Mr. Collins," Mila replied flatly. "I'll go with you to your meeting."

"Oh! Um... I guess you're right. Are you... Are you um... Are you sure?"

"It is my job, Mr. Collins."

"Right, of course! I'll be right out. Thank you."

Adrian was soon at Mila's desk and without them exchanging any further words, they were out of the office and on their way to Adrian's meeting. When they got outside of their building, Adrian looked up and down the street for a taxi when Mila said the first words between them since they'd gotten off the phone.

She pointed to the train station entrance across the street. "The train might be faster for this one, Mr. Collins."

"Oh um... That makes sense. Thank you, Mila."

It's also a lot less awkward than a cab ride would be if it were just the two of us, she thought to herself.

With it being early afternoon, the train wasn't too busy with rush hour just yet and Mila and Adrian ended up in a cart that had a few open seats. However, they still had to sit next to each other and their legs touched the whole time.

The fuck am I uncomfortable for? And what is this shit going on with my stomach? Mila's internal thoughts continued for the fifteen minutes they were on the train. *Oh right... This is what I always feel with him. Why him? Damnit! Body, brain... heart? Chill the fuck out.* She huffed her frustration and Adrian turned to look at her before quickly averting his gaze when he felt a tightness in his chest.

"Is... Everything okay?" he asked, still looking away.

"I'm fine," Mila replied curtly.

Following her response, the silence between them resumed for the rest of the train ride and during their entire walk from the train station to the building where the meeting was set to be held. Once they arrived to the office, Mila sat in one of the chairs behind the seats positioned at the conference table, as was the usual spot for note takers. Meanwhile, Adrian sat at the head of the table, as they were meeting with PMC Group's bankers.

Mila tried to distract herself by being diligent in her note-taking. However, each time Adrian spoke, the melody of his deep voice was a reminder of the sounds of him moaning into her. Then, she'd end up looking at him and would be reminded of his soft brown eyes that only added to the softness she felt for him. And finally, there were times when their eyes would meet momentarily and Mila would feel a fluttering in her stomach.

But along with those sensations, what she felt most of all was agitated with herself.

Why the fuck couldn't I have just developed these type of feelings for Eric when we were dating? Then when he proposed, I would've said yes, and boom! I wouldn't even be here in this fucking position.

The meeting went on for a torturous two hours before it finally came to an end. After saying goodbye to the other company's representatives, Mila and Adrian made their way to the elevators and as they waited for one, Adrian broke the silence between them again.

"Hey, so since it's close to five o'clock, anyway..." He drifted off when Mila looked up at him to meet his eyes. He didn't quite understand why, but she somehow appeared displeased. "I... I was just saying that... If you wanted to go home early, you can. I know you're not *too* far—"

Adrian was cut off when Mila abruptly grabbed his arm and pulled him down one of the hallways. She led him to a storage closet and pressed him against the door before pulling him down to meet his lips in an intense kiss. Adrian cupped her by the back of her neck to deepen it as Mila's hands drifted down his body and into his pants. He moaned into her mouth at the feeling of her hand wrapping around his dick.

As she stroked him and felt Adrian grow harder, Mila took his bottom lip between her teeth and pulled before making a path to his neck.

"I... I thought you didn't want me?" Adrian choked out.

"Don't fuck up the moment," Mila muttered. She took one of his hands and guided it inside of her tights so he could feel her directly. "Does it feel like I don't want you?"

Too caught up to worry about where they were in that moment, Adrian moved his fingers inside of her while Mila continued to stroke him.

"Ah fuck." He let out a sharp grunt at the feeling her teeth grazing his neck.

Just when Mila was on the edge of her release, she grabbed Adrian's wrist to stop him and dragged her tongue from the base of his neck up to his ear and nibbled on it. Pulling his hand from between her legs, Mila brought it up to her mouth and began sucking her essence from his fingers.

Holding eye contact with him while her other hand remained down his pants, Mila twirled her tongue around the tip of Adrian's fingers before she started moving her head back and forth, taking them further down with each movement. Adrian was in shambles as he watched her attentively.

After popping his fingers out her mouth, Mila pulled her hand out of his pants before he could approach his release and straightened up his suit jacket.

Pecking his lips one more time, Mila pulled away and scanned over Adrian's face.

"How about you come home with me?"

Make it Clear

Mila and Adrian stumbled into her apartment as their lips were practically glued against the other. Adrian moved his mouth down and kissed and sucked Mila's neck as she helped him remove his suit jacket before breaking away to pull her shirt off. Their mouths returning to each other, he reached back to unzip her skirt and pushed it down over her hips.

By the time they got to her room, Mila was down to nothing but her bra, panties, and heels, and Adrian was in his shirt, loosened tie, and briefs. Mila pushed him on the bed so he was laying on his back and crawled on top of him. She wrapped her hand around his neck to pin him down before taking his ear between her teeth and then placing teasing kisses along his jaw and bottom lip. Adrian reached back to grab two handfuls of her ass as she ground against his growing erection.

"What was it you said earlier, darling?" Mila whispered against his lips. "That I didn't want you?"

When Adrian took too long to answer, she tightened her grip around his neck.

"Y-yes."

"You were wrong..." Her kisses began to trail lower, leaving marks of her lipstick against his white shirt until she reached the hemline of his briefs. Adrian propped himself up on his elbows to make eye contact with her as she looked up at him with a mischievous gaze. "Let me make it clear."

Mila removed Adrian's briefs and held his length in her hand. He watched her as she stuck out her tongue and licked him from the base up. She spit on his dick and stroked him while flicking her tongue against his tip and Adrian's mouth opened wide with a deep moan.

"Oh fuck," Adrian breathed and his head fell back when Mila took his dick into her mouth and started bobbing up and down. He came back up to watch her, taking in every bit of the sight. "This feels so fucking g— God!"

Adrian failed to keep himself up when he felt Mila humming against his dick and was flat on his back again. When he reached down to hold her head, Mila stopped and removed him from her mouth.

"Hands above your head."

"Yes, Ms. Mila." Adrian did as he was told and kept his hands over his head as he stared at the ceiling, bathing in the euphoric state that Mila was putting him in. His mind grew cloudy and his eyes rolled back. His chest rose and fell with his heavy breathing and his stomach sunk in as he tried to keep himself from coming.

Just before he could come, Mila freed him from her mouth and crawled up his body to straddle his face. In no time, Adrian's mouth was eagerly working at Mila's pussy and she tangled her fingers in his hair. He wrapped his arms around her large thighs, one tight enough for him to reach to the front of her pussy and spread her lips apart, giving his tongue better access.

Adrian looked up at Mila as he flicked his tongue against her clit and nearly lost it at her erotic sounds and the sight of her head falling back.

"Fuck," Mila moaned. "You're so fucking good at this."

She started moving her hips to grind on his face and Adrian moaned into her. The feeling of being enveloped in her thighs as he devoured her uninterrupted felt just as good to Adrian as when Mila had gone down on him.

Her muscles tightened and her body shook as she came, but Adrian didn't let up, maintaining his tight grip on her legs. Mila pulled his hair harder and Adrian finally let her go. Easing back down to align their bodies and meet his eyes, Mila held Adrian's face. He moaned when she flicked her tongue against his lower lip before sucking it between her own and savoring the taste of herself on his lips.

"You taste so fucking good, Mila," Adrian muttered when she freed his lips. "Like your taste was made for me."

Mila simply smiled at him before getting off of Adrian and crawling to the top of the bed so she could reach the condoms in her dresser to hand him one. After he took it, she positioned herself to face the headboard and held onto it as she looked back at him on his knees behind her.

"Are you ready?" Mila asked.

"Yes," Adrian replied, eagerly pulling at his tie and unbuttoning his shirt.

Mila turned to him with sultry gaze, scanning him up and down. "Keep the tie on," she said. "I want something to hold on to while you fuck me from behind."

Adrian followed her instructions, only removing his button-up, and he quickly rolled on the condom. When he got in position behind Mila and held himself against her pussy, she reached back to take his tie while turning her head to look him in the eyes. As he and Mila held eye contact, he slowly eased himself inside of her.

"Oh... my... god..."

Feeling Mila wrapped around him for the first time felt otherworldly for Adrian and he released a drawn out moan when he was finally buried inside of her while Mila let out a satisfied hum. As he began moving, Adrian couldn't help the grunts that escaped him and when Mila had her first outburst, he was emboldened and started pounding her pussy.

Mila bit her lip as her face twisted in the pleasure he gave her. "Tell me how good it feels to finally get what you've been wanting all this time, darling."

"It feels... so fucking good," Adrian rasped. "So wet... my god."

Mila wrapped the tie around her hand and pulled Adrian in for a kiss. She moaned into his mouth and his hand drifted down to play with her clit and he brought the other one up to toy with her nipple.

"Fuck," Adrian groaned. "Your pussy is so fucking tight."

When his strokes slowed, Mila pushed herself back to meet him. He released her nipple to braced a palm on her ass in a failed attempt to guide her movements. Looking down at his hand, Mila noticed he kept raising it before gently placing it back down on her behind.

"Use... your words," she choked out.

"Please, Ms. Mila," he said through labored breaths. "Can I... *smack-yourass?*"

Mila kissed his lips again before letting go of the tie and using both hands to hold the headboard. "Smack it."

Adrian's first hit was too soft for her. Mila turned and reached back to hold his face.

"Is that it?"

He smacked her ass harder and Mila let out a satisfied hum before letting him go and leaning forward again. Adrian was losing it at the way it felt to be inside of Mila as he watched himself fuck her from behind and the way her ass rippled each time he smacked it. The stinging of his own hand from spanking her ass and the sensation of her walls spasming around him threw Adrian into a euphoric state more intense than when Mila first went down on him.

When he knew he couldn't hold it any longer, Adrian pulled out of Mila and sat back on his heels. He tried to catch his breath, but before he could, Mila pushed him on his back and got on top.

"Still think I don't want you?" she questioned softly as her face hovered over his.

Adrian gulped and shook his head. His eyes squeezed shut and he bit his lip when he felt Mila position him at her entrance before slowly lowering herself on him.

"You sure?" she teased as she started riding him. "I think I need to make it clearer." Mila used one hand to hold Adrian's neck and the other to guide his hand up her body to grab her breast. She moved her hips to bounce up and down his length and Adrian's moans turn uncontrollable. His sounds were intoxicating for Mila and she leaned forward to suck his neck so that his moans were directly in her ear.

He'd been wanting Mila for so long and now that they were finally together in the way he'd been dreaming about, Adrian's senses felt like they were going into overdrive. The feeling of her soaking wet pussy sliding up and down his dick, her thick thighs straddling him, her sweet and sexy moans caressing his ears, their bodies smacking together with each bounce—it all felt so *right*, like they were meant to be just like that. Adrian knew from that moment that he'd never get enough of Mila.

"I- I'm gonna come," Adrian choked out.

"Good." Mila held the side of his face and traced her tongue along his ear while she rode him faster. "I want you, Adrian... and I want you to come for me right now."

Mila's command combined with her teeth catching his ear lobe and biting down with just enough pressure to give Adrian the *right* level of pain, were enough to send him over the edge and straight into his orgasm. "Oh fuck!"

On command, Adrian's eyes fluttered closed and his body shook at his climax. Mila's hips continued to move until his intense panting turned into winces and she finally let up.

His eyes fluttered open and he took in the image of Mila hovering above him. She looked down at him with a small smile and held his face.

"Clear enough?"

Not Bothered

Macaroni noises filled the room, accompanied by the sounds of Adrian's body slapping against Mila's.

In missionary position, Adrian had Mila's legs up and open on each side of her, bracing himself with each hand on the back of her knees while he gave her deep strokes. Mila's intoxicating sounds kept him going and Adrian's mouth was wide open, unable to keep his own moans at bay.

"Oh fuck," Mila cried, throwing her head back. Her arms extended above her head and she pressed her hands flat against the headboard as she felt her release rising. With the way she was pulsating around him, Adrian knew she was almost there and he let go of one of her legs to rub her clit.

"You're... so beautiful... when you... come," Adrian said softly. Watching and feeling how Mila's body reacted to the pleasure he gave her was pure bliss for Adrian and just as he had been doing all night and into the morning, he took in every sensation of Mila hitting her orgasm. She'd often arch her back while a strangled, yet soft moan would cross her lips. Just when she'd reach her peak the whites of her eyes would give Adrian the assurance he needed that he was capable of giving her such an intense experience. The acrylic nails he loved to see on her would dig into his skin—the more painful, the better. Her pussy would tighten around him and he felt her essence wetting his groin.

"Oh god," Mila breathed as she came down from her high and Adrian slowed his movements.

Before she could reposition them so that she was on top, Adrian rolled Mila to her side and got behind her. He raised her leg up and to the side before easing himself back into her and let out a drawn out groan of pleasure fucking her from that angle.

"You feel so fucking good." Adrian sped up his thrusts and Mila reached back to tangle her fingers in his hair. He peppered kisses along her shoulder and collarbone as he fucked her. They continued just like that until Adrian's grunts grew more persistent and intense. His body started to tremble and his grip tightened on Mila's thigh that he was holding open.

"I'm... *fuck*... I'm coming..."

Adrian released a strangled moan as he came inside the condom. He rested, still inside of Mila and the pair sharing lazy kisses until he recovered enough to get out of bed. After disposing of the condom and returning to her, Adrian cuddled up with Mila and her head lay against his chest.

"So, does this mean you thought about what I'd asked you before?" he questioned as his fingertips caressed her shoulder.

There was a long pause and Mila could hear how fast his heart was beating. The last person she'd committed to monogamously was Eric and that was one of the hardest parts of their relationship behind the guilt that came with her failure to develop feelings for him. And it was her experience with Eric—combined with years of having already suspected as much and experimenting with non-monogamy—that confirmed for Mila that monogamy might not work for her. At the same time, while she had a better idea of what she wanted out of a serious relationship, she wasn't ready for one just yet.

"Of course I thought about it," Mila finally replied. "More than I want to admit, honestly... Adrian, I *like* you. And I want to take you up on that date. But to be fully transparent... I'm not sure if I'm ready for something serious."

"That's fine," Adrian replied without hesitation. "Mila, I don't want to rush you into something if you're not ready. I told you that I want to spend more time with you out of the office. I want to take you on real dates that aren't just coffees or lunches. Let's do that and see where things go from there."

He could feel Mila snickering against his chest before she stretched her neck to kiss his lower jaw.

"Well, I *guess* I can oblige," she quipped. "Let's make it happen, Mr. Collins."

MILA AND ADRIAN staggered their late arrivals to the office as not to draw too many suspicions—Mila walking in at ten-thirty and Adrian coming an hour later. Both were relieved when Caleb was nowhere to be found and Mila looked at his schedule to see that he'd be out most of the afternoon in meetings. Meanwhile, Justin was still in Los Angeles and wouldn't be back until the following day.

After the morning that they had, both Mila and Adrian were still on a high and had been texting nonstop.

This feeling is weird and new, but... I like it? Mila thought to herself. *I'm just going to enjoy it, if anything, I like what feels good. And this feels good as fuck right now... I'll figure out the other shit later.*

She looked down at her phone when it chimed with a message from Adrian.

ADRIAN

So... What's the rest of your afternoon looking like?

MILA

Matsuda is still out of town and Peterson is in meetings. You tell me, "Mr. Collins"

ADRIAN

Well, Ms. Mila. I could use your help with something in my office, please?

Mila scoffed lightly before putting her phone face down her desk and turning her attention back to her computer. With Justin out of town and Caleb away in meetings, Adrian was the only one of her three 'bosses' who she had to tend to. A notification came up with a meeting request from Adrian and Mila shook her head with a smile when she read it.

MEETING REQUEST: Annual Review Discussion - Mila Nelson

It was a clever move on Adrian's part. The nature of the meeting made sense given the time of year and Mila's position. Plus, such meetings could take as long as an hour, so there would be no questions from other colleagues about Mila spending that much time alone with Adrian in his office.

After responding to a handful of emails, Mila got up and went to Adrian's office. Locking the door behind her, she went straight to his desk where he stood to greet her.

Adrian wrapped his arms around her waist and pulled her body against his into a tight hug. He took a deep breath, enjoying the smell of Mila's light perfume that reminded him of her sheets. And then their lips met. Adrian loved kissing Mila, from the feeling of her soft lips to the taste of her peach lip balm to the sensation of her fingers tangling in his hair.

Mila enjoyed Adrian's full lips and how whenever and wherever he touched her, it felt intentional, yet natural—as if coming from a place of appreciation. Ever since they were together for the first time the night before, they couldn't seem to keep their hands off each other for long and just the few hours between them parting ways that morning and arriving to the office, they were craving each other again.

"Can you keep quiet?" Mila whispered as she unbuttoned Adrian's suit jacket.

"I can try," he replied before she turned him around so that he was leaning against the desk for support. Mila's lips started making a path down his neck, kissing and lightly sucking it. She pulled his shirt out of his pants reached up it to caress his bare skin. She took his bottom lip between her teeth and pulled it.

"Positive?" she muttered when she noticed his breathing grow heavy at the move. Just when Mila was about to undo his pants, they were interrupted at the sound of Adrian's door knob moving followed by urgent knocks.

"I know you're in there!" Caleb called from the other side. "Why is the door locked?"

Mila stepped away from Adrian who in turn grew agitated with Caleb. "What do you want?"

"I want you to let me in! Unless you want me to keep yelling at you through the door. I know the assistant is in there too!"

Not responding to Caleb, Mila and Adrian exchanged a glance and remained silent, hoping he would go away.

"Oh, so you're calling my bluff?" Caleb questioned. "Fine. Let me get started. I heard the two of you left for a meeting yesterday and then both of you were conveniently late for work this morning. You think I don't know that you f—"

He was cut off when the door flew open and Adrian was standing before him. Caleb pushed past him to walk into the office where he saw Mila sitting at one the chairs in front of Adrian's desk with her tablet in her lap, appearing as though she'd been taking notes.

"Nice act, but I don't believe it," Caleb commented, approaching Mila and taking the seat next to her.

Adrian walked over to his side of the desk, but remained standing. "What do you want, Caleb?"

"I want you to tell me the truth! You two fucked, didn't you?"

"None of your business," Mila and Adrian said in unison.

"The hell it isn't," Caleb said sharply. "Did you tell him about you and me?"

"You and me?" Mila gawked. "There is no 'you and me'."

"That's a lie."

"What? You think just because you have a habit of dry humping my foot, that there's a 'you and me'?"

Adrian watched their exchange, but couldn't quite identify how he felt about it. He found his lack of jealousy to be out of character for him, but he figured that his history with Caleb had a lot to do with it.

"I think you're a fucking tease, that's what I think." Caleb turned his head to look up at Adrian. "She's a tease and you know it. She's been teasing you too, hasn't she? I bet if we asked J—"

"So tell me, which one of us are you more jealous of?" Mila interrupted, catching both men by surprise. "Me or Adrian?"

"Jealous?" Caleb scoffed. "Yeah right. What would I have to be jealous of?"

Mila stood from her chair and walked over to Adrian's side of the desk to stand next to him while they both faced Caleb, who was still seated.

"Then why are you so bothered at the idea that Adrian and I might have been together."

"There's no 'might have'. You two definitely fucked. Hell, if I didn't knock on the door just now, I bet you would've been at it again... And I'm not bothered."

"Oh?" Mila tilted her head to the side, challenging him. "For someone who's 'not bothered', that sure is a lot of thinking to do about what may or may not be going on between two people."

"Well, umm..." Caleb crossed his arms stubbornly. "I'm just saying that I know what you did. It doesn't bother me."

Mila turned to Adrian and placed her hand against his chest before moving it up to run her fingers through his hair. "He says he's unbothered, but what do you think?"

Adrian glanced over at Caleb whose jaw was tensed as he watched how Mila touched Adrian so comfortably. She lifted herself up to whisper something in Adrian's ear that Caleb couldn't hear. Adrian looked at Caleb and then back to Mila before nodding. Caleb immediately went stiff when Mila and Adrian exchanged a brief kiss before his mouth moved lower.

"Does this bother you?" Mila asked, locking eyes with Caleb while Adrian's lips were against her neck.

Caleb slowly shook his head, but couldn't tear his gaze away from the scene. He watched as Adrian's hands wandered Mila's body. The way his fingertips caressed her curves before his hands drifted further down to grab two handfuls of her ass. Mila's head fell back to give him more access to her neck and Adrian's mouth grew more eager. It was like their bodies were already deeply familiar with each other.

Caleb took in the way Mila's slow blinks accompanied glazed eyes before she broke eye contact with him to turn back to Adrian. She held the side of his neck, her thumb caressing his jaw before pulling him in to close the distance. Watching the two of them and how their mouths moved together while their hands explored each other bodies, Caleb felt himself grow strained against his pants.

Adrian was starting to savor the moment. Although he was at Mila's mercy, he was also a possessive man and he wanted to show Caleb that Mila was his. He'd told her that morning that he wouldn't force them to move to fast, but he still didn't love the idea of anyone else thinking they could have her in the way that he did. Mila showed him a softness that he didn't see her show anyone else, even when she was nice to others.

When Mila whispered in Adrian's ear before, she'd said, "Let's see how unbothered he really is." Adrian's first reaction was one of slight surprise, not expecting that she'd be open to getting physical in front of Caleb. However, based on the heat radiating off of her and her shallow breathing, Adrian realized that she was turned on by the act.

"Still... not... bothered?" Mila's voice was breathy, her body reacting to Adrian's touch while Caleb watched.

Again, Caleb slowly shook his head.

Adrian flashed a glare in Caleb's direction before returning his attention to Mila. He had conflicting feelings. Something about Caleb watching them turned him on, knowing that he wanted to join, and knowing that if he tried in that moment, they both would deny him.

Mila's hand fell down down to the front Adrian's pants and she rubbed his growing erection. She traced her tongue along the edge of his ear and whispered, "If you want me to stop, just tell me."

Once Adrian nodded, she unzipped his pants, spit on her hand, and reached down into his briefs to stroke him directly. He grunted into her mouth when she took his lips with hers again. Mila then pulled away to kiss and suck his neck, allowing Adrian to hold eye contact with Caleb who was holding himself through his pants.

Mila slightly tightened her grip and Adrian let out a light moan. In turn, Caleb reached for his belt buckle and Adrian's gaze sharpened.

"Don't do it," Adrian warned.

Mila turned her head just in time to see a let down Caleb move his hand from his belt buckle and she gave him a taunting smirk. She was deeply turned on by the way in which Adrian spoke to Caleb and could feel his dick was pulsing in her hand.

Adrian's hand made its way up Mila's skirt and he tried to put pressure against her pussy through her tights. It wasn't lost on her how he seemed more aggressive when they were in front of Caleb.

"Tell me," she muttered. "Would you fuck me on this desk right now... in front of him?"

Before he could answer, Mila felt way Adrian's body reacted to the question.

"Without question," he rasped.

Mila looked at Caleb, still holding her snide smirk and stopped stroking Adrian. She pulled Adrian in for one last deep kiss before buttoning his pants back up and pulling herself away. Her eyes drifted down to Caleb's severely strained pants.

"You sure you're not bothered?"

EPISODE 35

More Forward

Justin was at one of his favorite restaurants in Los Angeles on the final day of his business trip. He didn't plan on having this dinner alone, but thanks to his business partners, he was forced to travel solo for his series of meetings in the city.

"Did you enjoy your dinner, Mr. Matsuda?" the waitress questioned as Justin looked over the bill. "We were sorry to hear that the other party you had planned to join you couldn't make it, but we hope that you still had a positive experience at our restaurant."

Justin nodded. "Yes, it's a shame that I wasn't able to surprise her the way I wanted to. But she had to stay back in Lenrod City due to work commitments. However..." He wrote a sizable tip on his two-hundred dollar tab and handed it back to the waitress. "The food was delicious and the view of the ocean was great. Either way, I wasn't going to miss out on this private dining experience."

"Thank you very much, Mr. Matsuda! We hope to see you again next time you're in Los Angeles and hopefully the lucky lady can join you."

"I hope so, too."

After the waitress left, Justin finished the last sip of his wine and ordered an Uber to go back to his hotel. Slightly wine-drunk, he slouched in his seat and closed his eyes. It was his final night in Los Angeles and he'd planned to bring Mila on the trip with him. However, Caleb and Adrian objected to the idea, saying Justin didn't have a strong enough argument to deprive them of an assistant for close to a week.

Had Mila joined him on the business trip, she would've been his date that night. He rented out the patio of one of his favorite seafood spots that had a perfect view of the ocean. Justin wanted to take Mila out on a proper date and saw it as a natural next move, especially given the way she'd been teasing him for weeks. From their first kiss, to that night she touched herself in his office while laying under him, to the smaller games she played whenever they were alone together, Mila ignited something in Justin and he wanted more. Although his plans to take her out in Los Angeles fell through, Justin was still set on making it clear to Mila that he wanted her.

Once he arrived at his hotel, Justin stripped down to his briefs and paced around his room scrolling his phone.

"Is it weird that I miss her?" he muttered to himself. "It's only been a few days and I'll see her tomorrow, but I've been wanting to video call her since I first got here." His thumb hovered over Mila's contact before he huffed his frustration and closed out of his contacts app. Justin then began browsing online for flower shops in Lenrod City.

"I should've done this days ago. I can send her flowers..." Justin sought to show Mila that he wanted more than just the heavy flirtation and teasings that occurred between them in the privacy of his office.

"Alright, so I remember Mila saying that she hates roses..." he pondered out loud. "And her favorite flowers are lilies. But it's not the season for them. Hm... I'm sure that florists probably use greenhouses or whatever, right?"

Justin eventually found himself in the couch of his hotel room as he browsed the internet, doing research on the process of growing lilies and looking for shops in Lenrod City where they'd be available. Finally, he ordered a bouquet of lilies online to have them sent to Mila's desk in time for her morning arrival to the office.

"I'll keep them anonymous, and then when I'm back in Lenrod City and see her tomorrow afternoon, I'll ask her if she liked them."

Justin swung his legs onto the couch and lay on his back with his hands behind his head as he continued to think about Mila.

"Maybe it's time for me to be more forward with her."

"So. Fuck-ing. Good," Mila moaned, her syllables punctuated by the way her body jerked each time Adrian thrusted into her. Both of them on their knees on the bed, Adrian's arms were wrapped around Mila's body, one hand holding her stomach and the other holding her breast. Grunting with each stroke, Adrian kissed and sucked Mila's neck between his own sounds.

"Oh shit. I... I'm gonna come."

Mila reached back to tangle her fingers in his hair with a tight grip. "Hold it."

Adrian attempted to do so as he kept going, but he strokes naturally eased to avoid coming too soon. Mila gently pushed him off of her so that Adrian could lay on his back and she got on top. She started by teasing him, rubbing her soaking pussy against his dick before holding it and rubbing her clit with the tip.

Mila continued just like that until she was on the edge of her release and slipped Adrian inside of her again. She threw her head back with a soft moan as she rocked her hips and Adrian lifted himself up to take one of her nipples into his mouth and grab two handfuls of her ass to guide her movements.

Her fingers found their way into Adrian's hair again and she pulled his head back to take his lips with hers while Mila started bouncing up and down his length. His moans were muffled against her mouth and she let him go just in time to hear his outburst when he met his release, the sound of Mila's name rolling off Adrian's tongue naturally.

Both of them out of breath, they collapsed side-by-side in bed, breathing heavy. Mila went to the bathroom and when she returned, she lay in bed next to Adrian and rested her head on his chest as he held her.

"This is our second day in a row leaving the office at the same time. Do you think people will start talking?" Adrian asked.

"Considering yesterday was because of a meeting, I wouldn't count it," Mila assured. "And either way, I'm sure we're fine as long as it's not an everyday thing."

"You're right," Adrian agreed. "Plus, we can always stagger our arrivals."

"Exactly."

There was a long pause of silence between them—Adrian staring up at the ceiling, still in awe at his past two days with Mila in and out of the office, and Mila with her eyes closed, enjoying the peace of the moment.

Finally, Mila was the first to speak. "So... We *still* haven't talked about what happened in your office today. Caleb was into it... and so were you."

Adrian's jaw tensed as he mulled over Mila's words. "Does it bother you?"

"Is that a serious question?" Mila propped her head up on Adrian's chest to look him in the eyes. "Am I not the one who started it?"

"How'd you know?"

"Know what? That you'd be down for it?"

Adrian nodded. "Yeah."

"I wasn't *completely* sure. You try to hide it, but I know you have a jealous streak, Adrian. However... There's something between you and Caleb. A mix of *tension* tension and sexual tension. Do you want to tell me about that?"

"You're a bit *too* good a reading people. Are you sure you're not psychic?"

"If I was, you think I'd be working at PMC Group?"

Adrian let out a low chuckle and caressed Mila's back. "Caleb and I do have... *history*. But it wasn't anything serious. We just messed around for a bit in the past."

"How long was 'a bit'?"

"A few months at a time for a few years. But things just didn't work out."

"Why not?" Mila questioned.

"I don't want to get into it..."

"Fair enough."

~

"Good morning, may I help you?" Mila asked the deliveryman who'd arrived on the twenty-third floor at PMC Group's offices early that morning. When she got a call from the reception that there was a flower delivery, for a split second, Mila worried that Eric may have somehow found out about her working there. However, watching the man approach with the flowers, she took a breath of relief when she saw that it was a bouquet of lilies, knowing that there was no chance it was Eric.

"Good morning," the man greeted. "I have a delivery for Ms. Mila Nelson."

"That's me." Mila's brows pulled together as she reached out and accepted the bouquet. She examined it curiously, looking for a card, but there wasn't one there. "Did it come with a message or anything?"

"No, ma'am. It looks like you have a secret admirer."

Mila scoffed. "Secret admirer? Am I a sixteen-year-old in the eighties? I guess whoever it is gets points for at least sending my favorite flowers. Thanks."

The deliveryman snickered and shook his head. "Have a good day, ma'am."

"Same to you."

After he left, Mila sat the bouquet of lilies on her desk and turned her attention back to her computer. About twenty minutes went by and Adrian arrived to the office. As he approached, his eyes went straight to the flowers on Mila's desk. He knew that lilies were her favorite. Considering he left Mila's place late that night and that there was no way to get out-of-season flowers *easily* so early in the morning on a weekday, Adrian concluded that they were a gift from someone else, rather than Mila having bought them herself.

"Where'd the flowers come from?" he asked when he made it to Mila's desk.

"Good morning to you too," Mila replied sarcastically. "And they were delivered this morning, like fifteen or twenty minutes ago. They were addressed to me, but it doesn't say who they're from."

"Oh, okay..." Adrian's nostrils flared as he released a deep breath and his eyes remained on the bouquet. He wondered who may have sent them to Mila—whether it was Caleb, Justin, or someone else in Mila's life with whom she may have had some romantic connection. Although Adrian had assured Mila that he wouldn't expect them to be exclusive, he still didn't like the idea of someone else romancing her.

Mila rested her head in her palm and looked up at Adrian who seemed to be in deep thought. "Is there anything else I can help you with?"

Adrian cleared his throat and his eyes met Mila's. "Yeah, I actually wanted to see if you'd want to um..." He leaned forward toward her and lowered his voice. "Do you want to come to my place tonight?"

"I'll think about it," Mila replied with a wink and Adrian gave her a small smile. "Have a nice day, Adrian."

"You too, Ms. Mila."

Not long after Adrian went into his office, Caleb arrived. His eyes were also intent on the bouquet on Mila's desk. Assuming that Adrian got them for her, Caleb simply huffed his annoyance, passed by her without saying a word, and went straight to his office.

Mila let out an entertained scoff at Caleb before turning her own attention to the flowers on her desk, wondering who may have been the sender.

So, it wasn't Adrian. Definitely not Caleb. And does Justin even know I like lilies? He's clueless half the time, so even if I did mention it, I doubt he'd pay attention since it wasn't business or sex-related. Considering they're not roses, it wouldn't be Eric... Could they be from that maintenance guy downstairs I was flirting with? Nah. He definitely wasn't the romantic type... Whatever, it'll come to light eventually.

As the day dragged on, Mila was bored out of her mind. Neither Adrian nor Caleb had meetings and were locked up in their respective offices focused on work. She couldn't take a full lunch break because she had a mountain of pending tasks herself. And the office itself was quiet as many colleagues were away for a conference.

"Only two-fifteen?" Mila muttered to herself sharply. "Why is today so long?" *And now I'm having sex flashbacks,* her ramblings turned internal. *Yeah, I'm definitely going to Adrian's tonight. In fact, maybe I'll see if he's down for a quickie right n-*

"Hey, Mila!" Justin greeted, interrupting her thoughts as he walked into PMC Group's offices. "How are you?"

"Oh yeah, I forgot you were coming back today... How was your trip, Mr. Matsuda?"

"Eh, it could've been better."

Mila noticed that like Adrian and Caleb, Justin's gaze was focused on the flowers on her desk as he approached.

"Before you ask, no, I don't know where they came from," she said dryly.

"Oh, I was actually going to ask if you could come with me to my office... Please?"

"You don't want to get settle first? Did you come here straight from the airport?"

"Yes." Justin nodded. "And it's fine. I just wanted to hit the ground running now that I'm back."

"If you say so," Mila sighed before getting up with her tablet and following Justin into his office.

Once the two of them got inside, Justin wasted no time in asking Mila what he'd been waiting to ask since the night before.

"Did you like the flowers, Mila?"

"Hm?" Mila hummed inquisitively as she sat in the chair in front of his desk. "I mean yeah, I'm just trying to figure out who sent them."

"It was me. Lilies are you favorite, right? I didn't want to put my name on them just in case someone else from the office intercepted them before you."

Mila's lips teased a smile and she tilted her head to the side. "How'd you know lilies are my favorite?"

"Well, you mentioned it one time. It was passive, but I remember you saying it a few months ago when we saw some flower arrangements at a meeting venue."

"Wow," Mila huffed softly. "I didn't call that one."

Justin walked over to stand in front of Mila and leaned against his desk. He'd pulled up his sleeves so that his arms were partially exposed and crossed them over his broad chest. "So, does that mean you're impressed?"

"Surprised does not mean impressed, Mr. Matsuda."

"I'll take it to mean you're impressed."

"Someone's getting cheeky," Mila teased. "You're generally aloof, so

I'm surprised that you remembered me saying anything like that so passively."

"I remember most of what you say, Mila. I like listening to you."

"Is that so?" Mila leaned back in her seat while she crossed her legs. "Now, I'm curious about what other trivia you have on me."

"Where do I begin? You like your coffee blonde roast with a dash of almond milk, unless you're just going for a treat, and then you prefer a flavored latte. When you're annoyed, your nose twitches and you cut your eyes to the right. You coordinate your outfits with whichever nail color you choose for the week. Your Japanese is already perfect, but after a few drinks, the regional accent comes out and you sound like a total native."

Mila maintained a neutral expression, but she was impressed that Justin had retained so much information about her. She assumed that he was more concerned with himself or their more flirtatious encounters, but the fact that he was able to give observations on even her most mundane preferences proved her wrong.

Justin continued. "You're a domineering woman, both in business and in pleasure. You enjoy being praised and you're able to easily coax it out of anyone. You like to tease because reactions turn you on, especially when you're the one controlling them. And there's something I've been wanting to ask you..." Justin leaned forward and braced himself on the arms of Mila's chair to get close enough to whisper to her.

"Oh, so you're getting *very* cheeky today. Go ahead, ask," Mila replied. It was her first time witnessing Justin being so forward and she couldn't deny that she liked it. She remained in her spot, waiting to see how far he would go. She felt his lips lightly brush her ear before he continued.

"I want to show you the praise that *every inch* of you deserves. Will you let me?"

His deeply toned whisper, the feeling of his breath against her ear, and conviction with which he spoke, caused heat to rush to Mila's core.

"Justin," she said softly turning her head to the side toward him. "Don't start something that you can't finish."

In turn, Justin turned his head and their lips lightly brushed each other. "I'm more than prepared to finish." He pulled away just enough to hold Mila's gaze. "... As many times as you want."

Mila scanned his face and was met with pure confidence that she'd previously only saw from Justin when they were in business meetings. Her eyes darted down to his lips before the acrylic nail of her index finger grazed under his chin and Justin took that as his signal to close the distance between them.

Holding each other's faces, Mila and Justin were in an intense kiss. It was unlike any other that they'd share before—there was no sign that Mila was teasing him and one of Justin's hands had wandered down to the front of her pants, cupping her core without being rejected.

The pair were so distracted that they didn't realize the sound of the door opening, but they immediately pulled away from each other at the sound of its slamming shut and the familiar voice that followed.

"What the fuck are two you doing?"

EPISODE 36

Yikes!

Adrian sat at his desk, unable to focus on work. He was scrolling through the Tiffany & Co. website looking for bracelets for Mila. After seeing the lilies sitting on her desk, he determined that whomever sent them knew that they were Mila's favorite flowers and considering they were out of season, it likely took more effort than a simple online order to get them sent to her.

He also realized that other than a bottle of wine and some soup, he'd never given Mila an actual gift. Adrian knew based on her apartment, the way she dressed, and how she carried herself that she was a woman with expensive taste. And he wanted to be sure to get her something that would leave an impression.

"Does she prefer rose gold or just gold," Adrian pondered to himself out loud. "I think she'll like this bangle. It's simple, yet elegant, and it's close to ten grand... I mean, I don't think she's a gold digger or anything, but maybe she'll look it up and see how much money I spent and be impressed."

He ran his fingers through his short brown hair and leaned back in his seat. "Or maybe I should do something that takes more effort, like what I did with the soup. She seemed really impressed that I cooked it from scratch. I could do something with my own hands, maybe making her a piece of furniture."

Adrian's computer chimed with a new email. It was from one of PMC Group's bankers confirming that the company was in good enough financial standing to pursue its next acquisition—the first company under Thompson Luxe Group it would aim to acquire.

Normally, he'd be ecstatic with the news, but he was too distracted with his musings of Mila. He didn't want to scare her with serious commitment, which was why he told her that it wouldn't be necessary for the time being. However, the idea of someone else—or even more than one person—pursuing her, slightly bothered him. Adrian knew he could be the jealous type, and he was trying his best not let it impact what he had going with Mila.

I wonder how long until she'd be willing to commit, he thought to himself.

Trying to return to his work, Adrian scrolled through more emails, and just when he thought he'd be able to concentrate, he heard shouting from Justin's office. He couldn't make out what was being said, but he knew that the other voice he heard was Caleb's. Looking out his open door, he also realized that Mila was missing from her desk.

I hope she's not in there with them.

Adrian slowly rose from his seat and made his way to Justin's office door.

"WHAT THE FUCK are two you doing?"

Justin was standing straight up, looking at Caleb apprehensively while Mila remained in the chair with her eyes closed and gripping the bridge of her nose.

"Ca-Caleb what are you..." Justin tried to speak through a shaky voice. "Why are you..."

"Why am I here?" Caleb finished for him. "Because I'm tired of you and Adrian having closed door meetings with the assistant after what we talked about."

Caleb turned to glare at the back of Mila's head as she kept her position. "So..." he continued. "You're fucking her too?"

"What do you mean 'too'?" replied an offended Justin. "And no, we're not having sex."

"Sure," Caleb snorted. "Did you know that she and Adrian are fucking?"

"What?" Justin looked down at Mila. "You're sleeping with Adrian."

Mila let out an exacerbated sigh and looked up at Justin. "Yes," she said curtly.

"Then why did you kiss me?"

Shaking her head, Mila cut her eyes at Caleb and then back at Justin. "Because, I'm a single woman and I can do what and *who* the f—"

She was interrupted by Adrian walking in.

"What the hell is going on here?" he questioned, closing the door behind him.

"Turns out that you're not the only one fucking the assistant," Caleb said matter-of-factly. "Don't feel so special now, do you?"

"I told you we're not having sex!" Justin countered.

"Then why the fuck did I walk in here and see the two of you having a definitely-about-to-fuck kiss? I'd bet you be doing her on the floor right now if I didn't interrupt."

"Why are you so obsessed with me, Mr. Peterson?" Mila asked casually. "You're constantly concerned with who I may or may not be fucking, you stalk me at my gym and record me working out, jack off to the video..."

"Shut up," Caleb said through gritted teeth.

Mila continued, anyway. "And then there are the times that you're humping my foot or sucking the heel. Oh! And let's not forget that night when you were on your knees in that office just down the hall counting—"

"Shut up!"

Mila's head jerked back at Caleb's outburst. "I'm just asking you a simple question, Mr. Peterson."

"You still didn't answer mine! What the fuck were you in Justin doing in here sucking face?"

"It sounds like you answered it yourself," Mila mumbled.

"What is this, Mila?" Adrian's voice was in total contrast to the exchanges that'd occurred between the others. His tone was soft with a hint of shakiness. "Y-you..." He swallowed hard. "And Justin? You were... You kissed? J-just now?"

Guilt came over Mila as she examined Adrian and she struggled to respond. If Adrian was anyone else, a simple 'yes' would've been her response, potentially followed by a reminder that she was single. But when it came to him, she had the urge to explain herself, and part of her wanted to apologize.

"Yes, Mila and I kissed just now," Justin confessed. "And we've had... *moments* over the past few weeks."

Adrian focused his glare to Mila, feeling a sharp pain in his chest and his eyes stung as they began to water. "What- Is it that you're just... just playing all of us? Huh? You like this game, Mila?"

"Hey," Justin interjected. "Don't get that tone with her. We haven't even had a chance to talk things out."

Mila finally stood from her seat to walk over and face Adrian with crossed arms. She'd never heard him take a tone like that with anyone other than Caleb and she was furious that was speaking to her like that.

Adrian's nostrils flared at Mila's lack of reaction. There he was, on the verge of tears, his voice cracking. Meanwhile, Mila simply approached, her arms crossed, and looked at him with a stone cold expression, devoid of any emotion.

Mila kept her breathing calm and steady. She felt the way her stomach was tying itself in knots at Adrian scolding her. She knew could've yelled back at him, engaged with the same energy he was giving her. However, if she did that, then Mila would have to accept the reality that Adrian was capable of bringing out as much in her. She wasn't the type to get into a shouting match with a sexual or romantic interest, and Adrian was the first to make her contemplate it.

"So, what is it, Mila? You like playing us? You like playing men in general don't you?" Adrian's tone went from heated to cold. "...or maybe you're just easy. Messing around with all three of your bosses... you open your mouth or legs for anyone who wants a taste, don't you? Desperate for any type of validation from any man..."

As soon as the words left his mouth, Adrian immediately regretted them. He saw a break in Mila's demeanor as her eyes went wide for a split second before turning neutral. She then nodded with pursed lips and looked him up and down.

"That's right..." she said calmly and turned to walk out of the room.

"No, wait! Mila!" Adrian sped over to grab her arm. Mila snatched it away and continued her path to the door. "I'm sorry, Mila. I was- I didn't mean—" His pleas unanswered, Adrian was met with the sound of the door shutting behind Mila.

"Oh shit," Caleb muttered.

"What the fuck, Adrian?" Justin spat.

"Shit!" Adrian shouted. "I didn't mean it, I was just..." He paused and rushed over to open the door to Justin's office so he could continue to pursue Mila. However, she wasn't at her desk. He looked over at the elevators to see one closing with her in it. Not wanting to make a scene in the office, he choose not to call out her and instead, rushed downstairs on his own.

When Adrian finally got to the first floor, he was too late. He ran outside to the street, hoping Mila might be waiting for an Uber or taxi, but again, she was nowhere to be found.

His shoulders slacked and tears brimming his eyes, Adrian swallowed the lump in his throat and turned back toward the building to return to his office.

"I am such a fuck up."

New Rules

After Mila left, Adrian, Justin, and Caleb relocated to Adrian's office. He was distraught, but tried keeping himself together as not to show Justin and Caleb that he was falling apart. However, the two men knew him well, and when he was hurt, it'd often result in him lashing out—and that was exactly what happened with Mila.

"Look…" Justin started, his eyes darting between Adrian and Caleb. "At this point, we have three choices: Fire the best assistant we've ever had. Continue to make these 'rules' that none of us are sticking to. Or… we can give up on the rules and let things play out on their own. My vote is with the last option."

Caleb scoffed and shook his head. "Yeah, of course that's your vote. You were just about to fuck her. Why ruin your progress now, right?"

"Could you stop being so vulgar about it? And no, we weren't… There was something else I wanted to do first."

"What the fuck was it you were gonna do first?" Adrian replied sharply, glaring at Justin. "By the way, stop assuming you and Mila were going to do anything."

"Oh, they were *definitely* about to do something…" Caleb said with a snicker. "Shit, they were doing something when I walked in."

Justin's gaze remained on Adrian as he stood with his head held high. "I want to take Mila out... for like, a lunch... or dinner."

"... and then fuck her," Caleb finished mockingly.

"Shut up," Adrian spat before he stubbornly crossed his arms "I think we should stick with the rules... None of us should have relations with Mila."

"Bullshit," Caleb countered. "You're just suggesting that because you know that Mila probably won't want shit else to do with you and you don't want either of us taking your spot. You've been waiting to fuck her for like a year, right? You finally do and then you ruin it after two d—"

Caleb was cut off when Adrian grabbed him by his collar. "Shut the fuck up," Adrian snapped.

"See, this is what got you in trouble in the first place," Caleb taunted. "You and that fucking temper. You were good at hiding it for so long, but now Mila got a look at the *real* you, and she doesn't like it."

"I told you to shut the fuck up."

"Adrian, please. You're the loudest one in this room right now," Justin reasoned. "We don't want the staff to hear this ruckus."

Adrian's jaw tensed as let out a long breath through his nose and released Caleb's collar before slowly backing away.

Caleb straightened up his shirt and looked at Adrian with a snide expression. "It's been some time since the *real* Adrian came out. I guess now that you've gotten in Mila's pants, you're finally able to let go of the nice guy act."

"You're just jealous because all you get is her fucking foot," Adrian seethed. "You saw how I touched her, how I kissed her? And how she touched *me*, how she kissed *me*? I bet you jack off at the thought of it. Those thoughts and her foot are all you'll fucking get."

"And I bet that foot is a lot more than you'll be getting after the shit you said to her today... Oh, and haven't you thought about it? First it's the foot, the calf, the thigh... Then boom! I am balls deep in her pussy."

"Not a fucking chance," Adrian retorted. "You're just a plaything for her- oh wait, I almost forgot... You're into that."

"Adrian, you're being a real dick right now, you know that?" Justin commented. "I know you're upset about what went down with Mila, but this is exactly why she's probably *very* pissed at you."

Taking a deep breath accompanied by flared nostrils, Adrian fell into the couch and lay on his back. He swallowed hard and closed his eyes. "Final vote... Caleb?" he said softly.

"Like you said... Being a plaything is my *thing*," he mocked. "So I'm with Justin. Let's just let shit play out."

"Well," Justin sighed. "There it is, we'll let the pieces fall where they may."

"Fine." Adrian remained laying in his couch with his eyes closed. "Now, get the fuck out of my office."

MILA PACED BACK and forth in her living room on the phone with her friend Naomi Laurent. What she experienced after Adrian's comments was unlike anything she'd ever felt before. Despite being in her late-twenties and with plenty experience dating, Mila never fell for anyone in the way that she fell for Adrian. And she didn't understand how she could've been on cloud nine just that morning with him in her bed, only to be crying over him that evening.

"I don't like this, Naomi," Mila said with a wince. "Is this what heartbre- No, I mean... Is this what it feels like when someone you um... like... hurts your feelings? Now, I understand why you gave up on dating when were in college!" she exclaimed. "I've never felt like this... My fucking chest physically hurts! And this fucking lump in my throat won't go away... And I'm... I'm... there are tears, Naomi. They won't stop!"

"I am so sorry, girl," Naomi replied. "You didn't deserve that. I can't believe boss A would say something like to you. He sounded so sweet."

Mila used code names when she spoke with Naomi about her bosses, only using the first letter of each of their first names.

"He is sweet. I mean, I suspected he had a temper, but for me to be on the receiving end of said temper? Especially when we've only been sleeping together for two days? I can admit that it probably hurt him more to find out that I've been messing around with his two business partners and best friends, but he knew that we'd kissed before!"

Naomi continued to listen from the other side of the phone.

"I'm a single woman, Naomi," Mila continued. "He knew that. He went too far with what he said, and he was so cold about it... He also said it in front of bosses C and J! The shit felt degrading!"

"Has he at least tried to apologize?"

"Yeah, right after he said it he tried, but I ignored that shit. And he's texted me like five times and even called... So I blocked his number. If he lashes out like that, then I don't want him to have access to me."

"What do you mean?" Naomi asked.

"I mean, this shit does not feel good. And you see how fast it went downhill? This morning was great and now I'm crying over this man! Naomi... what the fuck did I get myself into? Catching feelings felt good and now I'm regretting it. I didn't realize that your heart can literally, physically hurt. I thought that shit was figurative!"

For the first time ever, someone was capable of breaking Mila's heart. It was a vulnerability she'd never known before. And Mila saw it as a weakness she needed to fix.

Immediately.

"Boss A isn't going to have access to me in any capacity other than being my boss," Mila explained. "And my interactions with him can all happen over the work phone or email and be work-related only. From now on, he's completely cut off."

"Mila, are you sure about that?" Naomi questioned. "What he said was absolutely messed up and way out of line, but don't you want to talk to him about it before making such a big decision? I mean, you really like him, Mila. I've never seen you like this about anyone before."

"Liked!" Mila corrected. "Because that's over now. I usually ignore people who try to slut shame because they're usually mad that I don't want them or they're pick-mes who wish they could fuck as freely as I do. But for someone I actually like- er *liked* to say something like that to me? No, never again."

"Mila..."

"My decision is made, Naomi," replied a stubborn Mila. "Boss A will be simply that—boss A... Anyway, I need to go. Thank you for letting me vent to you. I love you, girl."

"Love you too, girl."

After hanging up, Mila poured a glass of wine and started running a hot bath.

"Fuck feelings," she whispered to herself.

EPISODE 38

The Plan, Mila

Sitting at her desk, Mila had a reinvigorated sense of determination to bring down PMC Group. She'd already been there for over a year—significantly longer than she originally planned, but the fun she was having with playing her three 'bosses' helped the time fly by. However, following the exchange with Adrian, Mila was brought back to reality. Despite the tension with Adrian, she had unprecedented trust with PMC Group, and now was more prime than ever to start taking them down.

I am going to be on some spy shit from now on, Mila thought to herself as she toyed with the thumb drive in her hand. *From here on out, anything I do with them will be for myself or my family's business.*

After tucking the thumb drive into her bra, Mila pulled out her phone and looked at the texts she'd exchanged with her sister Alexis the night before.

MILA

Hey, Lexi... You remember that thing you proposed like a month ago that I rejected?

ALEXIS

You mean when you laughed in my face,
asked if I thought I was 'the CIA or some
shit' and went on to roast me about being
such a 'hard ass'? 😒 Yeah. I remember.

MILA

But did I lie, tho? Anyway, I wanna give it a
try. Can you drop off that thing tonight?

ALEXIS

It is 11PM...

MILA

Okay? So pay someone to drop it off. It's not
like you're doing anything else for this
'mission'.

ALEXIS

I'm starting to wonder if you're doing
anything yourself. It's been over a year and
the intel you got hasn't been enough to take
them down. And they like you a bit too
much. They offered you a job? I had to pull
strings with my friend at the temp agency to
help you maintain that status.

MILA

Fine. How about you pretend to be an
assistant to these three assholes while trying
to covertly bring down their over-billion-
dollar business without endangering our
fam's business?

ALEXIS

Delete that text right now! And fine... I'll
have it dropped off at your place. You know
how to use it, right?

MILA

I just stick it in a hole, right? Don't you know
I'm a pro at that?

ALEXIS

Yeah. And I'm starting to think you're showing those bosses your skills at that considering how long you've been there… Anyway, it has to be one of their computers. And it needs to stay there for THREE MINUTES.

MILA

stfu. Just send my shit. 🙄

ALEXIS

Surely. And remember… THREE MINUTES.

When Mila heard the elevator bell, she quickly put her phone away and turned her attention to the computer screen to appear busy.

Adrian arrived to the office early that morning, hoping that Mila would be coming into work soon. After his outburst the day before, he tried calling and texting her, but his efforts were all ignored. He'd barely gotten any sleep the night before and Adrian resisted the urge to show up at Mila's apartment.

His heart fluttered and his stomach turned with his nerves when he saw Mila sitting at her desk. Her appearance was as if none of what occurred yesterday actually happened. Her face was perfectly made up, as usual. Her eyes weren't swollen like Adrian's were and she was in deep focus looking at her computer.

Unsure if that were a good or bad sign, Adrian tried his best to be optimistic when he approached Mila, hoping that it meant she was no longer upset about what he said to her.

"Hi Mila," he greeted. "G-good morning… M-may you um… Could you come to my of-office?"

"I've emailed you your schedule for the day, Mr. Collins," Mila replied dryly without removing her eyes from the computer.

"Mila, please… I want to ap- I want to apologize for yesterday, it was totally out of line and—"

"Hey Mila!" Shannon chimed, interrupting Adrian as she walked over to Mila's desk. "Are you ready for our coffee?" She turned to look at

Adrian who still had his eyes on Mila with a somber expression. "Oh! Sorry, Mr. Collins. Did I interrupt something here—"

"Nope!" Mila interjected, finally turning her gaze away from her computer and looking at Shannon. "I was just telling Mr. Collins that I sent him his schedule. I wanted to make sure to keep my morning open for our coffee. Thanks for coming in early!" She rose from her seat with a smile and pulled her wallet from her purse.

Adrian felt a sharp pain shoot through his chest when he saw how cheerful Mila was speaking to Shannon—in total contrast to her dry, disinterested demeanor when she spoke to him. He looked on as Mila walked away from him as if he weren't even standing there. And that was when he knew that things between them had officially changed.

As the day went on, Adrian couldn't pay attention to his work. With each minute that passed, he was hoping to hear from Mila. Whenever his phone rang, he heard a knock on his door, or he received a notification of an email or text, Adrian grew more anxious each time that it wasn't Mila. He took a deep breath and massaged his temples before reaching out toward the phone on his desk and dialing Mila's extension.

"Mr. Collins?"

Adrian's heart jumped into his throat. "Mila! You answered— er, I'm glad you answered! Mila, please I want to ap—"

"How may I help you, Mr. Collins?" Again, Mila's tone was detached, as if she weren't listening to anything he was saying.

"Mila... please," Adrian said softly. "I want to apol—"

"Mr. Collins, if this isn't work related, I am going to hang up."

"Wait!" Adrian hesitated as he tried to figure out a way to keep Mila on the phone. "I do need something for work, I um... I... I actually just got an email from some of our bankers who wanted to set up an urgent meeting. There'll be several of us on the phone and I could use help with note taking... and you're the best at it."

"There's no need for that, Mr. Collins," Mila replied casually. "One of the interns from the finance department told me that he's been wanting more exposure to see what his dream job is like. So, he'll be attending all of your meetings from now on."

"No. I said that I need you to take notes because you're the best at it, Mila. I can't risk having an intern mess this up."

"The intern will do a great job, I'm sure. His learning opportunities should not suffer because of your... *preferences.* I'll send him in shortly." Mila hung up the phone before Adrian could protest further.

Mila then called Greg, the finance intern, and sent him into Adrian's office. Not long after that, Justin came to her desk with a cheerful smile.

"Hey Mila," he called as he waved. "Are you ready for that lunch?"

With a small, closed-lip smile, Mila nodded as she picked up her purse and followed him to the elevator. Justin had texted her the night before about lunch. He apologized for the way things unfolded the day before and said that he wanted to take her on a proper outing. So, he carved out an hour in his schedule to take her to lunch at one of his favorite spots near the office. On the outside, it would look like a normal lunch meeting—similar to what Mila and Adrian had done a few times, but in reality, Justin saw it as a date.

Standing across from her in the elevator, Justin looked over at Mila, analyzing her face for any signs of uneasiness, but there were none. She looked the way she normally looked—unbothered.

A smirk pulled at Mila's lips when she saw the way Justin was looking at her so intently, though he hadn't said anything.

"Don't tell me you're nervous," she said. "You seemed pretty confident yesterday. I've never seen you so forward before. In fact, I did not expect that from you."

"I am a man full of surprises," he replied.

Mila let out an entertained scoff and shook her head. "We love a good cliche. Don't we, Mr. Matsuda?"

"What happened to you calling me 'Justin'?"

"Different names for different spaces, hon."

Justin's head jerked back and a quick breath crossed his nose when he heard the term. "'Hon'?" He walked over to Mila in the elevator and caged her between his arms as his face moved in closer to hers. "As in short for 'honey'? I like it," he whispered.

With a snide expression, Mila pressed her hand against his chest and pushed him away just in time for the elevator door to open.

"I knew you would."

Lunch between Mila and Justin flew by and the pair were enjoying a post-meal coffee at their table. She was at ease and their date helped her forget about the underlying pain she still felt from Adrian's words the day before.

"No almond milk today?" Justin questioned.

"Nope." Mila took a packet of sugar and held it up between her fingers. "Just a sugar this time... I'm impressed that you noticed so much about my preferences. You came off as the oblivious type."

"I wish," Justin sighed, looking down at his coffee as he stirred creamer into it. "I'm just damn good at making it seem like I am. It's easier that way."

"What do you mean?"

"Well... When we're talking business, sometimes the best negotiation tactic is letting the other party assume they're outsmarting you. Let them think they're steering and they won't even notice that you're the one who's pulling the strings."

"I see..." Mila gave him an impressed nod with pursed lips.

"Also... Sometimes, it's easier when I pretend not to know something..."

"Go on."

There were several moments of hesitation before Justin finally explained.

"It's the closest I can get to putting myself, to putting my life on auto-pilot. When you're oblivious—even when you're just pretending to be—you don't have to think about everything that endangers the expectations set on you... Like with Ashley... I knew she was with someone else, but it was easier for me to pretend she wasn't. It helped me ignore that our relationship was failing.

"But I still ended up breaking things off with her," Justin continued. "That was my first step in realizing that maybe the oblivious act doesn't work for *all* parts of my life."

"You think?" Mila questioned with a playful sarcasm.

"Hey, in my defense, it was going pretty well... But then I met you."

Please don't let this be some type of romantic confession, Mila thought to herself. *I've had enough of that this week.*

"I just mean that you opened my eyes, Mila," Justin clarified when he noticed the concern on her face. "You helped me realize that being honest with myself isn't just about *myself*. I was holding Ashley back just as much as I was holding myself back. So, thank you for helping me realize that, Mila."

Mila shrugged casually and leaned back in her seat. "What can I say. It's a gift."

"*You're* a gift."

Mila bursted out laughing and Justin followed.

"Okay, okay," he said through his chuckles. "That was a lot smoother in my head."

"I imagine so," Mila replied, still giggling. "I know you're trying... You know, so you can show me the praise that 'every inch' of me deserves," she added mockingly.

"Hey! I was proud of that line! I'm trying to be more forward with you."

"And I'm enjoying the effort, hon."

Again, when Mila called him 'hon', a sharp breath crossed Justin's nose. Something about the nickname, knowing she'd given it to him, felt pleasing to Justin. And he wanted to hear her calling him that more frequently.

"Mila, I also want to clarify that even with what I said yesterday... I enjoy our times when we're like this too... I mean, I just want to say that I don't only—"

"Don't make it weird," Mila interrupted. Her phone chimed and she looked down to see an email from Caleb. "It looks like Mr. Peterson needs me back in the office."

"You don't have to go if you don't want to."

"Actually... I do."

THREE Minutes

Mila returned to PMC Group with Justin and looked at her phone for the first time since they left. She saw a message from Alexis and immediately rolled her eyes at her sister's persistence.

ALEXIS

Remember: THREE MINUTES.

Mila shook her head as she deleted their entire chain and put down her phone. She then pulled the thumb drive from her bra, tucked it up her sleeve, and made her way to Caleb's office.

"I'm here for your meeting, Mr. Peterson."

"It's not for another fifteen minutes. And where the hell—" Caleb cleared his throat and straightened up. "I mean... Where were you?"

Slowly, Mila approached him. Over the past few weeks, he was becoming more well-behaved with her. She still disliked him and found him to be crude, but Caleb was nice to look at and Mila enjoyed degrading him.

"I was at lunch with Justin," she replied.

"Oh," Caleb scoffed. "I guess that means you two f—" Caleb

corrected himself again when he saw Mila tilt her head, a challenge clear in her eyes. "I mean... What did you do?"

"Like I said, we went to lunch. That was all." Mila leaned against Caleb's side of his desk and looked down at him in the chair—it had become the typical routine when she was alone with him. Usually, she'd tease him and he instinctively opened his legs, expecting her put her foot where it often landed.

"Not today, pet..." Mila cut her eyes at his computer and saw it was unlocked. With her fingertips, she caressed his jaw until she reached his chin and held it gently. "I'm feeling generous today. Remind me. What is it you've been asking for these past few weeks?"

Caleb gulped as he looked up at her, holding her gaze. "To taste you again."

Mila nodded thoughtfully. "And you've been patient... So, how about I give you a little test to see how much you've learned about patience." She turned around so that her back was facing Caleb and he was blocked from seeing his computer.

"How does this test work?"

"Well, I'm going to give you three minutes with me in this position while you stay there. And you can do whatever you think it is that you're allowed to do. Do you understand?"

"Does this mean I can kiss you again?" Caleb asked softly.

"I'm not turning around and you have to remain in your chair. So... use your imagination." Mila leaned forward and slipped the thumb drive out of her sleeve before speaking to cover the minor sound of the thumb drive sticking into his computer. "Go ahead, pet."

Caleb didn't know where to begin as he stared at Mila from behind. She was wearing a long sleeve burgundy velvet dress that hugged her body and fell just above her knees, along with a pair of black pep-toe pumps. As badly as he wanted to get more from Mila, he didn't expect her to come into his office with such a 'test' that day.

He reached out and toyed with the hemline of her dress before reaching under it. The tights she wore were thigh highs and Caleb pulled her dress up over her wide hips to expose the black lace panties she was wearing.

"Two minutes, pet," Mila warned. "I'm surprised you hesitated for so long." Her eyes remained on the screen, staring at the small pop-up window as the spyware from the thumb drive uploaded to the computer.

Caleb let out a deep breath through his nose and leaned forward to place a gentle kiss against the back of her thigh and when she didn't push him away, he continued until his mouth worked its way to her ass. While kissing one cheek, Caleb used his other hand to grab the other and his pants grew increasingly tight. With her lack of objections to his groping, Caleb took the opportunity to spread Mila's cheeks apart so that her panties sunk between them, allowing him a better view of the shape of her pussy.

His mouth returned to her, now making its way closer to her core. When she felt his fingers hook into her panties as he tried to pull them to the side, Mila reached back to grab his hair and stop him.

"Don't fail it now. You've got a minute-and-a-half left."

Caleb's hand retreated back to spreading her cheeks apart and his lips worked their way inside. He heard her let out a slight moan when his tongue glided near her asshole. He took that as a sign that he could continue as long as her panties remained on.

"One minute left." Mila kept her eyes on the screen, trying to focus on the spyware loading.

Not wanting to waste anymore time, Caleb pressed his tongue against Mila's other entrance through her panties as he used his hands to keep her spread open for him while groping her ass.

"I knew you were nasty," Mila said, her voice soft and breathy. "It's the only reason I entertain you, pet."

Caleb hummed his agreement against her ass while his mouth worked more eagerly. Mila's eyes squeezed shut and she silently took a deep breath, not wanting to make more sounds that would show she was getting pleasure from him. His head started moving up and down as he put more pressure against Mila through her panties, trying earn more sounds from her. Finally, when Caleb's mouth started moving down, closer to Mila's pussy, she pushed his head away.

Looking up at Mila as she turned to face him after pulling her dress back down, Caleb licked his lips. "Did I pass?" he asked.

"Barely," Mila sighed casually. She walked over to the opposite side of the the desk to take her seat, getting in position for their meeting. "Anyway, who are we meeting with today?"

"It's a first call with the CEO of this boutique fashion line. They're owned by a company like ours called Thompson Luxe Group, but we're going to see if it's worth it to buy this shop from under them."

Shit, Mila thought to herself. *At least I put that software on his computer. And now I'll take thorough notes and share them with Alexis.*

"Oh, before we start this meeting, there's something else," Caleb explained. "I need you to come with me to Atlanta next week."

Mila furrowed her brows and her head pulled back. "Excuse me?"

"There's a conference for C-suite executives. And I need you to come with me to help me stay on track. There are a ton of events I'm set to participate in."

Raising a perfect brow at him and leaning back in her seat with her legs crossed, Mila examined Caleb for several moments before finally responding.

"Oh yeah, I remember booking your travel for that... I guess I can use it as an excuse to visit some friends down there."

"Great. Then after we get out of here, you can book your tickets?"

"Fine. But I have two conditions... I only fly first class. And my hotel room will be on the *opposite* side of the hotel from you."

Caleb's jaw tensed as he nodded.

"Deal."

~

"WHAT THE FUCK do you mean you're taking Mila to Atlanta?" Adrian snapped. He, Caleb, and Justin were sitting in his office as Caleb explained that he would be taking Mila with him to the conference in Atlanta.

"I need her to come with me to keep me organized because there's a fuck ton of events going on. She'll help me stay on track."

"That's a week-long fucking conference!" Justin replied. "You can't keep her from us for a week. She's has to keep us organized too. And don't we have people from our PR team going to help you?"

"Then just use another assistant. There are plenty in this office. And the PR team is for press stuff and shit. Mila is for scheduling and logistics."

"That's bullshit and you know it, Caleb."

"What?" Caleb raised both hands innocently. "I need her with me and it's normal to bring assistants when doing big conferences like this."

"Oh please." Adrian waved him off. "We know you're just taking her with you because you're trying to get her in bed."

"So? We agreed to let things unfold naturally, right? Still upset that *you're* the one at the bottom of the totem pole now? Have you even had a conversation with Mila since your little tantrum?"

"Shut up."

"Want me to tell you about the moment we had just a few hours ago? I got more than the foot this time." Caleb raised and lowered his eyebrows suggestively with a snide grin. "*A lot* more."

"I told you to shut up."

"Yeah, yeah…" Caleb waved Adrian off dismissively. "Anyway, Mila's coming with me."

Justin shook his head. "Adrian and I didn't agree to that."

"It's too late. We've all been able to tell that Mila has expensive taste. She told me she only flies first class, so I dropped a pretty penny on last minute tickets for her."

"First class is almost always refundable," Justin countered.

"Well, Mila already agreed to it. She said something about using it as a free trip to visit her friends. So, *you guys* can tell her that you removed her from the trip. See how she takes it that you fucked that up for her."

Silence fell over the room and both Adrian and Justin's arms were crossed, glaring at Caleb.

"Not hearing any objections now from my wonderful business partners, am I?"

Calebs taunting was met with silence and so he made his way to the door with a triumphant stride.

"Have a nice day, guys."

After the door closed behind Caleb, Adrian and Justin exchanged a look before Adrian finally broke the silence.

"Justin... the conference is for C-suite executives. Caleb isn't the only one."

Justin's face lit up as he nodded. "I'll book our tickets myself."

EPISODE 40

Down Bad

Mila and Caleb arrived to Atlanta late Sunday night, with the conference set to begin Monday morning. It would be a busy week for the participants, with networking events, roundtable discussions, fireside chats, and plenty of mixers.

Despite what Caleb told Mila, Justin, and Adrian, he didn't need Mila there. It was the job of PMC Group's communications department to handle all of Caleb's engagements. But he wanted to take advantage of the conference to have Mila to himself without Adrian or Justin interrupting. Because Caleb would be occupied with conference events, Mila was set to have most days to herself, but he planned to keep her busy every night of their trip.

Walking into the conference center on day one of the summit, Caleb, Mila, and two people from the PR team went to the front counter to collect their credentials. As they approached, they saw two familiar figures and Caleb clutched his hand into a fist.

"What the fuck are you two doing here?" he blurted when they reached Adrian and Justin.

"Mr. Collins and Mr. Matsuda," one of the PR assistants said. "We didn't have you down for going to this conference, otherwise, we would've brought more people from the team to support you. Which events are you planning to participate in? Do you have any press engagements?"

"Don't worry, Kayla," Adrian assured, a kind smile on his face. "We're only here for some networking opportunities and to watch a few events. We don't plan on doing any panels, interviews, or press at all."

"Adrian is right. And just a little secret between us, it gives us an excuse for a bit of a vacation," Justin added with an uncharacteristic wink. "Plus, we can support our wonderful CEO at the events he plans to speak at."

Caleb's face tightened with agitation. "Convenient for you, isn't it?" He'd already done the math in his head. There'd be plenty of time during the trip for Adrian or Justin to be alone with Mila without the probing eyes of their colleagues or the demands of the office. Meanwhile, Caleb would be in events he'd committed to most days and therefore unable to interrupt their time with Mila.

Mila looked at the three expressionless, though her thoughts were in total contrast. She was still hurt about what Adrian said to her, she was impressed at Justin's ongoing forwardness, and she was entertained at Caleb's reaction to the two men showing up.

Passing by the three as if they weren't there, Mila continued to the counter to receive her credentials before turning around to go right back out of the door.

"Wait, where are you going?" Adrian questioned and Mila ignored him.

"Mila, wait!" Justin called and she stopped to turn her attention to him.

"Yes, Mr. Matsuda?"

"I thought you'd be attending conference events?"

"Kind of," Mila replied with a shrug. "Mr. Peterson is going to be busy with events and I'm mostly here on email duty and to help with smaller meetings here and there. Other than that, the PR team will support him and he said that I'm free to do what I want during the day. And right now, I want to go back to my room and take a nap."

"Mila," Adrian reached out his hand toward her wrist and she pulled it to her side before he could connect. "May I take you get coffee?"

Again, ignoring Adrian, Mila kept her attention on Justin.

"Even though I thought it was only Mr. Peterson who I'd have to deal with, I *am* still technically here on assistant duties. Was there something you needed, Mr. Matsuda? If not, like I said, I am going to take a nap."

Justin looked at Adrian and then back at Mila. "No, I don't need anything. Adrian and I were planning to do some networking before one of the events this morning and then *another* networking lunch after that."

"Great. In that case, I will see you three later."

Mila continued on her path to leave the building and Adrian watched with a lump in his throat. His sulking was interrupted when Justin put his hand on Adrian's shoulder.

"Come on," Justin said as he gestured to the crowd. "We need to go inside."

THE ATLANTA TRIP felt more like a vacation for Mila. While the men were in and out of various conference events, she took her nap and then did some shopping in the city. Mila planned to meet with her friends Naomi and Gianni later in the week and took advantage of what she could of her alone time.

Returning to the hotel with her hands full of bags, Mila reached the fifteenth floor where her room was located and started walking toward her suite. As soon as she arrived at her door, she heard a familiar voice calling her name and froze in place as she cursed internally.

What the fuck, universe? Is this supposed to be a sign or some shit? Or are you, too, playing games with me?

Mila slowly turned her head to see Adrian coming out of a room just five doors down from hers.

"Mila," Adrian called again as he got closer to her. "Hey, is this your room? I thought sure you'd be on the same side of the hotel as Caleb..."

In response, Mila's gaze turned into a glare and Adrian quickly tried to recover.

"Er— No, I just meant that I thought you'd be closer to his room because you're probably booked as part of his party or, you know, because of assistant stuff or something?"

"No," Mila finally replied. "I specifically wanted to be on the opposite side—" She stopped herself, wondering why she was explaining anything to Adrian. Mila returned her attention to her keycard for the door to unlock it.

"Mila, wait... please. I just want to apologize. Can you let me do that? What I said was w—"

"I have to prepare for the mixer this evening, Mr. Collins," Mila interrupted, holding a business-like tone. "It's a networking event for luxury industry professionals that PMC Group is co-sponsoring with a few of the other companies whose executives are attending. Mr. Peterson wanted to be sure that myself and the two people from our comms department also attend. I'm assuming you and Mr. Matsuda will be there as well?"

"Y-yeah. Caleb actually just told us about it."

"Enjoy the mixer, Mr. Collins." And with that, Mila went into her room and shut the door behind her.

With slouched shoulders, Adrian returned to his own room, going straight to the minibar to pull out all the dark liquors available.

"I'm not sure if this is an opportunity or a big 'fuck you' from the universe," he said to himself. "What are the chances of our rooms being so close together? But she's also obviously still pissed at me. What can I do to make things better between us?"

For the next hour, Adrian drank all of the liquor from the minibar as he scrolled his phone aimlessly before getting a notification that the mixer would start soon. He got up, took a shower and made his way downstairs, already drunk and unable to walk straight.

By the time he arrived to the event hall on the first floor of the hotel where the mixer was being held, it was in full swing. Bar-height tables were scattered throughout the space while waiters walked around to serve hors d'oeuvres and a large square-shaped bar sat in the center of the room. That was Adrian's first stop and he went there to order more whiskey, despite his already drunken state.

As he awaited his drink, Adrian scanned over the room looking for Mila. When his eyes finally landed on her, she was standing at one of the tables with three other people who appeared to be more PR support staff for other executives.

Part of him was relieved that she wasn't with Justin or Caleb or some other man, but another part of him felt even more hurt. Seeing the way she was smiling and energetic while socializing with others reminded Adrian that she wasn't like that with him anymore, and he wasn't sure if she ever would be considering how cold she'd been since his outburst.

What Adrian had with Mila, even before they were intimate for the first time, was unlike anything he'd experienced before and he missed her desperately. He deeply regretted what he'd said her and had been cursing himself every day since.

Adrian tapped the side of his thumb against the bar, anxiously waiting on his drink and keeping his eyes on Mila. There was an empty spot right next to her that he planned to take as soon as he could. He then went to scan over the rest of the room to look for where Justin and Caleb might be.

While Justin was nowhere to be found, Caleb was on the other side of the bar and had his arm wrapped around a tall thin brunette. He had a flirtatious smile as he whispered something in her ear and she in turn giggled. Caleb was a charmer and he excelled at it, as he had since Adrian first met him in college. With perfectly-straight teeth, a dimpled smile, deep blue eyes, dirty blonde hair that always fell *just right*, and a jawline that fit the description of every love interest in a romance, Caleb's looks were often the root of his easy wins.

However, the sight of Caleb in that moment reminded Adrian of why he ended things between the two of them in the first place.

Such a player, he thought to himself. Adrian finally received his drink and just as he began approaching Mila's table, he noticed Justin behind her and saw that he was also walking toward the empty spot beside Mila and Adrian sped up so that he could get there before him.

"Hey Mila," Adrian said as he joined her at the table. Between the smell of alcohol on his breath and the slight slur of his speech, Mila figured that Adrian already had quite a bit to drink before getting there. Meanwhile, the others at the table looked at him awkwardly.

"Adrian," Justin greeted when he got to the table and he reached out to place his hand on Adrian's shoulder. "Glad you finally made it…" He tried to gently push him to the side, as Justin had been standing next to Mila before he ran to the bathroom, but Adrian shrugged Justin's hand off his shoulder.

"Yeah, it was a bit of a rough day, so I wasn't so sure if I was going to come out," Adrian replied before taking a large gulp of his drink.

Mila exchanged a look with Justin and scooted over to give him a bit more room to squeeze in between her in Adrian, but when Mila moved, so did Adrian. Once again, Justin reached out to put his hand on Adrian's shoulder, and Adrian immediately pushed him off. It was clear that he was drunk and his hostility toward Justin brought tension to the table.

"Right…" Mila turned her attention back to the others. "So what were we talking about again? That new docu-series on that one designer, right?"

As Mila went on talking to the others, Adrian was trying to decipher exactly what they were discussing so he could join. Continuing to sip on his drink, he grew more agitated as he felt left out of the conversation. He was also envious at the obvious chemistry between Mila and Justin as they seemed to work as a team talking up the other guests.

Finally, Adrian had enough and turned to Justin with an intense stare.

"Are you sleeping with her?" he whispered sharply.

Justin, who was taken aback by Adrian's question and tone, shook his head. "You've had too much to drink, man. Maybe you should go to your room."

"You didn't answer me. Are you sleeping with her?" Adrian's voice was still low, but had grown loud enough for Mila to hear.

Not wanting to make a scene in front of the others at the table, Justin grabbed Adrian's arm to lead him away, but Adrian snatched it and stood there stubbornly.

"Answer my question. Did you f—" Adrian was cut off when his arm was grabbed again, but this time, it was Mila and he went with her as she led him toward the door. Justin excused himself along with the pair and quickly followed Mila and Adrian to the hallway.

"Adrian, what's was that…?" Justin drifted off when he noticed that both Mila and Adrian seemed to be focused on what appeared to be a closet door just a few feet away from them. "What's going on?"

Neither Mila nor Adrian responded to him and as Justin got closer, he could hear a man's grunts and a woman moans along with the sound of furniture banging against a wall or door.

Finally, Mila shook her head and Adrian scoffed—both familiar with the sound coming from the other room.

"Definitely," Mila said.

"Yeah," Adrian agreed with a nod.

That was all Justin needed to put the pieces together and realize they were talking about Caleb.

"He such a slut," Adrian groaned, his speech still slurred. "I should ruin this shit for him."

When he started walking toward the closet door, both Mila and Justin grabbed each of his arms and pulled him back.

"We should get you to your room," Justin suggested. "You're not in your right mind."

Adrian yanked his arm out of Justin's hand, but allowed Mila to continue holding him. "Don't tell me what to do!"

"C'mon, Adrian," Mila sighed. "Let's go."

"Oh? Does this mean you'll finally hear out my apology? You've been ignoring me every time I try to say sorry."

"Justin, can you please help me with Adrian?" Mila continued as if Adrian weren't speaking. "And Adrian, please don't make a scene. People are already looking."

"Don't talk to me like I'm a child. I'm not reckless like Caleb," Adrian grumbled. "I won't embarrass us. I'm just trying to talk to you, Mila. I just want to apologize."

"Then why were you asking Justin if he slept with me?" Mila questioned with venom dripping from her tone as she and Justin led Adrian onto one of the elevators. "That doesn't sound like an apology."

"It wasn't like that, Mila..."

"Shut up, Adrian."

"You won't even let me say I'm sorry," Adrian said with a wince. "Why can't you hear me out?"

"You're drunk."

"I've been trying to tell you sorry even when I'm sober and you won't listen to me!"

Justin gently rubbed Adrian's back. "Calm down, man."

"Don't tell me to calm down!" Adrian protested as he pushed Justin away. "I bet this is great for you. Now you can make a move on her without me being in the way, huh?"

"Adrian, you need to chill," Mila said calmly. "You drank too much and you're getting belligerent."

"Why can't you just let me apologize?"

"Because you can't even do that right!" Mila snapped. "Now, let's go to your room. And stop giving Justin a hard time. All of this is *your* fault."

Adrian cowered back at Mila's tone and and finally calmed down to allow her and Justin to escort him to his room. With a pout on his face while he sat on the couch, Adrian watched Mila and Justin work together to get him settled.

"I'll get him some water and he should probably eat something," Mila said to Justin. "Can you run down to the mixer and grab some food?"

"Yeah, of course," Justin replied without hesitation and left the room to go downstairs.

"Sit up, Adrian," Mila instructed as she joined him on the couch.

Adrian did as he was told and sat up with his arms spread across the back of the couch, his right arm behind Mila. She held a cup of water up to him, but Adrian ignored it and continued his attempts to apologize to her.

"Mila, please..."

"Adrian, you're drunk and we shouldn't be doing this right now. Drink some water and eat whatever food Justin brings so you're not *too* sick in the morning."

He took the water from her hand and started sipping it as they sat in silence. It was the first time they'd been alone together without her pushing him away since he insulted her. Although she was still upset with him, Mila missed Adrian. She knew that he was hurting over her and that it was part of the reason he'd gotten so drunk that night. With their proximity and his arm already around her, Mila's head fell on Adrian's shoulder and he felt is heart flutter at the move.

"Mila, I'm—"

"Adrian, please..." Mila pleaded. "Let's just have this moment... In silence."

Adrian sighed his defeat and kept his arm around her while she continued to lean on him and he sipped his water. As time passed, the emotions Mila had been feeling surrounding Adrian began to well up and just when she was about to speak to him, Justin walked back into the room with a plate of food.

"Hey, I brought over some food for you, Adrian."

As Justin walked over, Mila reluctantly lifted her head off of Adrian's shoulder and he sat up to accept the food from Justin.

"Thanks... And sorry about earlier. I was out of line."

"It's cool," Justin assured.

Mila's eyes remained on Adrian as she stood up from the chair, concern clear in her face. Without thinking about it, she placed a hand on his cheek and gently kissed his forehead before stepping back to leave the room with Justin.

"Take care of yourself, Adrian."

"Thanks," Adrian muttered with tears brimming his eyes.

Once they got outside of Adrian's door, Justin turned to Mila and asked, "Are you okay?"

"Yeah, I'm fine. I just don't like seeing him like that."

"Me neither. Are you ever going to forgive him?"

Mila looked at Adrian's door and then back to Justin. "Maybe we shouldn't talk about it here," she whispered. "I'm just a few rooms down."

"Of course."

Tip

In the short walk to her room, Mila decided she didn't want to talk about Adrian anymore and would rather entertain herself with Justin. Once they got inside, Mila leaned against the dresser in the room and watched him as he entered slowly behind her and admired the space.

Justin took note of the flirtatious gleam in Mila's eyes, but tried to remain on topic. While he was deeply attracted to her, he also didn't want her assuming that he only wanted sex from her.

"So... about my question... do you think you'll forgive Adrian?"

Mila ground her teeth and let out a sigh through her nose. "Honestly? I *want* to forgive Adrian, but at the same time, it's difficult. I don't really understand what I'm..." she paused before going too far. "Actually, can we not talk about this?"

"Oh, um... of course." Justin scratched the back of his head and awkwardly looked around the room. His eyes lingered on Mila's bed before they returned to hers. "But you know you can talk to me, right? I know things are kind of weird between the three- er *four* of us, but I can tell what he said is bothering you. And I don't want you feeling like you need to hold it all in."

"I have other friends, hon," Mila replied. She pushed herself off the dresser and walked across the room, passing by Justin, to sit on the end of her bed.

"'*Other*'?" A toothy grin grew on Justin's face and he followed her to the bed and sat beside her. "So, you admit that we have a budding friendship here?"

"I mean, you've confided in me and I've *kind of* confided in you. Plus, you're not *as* annoying as you were a few months ago... Going as far as saying 'friend'? That's still TBD."

"Fair enough... You really thought I was annoying?"

"You were annoying as hell," Mila responded flatly. "First, you were a total dick until you found out that I speak Japanese and I could help you with business. *And then*, when I was like 'maybe Justin's tolerable' you had to go and get weird about your girlfriend."

"Oh geez... Here we go."

"You're the one who started this conversation about our 'budding' friendship," Mila teased. "Don't you remember how you'd talk to me about her? You were all like, *'Mila, you're domineering... I wish Ashley were domineering. Why won't she wear heels like you, Mila? I'll buy her some. Damn, why won't she just be more dominate? I want her to choke me, Mila.'*" As Mila went on mocking Justin, he couldn't help but laugh along with her. She had a more playful side that rarely came out, but she and Justin did occasionally exchange banter.

"For what it's worth, I didn't realize what I was doing at the time."

"Sureeeeee," Mila dragged out.

"Also..." Justin paused and analyzed Mila's face before continuing. "I don't really know much about this stuff."

"What do you mean by 'this stuff'?"

"I just mean that I've always been vanilla and haven't tried much. I mean, Ashley liked it when I dominated her, but I was never really into it. I like when a woman is the more dominant one... Or at least I think I do... I mean, I like the way you are... with me. And I want to explore more of it."

"You mean your sexuality?"

"No." Justin shook his head. "I know that I'm straight."

"Sexuality isn't just about whether or not you're 'straight'," Mila explained. "It's about knowing and understanding your likes and dislikes and how you navigate sex. It's not always about which genders you may or may not be attracted to."

"Oh! Well um... I guess that's the case for me. What we've done—even though it's been pretty subtle—is new to me, but I like it... and I want to learn more. I want to do more."

"What a way with words you have," Mila said sarcastically. While she could see that he was trying, Justin was not the smoothest talker, though something about that was endearing to Mila.

Justin couldn't read Mila well in that moment and he began to get nervous and started speaking rapidly "Look, I know I'm not the best at expressing what I want to say. But what I mean is that I'm an open-minded guy. And I like you... and your approach to things. I also want to make clear that I don't see you as an experiment or anything. I don't want you to interpret it that way. I'm an Asian man, and I see how the women in my family get fetishized so I don't want you thinking that I'm being that way with you or anything. I'm just saying all this based on our interactions. And I trust you too, so I wanted to put that out there. You know? Plus, I feel like the attraction is mutual, so why not—"

"That's enough," Mila interrupted. "You're talking a mile a minute. Just go with the flow, Justin. Not everything needs to be approached like a business transaction."

"Right! Yes, I understand, I just don't want you to think I don't respect you or I'm just using you."

"Okay. Can we talk about it another time, though? It's been a long day and I'm ready to relax." She yawned before reaching down to start undoing her heels.

Mila was wearing a pair of five-inch, closed-toe black pumps that had a platform and a strap around the ankles. They were the only shoes that Justin noticed Mila repeated frequently. He watched her closely, as if she were moving in slow motion, and by the time she touched the ankle strap and was fiddling with it, Justin grabbed her wrist to stop her.

She looked up to meet his eyes with a raised brow.

"Can I take them off for you?"

Mila's lips pulled at the sides and she leaned back with her hands flat behind her on the bed. "Go ahead."

Getting on his knees in front of her, Justin cradled Mila's left calf and pressed his abdomen against the bottom of her shoe to hold it still while he reached for her ankle strap to undo it before slowly pulling it off. He repeated the motion with Mila's other shoe and held her foot as he began to massage it.

Mila watched Justin's hands move further up her leg, his fingertips pressing against all the right spots. He looked up to meet Mila's eyes and gave her a small smile.

"Does it feel good?"

"Mhmm," Mila hummed with a nod.

As Justin kept going, his excitement got the best of him and in no time, he'd reached Mila's thigh.

"Maybe you could lay down?" Justin suggested. "So I can reach under?"

Without responding, Mila scooted back on the bed to lay on her back and Justin joined, now on his knees between her legs. He brought her calf up to his shoulder as his fingers kneaded her thigh.

"You're beautiful, Mila," he whispered before his hands switched movements and he started caressing her. He turned his head to kiss the inside of her calf before turning his attention between her legs. "May I touch you?"

"Go ahead," she said softly.

While Mila's calf remained on his shoulder, Justin leaned forward and pressed his lips against hers while his hand drifted down to touch her through her panties. Mila grew increasingly wet while Justin's dick felt hard against the back of her leg.

"More," she breathed and Justin moved his hand under Mila's panties to touch her directly. At the same time, she reached down to unbutton his slacks and slip her hand inside. Although Mila had touched him in the past through his pants, it was her first time making direct contact with his length. Using his pre-cum, she teased his tip while Justin played with her pussy. He sunk a finger inside of her before slowly pulling it out and gently rubbing her clit.

Justin was the first to break their kiss as his lips made their way to Mila's neck and his fingers—now two curled inside of her—worked more eagerly. Mila spit on her hand and returned it to his pants, wrapping it around his dick and stroking him. Her eyes went wide when she realized the size of him and pushed Justin away.

He sat back up and held eye contact with Mila as he licked her essence off his fingers. "Is something wrong?"

"Take your pants off," Mila instructed and Justin did as he was told.

He got off of the bed to remove his pants and boxers, only to be further turned on by the way Mila licked her lips at the sight of his length. She then stood up in front of him and took her dress and bra off. Justin's eyes glided down to admire her body, seeing it bare for the first time. From the way her breasts fell naturally, slightly over her stomach to the curves of her hips where his hands rested perfectly, Justin admired Mila's body and since the first time he touched her, he knew that he wouldn't be able to get enough.

He pulled her in for a deep kiss and walked her back into the bed. Mila broke away and turned them over so that she was on top. She unbuttoned his shirt to remove what remained of his clothes while she was in nothing but her panties.

Mila stroked him while her mouth worked at his neck and Justin moaned her name when he felt her teeth graze against it. His hand went down to her pussy and he played with her clit, earning an outburst from Mila. She sat back up so that she was upright while straddling him and Justin could see clearly his fingers in Mila's panties while her hand moved up and down his dick.

He watched as she spit on his length and pulled her panties to the side before she started grinding her pussy against his dick.

"Fuck," Justin grunted. "That feels so good."

Mila's soaking core moved against him and both her moans and Justin's intensified as she rubbed his tip against her clit. It was a subtle pleasure, but the heat of the moment had both of them on edge. She used her fingers again to keep playing with his tip, even when her pussy was further down his length, not giving it a moment of rest.

Too far gone, Justin didn't realize until it was too late that he'd soon meet his release. He pushed Mila at her hips and she let up to look down at him while her fingers continued to toy with his tip.

"I'm... I'm com- shitttt," Justin moaned just as he hit his climax and Mila stroked him slowly until he finished. His eyes opened to see a slight look of disappointment in Mila's eyes and he was embarrassed that he came so quickly.

"I- I'm sorry, Mila. I didn't think I would... I've never come so fast or so easily..."

Mila sighed and got off of him to go to the bathroom so she could shower. When she realized he followed her, Mila turned to him before her eyes drifted down and saw that he was already getting hard again.

"Did you forget what I said before, Mila? About finishing as many times as you want?"

"Yeah. But it looks like only one of us got to finish."

Justin approached confidently and pressed Mila against the bathroom counter. He got on his knees in front of her and pulled her panties down before lifting one of her thighs to his shoulder.

"Let me make up for it," he rasped before his mouth was against her pussy. His tongue moved up and down her inner lips before he lightly sucked her clit and began pumping two fingers inside of her. With his free hand, Justin reached back to grab Mila's ass while his mouth worked more eagerly.

Mila's head fell back as she braced herself against the counter. Her hips pressed forward, moving with Justin until she hit her climax. Her body jerked and she let out a squeak when he didn't let up after she came. He gently pulled her clit between his lips hummed against her.

Both of them in a haze, they didn't notice the knocking at Mila's room until it was hard enough to shake the door. Justin pulled away and turned his head to look out of the bathroom toward the door.

Mila sighed her annoyance and took her leg off Justin's shoulder. "If that's who I think it is..."

"Open up, Mila!" Caleb called from the other side. "I know you're not asleep."

"I fucking knew it," she grumbled.

"He's always ruining shit," Justin griped.

Mila took Justin's hand and led him to the bed. "So annoying... Maybe if we don't respond, he'll go away."

However, their attempts to get back into their moment continued to be interrupted by Caleb's persistent knocking.

Finally, Mila got up, went through her suitcase and put on sweat-pants and a teeshirt before answering the door.

"Go the fuck away," she said coldly when she opened her door to an inebriated Caleb.

"I just wanted to give you something..." He handed her a box of chocolates and a wilted bouquet that appeared to have been bought from a corner store.

Mila looked at the gifts expressionless and reached out to accept them. "Is that it, Mr. Peterson?"

"No... Who's in there with you? Adrian or Justin?"

"None of your business."

"Why do you give them more than me? *I'm* the one who brought you here with me. I let you get first class tickets... and this nice room."

"All of which were on the company dime... And this room actually isn't up to my standards. I prefer a penthouse suite."

"Well you booked the travel, you could've got the penthouse if you wanted." Caleb could barely stand up straight and was holding himself against Mila's doorframe. He wasn't as drunk as Adrian had gotten earlier that night, but it was enough for him to show Mila a more vulnerable side of himself. Though, she wasn't in the mood to be open to it in that moment.

"Go back to your room, Mr. Peterson."

"No," Caleb replied stubbornly. "I want to stay with you tonight."

"The hell if you are," Justin blurted, walking toward the door and standing next to Mila in nothing but his boxers.

"Oh, so he's your favorite this week?" Caleb questioned as he glared at Justin.

Annoyed, Mila looked up at the ceiling and took a deep breath. *This shit is getting old,* she thought to herself. *I'm going to take care of everything this week.*

"You know what? How about neither of you spend the night."

EPISODE 42

What You Want

The second day of conference events had ended and Mila was in her room bored, scrolling through her phone while a TV show played in the background. She raised a curious brow when an email notification popped up from the hotel.

Dear Ms. Mila Nelson,
We are pleased to inform you that your room has been upgraded and you will be moved to the penthouse suite starting tomorrow, and you will be there for the rest of your stay. A member of our staff will come to your room tomorrow afternoon to move your things for you.
If you have any questions or need any other assistance, please do not hesitate contact us.
Sincerely,
Lavishly Hotel

With pursed lips, Mila nodded approvingly and before she could put her phone down, it chimed again. This time, there was a message from Caleb.

CALEB

I got you put in the penthouse. They said it won't be available until tomorrow.

MILA

Yeah. I just saw the email.

CALEB

Are you going to thank me?

MILA

No.

CALEB

Look at all this nice shit I'm doing and you're still cold with me. Why can't I get more? I know you like what we did in my office last week... Don't you want it again?

Mila shook her head with a hint of satisfaction on her face as she looked down at Caleb's message. Following what'd happened the night prior between Adrian's drunkenness, her moment with Justin, and Caleb showing up at her room and ruining it, Mila decided that the Atlanta trip would be her opportunity to finally establish with the men exactly where they all stood.

MILA

Or... How about I give you another test?

CALEB

Will this test end with me getting what I want?

MILA

Depends how you do. It's pretty simple, so even you should be able to pass.

CALEB

Tell me.

MILA

I want you to come here prepared for exactly what you want... Dress for the occasion.

CALEB

What I want doesn't require dressing at all.

MILA

Like I said, just come prepared.

CALEB

You expect me to walk across the hotel butt-ass-naked?

MILA

If what you want requires that... come at midnight.

After sending that final text, Mila went over to her suitcase to pick which piece of lingerie she'd wear for Caleb's arrival. She wanted to make sure he'd see her in something memorable and she had just the look in mind.

She pulled out a leather caged black bra, matching shorts, black fishnet tights and her tallest pair of platform heels. The set showed plenty of skin while keeping her breasts and bottom fully covered. Mila wanted enough to make an impression, but didn't want to allow Caleb to see too much.

Mila wasted a few more hours texting friends and watching reality TV before changing closer to the time that Caleb was set to arrive.

Right at midnight, there was a knock at her door and when she opened it, Mila held back her smile—Caleb did exactly what she expected him to do. He stood there in a black silk robe and based on the way it clung to him, he still had briefs on underneath.

Meanwhile, Caleb felt blood rushing straight to his dick at the sight of Mila in her lingerie. He was surprised that she went through the effort of wearing it for him and he was sure that it was a sign he'd have her in bed that night.

Mila feigned confusion before asking Caleb, "What is it, exactly, that you're dressed for? I thought you said the what you wanted didn't require any clothes."

Caleb's eyes remained on her form. Instinctively licking his lips, he admired the cut of the lingerie and the height of her heels along with the platform. He felt a subtle urge to get on his knees, but quickly pushed it to the side and turned his attention back to Mila's face.

"To fuck you, obviously," Caleb replied matter-of-factly. "C'mon. You didn't really expect me to walk over here naked."

In response, Mila crossed her arms and leaned against the doorway, simply looking at Caleb expectantly.

"Fine," he huffed after a long pause between them. He first untied his robe and handed it to her, leaving him in nothing but his briefs. However, Mila still didn't move from her spot in the doorway. "Seriously? I am literally two steps from being inside your room."

Again, there was a stretch of silence between them.

"You're so fucking demanding," he grumbled as he pulled off his briefs and also handed those to Mila so that he was completely nude.

He found himself feeling increasingly insecure as she looked him over with an indecipherable expression until his impatience got the best of him.

"Hello? I'm sure you like what you see. I passed the test, right? Let me in your room."

Mila's gaze came back up to meet Caleb's eyes and she let out an entertained huffed.

"I told you to come here dressed for what you wanted, and you didn't... so you failed."

"What?! What the fuck? Then give me—"

Caleb was cut off by the door closing this face while he remained in the hall completely naked. Mila took his robe and briefs with her. He knocked on her door, calling for her to answer.

"Open the goddamn door! You can't be fucking serious right now!"

However, despite the frustration he'd shown on the surface, Caleb's erection was growing as he stood out there in the hall. He liked being humiliated. It turned him on... *a lot*. The way Mila frequently did that to him was what had Caleb constantly going back to her for more. And although he hadn't explicitly said it, Mila could tell by their interactions that it was something he enjoyed—it was part of the reason she continued to entertain him.

Caleb's knocks were ignored and he could see from his peripherals someone from Mila's hallway coming out of their room. He quickly covered himself with his hands and his face turned even more red when he realized who it was.

"Caleb," Adrian called. "What the hell are you doing? I can hear you from all the way down here."

Taking a sigh of relief that Adrian was the first of Mila's neighbors to come out to the hallway, Caleb rushed down to his door and pushed past Adrian to get into his room.

"Could you get me some clothes?" Caleb requested urgently.

Without responding, Adrian closed the door behind him and went into his suitcase to get boxers, a shirt, and sweatpants for Caleb. Adrian's jaw clenched looking over him as he gave the clothes to him and he was frustrated that he was turned on seeing Caleb in his current state—completely naked and fully erect. If it were a little over a year ago, Caleb would be on his back in Adrian's bed, moaning his name while he pounded into him, as they often did during their 'business trips'.

"You still didn't answer my question. What the hell were you doing naked in front of Mila's room?"

"Chill out," Caleb spat. "I didn't fuck your girlfriend."

"She's not my girlfriend..."

"But you wish she was, don't you?"

"I don't want to talk about it," Adrian said softly.

"You're the one who asked about her."

Adrian shook his head and looked back at Caleb once he was dressed. Even with the sweatpants on, his erection was still very notice-able. Adrian swallowed his desire and averted his gaze.

"If you didn't have sex, then what *did* you two do?"

"What happened to not wanting to talk about it?" Caleb challenged before answering. "And nothing... *obviously*. She acted like she was going to let me fuck her. And then she made me strip down in the fucking hallway and left me there... She even wore some sexy-ass lingerie with these tall heels and I'm pretty sure I saw a set of handcuffs on the bed behind her."

"Wow."

"What?"

"I think that's the closest you've gotten to admitting you're attracted to Mila. Also... It looks like she's figured you out."

"Wanna expand on that?"

"You like getting fucked with," Adrian replied. "I knew you liked being degraded, but I didn't realize it ran *this* deep."

"I don't know what you're talking about."

"Oh, really?" Adrian walked toward Caleb until he was backed into the wall and caged him between his arms. "Because I don't think I'll ever forget that look in your eyes when I used to tell you how easy you were. Or the way your dick would twitch when I'd call you a dirty slut. Or the sound of you moaning whenever I came on your face."

Caleb was in a trance, looking into Adrian's eyes as he spoke and their faces were close enough for their lips to lightly brush and their noses to rub at the sides. He was already feeling vulnerable after Mila left him in the hallway and Adrian being the very next person he saw didn't help with his neediness in that moment. They were the only two people who seemed able to bring out that side of him.

"What does she call you?" Adrian whispered. Although he was often annoyed—and mostly jealous—about Caleb and Justin's advances toward Mila, Adrian was also interested in what exactly occurred between Mila and Caleb, especially after what happened in his office between the three of them. After he and Mila made out in front of Caleb, teasing him at the same time, fantasies started to fill his head about the three of them doing more together.

"P-pet," Caleb gulped. "She calls me 'pet'."

"And that turns you on?"

"Y-yes."

"See? You're still easy. What else do you two do?" Adrian leaned in to allow his lips to lightly trace along Caleb's neck.

"Tests..." Caleb let out a shaky breath and allowed his head to fall back to give Adrian better access. "She gives me tests... Last week, she gave me three minutes to do what I wanted and I couldn't take..." He drifted of when he felt Adrian begin to place kisses against his collarbone.

"Keep going."

"She kept her panties on. And I licked her..."

Again, Caleb drifted off. This time, Adrian cupped him over his sweatpants and his lips were working their way back up toward Caleb's.

"You're so hard right now," Adrian whispered as he pressed his own growing erection against Caleb. "We should do something about that."

Caleb's eyes were closed and it wasn't until he felt himself starting to grind against Adrian's hand that he stopped.

Wait! I'm not falling for this shit again, he thought to himself before pushing Adrian away.

Adrian stepped back and looked at Caleb, his eyes low and a voice to match. "What's wrong?"

"I'm not doing this," Caleb said sternly. "You're not going to get all hot and cold and shit with me again because you're upset or confused over Mila."

"But you want it too, don't you?"

"Doesn't matter. You told me months ago..." Caleb readjusted in his pants and walked past Adrian, shoulder-checking him as he went toward the door. "Platonic, right?"

"You weren't being platonic when you were with Mila and I in the office."

"That was different and you know it... And technically I wasn't *with* you... I was just watching."

"Watching with your hand on your dick," Adrian countered.

"Who said that was for *you*?"

And with those last words, Caleb walked out of Adrian's room and slammed the door shut.

"Jesus," Adrian groaned as he ran his fingers through his hair. "We need to settle this shit."

Let's Settle It

Adrian, Justin, and Caleb sat in awkward silence sipping coffee at their table after finishing lunch. Adrian was on edge about when Mila would finally take the time to listen to his apology, Justin was annoyed that Caleb had been consistently ruining his time with Mila, and Caleb was frustrated and confused about where he stood with Mila and Adrian.

"So," Caleb said, breaking the silence. "There's obviously tension here and we all know who caused it."

Adrian and Justin remained quiet and Caleb grew more agitated.

"Are you two really that whipped over our fat ass assistant?"

Justin's eye twitched and Adrian's hand balled into a tight fist, but they allowed Caleb to continue his rant.

"First off, she's big as fuck, so it's not like she's hot. Second, she's an *assistant*—not worth the drama. Third, there are hundreds of hot ass women here to fuck with a waistline that can actually fit in your hands."

Adrian leaned in toward Caleb with an intense glare. "You still pissed that she left you in the hallway naked? When are you going to stop talking shit about Mila? It's obvious you're attracted to her or you wouldn't be constantly embarrassing yourself for her."

Meanwhile, Justin remained hauntingly silent as he watched their exchange with flared nostrils and a tense jaw.

Caleb leaned back in his chair and crossed his arms. "I'm just doing what I need to do to fuck her. That's it. Hell, we can even fire her after that."

"You wouldn't go through all this just for a fuck. You're attracted to Mila. Every time you're around her, your dick is hard and she is constantly on your mind with the way you're always worried about what—or *who*—she's doing."

Caleb scoffed with a smirk and shook his head. "Of course you're staring at my cock. Is her big ass starting to get boring to look at now?"

"Mila's is a lot better than the ass I was getting before," Adrian countered.

Hurt flashed across Caleb's face before he threw his napkin on the table and stood up. "Whatever, enough about the assistant. This shit won't get settled over lunch, anyway. Let's go finish these last few events for the day."

With his statement, both Caleb and Adrian seemed to switch back into business mode, while Justin was still unresponsive, but stood up along with them.

"The meal's already paid for, right?" Adrian asked.

"Yeah, it's all covered by the conference. Probably cheap too, considering it's a literal hole in the wall not far from the venue. At least the food was good."

The three men filed out of the restaurant and started walking down a hallway that would lead them to the street just a block over from the conference hall. Before they got to the end, Caleb was abruptly grabbed by both collars and slammed against the wall by Justin.

Adrian was in shock as he saw the red undertone to Justin's tan face while he held Caleb. He hadn't seen him that angry since they were in college and their first business went under.

"Dude!" Caleb shouted. "What the fuck are you doing? What's wrong with you?"

"Caleb, you're a douche bag and we all know it, but I'm going to give you this *final* warning..." Justin's tone was cold enough that Caleb immediately stopped speaking and listened to him with wide eyes. "If you talk about Mila like that again, you're fucking done. Do you understand?"

Slowly nodding, Caleb could tell that it was not a moment for him to attempt to argue with Justin. Meanwhile, the tension in Adrian's shoulders was relieved watching the exchange. Seeing Justin get *that* angry for Mila's sake and go on to defend her gave Adrian a certain comfort he couldn't quite identify beyond his satisfaction that one of his best friends was looking out for Mila too.

After releasing Caleb's collar and straightening himself up, Justin cleared his throat and continued down the hall toward the exit.

"Now that that's all cleared up, let's enjoy the rest of our events for the day."

~

"WHAT DO you mean you're in Atlanta?!" Adrian's mother, Mary, scolded from the other end of the phone. "You could've done a stopover here beforehand. It's been months since we last saw you. And Emily is home from college on winter break."

Adrian walked around his hotel room as he spoke to his mother over the phone. Given that she raised him and his sister on her own, they were a close-knit family and spoke several times a week. Adrian also used to visit his mother regularly—at least every few months—but with PMC Group's growth, his visits became more scarce.

"Mom, I wouldn't have been able to stop on my way here, anyway," Adrian reasoned. "It was kind of a last-minute decision."

"Yes, I understand. I just miss you, is all. First, you went far away for college. But when you came back to North Carolina, even if you were in Lenrod City, you were much closer to us and at least in the same state, so I thought you'd visit more often…"

"You're right, I'll come visit soon. The three of us could do some hiking, maybe go see a movie or something. Just some good old quality time."

"That would be wonderful," Mary chimed. "And you can also spend that time telling me about the girl you met."

"What?" Adrian said with a slight gasp. "Wh- what do you mean?
"

"I know my son. Yes, of course business had you visiting less often, but as of recently, even your calls have become rare. My guess is that you met someone who has been holding your attention."

Adrian had temporarily forgotten about his anxiety over Mila while he was speaking to his mother, but now that she'd brought it him meeting someone, he was reminded of it all over again. "Something like that..."

"What's with that tone, Adrian? What happened?"

"Well... I kind of put my foot in my mouth. I let my temper get the best of me and I said something pretty mean to her."

"Have you tried apologizing?"

"Of course!" Adrian said quickly. "As soon as I said it last week I tried, and I've been trying constantly since then, but she won't hear me out. And then she finally told me a couple days ago that she needed space."

"How bad was what you said to her?"

"I pretty much called her a—" Adrian paused before going too far. He didn't want his mother asking more questions on what brought about the exchange in the first place. "It was just really disrespectful... and I said it to her in front of Caleb and Justin."

"Oh my god," Mary groaned. "I can only imagine how embarrassing that must have felt for her with other people around."

"Yeah... And I've been kicking myself every day over it."

"Well, just make sure you give her a sincere apology when she does come around."

A lump grew in Adrian's throat and he swallowed as he thought about what he wanted to say to Mila and his nerves surrounding the imminent exchange. "But what if that's not enough?"

"Cross that bridge if you get to it. And some motherly advice... it may help make it more genuine to apologize to her in front of Caleb and Justin. Especially since you committed the offense in front of them."

"I don't know about that. It's just that she—"

Adrian was cut off when his phone started ringing and he was receiving another call. He looked at the caller ID and his heart skipped a beat when he saw it was from Mila.

"It's... it's her," he said with almost a whisper.

"Answer it!" Mary exclaimed. "And I want you to tell me how it goes! Remember what I said about making the apology genuine."

"Thanks, mom."

Adrian switched over to answer Mila's call and with a shaky hand, held the phone up in front of him on speaker.

"Hey Mila, I'm glad you called. How are you doing?"

"I'm well. Though, I may have gone a bit overboard with my shopping since getting here," she giggled. "I'll have to bring another suitcase of stuff back up with me to Lenrod. How are you?"

"I'm... I'm alright. The conference events have been a bit boring, to be honest, but I don't regret coming."

There was then a pause that only lasted a few seconds, but felt like minutes to Adrian and he could feel his heart beating in his ears.

"Adrian," Mila finally said softly. "I know I've been a bit stubborn, but I'm ready to hear you out if you still want to talk. My room was moved and I'm in the penthouse on the top floor... Could you come here?"

"Yes!" Adrian replied urgently. "I'll be right up! I'm coming now. Oh! Um... should I bring anything? Do you want something like from the store or my room or—"

"Just you," Mila interrupted. "I just want you."

"I-I'll be there ASAP, Mila." After hanging up, Adrian rushed around his room to get dressed in jeans and a button-up. When he was about to close his suitcase, he froze when he saw a small box of condoms that he'd packed in the top. Adrian had an internal battle with himself about whether or not to take them with him, and ultimately decided to do so.

Once he got up to the penthouse, Adrian knocked on Mila's door and as he waited for her to answer, he continued to calculate the best way to apologize. At one point, he had an entire speech planned, but after having more time to think it over and speaking to his mom, Adrian just wanted to focus on giving Mila a sincere apology.

"Hey Adrian," Mila greeted when she opened the door. Oddly, she appeared dressed in a way that made her seem more approachable. She had on distressed jeans and a black scoop-neck top while her face was makeup-free and hair up in a bun.

"Mila, hi..." Adrian gulped his nerves as he tried to maintain his composure and keep his hands from shaking. "You look nice."

"Come in."

Mila led Adrian to the kitchen where the two of them stood at the counter.

"Do you want anything to drink? There's water, cranberry juice, tea, coffee..."

"Just a water would be fine. Thank you."

"Sure." Mila walked over to the fridge and pulled a bottle of water out of the door and handed it to him.

"Thanks..." Adrian took a sip of the water to get the dryness out of his throat before continuing. "And thank you for being willing to hear me out."

Mila gave him a simple nod and leaned against the counter to her side as she looked up at Adrian to listen to him.

"Right... um, to be honest with you, Mila, I had a whole speech planned before, but as I thought about it, I don't need to talk your ear off in order to give you a genuine apology. So... I'm sorry that I disrespected you, Mila. It was uncalled for and immature. Mila, I have the utmost respect for you and I care about you... *a lot.*"

Mila stepped back and crossed her arms. "Adrian, what you said... It really hurt. I've been insulted and disrespected before, but coming from *you*? That's what made it so bad. I knew you had a temper, but I never expected that you'd lash out at me like that."

"I am truly sorry... Please, Mila. I know I fucked up, and I promise to *never* disrespect you again."

Mila sighed and looked up and around the room as she considered Adrian's words, only putting him more on edge. When the silence became too much for him he decided to follow his mother's advice.

"And I was thinking... Since I did this in front of Caleb and Justin, I think I should apologize in front of them, as well."

Mila's gaze snapped to him and she gave an approving nod. "That makes sense. Plus, there's something I need to speak with the three of you about, anyway, so it works out."

"You need to speak with the three of us?"

"Mhm," Mila hummed. "There are a few things we need to settle."

"Oh um... Okay." Adrian reached into his front pocket to pull out his phone and call the men.

"Adrian, wait." Mila grabbed his arm to stop him. As she thought about it, she didn't want Caleb and Justin to see the side of her that she only revealed to Adrian, and so she gave him a response to his apology right there. "Actually, I'd rather get this settled before they come up... I can't say what you said is forgotten, but I *do* want to say that I forgive you... It'll just take some time before I can let you back in."

"That's fair," Adrian replied. "And Mila..."

"Hm?"

"May I take you a date tomorrow? I mean a *proper* date. The type of date I've been *wanting* to take you out on since before I asked you the first time."

"I'd like that." Mila walked up to him with small smile and nodded before she reached forward to wrap her arms around his waist while he took her face in his hands and tilted her head up before their lips met.

Mila and Adrian missed each other desperately and it was all coming out in that moment as their hands began to wander. Adrian used one hand to cup the back of Mila's neck while the other went down to her hip. At the same time, Mila's hands drifted lower from his waist and she felt something in his back pocket. Her eyes popped open when she recognized the shape of a small box and she pulled it out before breaking away.

"Adrian..." she said with a sigh and held the condoms in front of him. "Explain this to me."

"Mila!" Adrian exclaimed, his eyes wide with embarrassment. "I'm sorry. I... they were in my bag and I saw them and... I don't know. I wasn't thinking. I put them in my pocket just in case, but I wasn't necessarily expecting anything. I don't even know why I did something like that. I um... It wasn't in a—"

Adrian was silenced when Mila placed a finger over his lips and to his surprise, a smile was on her face.

"If you were anyone else *but* you, darling, I would've put you out."

"S-so you're not mad?"

"No." Mila shook her head and stepped back to get her phone. "Anyway, I still need to talk to the three of you together, so let's get Caleb and Justin up here."

Wanted to Be Ready

The first to knock on Mila's door was Caleb, and when she went to answer it, she nearly bursted out laughing before clearing her throat and regaining her composure.

"What in my text made you think this was *that* kind of visit?" she questioned as she looked Caleb up and down. He wore nothing but his silk robe and a pair of briefs, the same as what he had on for Mila's 'test' the night before.

"I just wanted to be ready in case—" Caleb paused when he walked in and saw Adrian who in turn glared at him. "What the fuck is this?" Caleb blurted.

Adrian gestured at Caleb's outfit. "What the fuck are you wearing?"

"Mr. Peterson misinterpreted the reason why I called him here," Mila replied before there were more knocks at the door and she opened it for Justin.

Looking between Adrian, Caleb, and Mila as he walked in, Justin was confused as to what was happening. "Um, Mila. Why exactly did you call us up here?"

"I need to talk to you—all three of you—about what's been going on." Mila leaned against the kitchen counter and rested her palms on the surface behind her as she looked at the men. They stood there just a few feet from her with attentive gazes. "All of you know that I've been messing around with the others and outside of Adrian's little fit last week, there haven't really been any reactions to that fact. And none of you have even *tried* to end things or at least tone it down. In fact, all of you have been more bold."

"So, what's the deal here? Are you trying to see which one of you I'll choose?" Mila continued. "Caleb has been a douche bag since day one. Justin isn't the *smoothest* man in the room. And Adrian is a sweet guy, but I'm not so sure about that temper... Also, I don't really like the idea of choosing, to be frank."

Adrian tilted his head to the side curiously. "Mila, where are you going with this?"

Justin's expression was inquisitive with pursed lips. "I'm not sure I understand."

Caleb crossed his arms. "Is this where you drop all three of us?"

Mila shook her head. "Not at all. What I'm getting at is that the four of us can help each other. I am a single woman who doesn't like the idea of choosing. Adrian came in here to apologize, but also with condoms in his pocket. Caleb came here half-dressed. And Justin, well... You were telling me the other day that you've been wanting to learn more about what you're into."

"What exactly are you proposing, Mila?" Adrian asked.

Mila took a deep sigh, pushed herself off the counter, and walked toward the men. "Follow me," she said and took Adrian and Justin's hands to lead them to the living room with her and the three stood in front of the couch while Caleb, who followed, was just a few feet away.

Reaching up to play with Adrian's hair, Mila looked at Caleb and said, "You remember what we did the last time the three of us were in Adrian's office, right?"

"... And?" Caleb replied.

"*And,* we could do more than that. *And,* Justin could join us too."

"What do you mean?" Justin questioned.

Keeping her fingers in Adrian's hair, Mila used the other to reach back for Justin's hand and gently squeezed it. "It's better that I show you... If you feel uncomfortable at any point, just say something."

After giving Justin that assurance, Mila pulled Adrian in for a kiss while continuing to hold Justin's hand behind her. He looked at them, slightly astonished at how comfortable Adrian seemed with kissing Mila in front of the two men before his eyes cut over to Caleb who was watching the pair with a tensed jaw.

Justin's gaze returned to Adrian and Mila, and to his surprise, he could feel a heat coming over him as he watched. *Am I into this?* he thought to himself.

Mila broke away from Adrian and turned to see Justin just as he was licking his lips. Holding his face, she asked, "What do you think, Justin? Do you want to try?"

Justin nodded and eagerly closed the distance between them. Adrian watched and oddly, didn't feel as much jealousy as he expected thanks to the memory of Justin defending Mila earlier that day. He noticed that when the pair stopped kissing, Justin looked down at Mila as if she were whispering something to him and he nodded before sitting on the couch behind them. Mila sat next to him and then pulled at Adrian's pants for him to sit on the other side of her.

Mila shot Caleb a sharp look when she noticed him getting closer to the couch and said, "Stay right there, pet."

Caleb did as he was told and Mila returned her attention to Justin to continue their kiss while she pulled Adrian's hand to her chest to signal to him that he could touch her. While her lips were occupied with Justin, Adrian focused on Mila's body.

Placing kisses along her neck and collarbone, Adrian massaged Mila's breast through her shirt. And when he heard her breathing grow heavier, he reached into her bra to toy with her nipple. Not wanting to waste time and feeling herself becoming wet already, Mila broke her kiss with Justin so that Adrian could remove her shirt and bra before turning to kiss him.

Justin took off his own shirt, desiring to feel skin-to-skin contact with Mila while he caressed her body as she and Adrian's mouths moved against each other. His lips made their way down to Mila's chest. Holding her breast in his hand, Justin flicked his tongue against her nipple before twirling it around her mound and taking it into his mouth. On Mila's other side, Adrian used his thumb to play with her nipple before lightly pinching it.

Meanwhile, Caleb pulled the accent chair in the living room to where he was standing so that he could sit down and continue watching the three of them.

When Mila turned to switch back to kissing Justin, Adrian refocused on her body, removing his shirt and getting on his knees in front of her. He removed Mila's jeans so that she was down to nothing but her panties and lifted her left leg up so that her foot was on the couch cushion next to her where he was sitting before.

Adrian then placed kisses on the inside of her thigh while using a single finger to tease her through her panties. Mila let out a light moan against Justin's mouth and her hand drifted down to the front of his pants to rub his growing erection. In turn, Justin pulled her right leg into his lap so that her legs were open wide.

Caleb held himself as he took in the sight. Mila and Justin were in an intense kiss while he massaged her full breasts and pinched her nipples. At the same time, Adrian's head was between her legs as his lips moved closer to Mila's pussy while he played with her through her panties.

"Oh shit," Mila moaned after pulling away from Justin. Adrian's tongue was moving up and down her lips through her panties. His eyes connected with hers when she looked down at him and Mila gave Adrian an approving nod.

He pulled her panties to the side so that he could start eating her out directly. Mila's attention went back to Justin and she caressed him down his chest until she reached the waistline of his pants.

"Is this okay?" she asked, her fingers pulling at his button.

"Yes," he breathed without hesitation as he helped her and pulled his pants down to free his dick. Mila spit on it and started stroking Justin while Adrian continued to eat her pussy.

The three went on as if Caleb wasn't there. He tried to get a peek at Mila's pussy, but it was blocked by Adrian. Caleb's eyes drifted down, examining the subtle movements of Adrian's back muscles as he ate her out while stroking himself. At the same time, Caleb reached into his own pants to rub his dick.

Mila's moans had become more persistent and Justin was grunting into her mouth. She broke away from him and let out a strangled moan upon hitting her climax and pulled Adrian's hair as she came on his mouth.

Justin looked down at Adrian who was holding Mila's gaze while he gently sucked on her outer lips and the insides of her thighs as she came down. It wasn't lost on Justin that her orgasm seemed more intense than when he'd eaten her out their first night in Atlanta.

His attention was broken when he saw Adrian's head pushed away and just before he could turn to Mila, her lips were scouring his neck as she whispered to him. "It's your turn, hon. Are you comfortable with that?"

"Yes," Justin breathed. "Er, I mean... from *you*, right?"

Mila lifted her head away from his neck to give him a small, closed-mouth smile. "Mhm." She then cut her eyes over to Caleb and gestured with her finger for him to come over.

The four of them repositioned so that Justin remained in the couch, Mila was on her knees in front of him while she straddled Adrian's face as he lay on the floor to keep eating her out, and Caleb was laying on the floor, but on his stomach so he could take Adrian's dick into his mouth.

The suite filled with the sound of their moans—Justin's uninterrupted, Mila's choked against his dick and Adrian's muffled on Mila's pussy.

"Fuuuuck," Justin dragged out as he threw his head back and ran his fingers through his hair. Mila released him from her mouth and looked up at him as she continued stroking his dick while flicking her tongue on his tip.

She then turned back to Caleb when she could feel Adrian moaning harder against her pussy.

"Don't... let him... come," she said through labored breaths before slightly lifting herself off of Adrian just enough to see his face. "You hear that? No fucking coming."

"Yes, Ms. Mila," he rasped and she settled herself back on his face.

Mila returned to working on Justin. Each time he was on the edge of his release, Mila eased her movements and he groaned a mix of frustration and pleasure.

She squealed on him and her body jerked at the unexpected sensation of Caleb burying his face between her ass cheeks and his tongue against her other entrance. Mila looked back, seeing that Caleb had crawled up Adrian's body so that their dicks rubbed against each other while he could join Adrian in eating her out.

Mila roughly grabbed Caleb by his hair and pulled him off. "What... the fuck... makes you think... you had permission?" She then pushed his head away and went back to Justin.

It wasn't long until she felt a second orgasm rising in her. She took Justin's entire length down her throat to choke on his dick, stroking him each time she came up. When she hit her release, Mila was sure to keep Justin in her mouth so he could feel the intense vibrations of her moaning her orgasm and it pushed him over the edge.

"Fuck... I can't... hold it," Justin choked out.

Right when he came, Mila pulled up just enough, opened her mouth at his tip and looked up at Justin, holding eye contact as she stroked him and he came all over her tongue and lips. He watched with low eyes and labored breaths as she swallowed all he had to give.

Justin had never been so turned on by a sight in his life. And in that moment, he knew...

Mila owned him.

She owned all of them.

Intrigued

Justin, Adrian, and Caleb sat in silence as they ate their breakfast. It was a different silence from their lunch the day before—now more awkward than tense. There were a lot of firsts for Justin the night before.

He knew that Adrian and Caleb had a relationship of sorts in the past, but it was Justin's first time witnessing them together sexually up close. He knew that Mila tended to be more dominant, but it was Justin's first time seeing her command the three of them, and it seemed like she was just getting started. He knew that Caleb wanted Mila despite his posturing, but it was Justin's first time seeing him behave so desperately.

Meanwhile, Adrian's silence was due to a mix of frustration, confusion, and excitement. He was frustrated that he wasn't permitted to come last night and he was unsure just how long his punishment would last. He was confused about how much he enjoyed the experience, even with Justin being there. He was excited about what might come next between the four of them.

Caleb couldn't bring himself to speak due to his conflicting feelings of shame and intrigue. He told himself before that he'd stop any and all sexual interactions with Adrian, but he still liked Adrian. And the dynamic with Mila gave him an excuse, and a cushion, to continue to be intimate with him. He was afraid of what Justin might have thought after seeing him in such a needy position with Mila. However, he was also intrigued by the experience of the four of them being together, and he only found himself wanting Mila more after seeing how she handled all three of the men.

"So um..." Justin was the first to break the silence. "About last night... Should we talk about it?"

"We obviously all liked it," Caleb said quickly. "Do we really need to talk about it?"

Adrian rolled his eyes at Caleb before asking Justin, "You weren't uncomfortable, right? Were you okay?"

Justing shook his head. "No, I wasn't uncomfortable. I mean, I was nervous and it was *new*, but not uncomfortable... You weren't... jealous?"

Adrian shrugged. "No, surprisingly enough... I think that's all that needs to be said... at least for now."

"Agreed."

MILA LOOKED over herself in the mirror, analyzing her outfit from head-to-toe. She wore a long-sleeved navy blue wrap dress with nude gladiator pumps that wrapped up to the lower part of her calf, and accessorized with a simple gold necklace and matching drop earrings. It was simple but elegant for her first date with Adrian. Mila had been feeling butterflies in her stomach all day with anticipation.

Behind Mila on the end of the bed sat her two closest friends, Naomi and Gianni. They had passed the whole day together, spending most of the time shopping and their bags were lined up next to them.

"What lip color do you think I should use?" Mila asked her friends. "I think I want to do something subtle. I know he likes a bold red, but this isn't the look for that."

"Do a gloss with a brownish tint to it," Gianni suggested.

"Yeah, I agree with Gi. You have a subtle-sexy-classy look going on tonight," Naomi added.

"Thanks Gigi. I'll go with that," Mila chimed. "And that's cute description, Naomi. It's what I'm going for, actually."

Gianni tilted her head to the side and smiled at Mila. "I've never seen you like this, girl. You seem excited about this date. Even though you won't let me in on who this mystery man is, he must have some sort of superpower to have you like this... or some magical dick."

"Boffum," Mila replied with a playful wink. "But for real don't play with me. I've been excited for dates before. You've seen it."

"Yes, but that was when you were being taken on super extravagant dates like getting flewed out and shit."

"In the twenty-four hours since I accepted the date, he rented out a private dining room in a restaurant for us. I mean, it's probably easier since its a weeknight, but still, I'm sure he paid a lot for that last minute. It's pretty extravagant."

"And you have enough money to do that on your own whenever you want. Just admit to me that this man is special, Mila. Don't be like Naomi and deny that shit like she did with Sebastien."

"Now, why am I in it?" Naomi questioned with her arms open and palms up.

"Look," Mila said pointedly with raised fingers. "I'm not going to go as far as saying he's 'special', but what I will say is that I am *intrigued* by what might be going on here."

"Yeah, yeah," Gianni replied, unconvinced. "Just let me know when y'all are exclusive. I know that's coming."

"Okay, Gigi chill out..." Mila looked at her phone and saw that it was almost time for her to meet with Adrian. "Anyway, I need y'all to get out because he's supposed to be picking me up soon."

"Oh! *And* you care about being on time?" Gianni challenged. "Yeah, 'intrigued' is code for enamored."

"Hush. I love you two, but you gotta go."

Naomi rose to her feet along with Gianni and walked over to give Mila a tight hug. "I hope you enjoy it, Mila," she whispered.

Once her friends left, Mila took a deep breath and looked over herself in the mirror one last time before there was knocking at her door and Adrian had arrived.

She couldn't help the smile that came to her face when she saw him.

He almost matched what she was wearing with a dark blue shirt and dark, almost black gray pants. He complemented his outfit with a gold watch, similar to Mila's gold accessories. In his hand, he held a bouquet of lilies and looking at his face, Mila adored his charming smile.

"You look beautiful, Mila," he said as he handed her the flowers.

"Thank you. Let me put these in some water and then we can be on our way."

RETURNING TO MILA'S PENTHOUSE, she and Adrian were on a high after their date. While he knew they weren't fully back to the way they were before, Adrian also felt that he took another step toward earning Mila's trust again.

He looked around the penthouse, admiring the floor-to-ceiling windows that overlooked the city, the modern decor with a minimalist style, the unnecessary fully-loaded kitchen, and finally the couch where he, Caleb, and Justin experienced their first shared moment with Mila the night before. Thinking back on what happened, Adrian didn't feel an ounce of regret. While he and Caleb had their own past, it was the first time that all three of the men were involved with a single woman at the same time.

"Wine?" Mila's offer broke Adrian out of his thoughts.

He turned to look at her as she poured herself a glass and nodded. "Yes, please."

Mila poured Adrian a drink and passed it to him across the counter. He took it and raised it out toward her and she returned the gesture.

"What's the toast to?"

"Oh, um..." Adrian was trying to figure out what to tell her. His initial plan to was to toast to the two of them. However, by the time it was too late, he found the idea of saying 'to us' a bit corny and presumptuous considering they were not technically an 'us'.

But he wanted them to be.

"A toast to what's to come," he finally said.

The two of them clinked their glasses before walking over to sit at the center of the large couch in the living room. Mila had taken off her shoes and brought her knees together up on the couch, pointing toward Adrian with his body facing hers. They both leaned their heads on their hands with their elbows on the back of the couch as they spoke to each other.

"Did you enjoy tonight?" Adrian asked. "I've been wanting to do something like that for you for so long and even though all the booking happened last minute, I hope you liked it."

"I did," Mila assured before taking a sip of her wine. There was a pause of silence after that and looking into Adrian's soft brown eyes, she noticed that he seemed deep in thought. "What's wrong?"

"Well um... We haven't talked about last night. I mean, me, Caleb, and Justin did this morning, but like... I mean with you... We didn't talk much after."

"You're right... It's obvious I enjoyed it. And I was sure that you three did too, but of course if you didn't, we should talk about that. It's fine if any of you want to stop."

"We enjoyed it!" Adrian blurted. "We liked it. All of us. It's just *new*. The three of us, we've never..." He drifted off.

"... been with a woman at the same time?" Mila finished for him.

"Yeah... I mean, Caleb and I have obviously been together, but this group thing is new. But it also felt kind of natural."

Mila could feel a heat come over her as she recalled what happened with the four of them the night before on that very couch. "Even with Justin around?"

"Yeah." Adrian nodded. "He's straight, obviously, but I don't know... The three of us still liked it."

"Then we'll do more. Now..." Mila took Adrian's glass and sat it on the coffee table along with hers before turning to him. He kissed her eagerly, pushing Mila until she was on her back and her dress rode up as he ground against her.

Mila's breathing grew heavy and her pussy wetter as he kept going and began to place kisses and lightly suck on her neck. She jumped when she felt something vibrating against her inner thigh and Adrian was too preoccupied to realize it was his phone ringing.

When the caller tried a second time, Mila figured who it was and pushed Adrian away. By the time he sat up, he was brought to his senses and he realized that his phone had been going off.

Mila exhaled as she looked up at him. "We both know who it is. Somehow, he always knows exactly when to call."

She reached into Adrian's pocket and pulled his phone out to pick up the call.

"Hello," she answered casually.

"I thought I was calling Adrian... You two are together, aren't you?"

"Obviously, pet."

"What are you two doing?"

Mila looked up at Adrian, the suggestion in her eyes, to which he nodded his consent. She let out an entertained huff before switching the call to video and turning the camera to show Adrian. "What does it look like we're doing?"

Caleb watched from his phone, seeing Adrian sit between Mila's legs and her free hand rub up his abdomen and down to the bulge in his pants. Adrian slowly unbuttoned his shirt, teasing Caleb through the camera. Mila's hand could be seen opening it and then caressing his bare torso. Meanwhile, Adrian's hand fell between her legs and he began teasing her through her panties.

Mila looked at the screen to see Caleb staring attentively at the scene. He was shirtless and his hair was wet, clearly fresh out of the shower. She toyed with the button on Adrian's pants before undoing it and unzipping them. A smirk was on Adrian's face as he removed his shirt and leaned forward toward Mila. She kept the camera on him as his lips returned to her neck before moving lower and he was at the the neckline of her wrap dress.

Caleb continued watching as Adrian's mouth made it to the inside of her dress and he kissed the exposed portions of her chest. He looked directly into the camera as he stuck his tongue out and licked the top of Mila's breast. Adrian then lifted himself back up so that he could untie her dress and open it, exposing the dark purple lingerie set that she was wearing.

"C-can I... join?" Caleb choked out with almost a whisper.

"What was that, pet?"

"Can I join?" he repeated louder.

Mila looked at Adrian and asked, "What do you think, darling?"

Adrian knew his answer already, but he paused as if mulling over the question.

"He's an eager one, isn't he?" Adrian replied, he voice low and breathy. "Let's indulge him for tonight."

"You heard him... and don't keep us waiting." After hanging up on Caleb, Mila slid Adrian's phone onto the coffee table.

Adrian got up to remove his pants and took off the rest of Mila's dress before they got back on the couch, now with her on top of him.

She looked down into his eyes and Adrian looked up at her and gulped before whispering, "I missed you."

Mila looked down at him with a small smile and held his cheek, rubbing it with her thumb. "I missed you too." She leaned back in to kiss him before her mouth trailed down to his neck. She didn't go on too long before sitting up to speak to Adrian.

"He'll be here soon."

"And you're okay with it, right?"

"I *am* the one who proposed it."

Adrian lifted himself up to place kisses along Mila's neck as he spoke to her. "He likes being used... and toyed with... And span—"

He was interrupted by Caleb knocking at the door and Mila got up to answer it.

"Hi..." Caleb's jaw tensed and he swallowed hard as he looked over Mila, standing there in the doorway with nothing but her lace bra and panties. "C-can I... come in?"

Mila nodded and let him into the penthouse before closing and locking the door. Adrian watched as Mila led Caleb to the couch while his eyes were glued to her ass. Now that he was sitting up, Mila straddled Adrian when she rejoined him.

"Take your clothes off and sit next to him, pet," Mila instructed and Caleb did as he was told.

When he sat next to Adrian, Caleb looked at him and Mila attentively as they shared a kiss before turning toward them to join. He grabbed Mila's ass and she broke away from Adrian to look at Caleb with a questioning brow raised.

"The fuck do you think you're doing?"

Caleb's hand quickly retreated and he struggled to answer Mila. "I-I thought I could... I thought I could join... you?"

Mila shook her head. "I didn't say anything about you touching me."

"I um..." Caleb gulped as he looked between them. Mila and Adrian were the only two people capable of putting Caleb in his current state. He was desperate, needy, and even a bit meek. "W-what about what we did in my office? I want to... taste you again?"

"Would you look at that, darling," Mila said to Adrian. "Looks like it's all about me..." She reached toward Caleb's mouth and slipped two fingers inside of it, moving them back and forth between his lips. Mila was deeply turned on as she watched him and felt his tongue twirling around her fingertips. "But what about last night, pet? You liked sucking Adrian off, didn't you?"

Caleb's gaze connected with Adrian's and he held eye contact as he nodded while Mila's fingers were still in his mouth. When she took them out, Adrian grabbed Caleb by the back of his neck and pulled him in for a deep kiss.

Still in Adrian's lap, Mila reached down into his boxers and began stroking him as she watched him and Caleb. She didn't sense an ounce of discomfort and could tell that the two had probably been intimate *a lot* before.

Once she heard their breathing become heavy, Mila pulled out Adrian's dick and spit on her hand before she started stroking him. In turn, with his free hand, he reached into her panties and started rubbing up and down her inner lips. Caleb grunted against Adrian's mouth when he felt Mila's other hand on his dick and she gently teased his tip.

When the two finally broke their kiss, Adrian pulled his fingers out of Mila's panties and put them directly into Caleb's mouth so he could have a taste of her. Watching the scene, Mila couldn't hold herself back anymore and she pulled her panties to the side, raised herself up, and held Adrian at her entrance.

"Oh fuck," Adrian moaned as he felt Mila slowly slide down his dick.

Caleb looked on as Mila began moving her hips in small motions back and forth. Aware that he wasn't permitted to touch her, he kept his focus on Adrian and started lightly sucking his neck while caressing his bare chest.

Soon, the sounds of Mila and Adrian's bodies slapping against each other filled the room as she started bouncing up and down his length. Caleb's dick twitched at the sound of Mila's sweet moans mixed with Adrian deep ones.

She could tell by the noises coming from him that Adrian was approaching his release and she wrapped her hand around his neck.

"You better not... fucking come," she warned through her moans.

Adrian's head fell back and the veins in his neck were gradually becoming visible as he tried to keep himself from coming while Mila rode him. She turned her head to see Caleb looking down at both of their groins as she fucked Adrian.

"You want... a better view... pet? On your... knees behind... me."

Caleb did as he was told and got on the floor behind Mila while she continued to ride Adrian. While she had one hand braced on the back of the couch, she used the free one to pull one of her ass cheeks apart so that Caleb had a clear view of Mila's pussy moving up and down Adrian's dick.

"Please..." Adrian choked out. "I can't hold it..."

"Are you telling... me... you need a... break, darling?"

He nodded and Mila slowed her movements to a stop and got off of him. She then got on the floor with Caleb and gently ran her fingers through his hair. He groaned his pleasure and looked at Mila with a plea clear in his eyes.

"Do you want to taste more, pet?"

"Yes... please?"

Mila looked up at Adrian, who was still recovering with heavy breaths and turned back to Caleb. She held Adrian at his base and kept her hand in Caleb's hair.

"Here you go, pet."

Caleb knew what that meant and he turned to take Adrian's dick into his mouth. Adrian grunted something unintelligible and Mila watched as Caleb's head bobbed up and down. She repositioned so that she was on her knees behind Caleb and reached around to stroke him.

"You were right, darling. He is an eager one."

As Caleb continued sucking off Adrian, Mila took in the sight of Adrian struggling to keep himself from coming and she wanted to see just how much he could take.

"You can do better than that, pet," she teased and pushed Caleb's head until he was choking on Adrian's dick.

"Shit!" Adrian shouted. "I don't know how much longer I can—"

"Fucking hold it," Mila interrupted with a cold tone before her voice softened again. "He gets so hard with your dick in his mouth," she said to Adrian as she continued stroking Caleb. "He's enjoying this... I bet he'd like it even more if I were fucking him from behind right now... What do you think, pet? You want me to fuck you while you choke on his dick?"

She pulled Caleb by his hair off of Adrian so he could answer.

"Y-yes," he choked out through labored breaths.

"Yes, what?" Mila questioned as she moved her hand from his shaft to grab his balls.

"Mistress!" Caleb blurted. "Y-yes Mistress."

"He really *is* an easy slut. I didn't even have to fuck it out of him... Maybe I won't need to fuck you at all, pet."

"Please... Please... fuck..."

"Hm?" Mila hummed inquisitively and wrapped her hand around his length again to stroke him.

"Please... may you fuck me?"

"Easy as fuck and *very* fucking needy," Mila taunted.

Once Adrian had come down enough, he looked at the two of them and immediately felt on edge again. Mila returned his gaze with a satisfied smile and stood up.

"Too bad neither of you are allowed to come."

With Ease

Adrian's eyes fluttered open and he exhaled on the back of Caleb's neck. His arm had fallen numb under him and he slowly pulled it away. He then turned to lay on his back and stretched his arms forward as he spread his fingers apart before allowing them to fall above his head.

After the scene they had with Mila the night before, the pair went to Caleb's room together and cuddled until they fell asleep.

Recalling what occurred, Adrian again took note of how easy it seemed to be intimate with Mila and Caleb without getting jealous, and it was another great night, however...

"Shit," Adrian groaned when he tried to sit up in bed. That was the second night in a row of Mila edging him and he woke up painfully erect. He lay back down and crossed his arms over his face as he muttered under his breath, "How long is this going to go on?"

"Do you wanna start taking bets?" Caleb whispered, the sleepiness heavy in his voice. "I feel your pain." He turned over so that he was on his back next to Adrian and lifted on his arms over his head.

"Bullshit." Adrian scoffed. "You had sex the first night of the conference."

"So? You had sex last night. Or did you forget I was there?"

"But I didn't come."

"And I didn't come that first night." Caleb said softly.

Adrian sucked his teeth. "Yeah, right…"

"I'm telling the truth. I haven't be able to come since… It's been like I'm the only one who can get myself off other than… whatever…"

"What do you mean?"

"I mean exactly what I fucking said," Caleb spat. "Whatever, I shouldn't have said anything to you in the first place."

"Don't be like that, Caleb. You gotta admit it's unlike you."

"Now what's that supposed to mean? You trying to say I come easy?"

Adrian turned on his side to face Caleb with a smirk. "For me, you always did."

"Yeah," Caleb scoffed. "Keep telling yourself that… More like the other way around, even if you are saying Mila's ass is 'much better' than mine."

"I was just saying that because you kept insulting Mila. It pisses me —and obviously Justin—off when you do that. Plus, it's not like you mean any of it. You're just being a dick because she intimidates you… and you like it."

"You sound pretty fucking confident in that assessment."

"Because I know you and I've seen how you are with her. She's handling you just the way you like."

Caleb simply turned his head to look up at the ceiling with his lips pressed together stubbornly, thinking about Mila. Adrian was right. The woman knew exactly how to deal with Caleb, and she was the first one to figure him out so quickly and so accurately.

Finally breaking his silence, Caleb said, "So you didn't mean it?"

"No, I didn't mean it," Adrian assured. "I was just saying that to get back at you… Being with you and being with Mila… they're two very difference experiences for me, but I like both of them equally."

"What about when it's both of us at the same time?"

"It's even better," Adrian replied as he lifted his head and rested it in his palm so he could look down at Caleb. "I'm enjoying this dynamic we're developing."

"She *does* have a nice ass," Caleb admitted. "You fuck it yet?"

"Do you always need to be so vulgar?" Adrian grumbled. "And no, I haven't."

"But you want to."

"So do you with the way you shoved your tongue in it the other night."

"Who's the vulgar one now?" Caleb countered. He took a deep breath as thoughts of Mila continued to swirl through his mind. "And where the fuck does she get her lingerie? What she had on last night was sexy, but what she was wearing that night she left me in the hall... *fuck*."

"What *was* she wearing?"

"It was black and strappy. I think it was a one piece? And the fucking platform heels she had on..." Caleb sucked in his bottom lip before he reached down under the covers to adjust himself in his boxers.

Adrian's gaze followed Caleb's hand and lingered on the spot where the covers were raised. "Of course you're hard, too," he said.

"Can you fucking blame me? At least you got some last night. All I got was her hand on my cock."

Adrian chuckled. "That's a big step up from her foot. You were obviously enjoying it and the way she spoke to you. Mila's dirty talk is..." He groaned something unintelligible before laying flat on his back again and keeping his hands behind his head as not to touch himself. "By the way... why were you calling me last night?"

A sharp breath crossed Caleb's nose and he kept his eyes on the ceiling. "Nothing... I was just checking on you."

"Right after your shower?" Adrian challenged. "Your hair was still wet when you got there last night."

Caleb took a heavy sigh and said, "You know what? Fuck it. I was calling to ask you to come over."

"Come over for what?"

"Don't play like you don't know... You were the last person I could get off with, so I figured why the fuck not."

"What happened to 'platonic it is'?" Adrian countered.

"First off, *you* were the one who said we should be platonic and kept playing hot and cold. Second, we can still get each other off... platonically."

"I'm not so sure it works like that..."

"Whatever, we both ended up getting blue-balled at the end of the night, anyway. I'm surprised you didn't make a move when we got back here. Trying to be good for *Ms. Mila*?" Caleb added mockingly.

"You're projecting... Watch it," Adrian warned.

"What? I'm just saying what's true. I bet you're hoping she'll give you a treat soon for being a *good boy*."

"Weren't you the one doing whatever she told you to do last night without giving her any lip? Pretty sure *you're* the one trying to be a good boy since you want to get fucked so badly."

Caleb cut his eyes at Adrian and looked down at the raised sheets covering him. "That's right," he replied casually. "I prepped and everything before I called you."

Adrian's jaw tensed at Caleb's obvious teasing as he tried to ignore his ongoing erection.

"But..." Caleb continued. "It looks like *Ms. Mila* has you completely wrapped around her finger and you can't do anything with your cock without her approval first."

"I'm not the only one."

"Yes, you are," Caleb teased. "I'm going to go get one off right now." When he removed the covers to get out of bed, he was stopped when Adrian grabbed his arm.

"Stay."

"And why should I—" He was cut off when Adrian pulled him back down and got on top of him. Their lips immediately met for an intense kiss. When Adrian finally broke away to start kissing down his neck, Caleb's breathing grew heavy and he opened his legs to give Adrian better access to grind against him. Making a path around his neck and back up to his ear, Adrian pulled Caleb's lobe between his teeth.

Caleb groaned his pleasure when Adrian reached into his boxers and used his pre-cum to stroke him before returning the move. Not long passed before Adrian removed Caleb's boxers and turned him over so that he was on his stomach.

"Where's the lube?" Adrian asked. "I know you have some."

"In there." Caleb pointed to the nightstand and Adrian reached over to open the drawer and pulled out a small bottle.

He put some on his fingers before getting back on top of Caleb and toying with his ass.

"When was the last time you did this?" Adrian whispered as he added a second finger and went deeper with each movement of his hand.

"You," Caleb replied with a gulp.

"But you feel so ready for me already."

"I told you I prepped... And I was thorough."

"Good. This won't take long." Adrian sat up and pulled Caleb back by his hips so that he was on all fours. He played with his ass as he put more lubricant on his length before slowly sliding himself inside. About halfway through, Adrian began giving Caleb slow strokes, going deeper with each turn as Caleb stretched out for him.

"Fuck," Caleb moaned. He sucked in his bottom lip and took deep breaths through his nose, keeping himself relaxed for Adrian.

Adrian let out a shaky breath before his own sounds ensued. "Shit... you feel so... fucking good."

Caleb leaned forward and rested on his elbows. Pleasure rippled through him when he felt Adrian buried inside him, but Caleb wanted more. "You're doing this... without *Ms. Mila's*... permission?" he teased.

"What... was that?"

"I *said*, you're doing this without Ms. M- *Fuck*!" Caleb had an outburst when Adrian smacked his ass and started fucking him harder.

"You think... I don't know... what you're... doing," Adrian said before pinning Caleb down to the bed by the back of his neck as he continued pounding him. "You wanted me to... fuck you like this... greedy slut."

Caleb's eyes rolled back as his moans grew louder. Adrian removed his hand from the back of Caleb's neck and pulled him by his hair so that he was on all fours again.

Not long passed until both of them felt their releases approaching and Adrian pulled out of Caleb and turned him on his back before easing himself into him again.

"I know... that face," Caleb said through labored breaths. "And you... said... I come... fast?"

Adrian muttered something under his breath and poured more lube on his length and Caleb's before he started stroking him while fucking his ass. Caleb breathed Adrian's name and threw his head back at the move.

Between Caleb's sounds and the way his body started to shake, Adrian knew he was on the verge of coming, and felt his own release rising too. He kept a steady pace until both of them hit their climaxes—Adrian coming inside Caleb and Caleb coming on his abdomen.

Out of breath, Adrian slowly pulled out of Caleb and collapsed next to him in bed.

Deeply satisfied and with a snide smirk, Caleb said, "What will you tell *Ms. Mila*?"

Satisfied

"Fuck," Mila moaned as she met her orgasm and Justin released a satisfied hum against her pussy. His lips made their way up her body until he reached hers and pulled her in for a deep kiss as Mila savored the taste of herself.

After they broke away, Justin whispered in Mila's ear, "Did you like that?"

Mila held Justin's face and looked into his eyes. "I don't fake orgasms... And I clearly just had one on your mouth."

She leaned forward to peck him on the lips before taking his bottom lip between her teeth and pulling it. He groaned with pleasure at the move, the slight pain a new sensation for him.

"Did you like *that*?" Mila questioned.

"I did," Justin replied. He analyzed Mila's face skeptically. "I just... I mean, I know that you came, but did you *really* like it when I went down on you?"

Mila sat up and looked at him attentively. "You wanna tell me what you're *actually* trying to find out here?"

"It just... it seemed like you had a... you came hard when Adrian went down on you the other day."

"I usually do when he eats me out..." Mila sighed when she realized the root of what Justin wanted to know. "Look, Justin... the way you and Adrian give head is different, that's all. Both are good... Adrian just gives me a more intense orgasm."

"How is it different?"

"It's just that..." Mila lay back down and turned on her side in the bed to face Justin while her head rested on the pillow. "You go down on me like you want to make me come, and you do and that's great. Adrian goes down on me like he enjoys the act. He's more focused on the journey there, like he savors it. Both are good but in different ways."

"Similar to when you went down on me?"

"Exactly..." Mila let out a slight giggle. "What an interesting conversation to have over 'lunch'."

Justin sat up and looked across the room at the table of uneaten food in front of them—two plates with salmon, broccoli, and mashed potatoes. He pulled himself out of the bed, walked over to the table, a dipped a finger into the mashed potatoes before putting it in his mouth. "Yeah, it's cold. I didn't even realize so much time passed."

When Mila didn't respond, he turned to face her and immediately gulped when he saw the look in her eyes. Biting her bottom lip, her sultry gaze wandered his body. He was shirtless and wearing low-riding gray sweatpants. Though he wasn't fully erect, he was still hard enough for it to be visible.

Mila's eyes came back up to meet his. "So, how long is it until you have that meeting?" Her voice was like velvet and Justin swallowed again. Mila's confidence both intimidated him and turned him on.

"It's... in thirty minutes."

Mila huffed her frustration. Her lips were tight as she examined him and it was clear what was on her mind.

Mila and Justin—though they had been intimate with each other—still hadn't had sex beyond oral. He wanted Mila. A lot. But he also didn't want their first time together to be rushed.

He walked over to stand next to her as she remained on the bed. She rested her hands behind her and leaned back to look up at him.

"Not this time," she said to him. "I don't want to rush with you... And I don't think you want that either."

Justin's mouth dropped open before his lips turned to a smile. "Your ability to read people never ceases to amaze me, Mila."

"One of my many talents. Go ahead to your meeting. I need to get ready for this afternoon, anyway."

AFTER TAKING A SHOWER, Mila walked out of her bathroom wrapped in a silk robe as she scrolled through her phone. She giggled to herself when she saw her calendar widget with Caleb's schedule showing he would be in meetings all day. Outside of the parties and dealmaking, Caleb was not a fan of big conferences—especially when he would spend hours on end in seminars with other business leaders sharing their opinions on topics he found boring.

Adrian was set to keep Mila company for most of the afternoon after getting out of his morning networking events. At first he suggested they go out and see the city, but both of them had already been to Atlanta several times before, and Mila had more exciting plans for them.

She went to her luggage and opened a large duffle bag. Although her plans in Atlanta did not initially include playing with her bosses, Mila was always sure to pack a toy bag if she was traveling to a city with people she had played with before, just in case she wanted to indulge while in town. Inside the duffle, she had a first aid kit, shower curtain, vibrators, a strap-on harness and dildo attachments, rope, a couple paddles, a flogger, and candles. Remembering her previous conversations with Adrian about his interests, Mila pulled out a magic wand, rope, and a set of scissors.

"We'll start with just this for now," she whispered to herself as she closed the bag and put it back away with her luggage. She then looked at herself in the mirror, examining how the silk robe fell over her body. It came down just above her knees and at the top, plunged to the center of her chest. Mila loved the feeling of the material against her skin and when she wanted to remove it, all she had to do was untie the single string holding it together. "This is perfect. I'm not in the mood for lingerie this time. Besides, today, it's about him."

The sound of a knocking on her door caused flutters in Mila's stomach. It was an odd sensation for Mila, but she tried not to think about it too much.

Taking her time walking down the steps and making her way to the door, Mila opened it to find the man she was expecting. Adrian stood there, leaned against the door frame with a smile on his face. He wore a simple white button-up and black slacks with dress shoes. His wavy brown hair fell over his forehead and his brown eyes had a clearness about them as he looked down at Mila. Reaching her hand up to hold his clean-shaven face, Mila brought Adrian down to kiss his lips.

When they broke away so that Mila could pull him into the penthouse and lock the door behind them, Adrian hummed with satisfaction. "Now *that* is a greeting I could go for every single day," he chimed.

Mila shook her head. "Of course it is… I'm in a good mood today, so I have something special for you, darling."

Adrian gulped when he saw the glimmer in her eyes, sensing some mischief behind them. His eyes then wandered down to take in the sight of her. The silk robe was all she wore, and he could see her nipples already perked up against the material.

"What do you have in mind… Ms. Mila?"

"It's better if I show you…" Mila took his hand and Adrian followed her lead up the steps and into the bedroom. When he saw the bed, he got an idea of what was going to happen. The comforter and top sheet were removed, leaving only the fitted sheet over the mattress. He looked over to the dresser and saw two bundles of rope sitting next to scissors and a magic wand and Adrian's face brightened, turning to Mila.

A hand flat against his chest, she pushed him toward the bed until it hit the back of his knees and he fell on it. Mila crawled on top of Adrian and looked down at him with a devilish smile. "Are you ready for what I have planned?"

"Yes," he replied quickly, lifting his head to look at her. His eyes wandered down her body to see that the bottom of her robe opened with her position, exposing her pussy. Mila sucked her teeth when she followed his gaze and pressed his forehead so he would lay back down flat.

Mila unbuttoned his shirt completely before rubbing up and down his chest. She then leaned forward to place soft kisses from his jaw, to his collarbone, to his chest. Her tongue made a path back up to his neck where she sucked the patch of flesh that sat just above his shoulder. Adrian reached forward to caress her thighs and Mila took both his arms and pinned them above his head as she hovered over him to meet his eyes.

"No, no..." Mila said softly, shaking her head. "Today it's all about you..." That was when she captured Adrian in an intense kiss, his lips parting with hers, her tongue entering his mouth and conquering his. He moaned against her and she broke away, releasing a satisfied hum. "Take off the rest of your clothes for me and then lay down on the center of the bed."

Adrian did as he was told. Laying down and looking at the ceiling, he already had an idea of what Mila planned to do after seeing the rope, and he spread his arms and legs apart so they were closer to each corner of the bed.

"Good boy," Mila cooed when she returned to the bed with ropes in her hands. Adrian watched her with anticipation as she took his wrists and put them together above his head to bind them before taking the leftover rope and tying it to the bed frame. She then placed the other rope next to him on the bed. "Not right now," she said when she noticed him eyeing the unused rope. "I want your legs to be free for this scene."

"Yes, Ms. Mila..." Adrian swallowed when Mila got back on top of him now that he was bound. She straddled his torso and he could feel the heat between her legs against his abdomen. His gaze drifted down to admire her form when she removed the tie from her robe, allowing it to open completely, giving him a better view of her body. He adored the way her plump breasts fell over her stomach and how the curves of her hips were perfect for holding.

Just as his mind started to wander, Adrian was interrupted by Mila covering his eyes. She used the tie from her robe as a blindfold for him.

Adrian felt Mila get off of him before four acrylic nails dragged their way down from his neck to his pelvis. Her lips scoured his jaw as she caressed his body. She came back up to meet his lips, gently kissing Adrian. When he lifted his head to press forward and deepen the kiss, Mila pushed him back down.

"Why so eager, darling?" she teased. Her lips lightly brushed against his before tracing his bottom one with her tongue. Adrian let out a shaky exhale at the sensation of her nails again making their way down his body, this time to his dick. Her breath against his ear sent a shiver down his spine. "I love how hard you get for me... you're always *so* ready."

"Thank you, Ms. Mila," he breathed. A sharp breath crossed his nose when he felt a finger against his tip, using his pre-cum to play with it.

Tempering his desire, Adrian managed to keep himself almost completely still as Mila teased him despite wanting to add more friction. He couldn't see it, but Mila's eyes narrowed and she tilted her head curiously.

That was when she completely removed her robe and straddled him again, now with her pussy rubbing against his length. When she started moving, he let out a soft moan. As she moved, Adrian's sounds became more persistent and he began lifting his hips to try to create more friction.

"Wh-what?" Adrian exhaled his frustration when Mila lifted away.

"It's been days of edging and you're nowhere near as needy as you should be... You should be desperate."

His eyes were uncovered to reveal Mila looking down at him skeptically.

"Tell me, Adrian..." She leaned in and grabbed his face gently, but with a firm grip. "Did you fuck Caleb?"

Immediately he swallowed before parting his lips to speak. "I... well I um..." His eyes fell, breaking contact with hers. "Yes."

"And you came?"

"We... we both did."

Adrian heard Mila suck her teeth before she let go of his face. He watched her get off the bed and walk over to where she had the ropes sitting before and saw her pick something up, though her back was to him.

"I-I'm sorry, Ms. Mila... We um... we were just... both of us were..." He drifted off when she turned around and to his surprise, she had the magic wand and small bottle of lube in her hands. Adrian kept his eyes on Mila when she returned to him. Without a word, she replaced the extra rope on the bed with the wand while using the rope to bind his ankles separately to the bottom of the frame.

"Did I give you permission to come, Adrian?" she questioned calmly.

"N-no..."

"Yet you did it anyway?" Mila scoffed and shook her head. "Caleb isn't the only greedy one, I see."

"He seduced—"

"Quiet," Mila said sternly and Adrian pressed his lips closed. "Don't worry, darling... this will only change our plans just a little." She crawled between his legs and poured the lubricant on his dick before taking it into her hand. "You see... I *was* going to allow you to come tonight. I wanted it. But instead, you gave that to Caleb."

"I... I'm sorry."

"Shhhh... It's okay," Mila assured as she began stroking him. "You're going to pay me back, aren't you, darling?"

Adrian nodded urgently. "Y-yes, Ms. Mila..." The sounds of his moans grew louder as Mila's hand moved up and down his shaft and the other played with his balls. She smirked when she felt them already begin to tighten.

"You better come for me soon, darling... unless you want me to stop."

"N-no," Adrian choked out. He could feel his release rising within him. "I... I'm close..."

"Close isn't good enough." Mila tightened her grip and moved her other hand up to rub his tip while she continued stroking him.

"Shhhitttt," Adrian exhaled through clenched teeth as he came all over Mila's hands. He looked up to see her licking her lips at the sight.

"Where are your manners, darling?"

"Th-thank you, Ms. Mila."

She looked down at him with a devious pull of her lips. "More."

Adrian arched his back and moaned again when she put the wand on a low setting against the tip of his dick. His breathing grew ragged as Mila kept going. "Oh god..."

"What's wrong, darling? You wanted to come so badly before... what's the matter now?" Mila turned up the toy and stroked faster.

Adrian was sensitive and the feeling was intense. He pressed his head back on the bed at another release, his body trembling with it. Mila put the wand away and continued to play with him.

"Th... Thank you... Ms. Mila."

"More."

"Fuck!" Adrian had a loud outburst when the lubricated tip of Mila's finger pressed against his ass.

Mila let out an entertained huff. "You wanted to come so *fucking* bad that you broke the rules, so I'm going to keep it going for you, darling."

"I-I... damnit." Adrian strained and squirmed and struggled against the restraints. "Fuck! Fuck!" He shouted at the sensation of Mila's finger further inside of him, pressing just the right spot.

Again, he came, the intensity of his orgasm bringing tears to his eyes. "ThankyoumsMila!"

"There we go... I know you've got more in there, so give it to me."

Adrian was losing himself to the pleasure that came over him, his moans loud and shameless. His heels dug into the bed as he braced himself, lifting his hips. Mila scooted closer between his legs, her hand and fingers unrelenting.

"Give me one more, darling... I'm helping you get what you wanted, aren't I?" Mila's tone was playful, teasing him and only turning Adrian on more.

"Oh fuck!" He choked out a loud moan with another orgasm. His hips dropped into Mila's lap as she finally eased her strokes, removed her fingers from him and allowed him to catch his breath.

Blinking the blurriness from his eyes, he looked down to see Mila with a satisfied smile, her hands and his groin covered in a clear mix of lubricant and his orgasms. She scooted back to allow his bottom to lay flat on the bed and crawled her way up to hover above him.

"Tell me... Are you satisfied now, darling?"

Needy

"Fuck," Adrian groaned. Lying in bed, he stretched out his arms and legs before bringing his hands back down over his dick through his boxers. "I'm sore."

"Good," Mila replied curtly. She was sitting up in bed next to him reading something on her phone. Without looking away from it, she continued to speak. "Maybe now you'll know better than to come when you were explicitly told not to."

Still laying down, he craned his neck to look up at her with a small smile on his face. "And Caleb? Are you planning to give him the same punishment?"

Mila sighed. "I haven't decided on one for him yet, but something tells me that milking him would feel more like a reward for Caleb."

"You've got that right. He's also a heavy masochist."

"I'm sure he is," Mila replied nonchalantly. She put her phone on the nightstand when Adrian finally lifted himself up to get out of bed.

"I still need to pack my bags before the flight. I'll see you when we leave?"

Mila shook her head. "We're going in separate cars, remember? You and Justin are getting a car and Caleb booked some transport for him and I through the hotel."

"Oh right, I forgot about that." Adrian walked over to Mila's side of the bed and sat down to face her while he took her hand. "When we're back in Lenrod, would you like to go on another date with me?"

Mila smiled at him in response and leaned in to kiss his lips. "That sounds like a plan to me. Now go pack your bags. I'll see you at the airport."

MILA AND CALEB sat in the back of the luxury Suburban van on their way to the airport. It wasn't her preference, but the ride had already been booked by Caleb days ago when he got her moved to the penthouse of the hotel where they were staying. *They had a special package deal, so I thought why not?'* was the rationale he gave Mila. While she didn't buy it, she also didn't care enough to make any changes.

Mila scrolled aimlessly through her phone, ignoring text notifications and opting to look through social media. Caleb stared out the window as he tapped his thumb against the car door.

The backseat was roomy enough for both of them to stretch their legs out and lounge without being uncomfortable.

However, Caleb was still uneasy.

Reflecting on the Atlanta trip, he was agitated. He booked it specifically as an excuse to get alone time with Mila, but Adrian and Justin ruined that for him. Not only did the two of them crash the trip, they both had alone time with Mila while Caleb was either in meetings, left out after failing Mila's 'tests', or stuck sharing her attention with the other two men.

But even with his agitation, Caleb also had underlying feelings of excitement. Being intimate with Mila and Adrian at the same time put him in a space he rarely got to enjoy—both of them ordering him around, using him, toying with him—he wanted more of it. And he hoped that now that the door for that had been opened, he'd have more opportunities with Mila and Adrian, together and separately.

Caleb's mind began to run wild with fantasies of their new dynamic and all that could come of it. His thoughts were cut short when Mila broke the silence between them.

"Adrian told me about the other night," she said, not looking up from her phone. The tone of her voice was indecipherable for Caleb. She didn't sound upset, but there was a hint of disappointment.

Caleb gulped. "What do you mean?"

"You wanna try that again?"

When she was met with silence, Mila looked up from her phone to turn her attention to Caleb. His mouth was closed tight and he ran his fingers through his hair as he looked forward in the direction of the driver.

"Excuse me, driver," Mila called. "May you roll up the partition, please?"

"Yes, ma'am," the driver replied before doing as he was told.

Caleb turned to meet her eyes—they did not hold an aura of disgust or annoyance as they often did when when Mila looked at him. Instead, her gaze was simply expectant, and with the partition closed, Caleb felt more comfortable whispering his answer.

"Yeah, we fucked," he admitted.

"Hm..."

"What did you expect? You edged both of us and then sent us to bed with each other. And it's clear you know we have a history."

"That wasn't what my 'hm' was for. I don't think I've ever seen you show shame, Mr. Peterson. Yet, you were afraid to let the driver hear our conversation?"

"I wasn't afraid," he replied quickly, still whispering. "And I'm not ashamed of fucking men. I haven't been since college... It would just be pretty fucking bad for anyone to know that the three heads of the company are involved with the assistant... at the same time... and sometimes together... and sometimes with each other... minus Justin."

"Interesting..." was all Mila cared to say in response. Now that she was facing him, Mila examined Caleb. He was undoubtedly a handsome man. Caleb had chiseled features, but not overly so, allowing his face to have a softness to it that made him look approachable. His lips were almost as full as Adrian's and from her few experiences kissing him, Mila was already aware of how skillful Caleb was with his mouth. Her gaze drifted lower down his body. He wore loose fitting jeans and a short-sleeve black teeshirt. The way it clung to his broad chest and tightened around his crossed arms had Mila subconsciously licking her lips.

It pisses me off that he looks this good, she thought to herself. *And it doesn't help that I also know he's just the type of sub I like. I could break him and he'd love every minute of him.*

"Come here," Mila said and Caleb snapped his gaze over to her.

"What?"

"You heard me. Don't make me repeat myself."

Without giving it another second, Caleb scooted closer to Mila so that he was right next to her in the middle seat.

"You're learning... even if it's very slowly." Mila's voice was soft and she ran the back of her hand down Caleb's face before her fingers rested at the neckline of his shirt, the sensation sending a shiver down his spine. "And for once you're not being a brat."

Caleb nodded, he kept his hands at his sides, but his eyes were on Mila, taking in the sight of her. She wore an olive green crop hoodie and matching sweatpants. The curves of her breasts were visible against the fabric of her top and the bottoms hugged her hips and thighs in a way that was enticing to Caleb. He was sure he'd be in trouble if he touched her without permission, so he dug his fingers into the seat cushion.

Mila crossed her leg in his direction and brought his hand that was closest to her to place it on her thigh. She leaned in to whisper against his ear as her hand worked its way down his body.

"It's okay, pet, you can touch me here, but only here..."

"T-thank you, Mis—"

"Shhh..." Mila placed a silencing finger over his lips. "No need for the honorifics right now, though I *do* enjoy how easy it is to get that out of you." Her hand then returned to drifting down his body.

"Thank you," he breathed.

"You're *really* easy, you know that? It's pathetic..." Mila toyed with the waistline of Caleb's jeans. "But it also turns me on," she added before catching his lobe between her teeth.

When he let out a shaky breath in response, Mila began to focus on the button of his pants as she continued to tease him.

"Adrian got his punishment last night, but I'm still deciding on what to do with you. I heard you're a pain slut, so a spanking might be more of a reward for you. So what shall it be, I wonder... More edging? Maybe a milking like him?"

Caleb took deep breaths as he listened to Mila, trying to keep himself calm.

"You're such a versatile toy that my options are almost endless." She moved her hand from the button on his waistline to rub the bulge growing in his pants. Caleb's head fell back, exposing his neck and Mila gently ran her tongue against it. She enjoyed teasing him, the moment just as much of a turn on for her as it was for him. And while she hadn't picked his punishment yet, she knew that toying with him was just the start of it.

"Are you enjoying this, pet?" Mila asked softly.

"Yes, Mila."

Mila's phone ringing interrupted them and she looked down to see Justin calling her. Breaking away from Caleb, she huffed her annoyance and muttered expletives under her breath before gesturing for him to go back to his seat. When she picked up the phone, she heard announcements for flights in the background. While she knew Justin was type-A like her sister and was always on time, she didn't expect him to show up at the airport for a domestic flight three hours early.

"Hey Justin," Mila answered. "What are you doing at the airport so early?"

"Mila!" he exclaimed. "Where are you? Our flight is about to leave."

Caleb was able to hear Justin's urgent voice through the phone and turned away from Mila to look out the window with a smug look on his face.

Her head jerked back. "What are you talking about? The flight isn't until five o'clock... Then again, I didn't book your flights since you and Adrian decided to come on your own."

"Yeah, and we booked our return on the same flight. Caleb said you guys were leaving at two-fifteen..." Justin paused with a deep sigh. Mila could hear him on the other side of the phone, his voice slightly quieter as if he pulled it away. "You were right, Adrian. Of course he fucking lied to us."

"Both of you have spent a lot of time with me and didn't think to ask? I just saw Adrian this morning and mentioned that Caleb and I were riding together this afternoon." He probably still wasn't thinking straight at the time, Mila thought to herself.

"We already had the information from Caleb, and it's not like our time together was spent talking about logistics..."

Mila chuckled, not bothering to hide her amusement. "And you believed him? Yeah, this one is on you guys. We're still about an hour from the airport. You know how Atlanta traffic gets."

"What an asshole," Justin griped, agitation clear in his tone. "I guess we'll see you back in Lenrod..."

"Bye, Justin." Mila hung up the phone and turned her attention back to Caleb. "Mr. Peterson, what did you think putting Adrian and Justin on a different flight would accomplish?"

Caleb turned to look at Mila with a slight pout on his face. He crossed his arms and sunk in his seat. "I didn't get any alone time with you," he mumbled.

"What was that?"

There was a long pause as Caleb stubbornly pressed his lips together. Mila reached out and ran her fingers through his hair, pushing it out of his face.

"Words." Her tone was calm. Caleb cut his eyes at her before he softened his face.

"We didn't have any alone time. You were with Adrian or Justin or your friends. I didn't get anything..." He paused when he saw Mila raise a brow at the last part. "I just mean... we didn't get any alone time. And this was *my* trip to begin with."

Mila, who had been playing with his hair since she'd pushed it out of his face before, brought her hand down to caress his jaw. The few times he would show his gentler side, Mila found him more tolerable.

"Do you blame me, Mr. Peterson? You've disrespected me time and time again since I've started working for you. Why would I feel inclined to spend alone time with you?"

"Please, you know you like it when I..." He cut toward the partition, unsure how much the driver could hear, so he lowered his voice into a whisper. "I know you're into me, Mila. You like the way I am... You said it yourself."

"None of what you said answers my question. What's the incentive to being alone? All four of us were intimate at once this week. Though you were more of a spectator, weren't you?"

"Shut up!" Caleb snapped and immediately regretted his decision when he saw the glare on Mila's face.

"Interrupt me or talk to me like that again and it won't end well for you..." Her voice turned cold, the coldest Caleb had ever heard it. "Maybe I'd spend more time alone with you if you knew the first thing about showing some *fucking* respect."

"I'm s-sor... That's just... I just..." Caleb let out a frustrated sigh. "I don't mean those things... I just say them."

Mila snorted as she shook her head and pulled her hand away from Caleb. "You think that's an acceptable response? Embarrassing..." And then it was she who turned to look out the window, effectively ending the conversation.

Caleb sunk himself further into his seat and kept his gaze forward. "I'm sorry," he said softly, though not loud enough for Mila to hear.

But For Now...

"That was a dick move lying to us about your return flight, Caleb." Justin scolded his co-founder as the three of them sat with each other at their favorite cigar bar. It was a routine the three established to go there the first Sunday of each month to talk business or personal life. Maintaining their friendship throughout their various ventures was important to them, and this was one of the activities they'd partake in to maintain their camaraderie.

Caleb took a shallow pull from the cigar and blew the smoke out his mouth. He looked at Adrian and Justin across from him who also had cigars of their own as be shook his head.

"If you guys didn't crash our fucking trip, that wouldn't have happened. It was supposed to be *my* time with Mila. Then you two showed up. And don't act like it was for anything other than her."

"I think we're well passed pretending when it comes to Mila," Justin replied. "And that includes you."

Adrian leaned forward toward Caleb, resting his elbows on his knees. "You can't keep denying you're attracted to her now. Not that your act was working in the first place."

Taking another puff of his his cigar and relaxing back against his seat as he spread his legs, Caleb smiled at both men. "You know what? Yeah, I'm into her. And I'm gonna take her from the two of you."

To that, both Justin and Adrian bursted out laughing.

"Yeah, yeah... Laugh all you fucking want now. You won't be doing that when *I'm* her favorite of the month."

Adrian and Justin continued, only further entertained by Caleb's assertion.

"You think this is so fucking funny like I'm not next up? And she likes that I'm a *versatile toy*... Even more than you two... Adrian knows... He used to say the same thing."

Adrian ceased laughing and cut his eyes at Caleb. While his expression was sharp, it wasn't one of anger or disgust. Instead, it was a knowing look. He and Mila had similar preferences when it came to Caleb, and he realized that she saw in him the same things that Adrian did.

"That reminds me..." Adrian relaxed back in his seat again, adding distance between himself and Caleb, but keeping his eyes on him. "Mila and I have been talking about you."

Caleb looked at Adrian expectantly, awaiting more words, more details on what exactly they'd talked about, but Adrian stopped there, taking another pull from his cigar as his gaze darkened.

Justin glanced between his two best friends and noticed there seemed to be some type of nonverbal communication going on. Normally, when they got into it like this, Justin stayed out of it. At times, he felt like a third wheel, especially over the few months when Adrian and Caleb seemed to have been spending almost every day together. He knew they had hooked up before, and suspected something romantic may have been happening, but things soured between the two men too quickly for Justin to really consider it.

Eyes locked with Adrian, Caleb's jaw tensed as he was flooded with memories from just a few days ago—the three of them with Mila, Adrian and Mila teasing him, his morning with Adrian, and that moment in the car with Mila.

"You're such a versatile toy that my options are almost endless."
Mila's words stuck with Caleb, and he held onto them. It wasn't just

what she said, but *how* she said it. Her voice was like velvet, she spoke with pure confidence, and there was an undertone that told Caleb she was thinking about some of those 'options' when she was speaking to him. He wondered if she'd fantasized about him as much as he did her. And when Caleb realized how well Mila and Adrian work together when playing with him, he realized they could give him exactly what he wanted: to be their toy.

Finally, Caleb was the first to break their staring match, looking away and asking, "Talking about me for what?"

The right side of Adrian's lips pulled into a smirk. "I'm sure you have an idea... *pet.*"

Caleb swallowed and put out his cigar—catching himself before his thoughts could run wild.

"Whatever," he said with a huff. "Let's get back to talking about business. We're going to need to ask our *benefactors* for more money so we can acquire another one of Thompson Luxe Group's brands. They're going to be the hardest competitor to remove from the picture, but once we crush them, we'll practically own the industry."

Justin nodded.

"I can make the call this time. I also need cash for something else."

MILA HUFFED AS she fell into the couch in her living room. She was exhausted... mentally. While reading Adrian, Justin, and Caleb was easy enough for her, what had her gears turning was herself.

Caleb—as much as Mila hated to admit it—piqued her interest. She enjoyed playing games with him the most. His brattiness was ample entertainment, and him being a heavy bottom gave Mila a mountain of ideas on scenes they could do together. He appealed to the sadist in her. There also seemed to be an underlying issue Caleb had, something other than the constant teasing that he was deeply frustrated about, and Mila wondered if it had to do with whatever past he and Adrian had.

Justin had become *almost* a friend to Mila. If she weren't trying to take down his company, she would've actually called him one. They had certain similarities when it came to parents with high-expectations and growing up as overachievers. However, that upbringing resulted in Mila seeking freedom and living life on her own terms, while Justin continued to try to keep his parents proud.

Adrian caused Mila to feel things she hadn't understood before—sensations she never thought she'd have again, nor did she care to. But it was too late. She liked the way she felt around him. She liked *him*... a lot. And Mila wasn't sure what that could mean for when she finished her time at PMC Group.

She shook her head and let out a deep sigh.

I'll just keep doing whatever I like... At least until I put this final puzzle piece together and bring down their company.

Mila had learned a lot about the inner workings of PMC Group while she was there. The company managed to complete acquisition after acquisition, taking down its competition by chipping away at other luxury conglomerates. However, that seemed to be the only purpose of buying the smaller companies. They did not serve a strategic purpose for PMC Group's business strategy. While cutting the competition was a huge benefit, buying other companies came at significant costs, and considering their profitability often faltered as they were neglected after being acquired by PMC Group, the benefit didn't seem worth what they were paying.

Yet PMC Group continued to have enough money to purchase more companies. Mila was sure that capital was received under suspicious circumstances, but she needed to know the exact details. And with those details, she'd be able to end PMC Group.

And her mission would be complete.

No more Adrian. No more Justin. No more Caleb.

Her loyalty was to her family. She entered PMC Group under the guise of Mila Nelson to take down the company from within. She had admittedly gotten distracted playing her games with the men who owned the company, but she still made progress, albeit slowly.

Mila knew she was dragging things out, and Alexis was growing increasingly impatient. The only reason Mila was able to keep Alexis at bay was by reminding her that she was doing all the work and taking all the risks.

Her contract should have been up a few months ago, but Adrian and Justin immediately extended it for another year, though what they really wanted was to hire Mila permanently. Mila knew she couldn't drag it out much longer, and once she got that final piece of the puzzle, she would need to end it all.

But for now, Mila would continue to have her fun.

As Told

"So, what's your schedule looking like today, Mila?" Justin asked. They were together in his office for their morning meeting, going over Justin's plans for the day. She was sitting across from him as he sat at his desk—positions they held that an outsider looking in would see as a typical boss-assistant dynamic. However, it had gone far beyond that for Justin and after their time in Atlanta, he was more distracted than ever each time he met with Mila.

"Not much. After this, I have..."

As Mila went on, her words faded out and Justin examined the woman before him. Her hair was slicked up in a bun, she went for a more subtle makeup look with brown eyeshadow that almost matched her skin, a single layer of foundation, and a nude gloss over her full lips. She wore a black button up blouse and Justin remembered how she said she had to get them custom made because 'button ups are not made for people with titties'. It reminded him of the rants she would often have about the fashion industry, poorly made clothes, and the inaccessibility of properly-fitted clothing due to cost restraints. Those rants of hers resulted in him and Adrian speaking privately about possibly launching an initiative—a specialized fashion brand—to address those issues, that Mila would lead.

However, they wanted to make sure that the intimate relationships they had going on with her weren't having *too* much of an influence on their business decisions.

Although Mila and Justin continued to mess around since returning to Lenrod City—at least in the office when they could share brief moments between business—they had yet to find time for a full night together of just the two of them.

Flashbacks from their trip often flooded Justin's mind when he was with Mila, and he kept thinking about how he wanted more. He wanted to feel her wrapped around him, give her praise for how good she felt, and receive some of his own for the pleasure he was confident he could give her. He wanted to feel her on top of him as she rode his dick, her hand wrapped around his neck, her teeth pulling at his lip, her nails digging into him and leaving marks behind. He wanted to hear his name rolling off her tongue as he was buried inside of her until she met her climax and gave him permission to have his.

"... Are you even listening to me, Mr. Matsuda?" Mila questioned, breaking Justin out of his thoughts. He'd seemed distracted as she spoke to him, running his tongue across his lips in a movement that appeared to be subconscious.

Justin readjusted in his seat. "Oh, um... Sorry, Mila. What were you saying?"

"Don't worry about that..." Mila tilted her head to the side with a small smile. "Now, I'm much more interested in what had you so distracted as I was answering your question."

"I just..." Justin gulped, looking down at his desk and then back up at Mila. "It's been a while since we had some time together... *ample* time together."

Nodding thoughtfully, Mila took out her phone, swiped through it and did some typing. "We keep trying to do nights but since that's not working, let's do a day. This Sunday work?"

Without missing a beat, Justin nodded his agreement. "Yes! That works for me. We can go to my favorite brunch spot."

Mila raised a silencing hand. "No need unless you can book us a private room in there. Let's just order out and come to my place. Between working here and as many business meetings we've been to with me as your assistant, we can't risk someone seeing us have Sunday brunch together. Lunch during a work day is one thing, but together on a weekend? Not a good look."

Justin blinked rapidly. "You're right. I'll pick it up and bring it over to your place."

Relaxing back in her seat and crossing her legs, Mila looked over at Justin with a glint in her eyes.

Whenever she'd look at him like that, Justin found himself frozen with a rapid beating in his chest and blood rushing to his dick. There was no doubting the hold that Mila had over him, Adrian, and even Caleb. He never thought someone could have him wrapped around their finger in that way, but between how impressed he was with Mila's business savvy, their friendship being in full bloom, and the fact that she had already given him new, mind-blowing experiences, Justin found himself completely smitten.

"Good. So, we now have a plan, Mr. Matsuda."

THE NOTIFICATION SOUNDED on Mila's computer to signal it was time for her meeting with Caleb. She pushed away from her desk, picked up her tablet, and slowly made her way toward his office.

Once Mila walked in, Caleb looked at her with anticipation. It was in stark contrast to the expressions he'd show her when she first started working for PMC Group over a year ago. The first time they met, he'd looked at her with disgust. The times that followed were lust, rage, curiosity, reverence—sometimes a mix of all four.

But since they returned from Atlanta, Caleb's expression each time he saw Mila was one of anticipation. She had finally decided on his punishment, and it was simple: Edging until she was no longer entertained by it... Or, until he was pitiful enough that she'd give him the mercy of a release.

"Hello Mila," Caleb greeted.

"Mr. Peterson," she replied.

Mila approached Caleb and placed her tablet on his desk before gesturing for him to move back from it and he did as instructed. She then moved to stand between Caleb and his desk, looking down at him with a mischievous smile. She dragged her knuckles along the side of his face, tracing his jaw until she reached his chin and placed her thumb against his bottom lip. His Adam's apple bobbed as he swallowed and kept himself still.

The anticipation had his heart racing and heat coming over his body. Every day for the past week and a half, it was the same routine. Mila would stand in the spot in front of him. She'd admire his appearance, with a clear expression of satisfaction at his obedience. Then, she would instruct him to release himself from his pants and stroke his dick for her as she talked him through it. Just before he met his climax, she'd stop him, he'd huff his frustration but do as told, she'd give him a few parting words, and then leave him in his office where he'd be unable to focus for the rest of the day.

However, the routine of it didn't stop Caleb's excitement. Although he rarely showed it, he was an attentive man, and it was the smaller, more subtle details of Mila's attitude and mannerisms that led to him falling to his knees for her. So, with each day he noticed the little changes. Mila had gone from watching with her arms crossed as she leaned against his desk to keeping them open and rested on the surface at each side of her. Her words as she talked him through the pleasure changed each day, her voice just a bit breathier, her tongue would run across her lips—lust lighting a fire in her eyes.

"Take it out for me, pet," Eve instructed softly. "And drop your pants all the way this time."

"Yes, Mistress..." Caleb did as he was told and released himself, allowing his pants to fall around his ankles. He had a partial erection where pre-cum was already leaking from his tip.

Just when he was about to reach for his desk drawer beside Mila to pull out lubricant to begin stroking himself as they'd been doing the days before, she stopped him.

"Not today..." Maintaining eye contact, Mila leaned forward, holding herself up on the arms of Caleb's chair and caging him in. Her gaze then drifted down to his length and she allowed spit to fall from her mouth onto it. Caleb let out a shaky breath when he felt it make contact with his dick. "Now, stroke it for me."

Again, Caleb followed her instructions. He slowly began moving his hand up and down his length, using Mila's saliva as lubricant. His head fell back against his chair and he opened his mouth to breathe.

Mila was deeply turned on at the sight of him as she took in every twitch of his face. "Tighten your grip."

"Fuck..." Caleb breathed. Over a week of edging had him highly sensitive, but he knew that if he wanted to spend more time with Mila, he'd need to last as long as he could before reaching the edge of his release.

Her lips parted, Mila brushed them over Caleb's before lightly running them along his jaw and up to his ear. "Watching you come undone like this really turns me on," she whispered before catching his lobe between her teeth. "Then again, maybe 'come' isn't the word in this case," she added, the taunting smile coming through in her tone.

"Can... can I please... c-come... today?" Caleb struggled to get the words out through his labored breaths. The answer was already clear when Mila let out an entertained huff.

"Oh, pet. You already know the answer to that." Mila spit on his length again before she dipped her head into his neck and lightly sucked and licked it from his right side to the left.

"Fuck," Caleb exhaled. "Your tongue feels so good."

Mila hummed her satisfaction. "You've been fantasizing about it, haven't you?"

Caleb opened his eyes to meet Mila's, his gaze filled with desire. "All the time... and a lot more than just that... I want you to use me."

"Use you? Expand on that for me, pet."

"I... I want to be your toy. I want- fuck..." Caleb was losing himself, trying to keep from approaching his release as he held Mila's gaze while fantasies about her ran through his mind.

"Keep going... I know you can hold it for me."

Caleb shuddered with his pleasure. "I want you to use me... my hands... my mouth... my coc- my dick... my ass... whatever you want from me... you and Adrian."

"I like the sound of that, pet."

Mila's hand dropped between Caleb's legs and she started teasing his balls. He had an outburst at the sensation and she silenced him with a kiss. A pool was forming between her legs as Caleb moaned into her mouth, their tongues moving urgently against each other.

When she noticed Caleb's arm stopped moving, Mila broke away. Her hand went up to his cheek so she could hold his face. His breathing was heavy and eyes closed while his lips remained parted. Caleb was completely at her mercy and Mila couldn't help the devilish grin that grew on her face. Her gaze drifted down his body until it reached his dick. The head was swollen and veins pronounced. Mila slowly dragged her hand from his balls, up his shaft, and to his tip.

"Please," Caleb moaned. "Oh, fuck..."

Mila removed her hand and turned her attention back up to his face.

"You did a good job today, pet. A *very* good job."

"Th-thank you, Mistress."

She placed a kiss on his forehead before standing up straight and giving Caleb a few minutes to catch his breath and gather himself enough to pull up his pants.

When he was calm again, now with a large bulge in his pants, Mila asked, "How are you feeling, pet?"

"Do you want an honest answer for that?"

Mila smiled and shook her head, the frustration in his tone gave her enough satisfaction. She pushed off the desk, picked up her tablet, and started making her way to the door.

"Same time tomorrow, Mr. Peterson?"

She heard a huff from Caleb before he answered.

"Yeah, put it on our calendars."

"Already done."

Risks

"Hey, Lexi..." Mila greeted her sister as she opened the door for her to enter the apartment. "It's been a while since I've seen you. I know I've been missing those brunches with mom... I'm not sorry about that, to be honest."

"Well, little sis. I'm not here about that." Alexis walked inside of the apartment, keeping her coat on and looking around the space. She hadn't seen her sister's new place since Mila moved following the scare with Eric. Alexis understood Mila's reluctance to give her new address away after what their mother did—she didn't approve of her sharing the information with Mila's ex either. And if she had done something like that to Alexis, she would've gotten a lot more than ignored calls and avoidance, as Mila had done. Their mother was lucky that Mila had a calmer nature.

"Then why are you here?" Mila questioned. "Wanted to see my new place? Just don't tell mom where it is, will you?"

Alexis sucked her teeth and crossed her arms. "You know why I'm here, Mila. You've been at PMC Group for over a year. And they've scooped one of our companies from under us. What are you doing there? What's taking so long?"

Mila walked over to her kitchen and started going through her cabinets. "They've been trying to move in on our companies for at least six months now, but *I've* been redirecting their attention to other brands… with the exception of that one of ours that sold insanely quick."

"And now?"

"And now they've gone through enough competitor brands that they've turned their attention back to ours."

"So what do you plan to do? '*Redirect*' them again?" Alexis used the term mockingly and Mila stopped her search through her cabinets to turn to her sister with a hardened expression.

"Do not catch a tone with me, Alexis. I'm the reason they haven't grabbed more companies from under us. Hell, *I'm* the reason you even know that they're trying to poach our companies again…" Mila huffed. "Do I need to remind you once again? *I'm* the one who's taking the risks here. *I'm* the one who has to work for them. *I'm* the one who has to deal with all this shit while you sit on your ass and wait for updates from me."

"Sitting on my ass?" Alexis raised her voice. "I'm running our family's company! And I refuse to let it fail under my leadership. You're supposed to be helping me—helping *our* family. Instead, it seems more like you're just helping yourself."

Mila crossed her arms and tilted her head as she gave her sister a sharp glare. "You wanna tell me what the fuck you mean by that?"

"Oh please, Mila! You think I don't know that you're fucking at least one of your bosses. Hell, knowing you, I wouldn't be surprised if it were all three."

There was a silence, Mila's lips pressed tightly together before she turned her attention back to her cabinets to pull out a bottle of red wine.

Alexis groaned and shook her head. "You *are* fucking all three of them, aren't you?"

"So?" Mila replied matter-of-factly as she searched through her kitchen drawers for a bottle opener. "I'm a grown ass woman. I can do what I want. And besides, you told me at the start that I can do what I want, as long as we bring them down."

"I didn't think it would involve you dragging it out for so long, Mila!"

"Okay, chill out," Mila cautioned. "Don't raise your voice at me in my home. Especially when it's *my* ass that's on the line."

Alexis calmed her volume back to a level tone. "Your *ass* is part of the problem here. You don't see that? You really don't think that the fact you've been messing around with your bosses doesn't have *any* influence on this task taking you so long?"

Mila let out a deep breath. She was frustrated with Alexis. As she already told her sister—she was the one taking all of the risk, while Alexis stood to get all the benefits. Even if it was for her family company, if they faced persecution, Mila would be at the highest risk for a harsh punishment. While Alexis assured her that the Davidson family could help if they did find themselves in legal trouble, Mila wasn't sure how much weight that actually held.

"They haven't hurt our company," Mila replied, not hiding the agitation in her voice. "And I'm smart enough to anticipate when they'll become a real threat. I'm almost done, so let me do my fucking job and you'll get what you want."

"Mila, please be fucking for real right now. You're talking about all this risk that you're taking, and you don't think dragging things out is *adding* to that risk? And it's only a matter of time until they begin to succeed at buying more of our companies from under us if they're not taken down soon."

"Lexi, you're annoying the fuck out of me."

"Because your judgment is clouded, Mila! Are you like a sex addict or something? You're quite literally letting pleasure get in the way of business."

She is still raising her goddamn voice at me in my *home.* Mila slammed her hand flat on the counter, the slap echoing in the room, startling Alexis who'd never seen her often chill sister lash out with such intensity. "Do you think I'm fucking dumb?"

Again, Alexis was reminded to lower her tone and her voice went down. "N-no..."

"Then why are you scolding me like you think that I'm stupid? The *one* time they actually looked like they *might* threaten our company, I redirected PMC Group from targeting our brands. Now that their sights are on us again, I'll either do the same thing or sabotage them some other way. Besides, we can afford to lose the less profitable companies we own, anyway. So, why don't we let them buy some of the trash, let them do some clean up for us, *and then* take them down?"

"Mila..."

"Lexi, when it comes down to it, you have no choice but to let me do what I want to do. *You're* not the one spying on them. What are you going to do? Pull me out of the company? Then what? The past year and several months that I spent there would be for nothing."

After a long pause, Alexis sighed her defeat. "Fine. You've made your point. But please, Mila... Finish this up ASAP. No more than a few months—*next* quarter."

"Mhmm..." Mila tucked the bottle of wine under her arm and held two glasses in her hand as she walked over to her dining room table to set them all down. "Now, drink this wine and tell me about the filthy rich single-dad-slash-crime-lord, Sean Davidson, you've been seeing. I know one thing... He must not be blowing your back out with that fucking attitude you got."

With the offering of wine, the tension in the room eased. Alexis relaxed her shoulders and took her coat off before joining her sister at the table. "Not a single damn filter on you."

"Oh, I can filter myself. I just know when it's appropriate."

"Fine, we can talk about him."

~

CALEB AGGRESSIVELY TYPED on his computer, responding to an email as Adrian sat across from them. The clicking of the keys was intense and Caleb was muttering expletives under his breath as he went on. Adrian shook his head at his frustrated demeanor.

"You're in a bad mood," Adrian commented once Caleb finished typing.

Caleb moved his mouse to click 'send' on the email before he cut his eyes at Adrian. "Do you blame me? I'm still being punished for something *you* did."

"Me?" Adrian scoffed. "You're the one who just *had* to tell me that you 'prepped' and everything."

A small smile immediately pulled at Caleb's lips. "So, we can agree that I'm not the only 'easy' one."

"Whatever. Let's just get through those Thompson Luxe Group files so we can pick our next targets and I can get out of here. Mila and I have a date night at her place."

Caleb's head jerked back and he gave a tight-lipped fake smile. "You really had to give that detail, didn't you? You're welcome, by the way."

Adrian raised a questioning brow. "For what?"

"I've been the one getting her worked up every day, and I bet *you're* the one enjoying it."

"You sound confident."

"You act like that's new. And don't play dumb. She's been edging me every single day—even on weekends when she just does it over the phone! And you know what she's been telling me lately? How much teasing me turns her on. I *know* she's wet by the time she's done with me. And who gets to enjoy it? *You.*"

"Please, you're loving every bit of this." Adrian leaned back in his chair and sharpened his gaze at Caleb. "Is this the longest you've ever been edged?"

"Of-fucking-course it is," Caleb spat. "*Ten* days. Ten-fucking-days. Shit, taking a shower almost makes me nut."

"Keep behaving for her and maybe she'll give you some relief."

"If it doesn't happen soon, I just might do it myself." Caleb's mouth shut when he heard the handle of his office door and looked over to see Mila walking in soon after. He straightened up in his seat and watched her as she approached them.

Adrian didn't need to turn around to know it was Mila. He could tell from Caleb's reaction and the clicking of her heels on the floor.

"I have those extra copies you asked for, Mr. Peterson," Mila said. "Adrian," she greeted when she walked past him to place the stack of papers on Caleb's desk. When she did so, she saw Thompson Luxe Group files sprawled across the surface and it confirmed her suspicion that the meeting titled "Target Tracking" without a listed description was indeed about selecting which companies they would target for acquisition.

Lingering in her spot next to Caleb's desk, Mila's gaze drifted from the files to the next thing that caught her eye. The bulge in Caleb's dark blue slacks reminded Mila of the session they'd had just an hour prior. She doubted his erection had lasted that long and concluded that him being in the room with Adrian had something to do with it.

Turning to Adrian, Mila said, "Has he told you about the fun we've been having, darling?"

Adrian looked at Mila before his eyes returned to connect with Caleb's. "Yeah. In fact, we were just talking about it. Caleb said he's been 'doing all the work' getting you worked up and *I'm* the one who gets to enjoy it."

Mila let out an entertained huff and shook her head. "*That's* what he's telling you? Well, for once at least our pet is half right. That's progress for him."

Adrian's jaw tensed and his gaze shifted to the front of Mila's skirt. They hadn't had sex in over a week and he knew she and Justin also hadn't had much time together. So, the 'half right' part that Mila was referring to had to be the fact that Caleb was getting her 'worked up'. Adrian craved Mila constantly, thinking about her all the time. She seemed a bit tense that day, but it seemed more stress-induced than a lack of release.

However, now that he was with the two of them, Adrian's mind began to wander about the extent of Mila's teasing. He wondered if she'd also been teasing herself through her games with Caleb. And if that were the case, he wondered if it meant she'd be 'worked up' for a longer time after their sessions. He wondered if she was wet in that moment.

Mila noticed the way Adrian was looking at her and had a guess of what was on his mind. She walked over to him and stood between his legs, placing her hands on his shoulders.

"It's true what he says about getting me 'worked up'," Mila admitted. "But you know how much I enjoy being a tease. You know how much I enjoy the look of desperation on a man's face. And you know just how desperate pet can be."

"I know, Ms. Mila..." Adrian reached out and held her hips before his eyes made their way back up to hers. "It's just been a while."

She placed a gentle hand on his cheek and smiled down at him. "We'll make up for it tonight."

Caleb examined the two of them behaving as if he weren't there despite being in *his* office. While he had the urge to make his presence known, he was also tired of constantly testing Mila. He was tired of being behind Adrian and Justin when it came to who Mila would give her energy to. And he was ready to finally earn her favor.

And that patience paid off.

After they exchanged a few more words that Caleb couldn't hear much of, Mila and Adrian both turned their attention to him.

Mila took Adrian's hand and led him from his chair to Caleb's side of the desk. As she'd been doing in their sessions, Mila gestured for Caleb to move back from his desk and she and Adrian stood in the space between it and Caleb. As the pair stood over him, Caleb found himself intimidated and turned on at the same time, which was not unusual for him.

Bending toward Caleb, Mila rested one hand on his chair's arm and another rubbed the bulge in his pants. Immediately, he grunted at the feeling of her touch.

"You've been keeping me entertained for how long now, pet?" she questioned.

"T-ten," he exhaled. "Ten days."

"That's right..." Mila nodded as she put more pressure against Caleb's erection and and he shuddered at the sensation. "Ten whole days you've been holding it for me. How much longer do you think you can take it before you lose control, pet?"

"I..." Caleb took a deep breath. "I don't kn-know..."

Mila released him and turned her attention back to Adrian. "How much longer do you think he'll hold it, darling? You're the one who told me about how much of a slut he is. And I know how needy he can get... I'm surprised he's lasted this long."

Adrian swallowed, keeping eye contact with Mila. "It's not like him. But I think for once he's willing to behave... for you, at least."

The energy in the room was already deeply sensual and those words from Adrian sent Mila over the edge. She brought him in for a deep kiss, using one hand to hold his face and the other to guide his hand down to her ass so he could grab it.

As Adrian predicted, Mila was teasing herself through Caleb, and she was taking out some of that pent up desire on Adrian right in front of the man who helped get her to that point. Breathing heavy against Adrian's lips, Mila was growing wetter with each moment and she *needed* a release.

Caleb watched as Mila broke the kiss with Adrian and whispered something in his ear before she turned around. Adrian then pulled Mila's skirt up over her hips so that her ass was exposed directly in Caleb's face as he remained seated.

Caleb readjusted in his seat, trying to give some relief to his severely strained pants.

"Take these off for me, pet," Mila said softly.

Without hesitation, Caleb reached forward and hooked his fingers in her panties before slowly pulling them down. Once he got to her ankles, she lifted her right foot, and then her left to allow him to remove them completely. He held the pink lace in his hands and looked down at it, the desire in his eyes. While Mila—who was still facing away from him—couldn't see Caleb, Adrian's gaze connected with his.

"Put them on your face." The command was clear in Adrian's tone and Caleb quickly obliged. He pulled the panties over his head so that the crotch area was over his nose, breathing in the smell of Mila's pussy. In front of him, Mila opened her legs and leaned forward, bracing herself against the desk. Her wet pussy was in clear view for him and as he stared at it practically salivating as he fantasized about easing himself into her. His thoughts were interrupted by the sight of Adrian's hand cupping her followed by a satisfied hum from Mila.

"God damn..." It came out as more of a sigh from Caleb, his breaths already slow and deep.

Mila turned her head to look over her shoulder at him with a sultry gaze, admiring his face covered with her panties. "Take it out, pet. We're going to play a game."

Caleb did as he was told and pulled himself from his pants.

Adrian moved his hand up from cupping Mila's pussy so that he was using his middle and ring fingers to play with her clit, rubbing it in slow, circular motions. Mila's head fell forward and light moans began to cross her lips. She was sensitive to his touch, still worked up from her time earlier with Caleb.

"Why don't you help me," Adrian rasped. "Put your fingers inside of her."

Eagerly, Caleb nodded and spit on his fingers before sliding two of them inside of Mila. He audibly groaned at the feeling of her tight pussy practically pulling his fingers in.

"Shhittt," Mila hissed. "Stroke yourself. And keep the pace with your fingers."

"I can help you too," Adrian rasped, a teasing clear in his tone. He leaned forward to spit on Caleb's length as Caleb moved his hand up and down his own shaft.

With Adrian playing with her clit and Caleb's fingers moving in and out of her, Mila bit her lip as she tried to keep her sounds down.

"Fuck," Caleb grunted before slowing his movements. "I... don't know... how long... I can..."

"You can hold it," Mila assured Caleb as her eyes connected with Adrian's. "And move faster."

"If you can make her come and hold it, we'll let you join our date night," Adrian added with a suggestive gleam in his eyes. The promise behind it only turned Caleb on more.

Moving his fingers and hand faster, Caleb fought against his orgasm as hard as he could—his grunts frustrated, muscles tight, face red, and breaths slow. Ten days of edging mixed with feeling Mila's pussy for the first time as she moaned with the pleasure he helped give her made not coming feel like an impossible task for Caleb. He *needed* Mila to come soon. He knew he wasn't going to last much longer. He curved his finger to stimulate Mila's g-spot, earning an outburst from her.

His mouth open with moans of his own, Caleb made the plea clear in his eyes to Adrian. Mila grabbed Adrian's shirt and pulled him in to kiss her, pure desire coming over her. He eased his fingers slightly down to stimulate the lower part of her clit—a spot he knew was the most sensitive for her. The move sent her over the edge and Mila moaned into Adrian's mouth as her body shook with her climax.

Caleb's breathing was heavy as he slowed his movements before pulling his fingers out of Mila. They were slick and covered with her orgasm. He licked her essence off of them. Meanwhile, Mila was coming down from her high, holding onto Adrian. She pulled him in for another kiss, only parting to pull his bottom lip between her teeth.

"Looks like our toy is coming home with us tonight, darling. And it's perfect timing... Have you been doing what I asked?"

Adrian nodded. "Yes, Ms. Mila."

"How many days?"

"Six."

Mila pulled her skirt down and turned to look at Caleb. She smiled at the sight of him still with her panties on his face and his painfully erect dick standing at attention.

"Fucking pervert," she taunted. "You're coming home with us."

Our Toy

Adrian opened the door to his apartment, Mila and Caleb walking in with him. Similar to Mila's apartment, his had an open floor plan. His unit occupied the entire top floor of his building with a perfect view of the Lenrod City skyline. The decor was that of earthy tones—shades of green and brown. From the entryway, the living room was to the left with a dark green velvet sofa toward the edge and at the center was a large rug of various shades of curved tan lines accented with a green that matched the sofa. On top of it sat a wooden coffee table that Adrian had built himself.

After the door closed behind them and they all removed their shoes, Mila took Caleb by his tie as she and Adrian led him toward the main bedroom. Once they were inside, Mila and Adrian had Caleb pinned against the wall. Mila teased him, holding his face in place while she brushed her lips against his. Meanwhile, Adrian explored Caleb's neck with his lips as he unbuttoned his shirt.

"You were telling me that you want to be our toy..." Mila muttered against his lips. "Tonight's your chance to show us if you're worth it."

"Please," Caleb breathed.

Mila flicked her tongue against Caleb's bottom lip before closing the distance between them. She continued her teasing, her lips massaging his, pressing then softening, then pressing again. Finally, her lips parted and she slipped her tongue into his mouth, causing Caleb to let out a light moan against her.

This was the most attention that Caleb had ever received from Mila—her kiss more intense, her tongue deeper than it's ever been in his mouth—and he was savoring every moment of it. His tongue tangled with hers as it explored her mouth. He knew that she liked kissing him, and Caleb wanted to show Mila just how good he could be for her.

Once Adrian unbuttoned Caleb's shirt down to the waistline of his pants, he pulled it out from its tucked position and opened it for Caleb to fully remove his top.

Not wanting to stop her kiss with Caleb just yet, Mila reached to tug at Adrian's shirt to signal him to remove his too. Adrian did as directed and quickly took off his button-up before returning his attention to Caleb. He kissed his way from Caleb's neck to his chest, flicking a tongue against his nipple, earning a groan from Caleb against Mila's lips.

Mila broke away from Caleb when he let out a more intense moan and she looked down to see Adrian's leg between Caleb's and his hand over his erection.

Adrian's voice was deep and breathy as he spoke. "He's really sensitive, Ms. Mila. We could probably make him come in his pants right now."

"Then he wouldn't be much use to us after that, now would he?"

"As long as he's been holding it in, maybe he'll be able to get it up for another round not long after."

"Only one way to find out..."

Mila's hand joined Adrian's in rubbing Caleb through his pants and she teased along his neck with her tongue before working her way down to his chest. Adrian kissed Caleb, his tongue immediately entering his mouth.

Caleb's breathing was heavy and his moans were muffled against Adrian's lips. Mila reached up to grab Adrian by his hair and pulled him away from Caleb. "I want to hear him, darling."

Adrian focused his lips on the other side of Caleb's neck while Mila had made it down to his chest. Her tongue circled his nipple before she lightly sucked it between her lips.

"God damnit," Caleb breathed. He squirmed and arched is back as the pressure built up inside of him.

"*Someone's* getting close," Mila crooned. "You gonna come for us, pet? Right now. In your pants?" She caught Caleb's nipple between her teeth.

"I think so," Adrian added before sucking on Caleb's neck.

Caleb lost it at the added sensations and had a loud outburst. "Fuck!" His entire body tensed and his hips bucked against Mila and Adrian's hands. He exhaled with a shaky breath.

Mila and Adrian both removed their hands from Caleb and looked down to see spots at the front of his pants.

Mila's eyes met Caleb's. "That better not be it, pet. Our night is just getting started."

Turning her attention to Adrian, Mila took him by the waistline of his slacks and pulled him toward the bed with her. Caleb remained against the wall, rubbing himself as he continued to come down from his orgasm.

Mila unbuttoned Adrian's pants and he pulled them the rest of the way off so he was down to just his briefs. She then turned around to face the bed and told him, "Go ahead, darling. Take these off for me."

Doing as he was told, Adrian eagerly worked to get Mila undressed. He unzipped her skirt, and allowed it to fall to the floor. Then, he reached around her to unbutton her blouse and pulled it off of her before undoing her bra.

Down to nothing but her panties, Mila crawled on the bed to lay on her back before gesturing Adrian over with her finger. He joined her, positioning between her legs with his hands planted on each side of her head.

Mila lifted her hand to slowly caress his lips with her thumb. "I've missed this mouth of yours, darling. You're going to put it to use for me tonight."

Adrian nodded. "Yes, Ms. Mila," he said and dipped his head down to meet her lips. They shared a deep kiss before Adrian's mouth worked its way down her body. When he made it to her pussy, Adrian pulled

Mila's panties off and opened her legs. Staring at her pussy, Adrian groaned at the sight. "You're so fucking beautiful." He settled himself between her legs, getting comfortable with one arm wrapped around her thigh and his other hand toying with her lips.

From his spot against the wall, Caleb watched the two of them on the bed as he continued to hold himself. Adrian spread Mila's lips apart and leaned forward to move his tongue up and down her pussy, circling her clit and going back down to move it in and out of her. When Mila started to moan, Adrian then slowly pushed two fingers inside of her and began moving them back and forth while his tongue flicked against her clit.

"You're so fucking good at this," Mila moaned as she tangled her fingers in Adrian's hair. He hummed against her, earning a breathless moan as Mila lifted her head to look down at him before her eyes locked with Caleb's as he watched them with a hungry gaze.

"Are you ready... to make use... of yourself..." Mila said through labored breaths and Caleb nodded in response. Lifting the leg that wasn't in Adrian's grip, Mila pointed her toes and Caleb knew just what she meant. Caleb walked over and joined them on the bed, sitting next to Adrian who was laying on his stomach, still eating Mila's pussy.

Caleb gently grabbed Mila by her ankle and brought his mouth to her foot. He licked her from her sole to to the ball of her foot before gliding his tongue along her toes. With Adrian's mouth working her pussy and Caleb's on her foot, the pleasure rippled through Mila and her head fell back on the bed as her moans grew louder.

"Fuck," Mila breathed. "You two are doing so fucking g—" she was cut off at the sound of her own outburst when both men adjusted their movements. Caleb pressed against the bottom of her foot with his thumb, massaging it as he continued sucking her toes and Adrian's fingers picked up speed.

Mila hit her orgasm, her body shaking, pulling Adrian's hair, and hips undulating against his mouth. He continued eating her, slowing his movements to allow her to come down from her high. Caleb released her foot to rest against his chest as he looked at her with hooded eyes.

Adrian crawled back up Mila's body to meet her with a deep kiss as the two of them worked together pulling his briefs down until his dick was free and rubbing against her pussy.

Caleb helped pull Adrian's briefs the rest of the way down. Just when he started spreading Adrian's cheeks apart to bury his face in them, Caleb was swatted away.

"Not tonight," Adrian said, his voice gruff. "We've got something else for you."

"And it's *perfect* for your hungry ass," Mila added before turning her attention to Adrian. "You said it's been six days, right, darling?"

Adrian nodded.

"Six days of what?" Caleb questioned with tensed brows.

"Adrian hasn't come in six days... I would've preferred longer, but that should still be enough to fill me up."

Adrian turned and cut his eyes at Caleb as he scanned him up and down. "Take the rest of your clothes off."

Doing as told, Caleb got off the bed to remove his pants and boxers so the he was fully nude like Mila and Adrian. By the time he returned to them, Adrian was already fucking Mila with intense strokes.

"Come down here and watch him fuck me, pet," Mila said. "Maybe you'll learn something."

"Yes, Mistress." Caleb positioned himself so that his face was next to where Mila and Adrian's groins met. Adrian had one of Mila's calves on his shoulder while Caleb held her other leg open as he watched Adrian pound her.

"Fuck," Mila cried. "Keep going. Just like that."

"So fucking good," Adrian said between grunts as he pounded into her harder. "I love your pussy, Ms. Mila. It's so fucking tight." Mila's wetness was audible and Adrian began trembling, on the edge of his release.

"Come for me," Mila breathed and on command, Adrian came inside of her, slowly inching his way out as he spilled over. By the time he pulled out of her, his orgasm was leaking out of Mila. Looking down, he was turned on by the sight and saw that Caleb was almost in a trance staring at it.

Adrian grabbed the back of Caleb's head and pushed his face into

Mila's pussy. "Eat up, bitch," he rasped and Caleb's mouth began eagerly working, licking and sucking Adrian's cum out of Mila.

Once he caught his breath, Adrian moved so that Caleb could have free range eating out Mila, slurping as much as he could get out of her.

"Fuck, you're nasty," Mila crooned, reaching down to hold onto Caleb's hair. His lips and tongue were relentless. Just as Mila guessed, he was skilled with his mouth, rivaling Adrian. "You're being a good fucking toy right now... maybe you're worth keeping around."

Caleb's response came in the form of him humming against her pussy. He felt Adrian lifting him by his hips to bring him from his position laying on his stomach, to resting on his knees with his ass in the air while his face remained buried between Mila's legs.

Adrian pulled lubricant from his side table and positioned himself behind Caleb. Adrian spread him apart and Caleb jerked his hips away, which Adrian took as a signal that Caleb hadn't prepped. Putting lubricant on his hand, Adrian then wrapped it around Caleb's length and stroked him as Caleb continued eating Mila out.

The vibrations of Caleb's moans grew more persistent until they pushed Mila over the edge and Caleb came soon after. He moved up next to Mila and Adrian positioned himself between. The three of them lay there in Adrian's bed—Mila and Caleb breathing heavy as they came down from their orgasms and Adrian caressing both of them as he and Caleb shared lazy kisses.

Once she finally came down, Mila went to use the bathroom and clean herself up before returning to bed with the two of them, who'd opened up so she could lay in the middle. After hesitating for several moments, Mila gave in and took her spot between them before the three of them drifted off into a peaceful sleep.

Had to Be

After her long night with Adrian and Caleb, Mila didn't make it back to her apartment until early afternoon the following day. Riding the elevator up to her floor, Mila scrolled through her phone. She saw several missed calls from a blocked number and huffed her annoyance. In the past when she received calls from blocked numbers, they'd come from Eric. He hadn't attempted to make contact with her since she moved, so Mila thought she was finally in the clear. However, once she saw what she assumed was him trying to make contact with her again, Mila grew tense.

Gripping her phone tight in her hand, Mila whispered to herself, "I'm changing my number *today*."

The elevator dinged when it finally made it to her floor and Mila walked to her unit. Once she reached the door, she immediately noticed something was off. While it appeared to be fully closed upon her approach, when Mila pressed against it, it opened without resistance—the lock and latch of the doorknob had been broken.

Cautiously, Mila remained in the doorway without entering her apartment. From the opening, she could see much of her open floor plan. There was a vase shattered on the floor by her dining room table—a puddle of water, glass, and lilies. A wine bottle was laying on its side on her kitchen island with the red fluid covering the surface. Two containers were open and flipped over on the floor, one containing what appeared to be spaghetti and another that appeared to be chicken alfredo.

There was a bouquet of roses on the floor near the door that told Mila exactly who it was that was there.

Eric. It had to be fucking Eric.

Mila balled her hand into a tight fist and a lump grew in her throat. Her heartbeats grew rapid and there was a burning heat behind her eyes. *Why the fuck is this happening to me?*

With clenched teeth and a tense jaw, she pulled her phone out of her pocket to book a hotel for the next few nights as she walked toward the elevator. Once she got to the bottom floor, she approached the concierge and showed him a picture of Eric.

"Did you see this man come around here tonight or this morning?" Mila asked.

The concierge gave the photo a good look, squinting his eyes at the image. "He *does* look familiar, but I can't quite put my finger on it... I do know that I definitely haven't seen him since I've been on my shift, so not this morning."

"What about last night? Who was on shift?"

"Teresa. You can ask her when she comes in tonight for her shift."

Mila sighed and pulled her phone away from the concierge before making her way out of the building. "I pay over five thousand dollars a-fucking-month for this place," she muttered to herself. "And they have half-assed security like this?"

After ordering a car to take her to her hotel, Mila then switched to her contacts and called her sister who answered after two trills of the line.

"Hey Mila—"

"Did you tell Eric my new address?" she questioned, cutting Alexis off.

"What? Why the hell would I do that?"

"I'm asking myself the same question! But you were at my place two days ago for the first time and now I suddenly get calls and a visit from Eric?"

Alexis gasped. "Shit. Are you okay? Did he do something to you?"

"I'm asking the questions here, Alexis. How else would he know my address? Mom doesn't have it. The only people who know where I live are you and PMC Group, but PMC Group doesn't know my identity, so that narrows it down to you."

"Mila, I swear to you that I didn't give your address to anyone. Don't you remember that I was just as pissed as you were when we found out she gave Eric your address the first time?"

"Then how the hell else would he get my address? And why won't that man just leave me alone?"

"Okay, okay..." Alexis failed her attempt to calm her voice, the urgency clear in her tone. "Mila, tell me what happened. Did he attack you or something? Please, just tell me you're okay!"

"No. Not exactly. I got home today and my door was open and my apartment was wrecked."

"Wait, then how do you know it was him?"

"There was a bouquet of roses on the floor just passed the doorway. The same flowers he'd get me all the time."

There was a pause on the other side of the line and with that pause, Mila's thoughts grew hostile. I swear if she questions this, I am going to cuss her ass out.

"Do you wanna come stay with me, Mila? I have plenty of room. It's safe here."

"Except that Eric knows where you live too.. I'm going to a hotel."

"Which one? Where?"

"I'm not telling you."

"Mila! I told you that it wasn't me. Don't you trust me?"

"I don't know... At least not right now. And I'm changing my number... I'll email you or something to let you know I'm okay, but I just need time, Lexi."

"Mila, please! Let m—"

Mila hung up the phone just as her ride pulled up in front of her building.

"This is such bullshit."

∼

MILA SAT up against the headboard of her bed in her hotel room, staring straight ahead with a dejected expression. She was confused. She was afraid. She was angry. Mila knew that Eric was overly persistent and had no respect for boundaries—it was evident when they were together. However, she had hoped he would've moved on by now.

She didn't understand his ongoing fixation with her. She couldn't get the image of her apartment out of her mind. He'd broken into it and thrown a fit—invading her home, what should've been her sanctuary, and desecrating it. It was a scary sight, one that showed her a clear picture of the fury he was capable of, a side of him she hadn't seen before. She was furious that he'd forced her—once again—to relocate. She was furious that authorities couldn't do anything unless he actually attacked her. She was furious that she was in the predicament in the first place, all of it on top everything else going on in her life.

But the worst part of her situation was how alone she felt. While Mila had a decent amount of money on her own, the type of money it would take for a *special third party* to intervene to keep Eric away from her would require tapping into her parent's resources. However, she couldn't go to her own sister, let alone her parents about what happened—she didn't know if they could have been involved in giving Eric her new address.

She didn't want to stress her closest friends about it. And while the thought of confiding in Justin—someone with whom she had built a friendship—came to mind, Mila knew that would be a poor decision on her part.

Mila felt helpless. And although there were other times in her life when she had such a feeling, this case was different—this helplessness had consequences that altered the way she lived. The thought of simply moving again to a new apartment crossed her mind, but that thought was immediately met with fear. She'd been thinking about what would've happened if she *were* home that night that Eric came to her apartment. If Adrian, Justin, or Caleb were with her, would he attack them? If she were alone, what could've happened to her?

Mila closed her eyes and took deep breaths as she tried to calm herself. *I can figure this out. I just need to concentrate, to think straight so I can decide what to do next. I can do this.* She repeated the affirmations to herself mentally, but they just weren't breaking through the cloudiness of her mind. *Maybe if I just rest, I can be better tomorrow...*

Sliding down from the headboard so that she was laying in bed, Mila realized that she was still too unsettled to sleep, not registering even the lightest bit of weight on her eyelids.

Red wine and melatonin would knock me out... But is it safe for me to leave this hotel? Maybe they'll have melatonin here... Room service will have wine for sure... Maybe I can order the melatonin on a delivery app... No, I can't risk it... Fuck! I still need to change my number. First thing in the morning, I'll do it. I'll go out during the busiest times, that way if he does somehow pop up, there'll be too many people around for him to do anything... at least I hope.

Mila's panicked thoughts went on like that for hours—calculating, playing different scenarios in her mind, going back-and-forth about what actions would have been safe and which ones wouldn't, trying to figure out what she would do about her living situation.

She didn't realize how much time had passed before she ultimately abandoned her idea to order wine from room service. So, Mila lay there in her dark hotel room with her eyes wide open, hoping that at some point, the fatigue would hit her hard enough to put her to sleep.

Just in Time

Justin examined himself in the mirror of the men's bathroom of his favorite brunch spot in Lenrod, where he was picking up a food order for himself and Mila. *Is this too formal for brunch at her place?* He had lost count of how many times he looked at himself that day, nervous about his date with Mila. He wore black slacks with a black button up shirt that had a red floral design decorating the right side of it. He specifically picked it out for his date with Mila, hoping she would like it. Justin knew Mila admired when someone could dress well, and he wanted to show her that he was just as capable of doing so outside of business.

A chime came from his pocket and Justin quickly pulled out his phone—it was the only thing he'd checked that day more than himself. His face fell when the alert wasn't from Mila.

"It's weird she hasn't texted me today," he muttered to himself as he typed on his phone. "Maybe she's just getting ready. I know it takes her forever."

JUSTIN

Hey, I'm picking up the food now and should be at your place in 20 minutes. We are still on, right?

He stuffed his phone back into his pocket before walking out of the bathroom and back into the restaurant.

"You're just in time, Mr. Matsuda," the host chimed as he turned to pick up the bag sitting behind him. "Your order just came out."

"Perfect!" Justin accepted the bag with a smile on his face before passing the host a hundred-dollar tip. "And send my regards to Chef Jay. I will be back for a sit-down meal next time."

The host nodded happily as he accepted the money. "Yes, yes. Of course, Mr. Matsuda! I'll be sure to let him know. Until next time."

Justin waved and left the restaurant to begin his walk to Mila's apartment. It wasn't far from the place and he budgeted enough time to factor in the walk, knowing he would need it to calm his nerves. No one had ever made him feel nervous until he met Mila. And when they first met, he never expected to be smitten with her in the way that he was now.

At first, Mila was just his assistant. Then, she was his *very* impressive, business savvy assistant. Then, she was his friend and confidant. Then, she was his infatuation. Now, she was all of that and more.

Thinking about Mila, Justin hadn't realized how quickly his walk had gone by and he already arrived at her building. He buzzed her apartment and waited several moments, but there was no response. *Is she in the shower or something? Maybe she's taking a bath?* While a past version of Justin would have assumed the worst, he'd changed since meeting Mila. She was reliable, dependable. When she told him she was going to do something, she did it.

He buzzed her apartment once more and again was met with silence. Looking at his phone, Justin saw that she still hadn't texted him back and so he called her. The line trilled and trilled, but there was no answer. That was when Justin finally let it hit him that something was off.

Justin looked through the glass door for the concierge, but no one was at the desk. Right when he was about to start buzzing random apartments until someone would let him in, a resident passed through the door and Justin followed behind.

"Forgot my key," Justin chuckled nervously when the resident looked back at him as he followed him onto the elevator.

Once they got on, Justin pressed the button for the fifteenth floor where Mila's apartment was located. His heart was thumping rapidly in his chest. He wasn't sure what to think about Mila's lack of responsiveness and her not answering her phone. He didn't want to think *too* much into it before getting to her place. He hoped it was just a case of her taking too long to get ready.

However, that hope was struck down when he reached the door of her apartment, knocked, and it opened at the small pressure. His eyes went wide and he dropped his bag when he saw the sight. A vase of lilies smashed on the floor next to some Italian food. Sticky, dried wine poured over her counter. Without hesitation, Justin entered the apartment, searching urgently.

"Mila!" he called. "Mila! It's Justin. Are you home? What happened?"

There was no response. A lump grew in his throat as he made his way toward her bedroom at the back of the apartment while he continued to examine the place. There were footprints on the walls of her hallway and on the doors, as if someone were kicking them. When he arrived to Mila's room, Justin gasped—it was torn apart. Her clothes were strung all over the place, her drawers were pulled out, the mirror above her dresser was smashed, and her large, walk-in closet was in a similar state. He noticed a hole in the wall next to her bed, appearing as though someone punched through it.

There was a burning at the tip of his nose and stinging in his eyes. "Mila!" he yelled out again. "Please, tell me you're here." Justin winced as a heaviness came over his chest. "Tell me you're okay!"

Justin pulled out his phone again to call Mila as he rushed through her apartment searching for her. This time, there was no trilling of the line, and instead, he got a message that the phone number had been disconnected.

"Shit! I need to call the cops," he said to himself. "Wait! Before I do that, maybe she's okay and whatever happened here was resolved or something. I hate to say it, but her being in the hospital right now would be a relief. I'll go downstairs and check if the concierge is back."

Justin ran to the elevator, pressing the call button nonstop until it stopped on the floor and he could take it down. Lucky for him, the concierge had returned from wherever he went and he rushed up to the desk.

"Hi, I'm looking for Mila Nelson. Apartment 1501."

Without looking up at Justin, the concierge replied. "Go on up."

"No! I already went up there!" Justin snapped, his fury earning a glare from the man. "Was there an incident or something? Her apartment's been wrecked. She's not there. She's not answering her phone. The number is disconnected. I can't get ahold of her."

The concierge waved his hands at Justin. "Okay, okay... Calm down. Who'd you say you were looking for? I can—"

"Mila Nelson! Apartment 1501!"

"Mila *Nelson*?" The concierge questioned. "We do have a Mila who lives here, but the name Nelson doesn't sound familiar..."

"I don't care! Just tell me if there was an incident and she was rushed to the hospital last night or something. Your building is supposed to be safe, isn't it? Rent starts at three grand a month here, and I'm sure Mila was paying more than that considering the size of her place. Why the hell does her apartment look like it was broken into? You have to know *something*!"

"Please, sir... Just calm down. I didn't hear about any incidents last night in this building."

"Isn't there a log or footage you could check to make sure? I tell you one of your residents is missing and that her apartment was wrecked and you're not showing the slightest bit of urgency!"

"Because it could've been a party or something. A lot of..." The man looked Justin up and down. "... *finance bros* live in this building and they throw wild parties sometimes."

Justin gawked. "Does 'Mila Nelson' sound like the name of a fucking finance bro to you? You're fucking useless! I'm calling the police—"

His rant was interrupted when his phone started ringing and he looked at the screen to see an unknown number. Justin's brows tensed. His thumb hovered over the ignore button as he contemplated calling the police, but something told him to answer.

With a shaky hand, he brought the phone up to his ear. "H-hello," he answered breathlessly.

"Justin..."

The sound of Mila's voice on the other side caused tears to finally fall from Justin's eyes. "Mila! Mila... what's going on? Where are you? Are you okay?"

"Yeah," Mila replied, her tone unbalanced. *"I'm fine. I'm sorry for going MIA like that. I know we had plans today."*

"No, don't worry about the plans. I came here to your place and it's been torn apart. Did someone hurt you? Are you okay? I nearly had the police on the phone just now."

"I'm not hurt, I'm just frazzled. I got home yesterday and saw my apartment and I... I just couldn't. I got a hotel and have been holding up here... I went this morning to get my number changed. With everything going on, I forgot to contact you."

"It's okay, it's okay. I'm just glad you're not hurt. Where are you? Do you need anything? Let me come to you. Whatever happened, I'll help you get through it. We can go to the police together."

"The police are useless!" Mila spat. *"The can't do anything! Not until I've actually been hurt!"*

"Then we'll figure something else out, Mila. Please, tell me what's going on. I want to help."

"Look, Justin... I just need the rest of the day to myself in this hotel. I'll be in the office tomorrow. Then, maybe we could talk a bit more. But I'm tired, Justin. I'm sorry for this. I wish I had more for you. I'm sorry I didn't contact you before."

"No, don't worry about that. What's most important is that you're okay... or at least not hurt. But we really should talk about this, Mila. I was worried sick. And I want to help. I have the power to help you, so let me."

There was a sniffle from Mila's side of the phone, but she played it off when she cleared her throat. *"Fine,"* she surrendered, exhaustion clear in her tone. *"We'll talk tomorrow."*

"And can I check in a few more times until then? Just to make sure you're okay?"

There was a pause that lasted for several moments before Mila finally answered.

"Yeah, that's fine."

EPISODE 55

What Now?

As soon as Mila got into the office on Monday, she was pulled into Justin's office to meet with him, Adrian, and Caleb. Justin was leaned against the front of his desk with his hands on each side of him while Caleb and Adrian sat on the couch to toward the far side of the office. With wide eyes, Mila looked between the men before her nostrils flared and her glare landed on Justin.

He raised a cautioning hand when he noticed the anger in her eyes. "Please, Mila... We just want to help you. I was worried sick when I saw your apartment. I was two seconds from flipping the city over to look for you when you called me just in time."

"And when I called you, I assured you that I was fine." Mila huffed her annoyance. "Someone had broken into my apartment, so I got a hotel and just needed the weekend to get myself together."

Justin crossed his arms and shook his head. "I'm not convinced it was a random break-in, Mila. There were plenty of valuables still in clear view in your apartment. It looked like someone just went in and wrecked the place. It looked personal."

Mila kept her lips tight. For the first time, the three men caught *her* off guard, and she couldn't figure out what exactly was on their minds.

Adrian stood from the couch and walked closer to Mila. "Mila, we're just worried about you. From what Justin told us, it sounded like a disturbing sight. And if it *is* personal, that's all the more reason to be concerned."

Mila's jaw tensed as she clenched her teeth and her eyes turned away from the men and out the window of Justin's office. She didn't know what to say to them. She couldn't tell them the truth—it could blow her cover if they connected her back to Eric. And even if she did say something to them, she didn't see a point to it. Again, without risking them learning her true identity, Mila wasn't sure if they could help her. And she still hadn't completely gotten her thoughts together as she remained frazzled from what Eric had done.

"The shit sounded freaky, and not the good kind. Do you have a stalker or something? Ow!" Caleb grabbed the back of his head and cut his eyes at Adrian. "The fuck was that?"

"Could you watch your fucking mouth for once?" Adrian scolded.

A small half-smile pulled at Mila's lips before they settled again. If her emotions weren't so occupied with the fact that Eric broke into her home, the guilt would've drowned her. Adrian, Justin, and even Caleb were clearly worried about her—they even seemed more worried than her own sister.

"What can I do, Mila?" Justin questioned. "What can *we* do to help you out here?"

"I'm not really sure if you *can* help. It's just a shitty situation that I'll need to get myself out of."

"Don't say that," Adrian countered. "We're here for you, Mila. Why don't you explain to us what happened so we can figure out a way to help?"

"Honestly? I can't share all the details with you. I think I know who broke into my apartment, but I can't say." Mila wanted to apologize for her lack of transparency considering the men's concern for her, but that was the least of what she was hiding from them, anyway.

"Have you at least gone to the police?"

"Yeah, and they were useless. They can't do anything about it unless the person causes me physical harm."

"That's such bullshit," Caleb commented.

"What *can* you tell us, Mila?" Justin asked.

"Look..." Mila's shoulders fell as she exhaled a deep breath. "All I can say is that I *do* potentially have a stalker, and that's who I think broke into my place. Now, I don't feel safe living alone, I have no one to go to, so I'm going to be living it up in hotels for the time being."

"Absolutely the fuck not!" Caleb exclaimed. "You can stay with me, I have plenty of room."

Justin and Adrian's gazes snapped to him and he was immediately met with their objections.

Adrian was the first. "What the hell? No, Mila can stay with me! She already knows my apartment well and has some stuff there. It'll be more comfortable for her."

Justin followed. "No, she can stay with me. I live the farthest from her old apartment and I'm sure she'd want to live as far away from that area as possible."

"Well, I have five bedrooms in my place, so there's plenty of space for her to bring as much as she wants," Caleb argued.

The three men continued to exchange their points on why Mila was better off with them and what she would want.

Looking between them, the whole scene reminded her that she was not herself in that moment. There they were, arguing about where Mila would want to stay as if she couldn't decide for herself. She didn't feel in control of the room—a first since she started working at PMC Group. Listening to them, Mila worked to put together her own thoughts despite her flustered state.

For Adrian's place, he made a good point that she was already familiar with it, and she even had her own drawer, some space in his closet, and a bag of toiletries that she kept there. However, while Mila was trying to hold out as long as she could in admitting it to herself, she had feelings for Adrian, and staying with him for more than just a day or two could only make it worse.

Justin also had a solid argument—if Mila could live farther away from her last known residence to Eric, it could make it more difficult for him to find her again. However, Justin was very particular, and Mila knew that would translate to his living space. While she was sure he'd be flexible for her, that could only last but so long.

As for Caleb, his point was the weakest out of the men. She'd never been to his place, but she heard about how large it was. Like Adrian, Caleb's unit also took up the entire top floor of his building, but Caleb's building had wider dimensions than Adrian's and made the most out of the space, including higher ceilings and a second floor in the home.

Massaging her temples and taking several more moments to think it over, Mila finally interrupted the men. "Don't try to speak for me," she snapped and the three of them immediately paused and turned to her, looking expectantly. "I'll stay with Caleb."

Both Adrian and Justin's heads jerked back in disbelief while a wide grin came to Caleb's face.

"Mila..." Adrian began. "I don't understand. Why would you want to stay with *him*?"

Mila let out a deep sigh as she tilted her head side to side thoughtfully before shrugging casually. "He made a valid point about having a big apartment. While now isn't the best time for me to live alone, I *do* still like having my own space. And from what I've heard about Caleb's place, I could have that type of isolation without being fully... isolated."

The victorious smile on Caleb's face only grew wider as he listened to Mila and watched the shock settle on Adrian and Justin's faces.

"I'm glad you saw it my way," Caleb replied while Adrian and Justin were still processing her words. "Let's take the rest of the day off so I can help you get settled in. How does that sound?"

Mila turned to meet Caleb's joyful blue eyes as she raised a curious brow. She'd never seen him like that before. Not only was he excited, but he was eager to help with something non-sexual for a change.

"Then, I'm staying with you," Adrian declared. "I... I'm not sure I trust you and Mila living together... alone. Especially considering how you used to treat her."

Mila's attention then switched to Adrian, squinting at him skeptically. She remembered he had a jealous streak, but considering she, him, and Caleb had officially started playing together, Mila expected him to be fine with the two sharing a space.

"The hell you—" Caleb paused, catching himself and mulling over what it meant for Mila and Adrian to *both* be staying with him and changed his tone. "Whatever... that's fine, I guess."

"Then I'm staying, too," Justin added.

Mila, Adrian, and Caleb all snapped their gazes to him at the same time with questioning expressions on their faces.

"If Adrian has already designated himself the fucking chaperone for me and Mila, why the hell do you need to stay there too?"

"Because I- because I," Justin sputtered, fumbling over his words. Caleb and Adrian had never seen him look so awkwardly nervous, but the display was not new for Mila.

"Let him stay," Mila suggested. "Like you said, Caleb, you have plenty of space. What is it? Five bedroom? That means one for each of us, plus there's still a spare room."

Caleb grumbled something under his breath before he straightened himself up and nodded. "Fine, whatever. Then all four of us will be roommates for a bit. But..." He pointed at Adrian and Justin. "Don't think this is fucking permanent. We were roommates once before and I hated that shit."

Adrian let out an entertained scoff and shook his head at Caleb, while Justin kept his attention on Mila.

"Hey Mila," Justin started. "Do you want me to go with you to your apartment to pick up your things? I imagine you don't want to go there alone."

"Yeah, you're right," Mila agreed. "Thanks, Justin."

"Always."

EPISODE 56

Assurance

Mila managed to keep her cool as best as she could in the taxi that she and Justin took from PMC Group's offices to her apartment. However, once they crossed into the building, her heart started racing. Walking through the lobby, the same concierge who Justin had spoken to the day prior was on shift and greeted them.

"Ah, so it was *this* Mila you were looking for!" he announced when he saw Mila and Justin before his eyes landed on her. "You friend here was all worked up looking for you. Is everything alright, Ms. Tho—"

"I'm fine," Mila interrupted, her tone cold.

"No-fucking-thanks to you," Justin spat.

They walked over the elevators and once they boarded one and were on their way up to her floor, Mila found herself growing even more tense. She drew her fingers into her palms and held her hands in tight fists while her eyes remained on the elevator doors. The image of her apartment flashed in her mind and she worried about the parts that she *didn't* see. She wanted to keep calm and play it cool, but she couldn't.

A large, warm hand wrapped around Mila's right fist and she tore her gaze from the elevator door to see Justin looking at her attentively.

"I'm here, Mila," he assured her with a nod and a squeeze of her hand before his fingers gently coaxed her to loosen and release her fist so that he could intertwine his fingers with hers. "Now, *let* me be here for you."

Mila broke eye contact, but did not pull her hand away as she looked everywhere in the elevator except back at Justin. The bell chimed when they arrived to her floor and keeping her hand in Justin's, the two of them slowly made their way to her apartment. Once they reached her door, Mila stopped in her tracks and Justin stood there beside her, analyzing her body language.

He'd never seen Mila like this before. She was uneasy. She was uncomfortable. She was afraid. She was undeniably shaken to her core.

"Hey." Justin rubbed Mila's thumb and squeezed her hand. "I'm right here. I won't let anything happen to you. I promise."

Mila swallowed and slowly nodded. She still hadn't made eye contact with Justin since they were in the elevator, her gaze now on her apartment door. After taking a deep breath, she stepped forward to push it open.

The sight was just as she remembered it. The shattered vase, flowers on the floor. Wine across the counter. She stepped forward into the apartment and Justin was right there with her, their hands still together.

Mila couldn't bring herself to look around as they walked from the doorway straight to her bedroom. She didn't want to see all the damage that had been done. Now that Eric had broken into her home and ruined it, she gave up on the place. And the more she saw his damage, the angrier she'd get.

Once she and Justin got into her bedroom, Mila choked up as soon as she set eyes on it. The space was in shambles—her clothes were strung all over the place, drawers pulled out and thrown on the floor, there was a hole in the wall next to her bed, and her vanity looked like someone took a bat to it.

Mila let out a shaky breath. "Fuck," she winced softly before her tone changed. "Fuck!" she shouted as she began pacing the room, her arms flailing with her rant. "I can't have shit! I just want to fucking exist. My home? My fucking *home*? And he ruined it! Fucking ruined it!"

Justin pulled her into his arms and wrapped her in a tight a hug. Without hesitation and without fighting back, Mila returned his embrace. Finally, she cracked, her body shaking against him as her tears wet his shirt. Mila's nails dug into his back as she held his shirt in a firm grip.

She was relieved it was Justin with her. She absolutely could not imagine Caleb seeing her in that state and while she trusted Adrian, she was still grappling with the way he made her feel and she didn't need that added confusion in that moment.

However, Justin was her balance.

While Mila had been hiding her true identity from the men, she had otherwise been honest with all of them, and especially open with Justin. They both confided in each other about growing up with distant parents and always feeling out of place in their families. Of the three men she'd grown to spend most of her time with, Justin was the only one she wanted there in that moment. The only one who she felt she could sob in front of without him seeing her as weak, or being overprotective... Justin was exactly who she needed.

Mila took a sharp breath and turned her head to the side as she rested it against Justin's chest. "Thanks for coming with me, Justin," she said softly. "Thank you for being here with me."

Justin caressed her back and rested his head on top of hers. "Always, Mila," he assured her. "You're one of my closest friends. I'm here for you. Whatever you need."

They stood there as Mila took deep breaths and Justin continued to soothe her. Regardless of the disaster of her desecrated home that surrounded them, Mila felt safe in Justin's arms. She found true comfort in his embrace.

Several minutes passed before she finally eased the grip on his shirt and let go of Justin to start packing with his help. He sat on the bed between two large suitcases and packed them with whatever Mila threw his way. In no time, both of the bags were filled and Mila disappeared into her closet after warning Justin not to follow her. The packing was an effective distraction from the uneasiness brought on by the state of Mila's apartment and she was feeling a little better than she did before she and Justin shared their moment.

Mila soon came back out with another large suitcase that Justin looked at curiously.

"You've already got two large bags filled with clothes, Mila, what's in there?"

A smirk came to Mila's face, the first time Justin had seen her smile that day.

"Activities for the four of us, of course."

Author's Note

Thank you. Thank you for taking the time and energy to read this book.

When I first decided to write this story, I wanted to write something fun and deeply unserious. I wanted ridiculous characters and scenarios. I wanted them being extra for extra's sake. I wanted a book that didn't take itself too seriously.

I wanted to share it with people, in hopes that they'd have just as much fun reading it. I hope this book made you laugh, I hope it helped you escape, at least for a bit.

Thank you to my beta readers, thank you to my ARC people, thank you to anyone who posted a review, good or bad (yes, that was a lil painful to say; but even negative reviews have their place!).

Be sure to follow me on social media (@janeramoon), as I will be posting previews of Playing the Bosses: Part II on my website.